Until the Day Breaks

California Rising
Book 1

PAULA SCOTT

UNTIL THE DAY BREAKS by Paula Scott
www.psbicknell.com

This is a work of fiction. Names, characters, places, and incidents are products of the author's imagination or are used fictitiously. Any similarity to actual people, organizations, and/or events is purely coincidental.

Cover Designer: Jenny Quinlan
Editor: Jenny Quinlan, Historical Editorial, www.historicaleditorial.com
Cover Image Credit: © ILINA SIMEONOVA / Trevillion Images
Typesetter: Jeff Gerke, www.jeffgerke.com

International Standard Book Number (10): 0-692-69534-6
International Standard Book Number (13): 978-0-692-69534-0

Printed in the United States of America

Part One

Behold, the eye of the LORD is on those who fear him,
on those who hope in his steadfast love.

Psalm 33:18

Chapter One

Rancho El Rio Lobo, California
Spring, 1846

The stranger appeared out of the darkness. She didn't notice him until he was standing beside the fountain, staring at her. He was tall and broad-shouldered, but bone-thin and covered in trail dust. Rachel thought him a vaquero. A long knife hung from his leather belt, and a pistol rode in his waistband. He wore the weapons gracefully.

Aghast at his arrival, she sloshed out of the fountain on the opposite side of where he stood. As soon as her bare feet hit dry ground, she dropped her skirt to cover her naked knees. "I'm sorry," she said breathlessly, shocked at how quietly he'd arrived, even with those long spurs strapped to his dusty boots.

"I'm not sorry. Did the fountain refresh you?" A smile softened his hard, handsome face as he slowly stepped around the fountain to her.

Heat flooded her cheeks, and then drained down throughout her body in a slow, torturous trickle. Her dress stuck to her damp legs. Should she put her shoes and stockings back on with him standing there in front of her, or wait for him to take his leave?

"Do you always wade in fountains?"

"No," she managed to answer. "We don't have these fancy water pieces back home."

The scent of leather, horses, and tobacco clung to him. He appeared to have just stepped off his mount. His perfect English made her suspect he was a fellow American. She certainly hadn't seen him thus far. Desperate to compose herself, she smoothed a loose curl behind her ear with a shaky hand.

Guitars and violins reverberated through the darkness. The aroma of roasting meat drifted on the air. Unseasonably warm weather and a full moon added to the allure of the fiesta. It was midnight, but the party in the front courtyard continued with more than a hundred Californios celebrating her father's marriage to Sarita Tomaso. Scores of lanterns glowed in the limbs of the live oak trees surrounding the adobe and timber mansion with its double porches. Yet in the walled garden behind the hacienda it was only the two of them.

He stared at her intently and then glanced around. "Where is your *dueña?*"

"I have no dueña." Her father informed her yesterday that Sarita's dueña would attend her after the wedding fiesta. Married women had no need for such servants, her father said.

"No dueña?" The man took her measure. A head-to-toe assessment of her body that quite shocked her. His scrutiny felt as if he'd reached out and touched her with his hands. Unnerved, she dropped her gaze to her damp skirt and then to the ground to study the dirt between his boots and her bare feet. Silence reigned until she could no longer stand the tension between them. She glanced back up at him.

His eyes, surprisingly light in color, blue or green, perhaps, stood out in his deeply tanned face. "Are you married? If you were my wife, I would not allow you to wander from my side." His mouth quirked into a half smile that melted her defenses.

She swallowed hard. Thoughts of Steven suddenly assailed her. Somehow she felt she'd just been unfaithful to him. As if she'd given this man something, or perhaps more accurately, he'd taken something from her. He'd certainly taken more than her measure. "I have no husband," she admitted.

Not yet. Steven was only her fiancé.

"What about your mother? Surely, she would not approve of you wandering about this way unattended."

"My mother died when I was a babe. My grandparents reared me."

"Your grandparents are of English descent?"

"New Englanders," she clarified.

"And they brought you all the way to California?"

"No. They remained back east. I traveled alone by ship around Cape Horn."

He leaned closer, this ebony-haired man drenched in weapons and the wilderness and a dangerous desirability she'd never encountered before. His voice, already melodious to her ears, softened even more. "Alone? There is only one kind of woman who journeys to California alone. Yet you do not strike me as this kind of woman."

She had no idea what kind of woman he spoke of, but the way he leaned so near left her feeling dizzy. Dark, dangerous men roved California like the cattle on a thousand hills here, but this man was different. He spoke with authority and the refinement of one born to lead men, and his manner conveyed strength and confidence and impeccable breeding. He completely unsettled her.

"Who is your padre? He is not wise to leave you unattended this way."

"Joshua Tyler is my father."

"Joshua Tyler?" Disbelief edged his voice. He stepped away from her.

"I am Rachel Tyler. Who are you, sir?"

His face grew hard. "I am Roman Miguel Vicente Vasquez." The name that rolled out of his lips was utterly Spanish. She was taken aback. He wore weapons and bore a Spanish name. Perhaps he served her father and was as mortified as she over this unseemly encounter between them.

"Do you work for my father, watching over his cattle? Watching over me?"

"I am not a vaquero. I would never watch over Tyler's daughter. Your padre is a thief and a foreigner. Where is he tonight?"

Stunned by these accusations, she glanced around for help, but the small walled garden hosted little more than the fountain, fruit trees, and several rosebushes struggling to bloom. She took a deep breath, pretending she wasn't frightened of him at all. In truth, he terrified her. "My father and his wife retired to their living quarters hours ago."

"He deserted his guests?"

"He . . . has a bride he must . . . comfort," she murmured.

"Your padre abandons his guests and leaves his daughter to wander about the night alone? A slip of a girl without her stockings?" He gave her bare feet a disapproving glance. "Unbelievable, even for a Yankee."

"Who are you to judge my father?" Hands atremble, she jerked her skirts out to cover her naked toes. "To judge . . . my . . . stockings?" She shook so badly she wondered if he could see her quaking. She'd never had an altercation with anyone in her life, least of all a man who left her fumbling for breath and reason.

He spoke tersely, "You should not be in California. Your father isn't wise to bring you here. War is coming. Women do not fare well in war. Especially women like you." His gaze locked with hers for a moment, challenging, warning, entreating. Then he spun away, limping into the darkness as quietly as he'd come.

A forceful rap on her door startled Rachel as she knelt beside her bed the following morning, trying to pray and still upset about the man she'd met at the fountain. Her thoughts scattered as her father threw open the door and strode into the room. Heart pounding at his arrival, she smiled up at him, remaining on her knees beside her bed.

"Why are you hiding in here? You should be entertaining my guests." He stared at her for a moment before continuing. "You remind me so much of your mother. She prayed often too."

Eager to hear something—anything—about her mother, Rachel rose to her feet, her stomach knotting at her father's impatient manner. "Tell me about my mother."

Turning his back on her, he walked across the room to gaze out the tiny window carved into the adobe wall. All windows in her father's wilderness home were small for protection. No Indian or animal could enter the hacienda unbidden through these little openings, she'd been told. At the window, he sighed deeply. "Leave the past in the past, my dear. I came to talk about your future." Her father moved to the handsomely carved writing desk beside the window, picking up a letter she'd left lying there. "What is this?"

"A letter to Steven." Oh, how she missed Steven. Would she ever see him again?

Her father's mouth formed a grim, hard line. "I've already said we will leave the past in the past. This young man is of your past, not your future." He crumpled the letter in one hand. "I have a brilliant life planned for you, my dear, and it begins today."

He kept the ruined letter in his fist, tucking it behind his back. "Mother has written that you sing beautifully. I want you to sing for my guests this evening. Singing and dancing are very meaningful to the Californios. Most of their celebrations involve these forms of entertainment. One of my servants will arrive shortly to instruct you in the Spanish way to dance." His voice gentled, and he turned thoughtful, even smiling. "I'm so pleased you can sing. Your mother had a beautiful voice. I used to have her sing to me when I was unsettled. Her voice was like an angel's. And you are so very lovely. As was she, God rest her soul."

Speechless, Rachel laced her fingers tightly together, praying for an appropriate response as her knuckles turned white. Nothing came to mind concerning what to say about Steven, so she focused on the singing for now. "But I only sing at church—"

He cut her off. "You are no longer with my parents, wasting your life on religious fancy. You will sing for my guests tonight. That is all there is to it." He threw the balled-up letter on the floor.

Her father wasn't a large man, but there was something larger than life about him. A will to be reckoned with that made him utterly formidable. He looked nothing like she had expected. What had she expected? A bespectacled old man like her grandfather?

In his prime with a headful of thick blond hair waving off a high, proud forehead, her father had the whipcord muscles of a twenty-year-old. His tanned face made his blue eyes all the bluer. Those blue eyes seared her now. "I want you to act like a well-raised Californiana. I didn't bring you here to place you in a convent. I brought you here to make a good union. When Mother wrote that you had grown into a beautiful girl set on marrying the young man taking over for Father, well, such a waste, I decided. My daughter marrying a minister. I vowed I would not stand for it. That's when I realized if you were appealing and untouched, you would be of great value to me here in California."

Value? Disillusionment swept over her. She searched her father's face for love, but found only ambition.

"Value," he repeated. "Land has value. Cattle have value. A beautiful, fair-haired virgin has incredible value in California." He motioned with his hand in her direction. "I want you to show the *gente de razón* you're one of them. These people are proud Spaniards. The blood of the conquistadors flows through their veins. Rosa will instruct you on our Californian customs and what is expected of a landowner's daughter. You will learn to ride and sew instead of spending all your time wandering along the river singing to the sparrows, as my vaquero has informed me you do each day. Did my good mother teach you to sew, perhaps? I recall she was quite a seamstress."

He didn't wait for her response. Didn't seem to care what she said or felt, just as long as she obeyed him. Walking over to the trunk at the foot of the bed, he threw open the chest and tossed several dresses onto the floor. Pulling out a peacock-blue silk gown, he shoved it into her trembling hands. "You'll wear this when you sing for my guests tonight, my girl."

She swallowed her apprehension, trying to remain calm as her father gave the simple black skirt and white peasant blouse she wore a disgusted glare.

"Change your clothes. No more servants' garb for you. You will dress like my daughter from now on. A refined young lady of the east." He handed her another gown, a modest but expensive yellow frock. "Put this on and meet me in the hall. You are not too old for a beating," he warned. "Californios whip their grown children with rods when they disobey."

He yanked open the bedroom door. "Rosa!"

A servant Rachel had never seen before rushed into the room. With her creamy brown skin and exotic caramel-colored eyes, she was striking. A few strands of silver ran like ribbons through hair as black as midnight. That thick mane was coiled tightly on her head in a regal way. Clearly, she was of mixed heritage, Indian and something else—English or Spanish, perhaps.

"Here is my daughter, whom we discussed this morning. See she dresses appropriately from now on," her father ordered as he left the room.

Rachel stared at the thick wooden door, stunned by the exchange. The thought of never seeing Steven again made her heart constrict. Terror washed over her. Marriage to a man she didn't know? Didn't love? *How impossible.*

"He is not so bad if you obey him," Rosa said kindly. "Hurry, *chica.* Señor Tyler hates to be kept waiting." She rushed Rachel out of her simple clothes and into the canary-yellow gown. The servant quickly pinned Rachel's long blond hair up in an artful display, then herded her from the chamber.

"Your daughter is beautiful now, no?" Rosa stepped out into the long, tiled hallway with Rachel in her wake.

Joshua inspected her briefly. "She'll do. You have three hours to teach her to dance. Then I want her out amongst my guests." Spinning on his heel, he disappeared down the hall, his spurs tapping the tile in dismissal.

Rosa squeezed Rachel's arm as she led her back into the bedroom and quietly closed the door. "I served as your father's señora before he married his new wife. Does this shock you, *niña*?"

Rachel's eyes widened. Even in her innocence, she knew what Rosa meant. "Yes," she whispered. "I am shocked."

"Good." Rosa patted Rachel's cheek. "You have a sweet spirit and your father's magnificent blue eyes." The servant's own amber eyes glistened with tears. "The *Patrón* can be kind when he has need of a woman, but kindness is not his nature. I did not think he would keep me here with his new wife. My sister lives in Monterey. I'd hoped to return there and live near her." Rosa picked up Rachel's shoes and motioned for her to sit down on the bed so she could place them on her feet.

Rachel stared at Rosa's bowed head as she knelt on the floor. She was closer to Rachel's father's age, the kind of woman she wished her father had married instead of the haughty, young Sarita.

After deftly placing the slippers on Rachel's feet, Rosa looked up at her. "You and I will dance because we are told to dance. We are women. Men rule over us. My mother was also a kept woman. And her mother before her. My grandmother was brought all the way from Spain by a conquistador who left his wife and children behind but could not live without my grandmother. This life as a kept woman is not so bad."

"Do you have children with my father?"

"No *pequeños*." Rosa smiled. "My womb remains barren all these years. A daughter will not share my shame, nor a son be unacknowledged by his padre." Rosa walked to the door, moving with quiet grace, her head held high. "Alejandro, our musician, awaits us. Come, I will teach you the Spanish way to dance."

Chapter Two

Roman pushed his way through the crowd as Tyler's daughter sang a ballad, accompanied by the Mutsun Indians trained to play the violin and guitar as youngsters at the missions. The music proved evocative, the night alive with the pulse of creation. Torches blazed in the courtyard, haloing Rachel Tyler and the Indian musicians in flickering golden firelight. Overhead, a million stars illuminated the night sky.

"What an angel. Listen to her sing. Have you ever heard a sweeter voice than that?"

"She is magnificent," another upper-class, hot-blooded young man answered the first. "Look at her. She sings for God, amigo."

Roman stared at the *criollos* for a moment before muttering, "Beware, boys. The beauty has the cross on her chest and the devil in her actions."

Everybody knew this saying; many claimed to serve God in California, yet their dealings often displayed a different bent.

He couldn't pin any wrongdoing on her yet, but she was Tyler's daughter. Though he had to admit he agreed with the drunken sons of the *gente de razón*. Rachel Tyler looked and sounded like an angel with her face tilted toward the sky. For a second, he too turned his face upward in search of something greater than himself, but only the stars piercing the darkness filled his plaintive gaze.

After several uncomfortable moments contemplating the heavens, Roman left the courtyard to continue his search for Sarita. He recognized many people at this fandango, some more influential than others. General Mariano Vallejo of Sonoma stood among the partygoers. Outrage burned through Roman that a man like General Vallejo, commander of the northern forces, would patronize this gringo gathering. Then again, many prominent Californios were here, thronging together like trusting sheep as the Yankee wolves prowled among them.

Roman shoved a hand through his hair, his hatred boiling over as he recognized Thomas Larkin. The wealthy, mutton-chopped merchant from Monterey stood under a large oak in conversation with several buckskin-clad frontiersmen. Noting the large bowie knives strapped to the frontiersmen's belts, Roman rubbed a hand across his shoulder, which now ached in cold weather. He knew the damage those big knives could do.

He tried to put Rachel Tyler from his mind, but her voice pursued him. Striding faster, he weaved through the fiesta until he could no longer hear her singing, the wound on his thigh pulsing with pain as he skirted the crowd, carefully avoiding those he knew.

He wandered behind the hacienda to the walled garden, where the fountain reflected the moonlight. Tonight it was filled with flowers instead of the Yankee *pequeña* with her shoes and stockings removed like a cantina girl. Far too often, she'd occupied his thoughts since finding her here alone last night.

In the tiny courtyard, he found dark shadows and lit a cigarillo, lounging impatiently against a cool adobe wall, pondering how to manage a meeting with Sarita. Should he even seek her out now that she was another man's wife? In the south, he'd learned from cousins that his family thought him buried in Texas after a number of men died in his regiment and a false report of his death made it all the way to California. Apparently the news of his return to the living hadn't made it this far north yet.

The scrape of wood as someone entered through the courtyard gate interrupted his contemplation. He crushed out his cigarillo, hoping the girl slipping into the walled garden hadn't noticed him. Rachel Tyler ventured so close he could smell the scent of her. Fresh and sweet and vexingly memorable.

She continued on through the walled garden, out another gate, and down a narrow path into the darkness. Against his better judgment, he followed her. The screech of owls came now and again, and music from the fiesta lingered faintly in the distance. He worried the scent of roasting meat might bring in a grizzly or two. Didn't she know how dangerous it was to wander off alone in these woods? Not only were wild Indians about, bears, wolves, cougars, and coyotes roamed these hills. The grizzlies proved especially fierce. The only safe place for women and children on the frontier, especially at night, was inside the hacienda's thick adobe walls. He edged closer to the foolish young woman, staying in the tangle of trees and vines along the path, where he hoped she wouldn't notice him.

The full moon on the horizon made it easy to navigate the surrounding countryside. This was the kind of night when

Indians from the Tulares thieved horses and killed those unfortunate enough to interrupt their thievery.

The girl walked to the riverbank and stood at the water's edge, staring out at the moonlit current, a silver strand running all the way to the sea. She looked like a marble statue, the blue silk of her dress turned silver like the river under the moon, her blond hair shining silver as well. Roman waited in the trees, doing the very thing he said he would never do, watching over Tyler's daughter.

On the bank, she didn't move for a long time. Had she not been standing, he might have thought she'd fallen asleep. When she finally raised her face to the stars and began to sing, his suspicion melted away. He hadn't been sure about the song at the fiesta, but he knew for certain this song was religious. A plea to God. And he was mesmerized.

The frogs and crickets and night birds stilled as her voice carried down the river. Goosebumps rose on his arms in response to her singing. A gentle breeze arose, whispering through his hair, cooling his fevered cheeks. He touched the bullet wound on his thigh, felt the hot dampness of the infection seeping through his trousers.

In Texas, he'd removed the ball himself with a white-hot knife and a bottle of brandy. He should have used more brandy on the wound instead of drinking most of it to ease the pain. It hadn't been much more than a flesh wound four months ago, but the lingering infection brought fevers he couldn't shake. The wound looked worse than when he'd acquired it.

With a deep sigh, he sat down, leaning his back against a large cottonwood tree, where he could watch her from the thicket. The peace that overcame him allowed him to close his eyes and rest like he hadn't rested in years as she sang that beautiful song.

How could this girl be Tyler's daughter?

His eyes snapped open when her song ended. She did not sing another, which disappointed him. He rubbed the back of his hand across his clammy forehead. Lupe would know how to treat the infection, but he wasn't ready to return home yet. He needed to speak with Sarita. And much to his chagrin, he'd grown utterly distracted by his enemy's daughter.

When the crickets and frogs reclaimed the night, joined by a nighthawk calling somewhere down the riverbank, Rachel Tyler slowly made her way back to the hacienda. He kept his distance, trailing silently in her wake like a shadow.

Once she reached the hacienda, the location of her bedroom surprised and incensed him. Her room was downstairs, near the walled garden where he first met her. The upstairs proved the most fortified part of any hacienda. Women and children always lodged on the second floor for the greatest protection.

She strolls alone to the river. Has no dueña. Is kept in a down-stairs room. Was her father a fool as well as a *bandido*?

Why should this upset him so?

Scores of people were here to keep an eye on this slip of a girl who had sung his demons away. Certainly, this was how she found the freedom to come and go as she pleased—a person could disappear in numbers. Wasn't he here at this fiesta doing the exact same thing?

A battle waged within him as he went to her bedroom door. If he frightened her enough tonight, perhaps she would return to New England before the U.S. soldiers arrived in California. After that, it would be too late for her to travel safely anywhere. Too late for any woman to venture out on the roads. He'd seen it often enough; men had two sides, good and evil, especially in war. What happened to women in war was unspeakable.

The Yankee *pequeña* wasn't much older than his sister. And just as foolish as Maria. But unlike Maria, chaperoned night and day by her diligent dueña, with every man in her family more than willing to die for her, Tyler's winsome daughter went wherever the wind blew, like a fawn without its mother. This wasn't the civilized east. Or even Monterey. This was the frontier. Tyler's folly in the wilderness.

At least her door proved solidly constructed. Planks of timber a foot thick. A man without a hatchet would have a difficult time getting through this entry when it was barred. To his relief, her latch string was pulled in when he checked for it.

Sweat trickled down his chest, and he shivered. Perhaps his fever was affecting his mind, standing here at her door like a besotted suitor. That he found her so appealing filled him with frustration. He needed to see Sarita. He knew she'd married Tyler because she thought him dead. He wanted to show her he was very much alive.

Chapter Three

Upon awakening to a room full of sunshine, Rachel lay in her bed, remembering that autumn day six months ago with Steven on the dock in Boston. It had been sunny that day too. A breeze off the ocean billowed her sky-blue skirts. She squeezed fists full of satin, willing her gown and spirits into order. Steven's trembling hands cupped her face. She couldn't believe he would finally touch her in the midst of so many. After all these months—years really, after it was too late to linger in his embrace. She opened her eyes to look up at him, and the tears slipped free, though she tried her best to rein in her emotions. Steven's thumbs captured the drops of grief and brushed them away, but he didn't remove his hands from her face. More tears coursed onto his fingers.

"Rachel . . ." When he breathed her name, she sighed with regret so deep she felt it in her bones. Surely, he'd kiss her now, but when his lips landed, warm and full of longing, they settled on her forehead. "I will find you. No matter how far you go, I will find you," He pressed his mouth to the vein that throbbed in the center of her forehead. She'd always hated that faint blue vein under her fair skin, revealing her anger or grief or any other deep emotion like a river pointing to the sea.

She wrapped her arms around his waist and wept uncontrollably for a moment with her face buried against his chest. He was tall and lean and felt like an oak, the solid presence of everything good and right in her life. How could she leave him? She couldn't see how God meant for this to happen now, after all these years wishing in vain for a summons from California.

Steven slipped his fingers into her hair and held her gently as she cried. Eventually, she settled down and looked up into his face, mapping his features into her memory. The aristocratic cheekbones and fine nose acquired from his English father. The dark, ardent eyes of his French mother. Never before had he taken her into his arms. Never before had he dared to kiss her or even put a hand to her hair. Even now, he touched her hair tentatively, like a shy child.

She hated to broach the subject of his mother, but if Yvette Gains succumbed to the wasting disease ravishing her once hardy frame, Steven could have his pick of sailing ships come spring. It was such a dreadful thought, really. How would they reunite after his mother passed on with a twenty-thousand-mile ocean voyage between them? Mrs. Gains remained steadfast that Steven not marry while she was sick, but the fervent Frenchwoman wouldn't live forever. She might not live a week. Then again, she'd lived several years now with one foot in the grave. The other foot was firmly planted on Steven, keeping him for God and God alone.

Late October sunshine warmed Rachel's back, but inside she shivered. She'd not felt warm since this unexpected journey was foisted upon her a month ago.

"Our Lord works everything together for the good of those who love him." Steven regretfully nudged her out of his embrace as he pointed to the vessel anchored in the harbor, soon to sail her away. "The *Rainbow* is new and fast, a clipper ship named for God's eternal covenant with us. Look at her sails. Isn't she grand, Rachel? We must search for our Lord's good plan in all this. The same hand that has protected us on dry land shall protect you on the mighty deep, my dearest."

Tears cooling on her cheeks, she glanced at the ship. Two middle-aged women boarded the steamboat that would convey them to the *Rainbow*. A weary-looking, red-haired woman holding the hand of a little redheaded girl, both too thin and dressed poorly, trailed the well-dressed ladies. A horn sounded, startling Rachel with the last call to board the steamboat. Tearing herself away from Steven, she moved in behind the red-haired woman and child. Passengers, all men now, surged forward, pushing her out of Steven's reach. Out of Steven's life.

After boarding the steamboat, she edged her way to the railing, searching for Steven where she'd left him on the dock. He wasn't there and her heart sank, but soon she found him not far off, waving to her from the dock as if in welcome instead of departure. That gentle smile she so dearly loved brightened his face. She waved in return, fresh tears flooding her eyes.

"Is that your husband?" The little girl, about seven years old, Rachel guessed, stood beside her, gripping the railing. The child's mother hung back, looking bone-weary, resting on the steamboat's deck near a pile of coiled rope.

"Not yet, but someday, I hope." Rachel blinked hard, her eyes stinging.

"We're searching for my father. He sailed for California three years ago. If we don't find him, Ma fears we'll starve to death come winter."

Rachel tucked a wisp of the little girl's tangled red hair behind her ear. "Then we will pray you find him." The girl's wide, despairing eyes were the hue of a stormy sea.

"Does God answer your prayers? 'Cause he don't answer mine."

"How do you know he doesn't answer?" Rachel did her best to keep Steven in view while acknowledging the child at the same time.

"He don't bring us more food. Don't give us a warm place to sleep. We barely get by, and he ain't brought my pa home. My sister just passed. God never done us any good. Ma had to sell her soul to purchase passage on this here ship for us."

Rachel didn't want to hear the details of a woman's soul selling. She put her hand on top of the child's head, trying to stop the flow of heartbreaking information spilling from that rosy little mouth.

As they steamed across the harbor, a bell ringing over the water from the ship reminded Rachel of bells across the snow. Just last winter, after an astonishing blizzard, she'd accompanied Steven in a horse-drawn sleigh to minister to snowbound parishioners about the countryside. She still thought of it as the finest day of her life, for he'd asked her to marry him that afternoon. Steven said she'd make a wonderful minister's wife, and he wanted her by his side always and forever. But Mrs. Gains continued to stand in their way.

Drowning in longing, Rachel waved to him one last time before kneeling beside the child unleashing her life story in spite of Rachel not wanting to hear it. "God is real, and he loves you. He will help you. I am Rachel Tyler. What is your name, young lady?"

"Molly O'Brian."

"Well, Molly O'Brian, you will have a warm place to sleep on the *Rainbow*."

"Ma don't think so. We're stuck in steerage with the rats."

Rachel swiped her cheeks dry before taking Molly's little hands in hers. "Well, we must see what we can do to remedy that. God has made us friends for a reason." She squeezed the little girl's hands in reassurance.

It shouldn't be too hard to tuck Molly and her mother into her stateroom. Paying to improve their meals would also help alleviate their misery. Her father had sent her plenty of coin to complete this six-month journey. She grew excited just thinking about writing to Steven to tell him how she'd rescued these poor Irish immigrants on the voyage.

"Do you know I am going to California in search of my father as well? It has been many years since we parted. I don't even remember what he looks like," she told Molly.

Molly's wide eyes widened even more. "Your pa done left you too?"

"He sure did. He went to make his fortune on that far-away shore, and he did just that. He's a landowner now in California."

"A landowner?" Molly was awestruck. "Only the rich own land. Does he keep slaves too?"

"I don't think so. Indians care for his cattle and crops."

"Indians?" Molly's eyes filled with fear. "Do they scalp white folks in California?"

"Of course not. Your pretty red hair is safe and sound on your head." Rachel stroked the girl's tangled tresses, hoping it was true. California Indians certainly didn't scalp folks, did they?

She considered the two fine-boned, ivory-handled brushes that had belonged to her mother. They were her greatest treasure. Every night before bed, she brushed her hair a hundred strokes while saying her prayers. She should give one of her brushes to this deprived little girl, but her heart recoiled at the idea. "Do you brush your own hair?" Rachel inquired.

"We don't own a brush. Ma says luxuries like that are for women who don't work their fingers to the bone. Ma's fingers are strong as cedars from scrubbin' folks' wash. When she combs my hair, it feels like tree limbs scrapin' my scalp off. Finola cried when Ma brushed her hair."

"Finola is your sister?"

"She was five and small for her age. Measles took her a month ago," Molly said in an adult-like fashion, as if it hardly mattered at all. "Mine weren't so bad. Only got me one pox on my face." Molly showed Rachel the small pinkish-white scar on her temple.

Rachel glanced over at Molly's mother. She could see the woman still grieved for her lost child. She had that hollow-eyed expression of having suffered a great loss. Helping Molly and her mother survive this ocean passage became Rachel's utmost priority at that very moment.

Rachel had nearly died on that voyage, growing weak and unwell as the journey progressed. Cocooned in a comfortable farmhouse with her grandparents outside of Boston, she'd never in her life faced trials such as on board the *Rainbow*.

She'd parted ways with Molly and her mother in Monterey, leaving one of her cherished brushes with Molly, and now here she was alive and well in California about to be bartered away as a bride to a man she didn't know and didn't love. Perhaps death on the ship and a swift journey to heaven would have been better.

Chapter Four

Roman awoke with Texas on his mind. The territory had been annexed to the United States and was now flooded with U.S. Army soldiers. Surveying his bandaged leg, he contemplated how long it would take the war to reach California. After two years fighting on the Texas front, getting home before American ships sailed into Monterey Bay was all he could think about. He had forgotten what it was like to wake up in California. Another day of feasting and celebrating did not appeal to him. Especially considering he rose from a bed of hay in Joshua Tyler's stables. He'd rejected the long, low adobe building that quartered the vaqueros. Some of Tyler's male visitors were bunking there. Families that didn't fit in the hacienda were housed in tents inside Tyler's high adobe walls.

Years ago, the wily foreigner had settled in these mountains with the mighty redwoods, sealing his fortune selling lumber, a precious commodity in California. Then he bought all the cattle he could get his hands on. With the missions secularized twelve years ago, men such as Tyler found their footing in earnest in California. The Catholic Church's plan had been to civilize the converted Indians—neophytes, as they were known—to allow the Indians to take over the mission lands themselves. This never happened. The mission resources—vast assets of cattle, sheep, and horses, orchards and vineyards, fertile fields of wheat and vegetables, and greatest of all, the neophyte workforce—fell into the hands of the *gente de razón* and those foreigners who took Mexican citizenship and became Catholic, "leaving their conscience at Cape Horn," as the Americans in California liked to say.

Roman had no respect for men who bartered away their citizenship and their religion so freely. Tyler, with his insatiable hunger for land and cattle. His empire growing as he bought out his neighbors one by one through the years. Only Roman's family had managed to hold their boundary lines in the valley against Tyler's merciless onslaught. But not without bloodshed. Hundreds of Indians and rancheros had been killed in the night raids stealing horses. Nothing could be proven, but he held Tyler accountable for his father's death in one of these raids. He couldn't believe Sarita had married the Yankee.

Having slept in his clothes, he got up and saddled Oro and then led his golden stallion from the stables at sunrise. Outside the grandest redwood stables Roman had ever seen waited Joshua Tyler, dressed like a Spanish don. He wore the unique garb of the privileged *gente de razón,* fitted trousers with flared legs and a short jacket of thick velvet over a billowing white shirt, topped off with a silk-lined sombrero decorated with brightly colored braid. Tyler spoke to an excited group of mounted *criollos,* superb horsemen in their teens and twenties, boys brash and bulletproof in their own eyes. Roman used to be this way as well, but no more. His father's death, followed by the battles in Texas, had changed him. He wondered if his carefree countrymen had any idea what awaited them once the United States' march of Manifest Destiny culminated on California's sleepy shores.

With Texas now annexed, the siege for California was all but a matter of time. Yet nothing seemed changed here in this pastoral land of lighthearted people. The *gente de razón* loved their fiestas: dancing, picnicking, gambling on everything from monte, a wildly popular card game, to horse races, cockfights, and other sporting events. This morning, the men planned a bear hunt, hoping to capture a beast for a bear baiting anticipated this afternoon. While yesterday seemed almost like summer, this spring morning dawned crisp, with an ocean fog besieging the sun.

Tyler leaned on a fence, telling the men how to find a canyon on his ranch where a grizzly had been sighted a few days prior. The group's concentration suddenly shifted across the field to a figure emerging from the woods. A breeze stirred the woman's simple black skirt. Her white peasant blouse was draped by a rough woolen shawl that covered her head, but one long blond tendril had escaped, streaming down her back. Only one woman had hair like that. *Tyler's daughter.*

Joshua Tyler cut short his speech upon seeing her. "You all have hunted bears before. I needn't say anymore," he finished abruptly. "*Vayan con Dios,* amigos."

Go with God indeed. Roman swore under his breath. Was the Yankee girl always wandering about unescorted in these mountains? The men stared at her openly. She was so fair and fetching and did not conduct herself as a proper señorita should.

What was she doing out so early this morning? Had she met someone down at the river? Why did her father all but ignore her presence? And above all, why of all wonders was an unmarried girl left without a dueña's protection? This was unheard of in California—unless she no longer had any virtue left to protect.

Roman longed to ride over to the river to see if she'd met someone there. A man, perhaps? Did she think the *paisano* clothes concealed her identity? Even dressed like a peasant, her blond hair proved a banner in the breeze. In a few more minutes, she would be out of his reach, safe inside the walls of her father's Yankee fortress. Allowing his heart to overrule his head, he spurred Oro after her as the rest of the men raced off to hunt bears.

Rachel Tyler saw him coming and hurried toward the hacienda in an attempt to escape him. She didn't stop and wouldn't look at him as he reined in his stallion beside her. He refused to speak to her until she acknowledged his arrival. He could see his stallion made her nervous. She kept moving sideways to distance herself from his horse. He urged Oro shoulder to shoulder with her, the way he herded wild mustang mares. She continued to ignore him, and his frustration grew.

Finally reining his horse to a halt, he stepped down from the saddle in front of her. The damp, foggy air caused a lock of fair hair, escaped from her shawl, to curl against her rosy cheek. Roman restrained himself from tucking the silky strand back under her head-covering. Her eyes were wide with trepidation.

"Who did you meet at the river?" He knew his voice was curt, but couldn't help himself. She must know that each time she left the hacienda's protective walls, she was in danger of being eaten by an animal or carried away by an Indian.

She hesitated for only a moment. "God."

"God? Really? No man waited for you there?"

"Only God was there." Her guileless blue eyes probed far too deeply. "Do you not pray to the Lord?"

Roman looked toward the river for a moment to escape her penetrating gaze. He removed a cigarillo from his shirt pocket and set about lighting it. "I pray for the Americanos to leave California."

"You do not like Americans?"

"I've killed Americanos." He puffed his cigarillo to life.

She said nothing until he leveled his gaze on her. "Why?"

"When the Americanos rose up in Texas, I fought for Mexico. I'll fight the Yankees again when war comes here."

"Why do you entertain war?"

"There is nothing entertaining about war." He blew smoke between them. She didn't flinch. Didn't back down one bit, but none of her gentle manner escaped her. Or him. Her sweetness took him aback. Sighing, he set his gaze on the distant horizon. "I hope to see California govern herself. Mexico does not deserve her, and America will only pillage her."

"Not all Americans are greedy."

He turned his eyes back to hers, longing to shake the innocence from her. "I haven't met a Yankee yet who can be trusted. Greed rules them all."

"I think you trust no man. Not just Yankees." Her words, though kindly spoken, incensed him further.

"You know nothing about me."

"You are wounded and sick, yet you pretend to be strong and whole." She pointed to his leg. "There is blood on your trousers."

He looked down at his soiled pant leg, his ire growing. "Are you a healer?"

To his surprise, she bent down and touched the dark stain on his pants with her fingertips. With her head bowed and covered by the dark shawl, she appeared a servant at his feet. The pressure she put on his thigh with her hand intensified, sending shooting pain through the aching wound. Had he not been so proud, he would have stepped away from her. "What are you doing?" he asked impatiently.

"You have an infection. Your flesh is on fire. I'm praying for God to heal you." She did not remove her hand from his leg. Instead, she put more pressure on the bandage under his pants. The sensation of her touch deepened. Heat climbed up his thigh, flooded his midsection, and pooled in his chest. For a moment, he found it hard to breathe.

Dragging in a fortifying breath, he grabbed her by the shoulders and abruptly pulled her to her feet. His wound pounded in a rhythm that matched his thudding heart. He felt out of sorts and held on to her for a moment to steady himself.

"How did you acquire the injury?" She put her hands on his upper arms, as if knowing he needed her strength. It almost seemed like an embrace between them.

After a stunned moment, he pushed away from her, gently but urgently. He'd never been superstitious like so many Californios, but something about this woman was otherworldly. His wound vibrated as if it had a pulse of its own now. As if she'd poured something into him. A spirit of some kind. He needed to get away from her.

"Let me help you." She reached out, but he jerked back. Was it his fever from the infection making him so perplexed in her presence?

With a last look at her standing there with the sun rising behind her, framing her in golden light, he mounted his horse in a hurry. "Leave me alone. You have done enough already."

Spinning his horse around, he spurred Oro out of the trees and down to the river.

Urging the stallion toward the mountains, he rode hard for over an hour. Across sprawling meadows, through shady redwood glens, and up into the pine and oak-studded peaks and canyons of a sprawling wilderness. When the stallion's gait stiffened and his ears pricked as they climbed the next hill, Roman knew his mount sensed danger.

Instinctively, he untied his riata from his saddle. Cresting the summit, he saw the grizzly digging in a squirrel hole just yards away. Too close. Much too close to avoid an encounter with the beast.

Roman cursed softly, quickly twirling the lasso up over his head. The big brown bear reared from his digging, standing on hind legs to better view his visitor. Roman threw the trusted rawhide. It uncoiled like a snake and settled around the bear's thick neck.

The captured brute charged, roaring his wrath. The stallion raced away, leaving the bear barreling close behind.

Nearby stood a massive oak tree. Laying his body over the horse's neck, Roman galloped Oro under a large limb, tossing the end of the riata over the branch and catching the rope again, allowing Oro to bolt just as the beast lunged at the stallion's backside.

In a nail-biting second, the bear was snatched back and dangled from the limb, hanging like an outlaw strung up by the town. Its hind feet clawed the ground, keeping the enraged animal from choking to death. Roman trotted his trembling stallion twice around the tree trunk, keeping the riata tightly drawn to hold the bear immobile. The animal roared, slicing the air with its claws.

Roman climbed off Oro and secured the end of his lasso to another low-hanging branch. Walking back to his horse, he realized his knees were shaking, though his leg didn't hurt as much now. Oro's muscles quivered too. The stallion dripped and foamed with sweat.

"It's been a while since we faced a bear together, huh?" He patted the stallion's soaked neck, feeling some of his manhood restored.

Oro blew through flared nostrils, his eyes never leaving the strung-up beast. Roman took a second riata tied to his saddle and returned to the bear. He lassoed the grizzly's paws and attached that riata to the tree as well. With the beast firmly bound, he mounted his stallion.

Letting out a breath, he realized he felt sorry for the bear as it twisted around growling in frustration. This bruin would be a perfect competitor for the bear baiting. The bear was young, which meant it wouldn't kill the bull too quickly. If the bull was old and wise, he might even win the match against the bear, though Roman doubted it. He'd only seen a bull win on two occasions, and those were against juvenile bears.

He didn't want any part in victoriously dragging this bear back to the Yankee hacienda. He figured the men would find the bear sooner or later. Hopefully sooner.

Chapter Five

Two riders from the hunting party found the bear tied to the tree. The *criollos* were ecstatic, calling out to Roman to join them in hauling the animal back to the fiesta. Roman rode in the opposite direction, ignoring their excited summons.

The *criollos* wasted no time. When Roman arrived at the fiesta that afternoon, having spent much of the day at a peaceful glen along the river where he bathed and shaved and spent some much-needed time resting, the bear and bull were chained together for the fight.

Roman slowly walked his horse toward the circle of spectators. From a distance, Rachel Tyler's golden hair shimmered in the sunshine. He didn't want to speak to her, but he couldn't stay away. She stood alongside a female Indian servant who whispered in her ear. It was obvious the little Yankee had no stomach for the savage fight between the animals. She covered her mouth with her hand and turned away as the bruin charged the bull.

By the time he reached her, she was crying softly into her hands. An overwhelming urge to comfort her assailed him. "You do not like the entertainment," he drawled gently, purposefully getting off his horse between her and the servant so nothing stood between them.

She looked at him in disbelief. "How can they do this to these animals?" She swiped at the tears on her cheeks, struggling to compose herself. The crowd cheered and clapped, egging on the warring beasts. Snarls of the bear and snorts of the bull filled the air. He stood close enough to smell the delicate perfume of rosewater on her skin and found himself at a loss for words.

"Which will win the bull or the bear?" She wouldn't look at the raging fight.

"The bear almost always wins, but this bear is young and stupid. He might lose," he spoke gently.

"How do you know he's young and stupid?" Rachel peeked at the fight and then, clearly regretting her glance, locked wide eyes on him.

"I captured the bear this morning. He wasn't much trouble."

"You did this?"

He didn't like her outrage directed at him. "Your father has done this." He waved his hand toward the animals trying to kill each other as the crowd roared its approval. "The Yankee takes without asking. Life, land, a woman who belongs to another man. Your father is like the grizzly." Roman scanned the crowd for Tyler and spotted Sarita beside her husband. Both of them cheered as the bear took the bull down by fastening its teeth around the bull's nose. The bull bawled as the bear muscled it to the ground. It kicked its legs, trying to free itself as the bruin moved his muzzle to the bull's throat, ripping open the flesh there.

Rachel's scream split the air, but Roman couldn't take his eyes off Sarita. She threw herself into Tyler's arms, kissing her Yankee husband as the bear finished off the bull. Their public display of unbridled passion stunned him. Though he'd been to many bear baitings, often capturing bears with Rancho de los Robles's vaqueros, never in his life had he been unsettled by the event as he was now. Watching Sarita relish the bull's death in the lusty embrace of her gringo husband unleashed something in Roman he'd never felt before. A deep, grieving regret over the human depravity he only now recognized in himself and those around him. It sickened him to see Sarita in another man's arms. True, she thought he was dead, but still it felt like a betrayal, and sliced his soul open.

Beside him, Rachel wept, her shoulders shaking, her face buried in her hands. She seemed so young and innocent, standing there sobbing in the midst of a crowd reveling in the bloodbath. The Indian servant waiting at her side watched him with knowing eyes. He recognized this servant, Sarita's old dueña, Chula. He'd always disliked this particular Indian. She practiced black magic and had led Sarita into her dark ways. In his younger years, he'd laughed at such nonsense. Now that he was older, and had seen plenty of death in Texas, he did not find the worship of devils so foolish and funny.

"I will see Señorita Tyler to the hacienda," he told the servant in Spanish.

Chula smiled. The gesture didn't reach her expressionless black eyes. "She is weak and fragile. A foreigner," she returned in Spanish. "She won't survive here. I believe the gringa will die this very year. Certainly, you of all men, Señor Vasquez, know I cannot allow *la niña* to depart with you."

Wrapping his arm around Rachel's waist, he pulled her from Chula's side in a swish of petticoats, leading his stallion nearly over the top of the dueña to get away from her. The servant jumped out of his horse's way, her cold black eyes suddenly flashing fire.

"The little gringa is safe with me. See to your señora. She is acting the harlot for her Yankee husband." Roman pointed across the crowd to Sarita and Tyler, relieved Rachel didn't understand the Spanish he spoke to the servant.

"I see you are alive," said Chula. "You should thank Tohic for sparing you."

"I do not thank devils," Roman returned in Spanish.

After escaping the dueña, he walked with Rachel at a leisurely pace away from the bear baiting. Moving slow eased the pain in his leg. She went along trustingly, tears streaking her cheeks, clutching his billowing shirt like a lost child.

In Spanish, he whispered comforting words he would never say to her in English, his arm firmly about her waist. Everything in him longed to protect this delicate girl. She didn't belong to her father's madness. He needed to get her away from the slaughtered bull. Away from the blood-thirsty crowd. Away from her father and Sarita with their passion displayed for all to see. Away from Chula and her devils.

It was late afternoon. A cool breeze pushed in from the coast. He could smell the ocean on the air. They'd held the bear baiting far out in the field, a safe distance from the hacienda in case the animals escaped and the vaqueros required open space to recapture the beasts. On the horizon, the hacienda loomed like a frontier fort, surrounded by high adobe walls with orchards, outbuildings, and stables sprawling across an open meadow ringed by giant redwood trees. Like all Californio ranchos, the wide clearing protected the occupants from a sneak attack. Enemies would be seen well before they reached the homestead.

As Roman and Rachel walked slowly to the hacienda, he led Oro with one hand, keeping his other arm around Rachel's waist until she stopped crying. He could have released the stallion's reins and let the horse follow, as Oro was trained to do, but he didn't trust himself with two free hands with this particular woman. The urge to carry her far away from this place was a feeling he couldn't shake. It would be so easy to sweep her onto his saddle and ride back to Rancho de los Robles where protecting her was easy. Under her fair skin, a blue vein throbbed in the center of her forehead when she cried. Her delicateness reminded him of his mother, who died of the fever when he was a boy. How he missed his beautiful, gentle mother. This girl's same beautiful gentleness tightened his chest, made him long for what he could not explain.

"How can they do that to God's creatures?" Rachel stopped walking, lifting her damp face to his. "How can people be so cruel?" Her tear-washed eyes shone as blue and fathomless as the sea. Those beseeching eyes pulled him far from the shore of his resolve to hate all Americans. With the sun on her face, he noticed a light sprinkling of freckles across her nose and cheeks he hadn't noticed at night. She was taller and slimmer than Sarita. Her head nearly reached his shoulder, her slender figure fitting his six-foot frame as no other woman's ever had.

"I don't know, *pequeña*." He didn't tell her this was the only bear baiting—besides his first one as a very young boy—that had horrified him. "The *osos grandes* can wipe out a sheep herd in one night. The cattle are rags in the great bears' mouths; one bite and the calves are gone. The mother cows grieve like women. They won't eat, won't sleep. They roam the hills bawling for the calves the bears have carried away." He needed her to understand why he'd killed so many bears. Why, though he felt sorry for the grizzlies, he had to go on destroying them. The welfare of his herds depended on it.

The sinking sun shining on her tresses turned her hair the color of California's golden hills come summertime. "You raise cattle and sheep?" she asked.

"*Sí.*" He stroked Oro's forehead. "And horses the color of your hair. This is Oro. His name means *gold* in Spanish. He has never sired a foal that did not match his color. We run one stallion with twenty-five mares in *manadas.* I own many of these small herds, placing chestnut mares with palomino stallions. This gives us the greatest return of palomino foals. Everyone rides palominos at Rancho de los Robles." He pointed across the mountains in the direction of his domain. "Rancho de los Robles has endless oak groves, pines, magnificent redwoods, and a crystal-clear creek singing through the land."

"What does Rancho de los Robles mean?" She smiled, and his stomach tightened.

"Ranch of the Oaks." A wave of wistfulness washed over him. He longed to show her his home. The rolling hills full of cattle and golden horses. The great oak trees that sheltered the herds during winter storms and warm summer afternoons. The creek so clear you could see the salmon swimming upstream from the ocean to spawn in the fall.

She stroked Oro's neck, her small white hand caressing his horse's flaxen mane. His mother had small hands too, soft and pale such as these. Giving into longing, he closed his eyes and feathered his fingers over the top of hers on the horse's warm hide. He savored the silkiness of her skin. When she didn't pull away, something deep inside him eased. He kept his eyes closed, relishing the comfort coursing through him in the presence of this gentle, young woman. There was such a sweetness about her. A serene beauty that captivated him.

"My father enjoyed watching the bear kill that bull." Her voice caught. "All the men enjoyed it. Even the women enjoyed it. I've never met people who savor cruelty this way."

He opened his eyes. Took a deep breath. In his mind, he saw Sarita cheering and lusting for blood alongside her gringo husband. He removed his dark hand from Rachel's fingers, so fair and delicate on his horse, gazing as far as he could across the horizon, wishing he didn't feel so raw inside. Wishing he didn't feel anything at all here with Joshua Tyler's daughter. "It is the Californio way," he finally said.

"What does *pequeña* mean?"

"*Pequeña* is small one." It was an endearment, really, the way he used it with her, but he wouldn't tell her so.

Her smile widened. "I'm not little. I'm tall for a woman. At least here in California, where the women are quite short."

"You weigh as much as my sister. She is a willow stick." He had no idea how his sisters, aunt, and uncle had fared in his absence. His uncle especially loved parties, and Sarita was Tia Josefa's niece. His family should have been at this wedding, even though Tyler was no friend of the Vasquezes.

"What was your mother like? When did she pass away?"

"Who told you she passed away?"

"My Father."

"Why would your father speak of my mother?"

"Not my earthly father. My heavenly Father."

"God?" Roman rasped out a laugh, but it unnerved him, the way she spoke of God.

"You don't believe in the Lord speaking to people?"

"Perhaps if you were a priest."

"The only mediator God requires is Jesus. His death on our behalf ushers us into the presence of the Almighty."

"Are you a Protestant?"

Her cheeks flushed. "I serve the Lord. Who do you serve, Señor Vasquez?"

"I have served you today, *Yanquia pequeña*. You should thank me for escorting you home." The whitewashed walls of her father's hacienda loomed ahead. The smell of roasting meat drifted on the air. Wine and brandy would be flowing soon enough, along with the sound of guitars and violins when the celebration returned to the house.

She glanced at the rambunctious crowd making its way toward them in crude wooden carts and atop prancing horses, then turned back to him. "You are mocking my faith?"

"I do not mock faith."

"So you are Catholic?" Her voice trembled.

"Everyone in California is Catholic." He tossed the challenge out to her, waiting for her to deny an allegiance to the Catholic Church for herself or her father. He smiled even as his eyes narrowed against the glare of the sun and the real trouble religion could bring. Perhaps he could wipe her from his mind if she admitted to being Protestant. A Protestant woman was about as appealing to him as a prairie fire.

"My father is . . ."

His heart stalled and then beat thickly, anticipating what she would say. He couldn't let her say it. "Catholic," he finished abruptly for her in spite of himself. Denying Catholicism was a serious matter in California. She appeared taken aback by his forceful interruption. Her mouth opened and closed and then opened again.

"All landowners in California must belong to the Church," he finished before she could utter a word.

"The Catholic Church," she clarified.

"Yes." Favoring his wounded thigh, he swung onto his horse, settling himself in the saddle to look down at her. On top of his mount, he felt invincible, even with his bad leg. But staring at her, her wide blue eyes locked expectantly on him, his chest tightened. Who would watch over the Yankee *pequeña* once he was gone? Surely not her foolish father or Sarita's wicked dueña.

He recalled Sarita's fascination with the Indian shamans. Her dueña was a soothsayer. Intuition had saved his life on countless occasions, and he sensed Rachel was in danger here. *I believe the gringa will die this very year.* He scanned the approaching crowd and found the Indian servant watching them but a stone's throw away, waiting like a snake to coil back around the little gringa.

"Stay behind these walls." He pointed to the whitewashed adobe bricks behind her. "And tell your father to find you a different dueña." He pointed to the servant. "That one serves the devil." Reining Oro around, he rode away without looking back.

Chapter

Six

Rancho de los Robles, California
Spring, 1846

His family was thrilled to have him home alive. Roman spent a month doing little more than eating everything Lupe set in front of him while keeping his sisters company as they sewed and studied their lessons in the *sala*. While he was in Texas, Maria and Isabella had changed. All Maria talked about was traveling. Each day, she begged him to take her to Monterey, to Mexico City, to Spain to see their grandparents. His red-haired sister was a beauty, but she was stubborn and spoiled, and her fondest wish was to leave Rancho de los Robles. He couldn't stand the thought of letting her venture out into the world without a husband. And he couldn't think of one man in California he'd allow Maria to marry.

His younger sister, Isabella—his cousin really, for Izzy was Tio and Tia's adopted daughter—was growing up quickly as well. Much to his dismay, she no longer wanted piggyback rides. Instead, she skipped along wherever she pleased, carrying a chicken named Señora Poppycock in her arms.

Thanks to Lupe's oily salve, his leg was nearly healed. Coupled with the old Indian woman's constant care and hearty cooking, along with plenty of rest in the *sala* with his sisters, he felt stronger than ever. Aside from his concerns over Maria and Isabella, it was good to be home. Today, he'd been more than ready to escape the hacienda, to mount up and ride out into the fields with his uncle and the vaqueros to oversee the livestock.

Hills covered in the lush green grass of spring rolled as far as the eye could see. A herd of cattle numbering over a thousand head grazed peacefully at the property's northwestern border. The land hadn't changed, but the stones that marked the property boundaries had. Joshua Tyler now claimed this territory as his own. The cattle milling here belonged to both ranchos. The *fierros*, the iron brands, on the cattle appeared similar. Many wore sale brands marking them as Tyler's animals now. The cattle's ear marks, the *señals*, could be altered as well. Tyler's cattle were missing most of their left ear. Rancho de los Robles cattle were also marked in the left ear with a slit: a *señal* that could easily be cut off to become Tyler's half-ear mark.

His easy mood evaporating, Roman shifted in his silver-studded saddle that had seen better days. "What has happened here?" he asked Tio Pedro and Juan, Rancho de los Robles's *mayordomo,* riding beside him on palomino stallions. A dozen vaqueros rode in the three men's wake, all on golden horses as well.

"We have lost hundreds of cattle. Tyler is changing the brands," Juan explained. "Those over there," Juan pointed to a herd of nearby longhorns, "they all have the foreigner's sale-brand. What should we do, Patrón?"

"Take the vaqueros and mark the new calves," Pedro told Juan. His uncle was nearly too heavy to sit a horse now. Roman could hear him breathing from several feet away. He waved his pudgy hand at Juan to do his bidding.

The *mayordomo* looked to Roman for confirmation of the command, something Juan had never done before he left for Texas. Time had not been kind to his Uncle Pedro. The golden rings were absent from his fingers, probably gambled away. The *aguardiente*, California's brandy, had taken its toll, making him an unfit leader for Rancho de los Robles. Roman could see Juan and the other vaqueros no longer respected Tio Pedro. The herdsmen waited for his nod of approval before galloping off to the task his uncle assigned them.

"Juan is right. The brands have been changed." Tio Pedro sighed heavily.

Roman shifted again in his saddle, raking a hand through his hair. Though he'd left war-torn Texas, he still felt embattled here. "Tell me the truth, Tio. Why has Tyler branded our cattle?"

"The Americano has stolen from us, but it is not as Juan believes." Tio Pedro sighed again. Roman wondered if he could make it back to the hacienda on his horse or if they would need a cart to carry the don home today.

"What does Juan believe?" Roman asked patiently. It was the Californio way to honor one's elders at all times. If nothing else, Roman was Californio to the core. And he did love his uncle, who had raised him since his father's death over a decade ago when Tio Pedro took over as the Patrón of Rancho de los Robles.

Tio Pedro waved a plump hand in the *mayordomo*'s direction. "Juan's father was our *mayordomo* for twenty-eight years. Not once did Junipero question me or your father. But that one, the son, he is disrespectful. I miss Junipero. Oh, that the bull that killed the father would have killed the son instead."

"What are you saying, Tio?"

"I'm sorry about Sarita. She chose the Americano on her own accord. I had nothing to do with her marriage to Señor Tyler."

Roman did not acknowledge his uncle's condolences. When he refused to speak, Tio Pedro continued. "You should be happy Sarita agreed to that union. Señor Tyler had his heart set on Maria. It was all I could do to hold the foreigner at bay. We thought you were dead and it was hard to go on without you."

"Tyler wanted my sister for a wife?" Roman was stunned. Maria was younger than Tyler's daughter, for heaven's sake.

"It cost many cattle to pacify the Yankee; alas, the changed brands." Tio Pedro waved his hand over the herd in explanation.

The leather of Roman's saddle creaked in protest as he shifted his frame, every muscle in his body tightening in anger. He knew his uncle's fondness for monte. But certainly Tio would never gamble with the Americano, would he?

"Why must we pacify Tyler?" Roman's heart pounded as he waited for his uncle's response. Tio would not be the first Californio to lose his family's holdings to gambling.

"The Americanos are threatening to wrest California from Mexico. If this happens, it will be wise to have a powerful Yankee aligned with us. I have done everything I can to see this accomplished for Rancho de los Robles."

"Micheltorena will not let this happen," Roman said with more merit than the statement deserved. He'd been a soldier with California's governor in the Texas campaign. Though he defended Micheltorena, he doubted the governor and his *cholo* troops could stop the Americans if the United States declared war on California.

"Micheltorena's troops are nothing but convicts from Mexico." Tio Pedro spat in disgust. "I consider the *cholos* a bitter insult. That Mexico would send us such worthless men to defend California is despicable. The *cholos* are the only outlaws Alta California knows except for the bears and horse-thieving Indians. Not only do the *cholos* molest women, they steal everything from clothing to chickens. Because of this, Micheltorena is no longer popular here."

"California should be a free province governed by the *gente de razón*," Roman said. "Is it true Micheltorena has aligned himself with the Americans in the north?"

"Micheltorena granted huge tracts of land in the Sacramento Valley to a number of foreigners to secure their loyalty. John Sutter has now built a fort on the Sacramento River. The Swiss bows to no authority but his own and is training the Indians to be his soldiers, and Micheltorena has been run out of California," Tio Pedro said dismally.

Roman swore under his breath and pounded his saddle. "Why did you not tell me this a month ago? Who has become our governor? With the United States declaring their doctrine of Manifest Destiny, we must be united now more than ever!"

Oro laid his ears back at Roman's outburst, but didn't move a muscle.

"You were sick a month ago, *mi hijo*. You needed rest. I'm sorry, but Josefa forbade me to speak of this matter with you until you were strong enough to return to the saddle."

"Since when do you take commands from your wife?"

"Since I realized she has better sense than I do." Tio Pedro smiled and then grew serious once more. "Pio Pico is governor now. General Castro has been made military commander. You know there is bad blood between the two. Castro has settled in San Juan Bautista and Monterey, shuttling back and forth between the villages. Pico remains rooted in the south. He has made Our Lady of the Angels the province's capital. Already Pico and Castro's petty squabbles are splitting the province. Pico wants California to become a British protectorate. Castro seeks a semi-independent status for Alta California. General Vallejo says we should submit ourselves to the United States. He sees this as the best path for California."

"Vallejo wants the United States to rule us?" Roman's anger grew.

"You've been gone a long time. Much has changed since you left, *mi hijo*. The Americanos arrive by land now as well as by sea. The Sacramento Valley is teeming with settlers. The Yankees come in wagons over the mountains with their women and children. Mexico cannot hold on to California much longer."

"We don't need Mexico. We will govern ourselves." Roman leaned back in his saddle, rubbing his leg. Hours on horseback left his thigh stiff and sore. "The *gente de razón* can rule California better than Mexico. A mule could rule California better than Mexico!" Roman did not bother to control his temper. "I will ride to Monterey or San Juan Bautista, wherever the general is residing at the moment, and offer my services as soon as possible. Certainly, Castro will ride north to confront the Americanos—"

Tio Pedro interrupted, "This is a war we cannot win, *mi hijo*. Not by the lance. Nor the *riflero*. The United States has grown too strong. I have arranged a marriage for you. A good match. A union that will safeguard Rancho de los Robles from the Americanos when they overtake us."

Alarm of a different kind swept through Roman. Tio had allowed him to choose Sarita for his wife before he left for Texas. She'd pushed hard for the marriage, but he was not ready to wed then with his heart set on war, not marriage. Certainly, Tio would let him choose another fiancée when he decided to marry. Perhaps when he got over the sting of losing Sarita, he would find another Californiana wife. Or maybe sail for Spain to acquire a bride to bear his children. Roman wanted *niños*, sons to ride Rancho de los Robles's golden horses and daughters to grace his hacienda parlor. Rachel Tyler's image flashed in his mind, but he squelched the ludicrous notion.

"I am not ready for a wife, Tio."

"The match is already set. You will sign the betrothal papers when you meet your *novia* in a fortnight," Tio Pedro said quietly.

"Two weeks?" Roman ran a hand through his hair again. No matter how much he hated it, Tio Pedro ruled the Vasquez family. Roman prided himself on being a Californio. Arranged marriages were the Californio way. Yet he never thought Tio would interfere in matters of the heart this way.

"You are like my son, Roman. I have raised you as my own since your father died, the Blessed Mother rest his soul. I love you, and I have prepared a good marriage for you."

"Who is she that her family can safeguard our land?" To his own ears, his voice sounded calm. Inside, he was coming apart.

"She is an Americana. You will meet her when we sign the betrothal papers. I'm sorry, Roman. It was you or Maria who must marry into an influential family. I thought you would rather be the sacrificial lamb than your sister. Maria is young and spoiled. She would not fare well in a marriage with a foreigner."

Roman could no longer stand to look at his uncle's puffy face. Disgust rioted through him. Rancho de los Robles deserved better than this union with the Yankees. A sudden realization hit him. His uncle must be indebted. "How much do you owe this Yankee?"

"More than you could imagine, *mi hijo*."

"Monte?"

"And horse racing and cockfighting and . . . the Yankee always wins," Tio Pedro said dismally.

Roman raised his hand to silence him. "Don't tell me more. You are not the only Californio sick with this disease of gambling. Why, Tio? Why did you bet with an Americano?"

"I wanted to take from the gringo." Tio Pedro smiled wistfully. "Why take from my Californio brothers when I can take from a Yankee?"

Tio Pedro turned his horse toward the hacienda. It was several hours away. "I have become an old man. I cannot ride with our vaqueros the way I used to." Tio Pedro maneuvered his horse next to Roman's mount. "I've never seen men take the

way the Americanos take. The Yankees are wolves at our door."
Tio Pedro shook his head. "I pray your gringa wife protects us
when war comes here."

Chapter Seven

The guests in their finest Californian clothes arrived on golden horses accompanied by a sea of servants and Indian vaqueros. A red-haired young woman in the party captured Rachel's rapt attention. She stood out amongst her dark-haired family like a lamp burning at midnight. Though, like the other women, she rode sidesaddle, she handled her prancing palomino like a vaquero. A richly garbed younger girl rode beside her on a smaller palomino, a large pony, really. Never had Rachel seen such a magnificent sight. All these golden horses and the striking redhead so sure of herself in the midst of that parade of splendor.

"Maria Vasquez, my fair cousin." Sarita stepped up behind Rachel on the second-story porch that looked out over the front yard filled with guests. "I hate her."

Rachel moved aside to let Sarita swoosh past on the balcony. Her stepmother's gaze tore through the crowd, her fingers clawing the wooden railing. "He's not there," she breathed.

Then more confidently, "He hasn't come." She gave Rachel a triumphant smile, her ebony eyes blazing with contempt.

Under Sarita's unexpected wrath, Rachel found it hard to breathe. Her heart began to gallop in terrified anticipation of meeting her betrothed. Her father had told her so little about him, only that he was a neighboring rancher and nearer her age than his. She didn't even know her Californian fiancé's name. For weeks, she'd wondered how God could allow this to happen when she loved Steven. And even now he waited for her in Boston with the confidence they would wed one day.

Sarita waved to a plump, older woman riding beside an even heavier man on matching palominos. They rode their golden horses regally, dressed in the traditional Californian fashion alongside the red-haired beauty and the pretty little raven-haired girl on her pony. Sarita's animosity crouched like a living thing between them on the balcony. Rachel chose her words carefully. "My father arranged this match for me. I had no choice in the matter. I don't even know who my future husband is."

"He is my cousin." Sarita's crimson dress clung to her generous curves and accentuated her wasp-like waist. Her eyes appeared so black and soulless Rachel could not make out where the pupils ended and the irises began. "Your father is a fool. He will pay for his folly and so will you." Sarita reached out and yanked a handful of hair out of Rachel's head as she strode off the balcony.

Rachel stumbled back, holding her injured scalp.

Rosa hurried out onto the balcony, looking after Sarita and the strands of blond hair hanging from her fist.

Rachel blinked away tears. "She pulled my hair for no reason."

"Oh no, *chica*." Rosa covered her mouth with her hand, eyes big as copper coins. "She has a reason. A very bad reason. I must retrieve that hair from her." Rosa rushed away, leaving Rachel even more confused.

Below, her father greeted his guests as they dismounted their horses near the front door. Should she tell him Sarita had just attacked her and that his mistress was chasing after his wife, trying to retrieve his daughter's hair? What a disaster. Of course she couldn't tell her father this. In a short while, he expected to find her in the parlor, politely pouring wine for his guests. Apprehension filled her, and she could hardly swallow.

A soft, warm breeze rustled her skirts as she watched the vaqueros gather up the golden horses. The redhead's mount balked when the girl turned the reins over to an Indian cowboy. The horse reared on its hind legs, pawing the air in fiery defiance. The redhead impatiently yanked the reins from the vaquero's hands and led the agitated horse toward the redwood stables herself, though the plump, older couple called after her to give the horse to the vaquero. The girl ignored them, continuing on to the stables with the vaquero trailing after her.

Rachel's father stood with the Californian couple, watching the redhead. The unbridled interest on her father's face sickened Rachel.

So much lust in this land. Everyone hungry for everything but God. She walked from the balcony and returned to her room, where she knelt beside her bed. *Strengthen me, Lord, to fulfill the purposes you have for me here.*

Roman Vasquez tumbled into her thoughts, as he often had of late at the oddest moments. Especially before she went to sleep and when she first awakened in the morning, she found herself praying for him. The man who captured bears single-handedly and questioned her about God and made her knees tremble with fear and something else she wouldn't name.

She wondered if he'd recovered from the infection in his leg. She'd asked Jesus to heal him and kept thinking about how he had gently comforted her after the dreadful bear and bull fight. The memory of his hand on hers as they stroked the horse together sent warmth throughout her. The heat settled in her face, making her cheeks burn. Pleasure had filled her at his surprisingly tender touch that day. What was he searching for? A woman's kindness? A woman's gentleness? Perhaps a woman's love?

She stopped the thought right there. Steven's face rose before her. And then the unknown face of the man her father had chosen for her to marry. Dread flooded her. *Help me, Lord. Please help me. I'm afraid of meeting him.*

As she prayed, Rosa burst into the room as flustered as when she'd bolted after Sarita thirty minutes earlier. "I could not find the señora. She has taken your hair and vanished!"

Rosa draped a crude wooden rosary around Rachel's neck. "You must wear this now for protection."

Rachel removed the beads and crucifix. "This is but a necklace. It cannot protect me, Rosa."

"Do not say that, señorita!" Rosa attempted to replace the rosary around her neck. "You must wear it until I find the hair she took from you. Hair is used for spells. That one, she is a witch! I see the dark calling in her eyes. She worships the evil one."

Rachel shook her head. "God is sovereign. The devil can only do what God allows him to do. I was told you cannot wear a rosary around your neck. It is only for prayer to be held in your hands."

"Dios wants you to wear the rosary. The evil one is afraid of the rosary! My mother told me so," Rosa pleaded.

Rachel handed the rosary back to her. "This is made of wood. It cannot protect me from evil."

Rosa wrung her hands. "Please, *chica*, keep it. Sleep with it under your pillow if you will not wear it."

"Will it make you feel better if I sleep with it?"

"Yes." Rosa appeared on the verge of tears. Rachel had never seen her flustered like this before.

"I will put it under my pillow right now." She walked over and tucked the rosary under her bedding. "Now I'd best go to the parlor. My father wants me to pour wine for the guests."

Rosa tried to smile, but her eyes remained frightened. "When the evening is over, I will check on you. And I will pray as you meet your betrothed for the first time. He is a sight for sore eyes, as your father likes to say."

"I have seen no man who could be my betrothed amongst the guests who arrived a while ago."

"He just rode in on a golden stallion. He rides like the devil but looks like an avenging angel. Never have I seen such a man." The smile trembled on Rosa's lips.

"Will you help me dress?" Rachel held out shaking hands. "I'm so nervous I can't see straight. What if my betrothed is cruel and proud and fierce?"

"He does not look cruel. But proud and fierce, yes. I will pray for you." Rosa began to unhook the buttons on Rachel's day dress and assisted her as she donned a quilted pink petticoat and a delicate corset with sixty linen stays. After lacing her up tight, Rosa slipped a delicate rose-colored silk gown with vanilla lace trim over her head. Then she piled Rachel's hair in soft ringlets that spilled down her back. "You look like a European princess. How beautiful you are, *chica*."

"I feel exposed in this dress." Rachel tried to pull up the plunging neckline where the lacy corset enhanced her cleavage.

"Men like exposure." Rosa attempted another smile, but her eyes brimmed with worry. "I'm sure your betrothed will find you irresistible."

"The men I'm accustomed to prefer modest attire and do not ride golden stallions. My grandfather and Steven would be shocked to see me in this gown." Her heart ached thinking of Steven. What would he do when her letter reached him? It had taken her days and countless tears to write it.

Rosa nodded in sympathy and then pushed her from the room. "Go. Your padre is not a patient man."

Rachel adjusted her bodice again as she walked down the hall, her nerves and the snug corset making it hard to breathe. Glancing down into the valley of the gown's audacious neckline, her cheeks caught fire. She had gained some of the curves back she'd lost during her sickness on the ship. Never would she look like Sarita, with her voluptuous figure, but at least she no longer resembled a boy.

Aside from the neckline, this really was an exquisite gown of silk and lace. She did feel womanly in it. The dress was beautiful. Remembering her time on the ship making gowns for Molly, she realized Molly would have loved this dress the color of her rosy, rounded little cheeks.

For the hundredth time, she wondered how Molly and Anne were faring in Monterey. Had they stayed in the seaside village? Had they found Molly's father? If no other good came of this journey to California—the startling loss of Steven, the uncertain future she now faced married to a stranger—at least Molly and Anne were alive and facing a fresh start in the pretty pueblo town.

There is no greater love than to lay down one's life for a friend. The thought strengthened her as she approached the *sala*. She wasn't dying, but marrying someone other than Steven felt like a death.

Chapter Eight

Her father and another man waited near the *sala* door both extravagantly dressed in short embroidered jackets and fine knee-length, velvet britches favored by California dons. Elaborately stitched deerskin boots adorned the men's feet. Their conversation ceased as Rachel stepped into the long room designed for entertaining guests. In the corner of the *sala,* a man slouched in one of her father's carved mahogany chairs. Dressed like a vaquero, he was in the middle of downing a glass of wine. Recognizing his ebony hair, his startling light eyes in his deeply tanned face, that big, strong body with weapons tucked into his belt, she stopped cold.

The red-haired girl beside him drank wine as well. Up close, she looked younger. And petulant. Again, Rachel was struck by her beauty and boldness, but not nearly as struck as she was by the man sitting beside her.

Roman Vasquez.

His long legs were stretched out before him, his dusty, spur-strapped boots propped on one of her father's expensive rugs. Rugs were a rarity due to the fleas in California. Her father often had his rugs hauled out of the hacienda and beaten in the yard by the servants to keep them pest free. Beside them sat the older woman Sarita had waved to from the balcony. Short and round like her husband, the older woman smiled when Rachel arrived. She held the hand of the little girl, who smiled too, a bit shyly but with a vivacious sparkle in her eyes. The girl was quite pretty with blue-black hair, dusky skin, and a delicate build, but it was her eyes, a startling crystalline blue, that surprised Rachel. Clearly, the child was of mixed heritage.

"Rachel," said her father, his voice laced with reproach. "It is well you have finally graced us with your presence."

The plump Californio gentleman stepped forward to take her hand. "Señorita Tyler, you are well worth the wait. I am Don Pedro, and your beauty has vastly exceeded my expectations. Your hair is the color of Rancho de los Robles's horses and your eyes as blue as Monterey Bay." The don's ample cheeks puffed with his heavy breathing as he kissed the back of her hand.

In the corner, Roman Vasquez slowly clapped his hands, applauding the older man's introduction. His rudeness startled the sweating don leaning over Rachel's hand. The redhead laughed, muffling the giggle when the older woman rebuked her with her gaze. The older woman then tapped Roman on the head with the fan she held in her hand. She said something in Spanish that Rachel didn't understand.

Roman slowly got to his feet, swaying as he rose from his chair. He shoved his empty glass at the redhead and then made his way across the parlor, walking a crooked line that led to Rachel.

"Señor Vasquez," she said cautiously, confused by his behavior.

"*Chiquita Yanquia* . . . like my uncle says . . . you are as beautiful as my horse." He made a sweeping bow, staggering as he did so.

Both girls giggled; the redhead no longer bothering to stifle her mirth when the older woman glared at her. The blue-eyed girl laughed behind hands cupped over her rosy mouth.

"Roman Miguel Vicente Vasquez," Don Pedro said sharply. "You will address your betrothed as Señorita Tyler. And you will cease with this atrocious behavior at once!"

Roman captured Rachel's hand. His eyes, a startling green in his deeply tanned face, shone unnaturally bright and blood-shot. Instead of kissing the back of her hand as the plump man had, he turned her hand over and kissed the open palm, the very center of it, his lips searing all the way to her soul.

Horrified, she attempted to jerk her hand away.

"Enough, Roman." Don Pedro tried to step between them, but Roman moved with surprising swiftness, sweeping her against his body while stepping beyond the older gentleman's reach. She lost her breath as he tucked her roughly against his hard frame. He'd gained muscle since she'd last seen him, and his strength astonished her.

"My *novia* and I are well acquainted. I have seen her naked knees." Roman ran his hand along Rachel's cinched waist, then down over her hip with shocking intimacy.

Appalled, she attempted to move away from him, which only caused him to tighten his grip on her. "Drunkenness is a sin," she hissed in his ear, struggling to free herself of his vise-like hold.

"One of my many sins, my protesting little dove." He gave her waist a rakish squeeze as he grinned at her.

"Let's get on with signing the betrothal papers so we can all enjoy the celebration as much as my future son-in-law already has." Her father walked to the table where the engagement papers were laid out on the polished mahogany wood.

Don Pedro motioned for Roman to do the same. For a moment, Rachel thought he would resist, but instead, he released her and approached the table. Don Pedro offered his arm to her like a gentleman. His brown eyes extended a wordless apology.

Gratefully, she tucked her hand in the crook of his elbow and allowed him to escort her the short distance across the *sala* to the table. She did not trust her shaking limbs to carry her there alone.

Roman signed first, dipping his quill in the ink and scrawling his name in a bold flourish. Rachel concentrated hard to put her signature beside his, her hands trembling as badly as her legs.

Then her father poured everyone more wine and toasted the engagement. "To a grand alliance and grandsons," he said with a smile.

The Vasquezes emptied their glasses, all except Roman. He refused to participate in the toast. Rachel's glass also remained untouched.

Her father set his glass on the table beside the sealed betrothal agreement. "I have arranged a private fiesta for tonight. My daughter has agreed to sing for us. She has the most beautiful voice. But first we will take a siesta, as the ladies need time to refresh themselves after their travel.

"Rachel, escort Señora Josefa, Señorita Maria, and Señorita Isabella to their rooms," her father commanded.

"Certainly." Rachel did not like the way her father's gaze lingered on the red-haired Maria.

"My study is open for you," her father told Don Pedro. "I will send a servant to you shortly with the article you requested."

"Thank you." Don Pedro looked grimly determined. "Roman, you will apologize to your betrothed for your shameful behavior before she departs."

A muscle jerked in Roman's cheek. His green eyes shone bright as jade as he addressed her. "*Lo siento mucho, Yanquia pequeña.*"

There was no regret in his eyes. What she saw there chilled her. Drunkenness allowed the devil an open door to a person's spirit, her grandfather always said. "Please don't drink any more," she whispered, hoping only he could hear her.

"I will need whiskey when my uncle's through with me," he said just as softly. Then raising his voice for everyone to hear, "Won't I need whiskey, Tio?"

Don Pedro's lips tightened, but he said nothing.

"Escort the ladies to their rooms, Rachel." Her father motioned for Don Pedro and Roman to follow him. The men waited for the women to exit the *sala* and then trailed the ladies out the door.

The men headed for her father's study as she led the ladies down the tiled hallway to the first wing of bedrooms. "Do you know what the men will do in the study?" Rachel hesitantly asked Señora Josefa.

Before the older woman could respond, the little girl, Isabella, interrupted. "They will beat my brother soundly!"

"Isabella, shush," Señora Josefa whispered.

"She's only telling the truth," Maria interrupted.

"You shush too," Señora Josefa retorted.

"Roman never drinks wine. Why was he drinking today?" Isabella asked.

"He doesn't want to marry Señorita Tyler," Maria answered. "Our brother is drunk because he's miserable at the thought of marrying an Americana."

"*Niñas,* enough!" Señora Josefa fanned herself.

"It's the truth," Maria said. "Don't you think Señorita Tyler should hear the truth, Tia?"

"I'm sure Señorita Tyler noticed your brother's misgivings," Señora Josefa acknowledged.

"Why wouldn't Roman want to marry you?" Isabella was practically bouncing up and down. "You're so beautiful with your fair skin and golden hair. Even the freckles on your nose are pretty." The little girl wrinkled her own nose, as if freckles were a curse.

"Thank you." Rachel felt sick to her stomach. "How will they beat him?" she ventured.

"With a rod." Isabella's blue eyes widened. "A heavy wooden rod that will leave lumps like squirrels on his back. He'll probably even bleed."

"But he's a grown man." Rachel stopped walking. She couldn't believe what she was hearing.

"In California, a child is never too old for discipline," Señora Josefa explained. "Roman is like a son to us. I have raised him as my own since I married Don Pedro." She lowered her voice. "His poor, protesting mother was buried by then."

"My mother embraced Protestantism before she died." Maria appeared scandalized, though Rachel sensed the red-head only pretended to be shocked. "An American ship captain and his wife converted my mother. My father threatened to kill the captain before he sailed away. Are you a protester to our religion, Señorita Tyler?" Maria cocked one of those finely arched red brows at her.

"You may call me Rachel, and I will call you Maria." She ignored Maria's question about her faith. Before the priest who married her father returned to Monterey, her father had insisted on a Catholic baptism for her. She signed some church documents, the sign of the cross was made on her forehead with oil by the priest, and then water was poured over the crown of her head. Afterward, she went to her room to sit with her Bible. Being Protestant or Catholic didn't make a person serve Jesus any more or any less, she'd decided after praying about it. Sin must be forsaken and a life consecrated to the Lord. That's what mattered to God, not one's religion. Rachel opened the door to the first bedroom, the one with a large bed intended for a couple.

"Rachel can't be Protestant." Isabella said. "Roman would not marry her if she was a protestor!"

Señora Josefa looked at Rachel, waiting for her answer. Rachel felt embattled since she still considered herself very much a Protestant, even after her Catholic baptism.

"You are not a . . . Protestant . . . are you?" Señora Josefa whispered the word while furiously fanning her flushed face.

"I was baptized Catholic upon coming to California." Rachel did not want to cause Señora Josefa further distress.

"Oh, thank the Blessed Mother!" Señora Josefa snapped her fan shut. She smiled and patted Rachel's cheek. "You will make a fine wife for Roman. He has grown so hard. The Texas war was not good for him. By the grace of God, you will soften him with little ones. He so longs for *ninos*."

Señora Josefa stared lovingly at the little girl now glued to Rachel's side. "Isabella is our miracle. For years, we had no children. Then one afternoon, Father Renalgo rode up on his donkey to deliver this blue-eyed baby to us. Roman fell in love with her at first sight. Maria was very jealous of her new sister, but Roman dearly loves both of you, doesn't he, *chicas*?"

Isabella nodded in agreement. Maria appeared bored and annoyed, as if she'd heard this adoption story a hundred times and still didn't fancy it. Rachel was grateful for this insight about her future husband. If he loved children and his sisters, then there must be kindness in him. But why would God yoke her to an unbeliever? A man who touched her so shamefully in his drunkenness, setting her senses afire?

All her life, she'd dreamed of the man she would one day marry. For years, she thought Steven would be that man. Gentle Steven would never touch her as Roman Vasquez had. Even now, she could feel the heat of his hand running up and down her side, stroking her in places she'd never been stroked, stirring feelings in her that had never been stirred. And that warm, lingering kiss on the inside of her palm. Reprehensible!

"I hope Roman comes to love you the way he loves me. He loves me more than anyone," Isabella said with the greatest confidence.

Rachel swallowed the tightness in her throat. "I hope so too. You may call me Rachel. May I call you Isabella?"

"Yes, please. Or Izzy, if you wish."

Rachel felt the heat of the redhead's gaze. "Are you afraid of my brother's bed?" Not an ounce of shame colored her beautiful face. Maria's features were classic and refined, though her lips curved fuller than most, adding a lushness to her face that was earthy and enchanting. Her eyes were nearly identical to her brother's. Green, heavily lashed, and striking.

"Maria!" Señora Josefa snapped the fan against her palm. Rachel thought she might smack the girl on top of the head as she had Roman in the parlor.

A pout formed on Maria's mouth. "Do you have a mother?" Maria asked Rachel. Without waiting for her response, she turned to her aunt. "If she doesn't have a mother, Tia, then you must warn her about the marriage bed. Look at her. Obviously, she knows nothing of men."

"The Lord will prepare me for my marriage bed," Rachel announced with a bravado she didn't feel.

"Isn't that funny? She thinks Dios can prepare her for the marriage bed." Maria laughed.

Isabella patted Rachel's skirt, whispering loudly, "Roman won't hurt you. He is not like the men who wear out their horses."

Though she felt like crying, Rachel smiled down at Isabella. The little minx had quickly become her champion.

Señora Josefa plopped down on the bed with an exaggerated sigh. "Maria, pull off my boots before my feet swell up. If that happens, they'll have to bury me in these awful hides."

Maria did as she was told, though it was obvious she found the chore utterly distasteful.

"No more talk of the marriage bed." Señora Josefa fluffed the pillows behind her head. "*En boca cerrada no entran moscas.*"

"Flies do not enter a closed mouth," Isabella translated for Rachel.

"Would you like to see yours and Maria's room?" Rachel asked Isabella. These Californian women were so different than the women she was used to. Never would her grandmother or the ladies of their church have discussed the marriage bed so freely.

"Can I sleep in your room with you?" Isabella widened her big blue eyes in sweet appeal. "We are going to be sisters. I sleep with Maria all the time. I want to sleep with you tonight."

"Please, Tia Josefa, let Izzy sleep with Rachel. I'm tired of her kicking me all night long. She is such a little goat." Maria dropped her aunt's boots on the floor with a thud.

"It is Señorita Rachel's decision." Josefa pointed at the boots. "Tuck those under the bed, *mi hija.*"

Maria wrinkled her nose, pushing the boots out of sight with the tips of her own boots.

"Of course Isabella can sleep with me." Rachel touched the little girl's head with tenderness. Isabella reminded her of Molly, only a few years older than the little Irish girl.

Isabella nestled her small brown hand into Rachel's and tugged. "Let's go see your room."

Rachel allowed the little girl to lead her down the hall. "Maria calls me *little goat.* Do you think I have goat ears?"

Isabella cocked her head, using her free hand to push the long black hair away from a little ear for inspection.

"I think you have lovely ears." The child had perfect ears. Like little seashells.

"I think my ears are nice too." Isabella giggled happily. "Maria will end up eating with pigs. I know she will."

"Why do you say such a thing about your sister?"

"Because people reap what they sow. Maria is always sowing slop, so she will reap slop one day."

"That expression is from the Bible. Do you read the Bible?"

"The padres read the Bible during Mass. I don't like going to Mass."

"Why not?"

"Because Señora Poppycock is not welcome at Mass."

"Who is Señora Poppycock?"

"My chicken."

"You have a chicken?"

"Oh yes, and she is beautiful and smart and eats flies off the wall. When you come to live with us, I will bring her to your room so she can eat up all the flies, and then they won't bother you."

"That will be wonderful." Despite her anxiety over her betrothal, Rachel couldn't help but smile, enjoying Isabella's company very much.

Chapter Nine

Rosa massaged the herbs and oil into Roman's lacerated back. He didn't talk or make any sound as she dressed his wounds, but he drank all the patrón's whiskey she'd brought along to take the edge off his pain. Never had Rosa seen such a magnificent man, nor one so harshly flogged. He thanked her with a grateful smile, flashing perfect white teeth when she finished attending him, then he rose from the wooden chair he'd straddled while she ministered to his wounds and lay down on the bed with only his pants on. He appeared to already be asleep when she departed. After quietly closing his door, Rosa nearly screamed out loud, coming face-to-face with Sarita.

"*Silencio,*" Sarita hissed, calling Rosa a terrible name as well.

Rosa crossed herself, backing away from the woman. "You must give me Señorita Tyler's hair," Rosa demanded in a trembling voice.

Sarita laughed, making a growling sound that unnerved Rosa. "I will use the *Yanquia's* hair to worship Tohic when the new moon rises."

Rosa made the sign of the cross again. "I will tell the patrón," she threatened.

"Tell him." Sarita smiled, eyes black and hard as onyx. "I will steal his hair and yours too and offer it all to Tohic if you don't stay out of my way, you stupid fool."

"Why did you come here?" Rosa kept her voice low so as not to disturb her patient on the other side of the door. Rachel's betrothed had been placed in the *mayordomo's* quarters behind the sprawling redwood stables outside the hacienda's walls until he sobered up.

"I have come to attend his wounds." Sarita held up a deerskin pouch that was bloodstained. Rosa shuttered at the thought of what might be in that bag.

"I have already attended Señorita Rachel's betrothed." Rosa mustered all her courage. "He does not need your help."

The señora's eyes grew even blacker, if that were possible, narrowing in fury. "Roman Vasquez belongs to me. He has always been mine. He will always be mine." Glaring a warning at the servant, Sarita pushed past her, cracking open the *mayordomo's* door. "If you tell anyone I was here, I will have you killed." Slipping into the room, the señora shut the door in Rosa's face.

Rosa made the sign of the cross again as she hurried back to the hacienda. Poor Señorita Rachel, an innocent angel tangled in that witch's web. Knowing the señora probably would not return to the hacienda for some time, Rosa hurried to Sarita's room and frantically searched for Rachel's hair. She found charms and woodpecker feathers and numerous herbs, sinister little carvings of animal figures and evil faces, and tiny woven medicine baskets made by Indian women, but not a lock of blond hair.

Distraught and discouraged, she considered going to the patrón, but she didn't want to attend to his desires if he happened to be in the mood. After years with him, Rosa knew he was not in the least superstitious. Informing Joshua that his wife was a witch would do no good. But if she told him about Sarita in Rachel's betrothed's room, certainly that would stir up enough trouble to keep the señora from casting her spells right now, but who knew where this telling would lead?

Rosa still hoped she could return to Monterey and the little red tile-roofed house he had built for her there this past winter as he planned his wedding. Upon giving the situation more thought, Rosa decided to return to Señorita Rachel to help her dress for tonight's celebration without saying anything to anyone. She was a servant after all, and servants kept their mouths shut and did as they were told.

The siesta was nearly over. Soon it would be time to prepare for the evening activities. After she arrived at the señorita's room, Rosa helped Rachel into a corset and petticoat, though the women of California rarely wore corsets these days. The peacock-blue silk gown with its scooped neckline and laced-up bodice made the most of Rachel's slender curves. The girl's long hair tumbled in golden waves to her waist. Washed and dried now, Rosa brushed the beautiful hair till it shone like sunshine, then pinned it up in artful curls. Thankfully, Señorita Rachel didn't press her for any information about her betrothed. Rosa's thoughts swirled about what she could do to help her young charge, but nothing came to mind that would protect the Patrón's daughter from the wicked woman he'd married.

• • •

"You missed Rachel's singing. You must hear her sing," Isabella said excitedly upon Roman's arrival that night at the family's fiesta. His sister tugged him farther into the courtyard lit by candle lanterns. A table laden with food filled the air with the smells of a feast, but he wasn't hungry and made no pretense of wanting to be there, resisting Isabella's pleas to go see Rachel. He'd only come because Tio Pedro insisted on it.

Isabella finally gave up trying to drag him over to where Rachel stood near the musicians and instead rushed over to Rachel's side. After pleading with her to sing again— without success, it appeared from Roman's vantage point, Isabella scampered over to Tio Pedro and Don Tyler, who were smoking cigarillos and drinking brandy where they sat in two carved wooden chairs probably carried out from the house into the courtyard.

Hands on hips, Isabella planted herself before the two men. That determined look was on her little face that Roman knew all too well. He couldn't make out the words she said, but he had an idea of what she told them.

Tio Pedro crushed out his cigarillo, and Joshua Tyler did the same. "Have you asked her to sing?" Tyler's voice rang out loud enough for all to hear.

Isabella answered him, but Roman couldn't hear what she said. He'd retired to the darkest corner of the courtyard, planting himself against a cool adobe wall where he set about lighting his own cigarillo.

After speaking with Isabella, Joshua Tyler walked over to his daughter, who was standing with the Indian musicians. She did not look comfortable there. She looked like he felt, forced into something neither of them wanted.

Isabella bounced back over to where he sat on the cobblestones, leaning gingerly against the wall. "I am sleeping in Rachel's room tonight," she teased. "Don't you wish you were me, *hermano*?"

"You should not talk of things you don't understand, *pequeña*. And look, you got the señorita in trouble with her padre." Roman pointed to Tyler chastising his daughter now.

A hurt look on her face, Isabella flounced away.

It wasn't long before the fiesta quieted as Rachel stepped into the middle of the courtyard once more. The Indians strummed the violins, softly, slowly, and then stronger, with the guitar joining in as Rachel began to sing.

Isabella skipped back over to Roman, crawling up into his lap. Roman crushed out his cigarillo. He did not wish to smoke in front of his sisters, for he did not want them taking up the habit like some women did.

"Isn't Rachel's singing beautiful? She sings like a bird. A nightingale, I think."

He said nothing.

"I feel like weeping when she sings. Do you not feel like weeping?" Isabella leaned against Roman's chest. He flinched as her weight pressed his injured back into the hard adobe bricks. He didn't take his eyes off of Rachel.

"You smell funny," Isabella announced. "You smell like a woman."

"It's medicine. Sit still, Izzy, you're hurting my back."

"You smell like perfume," she accused.

"If you don't like how I smell, go sit somewhere else."

Isabella pressed her warm little body snugly against his. "No, I like sitting on you, *hermano*."

The two listened to the rest of Rachel's song in silence. When she finished singing, Rachel left the courtyard with her head bowed. Roman sensed her defeat. Her haunting song continued to ring in his ears. She really did have the sweetest voice he'd ever heard. He stood up, dumping Isabella onto her own two feet.

"Where are you going?" Isabella asked.

"Isn't it your bedtime yet?"

"I'll go to bed when Rachel goes to bed. I'm sleeping with her tonight."

"Perhaps she just went to bed." Roman walked from the courtyard. Isabella trailed along behind him.

"I think you're mad," she told him.

"Why would I be mad?"

Outside of the walled patio, at the edge of the darkness, Isabella tugged him to a halt. "You are mad because nothing is going the way you planned. You lost the war in Texas. Sarita married the gringo. And now you must marry Rachel. Perhaps California will be conquered by the Yankees, and then you will be happy you married a gringa because Papa says an alliance with the Americanos will protect us."

Roman knelt down beside her, putting his hand gently on top of her head. "Do you fear the Americanos coming, *pequeña?*"

"Maria prays the United States will conqueror us quickly. She says she will sail away on one of those Yankee ships that bring us sugar and satin shoes." Isabella's voice trembled, and her eyes filled with tears.

Roman pulled her into his arms. "I won't let that happen, *chica*. Maria will never board a Yankee ship and leave us. Never."

Isabella wrapped her arms around his neck. "Promise?"

"I promise." Roman held her for a moment and then set her away from him as he rose to his feet.

"Did Papa whip you harshly?"

He smiled to ease her concern. "I am fine, *pequeña*. Let me go to bed now. I'm very tired tonight."

"Is that really where you are going? To your bed?"

"Look at the moon. The second night watch is already here. You should go to your bed too."

"Will you walk me to Rachel's room?"

His smile disappeared. "Can you not find your own way there?"

"No. I need your help. How will I sleep tonight without Señora Poppycock?" Isabella appeared on the verge of tears again.

He reached for her hand and led her through a colonnaded patio lit by more candle lanterns. "I hope Señorita Tyler does not snore like Señora Poppycock."

"Señora Poppycock does not snore."

"No, she clucks. How do you sleep with all that clucking your chicken does?"

"She only clucks if something frightens her."

"Then she must be frightened all the time."

"Señora Poppycock is not frightened all the time. She is a brave hen." Isabella tugged him toward the east wing.

After passing several closed doors, Isabella abruptly opened a door and pulled Roman into a candlelit room. Clothed in a white nightdress, Rachel knelt beside her bed. Her unbound hair tumbled to the floor. She rose swiftly to her feet upon their arrival, her hair swirling about her in glorious display.

"You left without me," Isabella chastised her.

Rachel glanced at Isabella and then fixed her gaze on Roman. He attempted to free himself from Isabella's grip, taking in Rachel's unbound hair and thin white nightdress, as well as the shocked look on her face. As he stared at her, she gathered her hair with both hands and swiftly braided it over one shoulder.

Isabella would not let him go. He finally yanked his hand free of hers and shut the door behind them so no other guests saw him there. "Can't you see we have interrupted Señorita Tyler as she prepares for bed?"

"She wasn't sleeping, just praying," Isabella said.

"You should never barge into a señorita's room." Roman glared down at her.

Isabella backed away from his disapproval until she stood in the sweep of Rachel's white nightgown.

Rachel put her arms around Isabella. "It's all right. I told her my room was hers as long as she stayed here."

Rachel looked so vulnerable and fetching and determined to stand her ground that he couldn't help but admire her. "I'm sorry you were forced to sing tonight," he said.

"I am sorry you and I are being forced to marry. I do not want this marriage any more than you do," she answered.

"Don't say that!" Isabella turned and wrapped her arms around Rachel's waist.

"Isabella, this is an adult affair." Roman moved toward the door.

Rachel stroked Isabella's hair, staring down at the child now, no longer meeting his gaze.

"I have requested you stay at Rancho de los Robles until the wedding so we may have the chance to get to know one another before we marry. Your father has agreed to this, which amazes me. If you were my daughter, I would never allow such a scandalous arrangement."

Rachel raised her eyes to his, and though he didn't know her very well, he could see he'd made her angry. "Then why did you ask for this arrangement?"

A rueful smile twisted his mouth. "Why not? We are all but wed in California. A betrothal is as binding as rings here. You may as well be my wife."

"You can sleep with me and Señora Poppycock at our house," Isabella volunteered brightly.

"I will speak to my father about this." Rachel's voice trembled as she twisted her braid in her hand. She kept her other arm tucked around Isabella.

"I am leaving tomorrow. I don't care what you say to your father. You will leave with me when I ride out in the morning."

Isabella giggled. "I am so happy you are coming to Rancho de los Robles. We will plan your wedding there. You should marry quickly and begin having babies."

A blush colored Rachel's cheeks at the mention of babies. "How old are you?" she asked Isabella.

"Eleven." His sister squared her little shoulders.

"Really?" The child's age obviously surprised Rachel.

"I am small for my years. My mother was small this way too. She died giving birth to me. I was brought to Rancho de los Robles on All Saints Day, along with my wet nurse because I was but a month old. My father decided he could not live in California and care for me after my mother passed. He was a Russian fur hunter who lived at Fort Ross. Padre Renalgo said he truly loved my mother. Padre Renalgo said everyone loved my mother. She was so very beautiful, but so very young. Just fourteen years old when she died at Fort Ross while giving birth to me during a terrible storm that made the ocean rage. This is only a few years older than me. See, I am quite grown up after all."

"Grown up enough to understand Señorita Tyler must be given time to get used to this idea of marrying a stranger," said Roman, narrowing his eyes at his sister. He wished she wasn't in the room with them.

"You are not a stranger," Isabella told him.

"I am a stranger to Señorita Tyler." Smiling in spite of himself, Roman opened the door. He could stare at Rachel in her winsome white gown all night long, but he knew he needed to go. "Goodnight, *pequeñas*," he said, shutting the door behind him.

Chapter Ten

The knock on her door came before dawn. Rachel was already awake, curled on her side in the bed beside the sleeping Isabella. After lighting a candle, she tiptoed on bare feet to open the door. Roman stood there dressed for the trail, along with a very sleepy Maria still in her nightclothes. He pushed his sister into the room and quietly closed the door behind her.

"You must dress for travel," Maria said as if she were talking in her sleep. "Don't worry about your belongings. Everything will be packed up by our servants and brought along when we return to Rancho de los Robles. Roman says you must hurry." Maria headed for the bed, crawling into it to snuggle down beside Isabella, still sleeping soundly there.

"Maria," Rachel whispered in rising panic. She went to the bed and gently shook the girl awake. "What has happened? Why is your brother here so early?"

Maria mumbled something in Spanish. Rachel had no idea what she said. "Maria!" She shook her again. "Why is he here so early?"

Maria rolled toward Rachel. "Roman's ready to leave. How do I know why he gets up so early? He always rises early."

"But what about the rest of you? Aren't we all traveling together today?"

"We won't be leaving for several more days. Unlike my brother, Tio and Tia would never behave so rudely." The red-head flipped onto her stomach, burying her head under the covers.

"Maria." Rachel shook her again, hoping she had the red-head by the shoulder under the bundle of covers. "Certainly, your brother knows I can't travel alone with him."

The covers flew back, hitting Rachel in her face. Maria sat up, a stream of indignant Spanish spilling from her lips. Rachel marveled Isabella didn't wake up in the midst of the ruckus. "I have no idea what you are saying," she patiently told Maria. Inside, she was frantic.

The bedroom door opened. "She said you will travel with me or else there will be the devil to pay. I am your betrothed, and you must obey me as you would obey your husband." Roman walked into the room, translating for Maria.

"I did not say that," Maria replied in irritated English. "If you've had your ear pressed to the door like a snooping servant all this time, why didn't you just come in and fetch her yourself so I can go back to sleep!"

"Lower your voice," Roman commanded. "I told you to help Señorita Tyler dress. She doesn't look dressed to me." He kept his eyes on Maria. Rachel was still in her nightdress.

"I told you, I am not a servant. She can dress herself." Maria smirked. "Better yet, you dress her, *hermano*. It won't be long before you undress her as well." Maria laughed.

Roman took a threatening step toward the bed. Maria dove under the covers, bumping Isabella. Amazingly, the child slept on.

Glancing around, he focused on Rachel's traveling trunk and strode over to it with a purpose, his spurs clicking against the plank floor.

"What are you doing?" Rachel grabbed a shawl to wrap around her shoulders as he rifled through her things.

He ignored her until a bundle of clothing filled his arms. "Come with me." He gripped her by the elbow, dragging her toward the door.

"How dare you!" She fought to escape him, resolved to keep the shawl covering her nightgown.

He wrestled her to the door.

"I will not leave with you," she cried.

The blankets again flew back from Maria's head. She sat up, still laughing at them.

Finally awake, Isabella untangled herself in the mess Maria had made of the bed.

"*Silencio*, all of you!" Roman pushed Rachel out the door.

"I must have my Bible!" She twisted away from him.

Their gazes collided and then held in a contest of wills. "Does the Bible mean that much to you?"

"Yes!" She yanked out of his hold and rushed back into the room.

He followed her. Both his sisters sat up in bed, watching them, Maria clearly entertained, poor Isabella rubbing her eyes like a child roused from a long summer nap.

"Hurry," Roman told Rachel.

She grabbed the worn leather Bible off the table beside her bed where the candle burned and then refused to budge. It wasn't even dawn yet. "I will not travel alone with you."

Maria laughed out loud.

"What's so funny?" Isabella asked.

Roman strode over to the bed. He shoved the bundle of clothes at Maria. "Be quiet and follow me," he ordered. The redhead dove back under the covers, taking the clothes with her.

Rachel backed away from him when he approached, his face absolutely unwavering. When he attempted to grab hold of her arm, she raced around the bed with her Bible clutched to her chest. He ended up with just her shawl in his hands. He let out a curse. Throwing the shawl to the floor, he pursued her from the room.

He caught her in the darkened hall, cupping his hand over her mouth as he pulled her into his arms. "You must not scream." Her thin nightdress offered very little covering between their two bodies. God bless her Bible for it was the only thing keeping an ounce of distance between them as Roman pressed her against his hard, immobile chest.

"Nod your head if you will not scream."

She shook her head *no* instead. He pulled her more tightly against him, if that were possible, his breath hot against her ear. "Do not resist me, Rachel. I am trying to protect you, and I cannot do that by leaving you here with your father. You have enemies in this place."

It was the first time she'd heard her name on his lips. He said it so invitingly. The enemies he mentioned confused her. Who would be her enemy in her father's house? She thought she might faint in his arms, his body, so hard and warm and masculine, pressed against her frame. Never had she been pressed to a man's body before. The rawness of it stunned her, the muscle and bone and strength of him. She couldn't see his face in the darkness, but she could feel his anxiety. His breath warmed her ear as he whispered, "Your father was well into his brandy last night. If he's any kind of father at all, he will have changed his mind this morning about allowing you to leave with me. I want to be long gone when he rises."

Slowly, he removed his hand from her mouth. She opened her mouth to scream, but the moment she made a sound, his lips covered hers. His kiss muffled her cry. He kept on kissing her until she stilled in his arms. Until she could no longer resist the heat washing over her. His kiss was nothing like she'd ever imagined a kiss could be. At first fiercely consuming, then shockingly intimate, now his lips gentled, becoming so tender she could taste his longing for her to yield in a way she didn't know a woman could yield to a man.

When she tentatively responded to his tenderness, he released her, cradling her face in his large, calloused hands. "Please don't scream," he said and then kissed her again, this time deeply, intimately, his body trembling against hers. This hard man was trembling from head to toe. She trembled too.

With a soft groan, he scooped her up into his arms.

"Come with me willingly, *pequeña*." He sounded as breathless as she felt.

"All right," she answered, shocking herself.

His lips found hers in the darkness once more, and he kissed her swiftly. Possessively. Passionately. Then he strode through the shadowy hacienda and out into the cold, moonlit morning with her in his arms.

The brisk air brought Rachel to her senses. She pressed the Bible against her chest as he carried her to the stables like a captive. She began to shiver uncontrollably. In response, he tucked her closer to his chest, trying to warm her, it seemed.

In front of the stables, four mounted riders waited with two saddled horses in the blue-black darkness. Roman spoke Spanish to the men.

One of them dismounted and disappeared into the stables.

A second man dismounted and took Rachel from his arms as Roman swiftly leaped into one of the saddles. The vaquero placed Rachel back into Roman's arms in front of him on the horse.

The other vaquero came from the stables carrying a woolen blanket, which he handed to Roman. He threw the blanket over Rachel, tucking it around her. The vaquero then placed another cloth bundle into a leather bag on the horse without a rider before mounting his own horse.

One of the men led the pack animal out into the darkness. Rachel scarcely had time to gather her thoughts before they were off at a gallop, horse hooves thundering in her ears.

They were a mile from the hacienda before her situation truly sank in. How Roman kept them both in the saddle with the blanket tucked around her astounded her. This man seemed part of the horse, and she a part of him, pressed intimately against his body. The group did not slow when dawn broke upon the hills. By then, Rachel had worked herself into a state of absolute panic.

"I lift up my eyes to the hills. Where does my help come from? My help comes from the Lord, the Maker of heaven and earth."

Repeating this verse from the Bible again and again brought calmness like nothing else could. Neither she nor Roman had spoken a word to each other since she agreed to go with him outside her bedroom door after his kisses.

Had she really agreed to travel to his home alone with him? She needed to stop thinking about what had happened in his arms. *Lord, help me. I have lost my mind, surrendering to him this way.*

Staring at the sun breaking over the hills, tears of shame filled Rachel's eyes and then washed across her cold, wind-blown cheeks. How could she ever face Steven again now that she'd yielded herself to another man? This Spaniard, whose rock-hard body cradled hers as if they were one in the saddle. The smell of him. The feel of him. Her lips still throbbing from his kisses. All of it so pleasurable. So seductive. She hated herself for feeling this way because she loved Steven.

After several hours, the horses came to a halt in a grassy meadow. At Roman's command, two of the vaqueros rode on across the meadow, disappearing into the woods.

The vaquero who had lifted Rachel into the saddle still led the packhorse along with them. He spoke with Roman as the sweat-soaked horses rested. Rachel did not understand their Spanish. The vaquero was definitely Indian. He was about the same age as Roman, darker in complexion, and powerfully built. Clearly, the two men were very fond of each other. The Indian remained careful not to look at Rachel. Most likely embarrassed they'd all seen her in her nightdress. At least it was dark then, she reminded herself. The blanket covered her now.

In the time they'd been riding, she'd worked herself into a fine fit of outrage. What was he thinking stealing her away from her father before he changed his mind? Forcing his attentions on her as if she was already his wife? Worse, as if she was some wanton woman without any sense of morality. Shame flooded her anew as she remembered how she'd responded to his kisses.

"Antonio is going to lift you down. Hold on to your blanket," Roman interrupted her anxious thoughts.

The vaquero was off his horse now, reaching for Rachel. Roman said something to him in Spanish. She could tell it was something teasing about her.

"What did you say to him?" she demanded, moving away from Antonio after he set her feet on the ground as Roman dismounted.

"I said be careful. She is mean as a wild hog and bites like one too."

"You did not tell him that."

Roman laughed. "I said you weigh as much as a feather and are gentle as a dove." He repeated this in Spanish for Antonio, who responded with a smile.

Roman went to the packhorse and retrieved what Antonio had stuffed in the saddlebags back at the stable. He spoke in Spanish again, and Antonio mounted his horse and rode off without another word, leading the pack animal along behind him.

"Where's he going?" With shaking hands, Rachel pushed her wild curls into some semblance of order.

"We'll catch up to him later. You don't want Antonio to see you changing out of your bedclothes, do you?" He came to her, carrying what he'd removed from the saddlebag. A pair of small pantaloons and one of the blousy white shirts the vaqueros wore, along with wool socks, and a pair of little leather boots. "I'm sorry this is all we could find in the stables. They belong to a boy."

"You don't expect me to wear a boy's garments?" She pulled the blanket more firmly about her.

"You must be cold in that nightgown." He smiled. The first genuine smile she'd seen on his face since she told him she was Joshua Tyler's daughter. She didn't know him that well—hardly at all, really—but sensed he was strangely happy standing there alone in the wilderness with her.

"You need to put on something more substantial." He kept on grinning.

Her face flamed in embarrassment. He had dimples in his cheeks when he smiled. How unnervingly handsome he was. And how deeply he frustrated her. Tears sprang to her eyes.

His smile disappeared. "I should not have kissed you this morning. I'm sorry, *chica*."

She bowed her head and began to cry.

He tried to put his arms around her, but she jerked away from him. "Don't touch me. We have said no vows." Dreams of a life with Steven turned to ashes, filling her with immeasurable grief. Mounting shame rose as well that Roman Vasquez had awakened something in her she hadn't known existed. *Lust.* It had to be lust.

So often she'd dreamed of Steven kissing her, what his embrace would feel like, what it would be like to be in his arms. Loved and cherished by him. Now she'd been held by a stranger. Kissed and caressed by a stranger. Roman Vasquez really was that to her. A dark, dangerous man she knew nothing about. A man who took unbelievable liberties, and she couldn't seem to resist him.

Where on earth did he expect her to change her clothes out here in this open meadow? And into a boy's apparel of all things? Had he lost his mind? Perhaps she was losing her mind. She pressed the Bible to her face and cried harder.

Chapter Eleven

Roman didn't know what to do in the face of her tears. He didn't try to touch her again, knowing he'd already touched her far too freely. He'd never been with a woman like her before—someone he wasn't supposed to want, but for the life of him, he couldn't stop wanting. Even now, all he wanted to do was take her in his arms. The sun shone warmly down on them in the green field surrounded by towering redwood trees. Birds frolicked in the willows along a nearby creek that tumbled musically through the meadow.

Oro grazed where Roman left him after removing his bridle. The horse was well trained, his primary mount for the past four years. Many Californios wore out their horses in a very short time. Roman was not this way. He loved Oro and refused to use his mount harshly. The chance to graze would do the stallion good since he carried two riders this day. Oro remained saddled, the bridle hanging from the saddle horn in case they needed to be off in a hurry.

Rachel finally stopped crying. She sank down on the grass and opened her Bible, then sat there quietly reading with her hair veiling her face. He settled down beside her and lay back on the grass, folding his arms behind his head, staring up into the endless sky, thinking of God. It was hard not to think about God in her presence. She was such a religious person, but not in the way he was used to. He remembered his mother praying the rosary every night. How she taught him to kneel beside her when he was very young. Before she died, he'd liked religion. Now it made him uncomfortable and sometimes sad because religion reminded him of his mother.

After a while, there in the meadow, a peace like he'd never known settled gently upon him. He breathed in the fresh spring air, feeling more content than he had in years. The sky looked bluer. The meadow greener. He glanced over at Rachel. The sun shimmered on her fair hair, haloing her in golden light. Was this light upon her a holy thing, a touch from Dios? He wanted to understand the religion she cocooned herself in, but he was wary of it too. He wasn't quite sure what to do with her.

"What are you reading?" he asked.

She wrapped the blanket more tightly around herself. "I am reading from the Psalms and confessing my sins to God." Her eyes accused him when she turned her face to his.

"What sins? I have seen you do nothing wrong."

She looked back down at her Bible. "You have made me do wrong," she whispered without looking at him.

Understanding finally dawned. "I only kissed you. I did not make you my woman."

"I know what a kiss is. That was not a kiss. That was sin between us this morning."

Fire flamed in his belly, remembering the softness of her mouth as she yielded to his desire. The surprising flare of her own passion in his arms. He wasn't used to feeling consumed by a woman. With her in his arms, he completely lost his head. That had never happened to him before. And now to his discomfort, he found himself questioning his motives and doubting his actions where she was concerned. With her tear-filled eyes upon him, he felt convicted by his own behavior. He'd always prided himself on his respect for women, how he protected them with his very life. Never had he forced a woman to do anything she didn't want to do. Women had always wanted him. Sarita had practically begged him to marry her before he left for Texas. But here was Rachel, staring at him like he was an outlaw. She'd agreed to go with him. He hadn't kidnapped her.

Rising to his feet, he left the little boots and boy clothes there beside her on the grass. Walking over to Oro, he dug through his saddlebags. Pulling out dried meat, he ate just a little, saving most of it for her. He didn't want to think about what he was doing. Didn't want to admit that in a way, he was no better than her father, dragging her into this wilderness on a whim he wasn't sure about. Surely, she was better off with him than with her father and Sarita's *dueña*.

When he turned her way, she was trying on the little boots. Hopefully, they would fit her, but if they didn't, it would serve her right. She shouldn't have fought leaving with him this morning. Between her and Maria, he'd longed to throttle them both. He had shoved Rachel's clothes at Maria with the plan of having his sister accompany them to the stables. But every scheme in his head evaporated as soon as he kissed Rachel to stop her from screaming in the hall. He was just going to quiet her; instead, he found himself hungry to consume her.

Now she was trying to shimmy into the pantaloons under her nightdress. He looked away. The last thing he needed was a glimpse of that fair skin that felt like silk under his calloused hands. He turned back to his mount and rummaged through his saddlebags some more, realizing most of his supplies were with the packhorse.

A few minutes later, she tentatively approached him. In her arms, she carried the blanket, Bible, and her nightdress. The masculine clothes fit her like Roman never imagined they would. She looked so appealing he nearly groaned.

Her hair remained loose, falling to her waist in waves of gold. The pants hugged her slim hips. She'd tucked the white shirt into the waistband of the pants. Fortunately, he could not see her bosom, for she held the items against her chest.

"This is scandalous, you know," she said, and he sensed a teasing in her tone that utterly surprised him. His darkened mood lightened in an instant.

"*Si,*" he acknowledged. "You do look scandalous." He took the blanket from her, trying not to grin. The nightdress and Bible she kept tucked to her chest. He handed her the dried meat, which she began to eat very delicately. How things eased between them so quickly, he didn't know, but he was more than thankful for this truce settling over them. Being honest with himself, he had to admit that he deeply enjoyed being alone with her.

The sound of approaching riders carried to them there in the meadow. He could tell by the look on Rachel's face that she heard the sound too but didn't recognize it for what it was. A small army approaching. "You will ride astride in front of me," he said, dropping the blanket to the ground and swiftly bridling his stallion. Grabbing Rachel around the waist, he threw her up onto his saddle. In a heartbeat, he was behind her, urging Oro to run like the wind.

Part Two

"He is my stronghold, my refuge, and my Savior—
From violent men you save me."

2 Samuel 22:3

Chapter Twelve

Pausing deep in the trees, Roman and Rachel watched as the army of vaqueros, led by Rachel's father, stopped to investigate the abandoned blanket in the middle of the meadow. Tio Pedro, on his palomino mount, stood out amid Rancho El Rio Lobo riders on all their dark horses. Roman knew there was little chance of outrunning Tyler's vaqueros riding double with Rachel. And he wasn't about to turn her over to her father today either. He wasn't sure what he would do.

Antonio waited on the other side of the next hill. Roman turned his mount and spurred Oro through the woods in that direction, one arm firmly holding Rachel before him in the saddle.

Finding his vaquero, with the packhorse now ready for Rachel to ride, exactly where he'd told him to wait, Roman decided they would not continue to run. It would be too dangerous for Rachel if she wasn't an experienced rider. And he had no idea what kind of rider she was. Just like he had no idea what kind of woman she really was, though his opinions were changing quickly about her.

Reaching Antonio, he took his time getting down from the saddle and lifting Rachel down as well. He would miss her warm body pressed against his. She was delicately built, slender, but soft in all the right places. Helping her down, he smiled reassuringly into her frightened face. "Let me put your gown and Bible in the saddlebags." When she hesitated to turn them over to him, he explained, "You will need your hands free to ride your own horse now."

After placing the book and nightgown in the bags, he helped Rachel onto the pack horse. The three then rode at a leisurely pace, waiting for their pursuers to catch up with them.

They rode for several hours without being overtaken. By then, they had traveled onto Rancho de los Robles land, following the creek that ultimately flowed past the Vasquez hacienda. Roman grew certain they were no longer being pursued. He had no idea why Tyler gave up the chase, but was happy for it. In Spanish, he told Antonio to ride on home without them.

Antonio nodded and spurred his horse into a gallop.

After he rode off, Roman turned to Rachel. "Do you need to rest?" He pointed to the inviting creek. "We could get a drink of water and stretch our legs for a spell."

"Are we far from your home?" she asked with concern.

"Not far." He stepped down from Oro and approached her horse. When he reached out for her, she tentatively leaned into his arms. He lifted her down, all the while searching her eyes for acceptance of his advances.

But as soon as her feet were on the ground, she stepped away from him, avoiding his gaze. The boy's shirt offered about as much modesty as her nightgown had. She didn't look back to see what he was doing with the horses, just quickly headed for the creek with its lush undergrowth and towering oak and cottonwood trees that would allow her some much-needed privacy, he supposed.

The growl came low and menacing from across the stream where Rachel knelt drinking water from the cupped palms of her hands. Looking up, she stared directly into the gleaming eyes of a large gray wolf. She scooted away from the water, not taking her gaze off the threatening animal across the creek. When the wolf didn't move, she slowly rose to her feet, backing up as best she could in the tangled vines that matted the creek bed.

When strong arms wrapped around her from behind, she screamed in terror.

The wolf turned and disappeared into the dense undergrowth. Roman spun her around, tucking her tightly against his chest.

"The wolf, where is it?"

"He's gone. A lone wolf usually will not attack unless something's wrong with it. Like you, he was just satisfying his thirst."

"This place is so wild."

"*Si,*" he agreed. "You must stay where I can always protect you." His hands began to explore her back under her unbound hair. Through the shirt, the heat of his hands seared her skin as if nothing shielded her body from him.

"I am not your wife yet." She leaned sharply away from him.

He tightened his hold on her, his hands pressing her closer to his chest.

"You have already taken what only belongs to a husband. Do not take any more from me."

"Truth be known, I have taken very little from you, Señorita Tyler."

"My father will not allow you to misuse me. He is an honorable man."

"Your father has already proved he has no honor whatsoever. I would kill a man for carrying my daughter away. Your father has already returned to his brandy. He and my uncle are probably drunk by now. Perhaps gambling over whether or not I will take your virtue tonight."

"You wouldn't dare."

"Don't underestimate me, dove." He ran his long, dark fingers over her ribcage, his thumbs caressing her sides. The boy's shirt offered her up so freely. Shivers raced down her spine at his daring touch. Her stomach swirled wildly. Fear made her head spin. When he lowered his warm mouth to her neck, running his lips along her throbbing pulse, she stopped breathing. When his hand reached for her breast, her world went dark.

He poured water from the creek onto her lips to bring her out of her dead faint. Holding her in his lap, he scooped more water onto her face. For a moment, she remained disoriented, unsure of where she was and what had happened. He carried her away from the water, placing her on a bed of cushiony grape vines. When she tried to escape, he pinned her there with his body, yanking the cotton shirt free from the waistband of her pants, exposing the pale skin of her midriff as his lips sought hers once more.

A crow squawked in a tree above their heads. The big black bird startled Roman. He stopped kissing her and looked up at the incensed bird.

"Please," she pleaded. "Let me go." Tears filled her eyes.

He rose to his feet in a rush, hauling her up with him. He didn't say anything, just held her protectively in his arms, smoothing down her tangled hair with trembling hands. She could tell he was shaken. She was shaken too.

The crow squawked again before flying away.

The sound of rushing water was the only sound in the grove now. "I'm sorry, *pequeña*. I don't know what came over me. The spirit of the wolf, perhaps." He reached out to retrieve a leaf caught in her hair.

She shied away from his touch. When he released her, she hurried out of his arms.

In a flash, he grabbed hold of the waistband of her pants, yanking her back into his embrace, a wounded look on his face. He took the leaf from her hair at leisure and then leaned his forehead against hers in regret. "I said I was sorry. I won't hurt you, Rachel."

"You have already hurt me."

Cursing in Spanish, he released her. He strode over to the stream. There at the water, he yanked off his shirt and began bathing his face and upper body as if he was a man on fire. His torso was much lighter than his tanned arms and neck, all of him corded in hard muscle. Great bruises and broken skin marred his back. For heaven's sake, he was so appealing yet so injured. She'd had no idea. He'd not once winced or acted as if in any pain today. She stared at the wounds on his back with wide, shocked eyes. He'd been terribly beaten. The sight of his injuries appalled her. Had his uncle done that to him on account of her?

Trembling all over, she tucked the bottom of her shirt back into her pants as she turned away from the only half-naked man she'd ever seen and walked out of the undergrowth growing in abundance along the creek.

Their horses were tied together with a long rope in the open field. The buckskin mare Rachel rode would have bolted away when she approached, but Roman's palomino stallion refused to run, holding the other horse in check.

A whistle from the trees caused the palomino to trot away from her, dragging her horse to where Roman walked into the clearing. His shirt was back on, his jet-black hair wet and slicked away from his unsmiling face. He untied the horses, rolled up the rope, and bridled both of them. After swinging up on Oro, he rode over to her, leading her mount. His shirt clung to his wet skin outlining muscles Rachel now intimately knew the strength of, even injured, he was unbelievably strong, both physically and in will and constitution. She couldn't believe how unaffected he was by all those bruises on his body.

"Do not try to return to your father without an escort. The way would be too dangerous for you," he told her flatly.

She could see he'd misunderstood her approaching the horses while he was at the creek. "I only wanted my Bible."

He got off Oro and took her by the elbow. "I will return your Bible tonight when we reach my hacienda." He led her to the buckskin and lifted her without fanfare into the saddle. His eyes revealed not an ounce of emotion, good or bad.

When he turned away to mount his own horse, Rachel saw blood seeping through his wet shirt.

"Your back is bleeding." She gathered the reins in both hands, keeping a firm bit on the mustang and her feelings.

He settled into his saddle. "It is nothing."

"I didn't know you were hurt so badly."

"Would you have surrendered to me on account of my wounds?" His gaze bore into hers.

"No."

"I didn't think so." He nudged his horse ahead, leaving her to follow.

Her horse naturally fell in behind his. For the following hours, they rode in silence as she watched the blood dry on his shirt. During that time, she prayed for him. He was like two different men. One protective, caring, and tender, the other driven by demons.

Chapter
Thirteen

A flock of chickens scratching in the dirt near the porch greeted Roman and Rachel when they arrived at the hacienda late that afternoon. Antonio came and took their horses away after Roman removed their possessions from the saddlebags. The two-story adobe with its red tile roof stood amid a grove of towering oak trees. Blooming magnolia trees thrived around the house. An olive grove flanked the home on one side, and a vineyard spread out along the opposite end of the sweeping residence. Roses of Castile and jasmine climbed the whitewashed walls. The creek they'd been following for hours flowed behind the estate, farther down the hill from the impressive dwelling.

"Most of the house servants are with my family at your father's rancho. When they return, you will see this place is not so quiet." Roman released Rachel's elbow inside the front door and allowed her to look around.

The furniture, though sparse, had been shipped around Cape Horn from Spain. Religious paintings adorned every room. Rachel walked up to each painting reverently, taking her time regarding the biblical images beautifully painted by some talented artist.

"My mother brought the paintings with her from Spain. She cherished them." Roman stepped to Rachel's side, where she studied a scene of the Madonna and baby Jesus on a donkey being led by Joseph. The painting bore a title, but the words were in Spanish.

"What does this say?

"Out of Egypt," he translated. Many Californios could not read or write, nor did they speak English. The tutor Roman's mother had hired when he was six years old lived at the rancho for twelve years. He was young, a highly educated Spaniard who happened to fall in love with one of Rancho de los Robles's Indian maids. So he stayed. The two never married, probably never consummated their strange love affair, but after the maid died from a fever, the tutor finally returned to Spain. By then, Roman and Maria spoke several languages, along with having gained the ability to read and write with great fluency.

"May I see all of the paintings?" Rachel asked eagerly. She appeared to have recovered from their conflict at the creek, which pleased him.

"The hacienda is yours. Go wherever you like." He couldn't help but smile. It made him happy to have her in his home. When she wandered off down the hall looking at the paintings, he followed her, admiring her beauty. He doubted his family would stay at Rancho El Rio Lobo for very long. Tia Josefa would be embarrassed and want to leave as soon as possible without causing greater offense when she found out he'd taken Rachel and ridden home. Fortunately, the journey was a hard day of travel, especially for the entourage accompanying his family. The smile grew on his lips. He had Rachel all to himself under his own roof tonight. The thought delighted him.

He followed her from room to room, allowing her to find her own way in the sprawling hacienda while he quietly walked behind her. When she finally came to his room, he found himself eager for her response to his painting—one he hardly noticed anymore, though when he was a boy, it had frightened him.

Just as she had done in every other room, she went straight to the painting and stood there before it silently for a time. Roman waited to translate the title on the bottom of the frame when she was ready. He didn't need to read it. Every title in this house he knew by heart. After he'd translate, she'd briefly tell him the biblical story behind the painted scene. He'd come to enjoy this little game with her very much as they went from room to room. Nobody had really appreciated the paintings since his mother had passed. His appreciation for Rachel grew as she studied each art piece with a thoughtful gaze.

For a long time, she stood before his painting without saying anything. When she finally turned to face him, she did not ask him for the translation as she had in every other room. Instead, she walked around the spacious chamber, studying its furnishings, even looking out the window for a while without speaking to him.

Because it was an upper-story bedroom, the window was large, offering a wonderful view of the vineyard and creek. The only thing she ignored was the magnificently carved four-poster bed from Spain he'd been born in. He could so easily imagine laying her down there, softly caressing her, slowly awakening her passions. He knew great passion was in her, he'd felt it when he kissed her in the hall. This surprised him about her. His little religious dove was made for love.

"This is your room," she said when he could hardly stand her silence any longer.

"How did you know?" He walked to the window, turning his back to her as he waited for her answer. For some reason, he suddenly felt vulnerable. A thousand times before, he'd looked out this window, but this evening, with the sun dying on the horizon in a burst of golden fire, the vineyard swept with rosy twilight, all he could think about was this woman here with him. *His betrothed.* Already, he felt fiercely possessive of her— and constantly had to turn his mind away from wanting her.

When she didn't answer him, he moved away from the window and went to his painting, standing before it, studying the artwork in a way he had never done before. It was the only painting in the house that portrayed the devil.

"The mighty guardian angel Michael is wrestling Satan out of heaven in your painting." Her soft voice washed over him like silk against his skin.

He did not turn to look at her, sensing she stood right behind him now. The way she spoke of heaven and hell and angels and demons made him uneasy. Made him more determined than ever not to reach for her now, not to introduce her to his bed, as he ached to do this very moment.

"When I was a boy, I hated this painting," he admitted, staring at the face of Satan.

"I can see why a child would be frightened of it." She stepped up beside him and ran her hand along the inscription.

"The Great Battle," he translated. "After both my parents died, I moved into this room. I was born in this room. Tio complained about me having the master's quarters, but Tia said, 'Let the boy alone. I do not want the devil's room anyway.' My aunt did not know I heard her say this after my father was killed."

Rachel placed a hand on his forearm, offering comfort he didn't expect and wasn't sure he wanted. His muscles tensed under her gentle fingers.

"I am sorry your father was killed," she said with feeling. If only she knew he held her father responsible for that night. Tyler was behind the Indian attacks that cleared out their neighbors. He ended up with all their land and holdings.

It wasn't her fault her father was a thief and probably a murderer. And he'd never tell her of his suspicions involving his father's death. He pulled his arm away from her and walked back to the window and then restlessly strolled over to a feminine blue trunk shoved in one corner. A row of whimsical birds had been painted across its front. He hadn't really looked at the trunk in a long time. It was his mother's.

Heaving the heavy trunk away from the wall, he opened the lid. After staring at the contents for a thoughtful moment, he turned to Rachel, standing there in her boy's attire. He loved the way she looked, even in the masculine garb. She was like a well-bred filly, long-legged and fine-boned, the same as another woman he'd dearly loved, if he remembered correctly.

He could see her growing uneasy under his perusal. "These were my mother's clothes," he said to ease her mind. "They are yours to use until your own trunks arrive. I will see if there are any servants to prepare our supper. I enjoyed our time with the paintings. Thank you." He quietly shut the bedroom door on his way out.

Chapter Fourteen

After he left, Rachel explored the items in the trunk. He'd been like an expectant boy, hungry for her approval as they went from painting to painting talking about the Bible. She felt that tug on her heart to minister God's love to him, though he unnerved her. His emotions boiled just below the surface, his passions barely restrained, his temperament two-sided. On one hand, he was strong and protective and kind; on the other, he was dangerous and swift to anger. Steven was nothing like this. She'd never seen Steven angry in her life. Steven never allowed his passions to reign except on the pulpit, when he poured out God's word to the people. What disturbed her most was how she felt with Roman. In his arms, she completely lost her mind. Absolutely, positively lost herself in his embrace. Was this what happened between a man and a woman in the marriage bed?

She glanced over at the four-poster bed in his room, covered in expensive bedding, draped in velvet curtains, and heat filled her face, spreading to the core of her being and out into her limbs, weakening her knees and making her head spin. She averted her eyes from the bed, a grand island unto itself, and concentrated on the trunk filled with a wealthy woman's wardrobe.

His mother's gowns were still beautiful, many appearing never to have been worn. She held one up in front of her. The fit looked perfect, though the length was too short. These gowns would have to do unless she stayed in the boy's garments, which wasn't even an option. The only reason she'd put them on was because they afforded more coverage and durability than her nightdress, especially riding the horse.

But it was the delicate undergarments packed beneath the gowns that delighted her. They were exquisite and silky soft. Several jewelry cases nestled amongst the underclothes. These she didn't touch. Carefully, she selected several of the most serviceable dresses and a handful of the lovely undergarments and laid them out on the bed. She looked for a sturdy shawl but couldn't find any not intricately woven and delicate beyond measure. She pulled a pair of slippers from the trunk, but they were too small. Disappointed, she placed them back with the other tiny shoes at the bottom of the trunk.

After riding all day, she felt too dusty to wear any of these luxurious items. Walking again to the window, she noted the creek wasn't far off, and the sun had only just now disappeared behind the horizon. If she hurried, perhaps she could bathe and return before it grew dark without him knowing.

At a washstand in the room, she found what she'd hoped for: a towel and bar of soap. The soap was more refined than any she'd seen in California thus far. It had a pleasant smell and was not rough like her father's soaps.

Gathering a pair of lovely undergarments and the simplest dress in the pile, a brown woolen one, along with the towel and soap, she rushed from the room and down the stairs as quietly as possible, praying she didn't encounter him on the way. The last thing she wanted was his company at the creek. After their last episode, she didn't trust him one bit.

The stream was cold but crystal clear and deep enough in the middle to submerge herself completely. She was a good swimmer, so she didn't worry about slipping on a rock or being swept away by the current. What made her nervous was how fast darkness fell upon the land. She tried not to think about wolves or other large animals like bears. Scrubbing her body vigorously, she realized she'd not had a bath in a fresh stream in far too long. She even washed her hair, though now there would be no way to hide her visit to the water. In New England, when weather permitted, she and her grandmother bathed in a nearby stream. As a child, she loved those bath outings and savored the chilly water, even though gooseflesh covered her body and she shivered as she left the water.

Upon returning to the rocky bank, she dried herself as best she could, wrapping her hair in the towel before donning the silky undergarments and then the gown, which was soft and warm and clung to her frame in an appealing way.

Pulling on her boy's boots, she scooped up the stable boy's clothes as darkness closed in fast. The night air carried a distinct chill. Maybe winter was not finished with California yet. The screech of an owl startled her so badly she let out a small scream. Roman appeared from behind a tree and joined her. She was so taken aback she couldn't speak for a moment. The lengthening shadows made it impossible to read the expression on his face.

"Were you spying on me?" she finally managed.

"I was protecting you."

"You invaded my privacy."

"Your privacy means nothing to me. It's your life I care about."

Angry and embarrassed, she yanked the towel from her damp, tangled hair. "My modesty matters much to me, as you well know."

"Modesty can kill in California."

"Do not your aunt and sisters bathe by themselves down here?"

"They don't bathe at night, nor do they bathe alone." He snatched the towel from her hands.

She shoved the soap at him too. "You should have made your presence known, as any gentleman would have."

"You should not have left the hacienda by yourself, as any lady wouldn't have."

"How did you know when I left the hacienda?"

"I followed you."

Heat flooded her. He'd watched her bathe. She was horrified. Dropping the stable boy's clothes, she slapped his face. The sound of her hand connecting with his cheek rent the still of the night.

He didn't react to the blow at all. She may as well have hit a stone wall, his cheek felt that unyielding.

"You watched the whole time!" It was not a question, but a furious accusation. Her voice shook with indignation.

"What has happened to my gentle little dove? Is not anger a sin, *pequeña*?"

She scooped up the boy's clothes, and rushed ahead of him, running to the hacienda to escape him. Tears streaked her cheeks, though she was mad as a wet hen. She felt like a wet hen. Her damp hair drenched the back of her dress. A chill filled her that she couldn't shake. Chickens squawked in the oak branches when she raced into the yard. Startled by their flurry, she swallowed another frightened cry and hurried into his house, shivering uncontrollably.

Chapter Fifteen

At first, he was furious when he saw her rushing away from the hacienda, endangering herself out there alone, but then he was so captivated by what unfolded at the creek, he couldn't bring himself to announce his presence. Now he regretted what he'd seen. He couldn't get the image of Rachel naked and all too beautiful out of his head, and it fueled his desire to have her and be done with it. What was wrong with her? Did she have no regard for her life? He'd never met a woman so fearless of the outdoors. Maybe it was her East Coast upbringing. Maybe wild animals and untamed men weren't a problem in New England. But he doubted that. Most men could become untamed given the right circumstances.

He walked several loops around the house to cool off, checking the windows and plank doors for security. A black cat raced out of the Roses of Castile. The cat ran across the path right in front of him, stopping him in his tracks. He resisted superstition, but the vision of the devil in the painting rose in his mind. A fresh wave of anger hit him that she insisted on running off alone into the woods. He would put a stop to that here. If she insisted on baths in the creek, she could wash herself with him there. Better yet, they could bathe together. He made several more jaunts around the house to get a grip on his emotions. Never had a woman inflamed him this way. She was like a fever in his blood. A sickness he couldn't shake.

The aroma of roasted meat wafted to him as he walked through the hacienda door. Heading for the dining room, he found the table set for two, the food already there, looking delicious. Several servants waited for him. The Indian women smiled with pleasure upon his arrival. He was popular with the servants, especially the women.

"Don Roman, you are ready to eat now?" the older servant inquired.

"*Sí,*" he said. "I will return shortly with the señorita."

He went in search of Rachel. She wasn't in his room. His mother's trunk was closed. Except for being pulled away from the wall, it appeared never to have been disturbed. The room appeared untouched, with everything in order. The other upstairs bedrooms were empty and in order as well.

In the *sala,* he found her sitting in a chair, reading her Bible by candlelight. The servants always lit the candle lanterns throughout the hacienda just after sundown. A damp golden braid draped over her shoulder. He missed her hair tumbling in waves down her back as it had all day. Or wet and slicked back, clinging to her shoulders like a golden veil after she'd submerged herself in the stream.

"You must be hungry," he said from the entryway, reining in his thoughts as he looked her over. She was lovely in his mother's dress. Something inside him softened.

She didn't glance up from her reading.

"The servants have prepared our meal. Come and eat with me."

She ignored him, continuing to read. He watched her, his regret rising. She brought out the best and the worst in him. He sighed, wishing for the ease between them that had been there earlier today.

"We must get something straight between us." She rose from the chair, snapping her Bible closed and clutching the book to her chest. "We are not married. The liberties you take with me are sinful." Color stained her cheeks. Her chest rose and fell, constrained by the bodice of his mother's dress, highlighting her slender figure and the gentle swell of her bosom. The gown was too short for her, and she still wore the stable boy's boots.

Again, he deeply regretted surrendering to Sarita's seduction at Rancho El Rio Lobo. The deep scratches on his back causing blood to seep through his shirt were also from Sarita's nails, not entirely his uncle's beating. When Rachel mentioned the blood on his shirt today on their ride home, he felt shame. And shame again now as she accused him of sinfulness with her. She had no idea what sinfulness really was between a man and a woman.

After giving in to Sarita, he'd felt sickened. He'd ordered her to return to her gringo husband, and then he lay there on the bunk in El Rio Lobo's outbuilding thinking only of Rachel. It was then he decided he'd take her to his home. By law, she was his now. He didn't trust Sarita or her evil-eyed *dueña*. Nor did he trust Rachel's father. He wasn't about to abandon her to the likes of the lot of them. Nor was he used to feeling ashamed of his actions. Nothing had bothered his conscience in a long time. And nothing had so stirred his heart as this woman holding a Bible before him now. With everything inside him, he longed to protect her, but perhaps the real protection she needed was from him.

"Say something," she demanded.

"Read to me."

"Read what?"

"What you were reading when I interrupted you."

She opened the Bible, flipping through a handful of pages before settling on the verse. "Blessed are the merciful, for they will be shown mercy."

"Read more."

"Blessed are the pure in heart, for they will see God."

"My heart is not pure," he admitted, feeling chastised by a God he couldn't see and couldn't feel.

She closed the Bible. "Only the blood of Christ can purify a heart. No matter how great or small our sins may be, his blood makes us clean."

"What sins do you have?" He couldn't help but smile thinking about her sins. What could she do to make God angry?

She bowed her head and would not answer him.

"Please tell me how you could possibly sin, *pequeña*."

"You."

She spoke so softly he wasn't sure he heard her correctly.

"You," she said louder. "I have sinned with you."

How he wanted to take her in his arms, comfort her, but he didn't dare. In his home, she was under his authority. He vowed to treat her with the utmost respect, like a guest. Guests were treated like kings and queens in California.

He noticed the shimmer of tears in her eyes. She was such a gentle spirit, another quality that reminded him of his mother. "Do I grieve you?"

"What I feel with you grieves me." When she blinked, tears slipped down her cheeks.

"Do I repulse you then?" His heart pounded in his ears, waiting for her answer.

"You do not repulse me," she admitted.

"Do I please you?" He put his hand on his chest, willing his heart to stop racing.

Their gazes locked and held. She broke the trance between them by looking down at the Bible in her arms. "Lust is a sin," she said, not meeting his eyes any longer.

"Then my sin knows no bounds."

She reached out a hand to him. "Pray with me."

He didn't move any closer, didn't take the hand she offered. Now that he was certain she felt passion for him too, he didn't know how he'd resist not pressing his affections upon her while they were alone in this house.

When he didn't move toward her, she came to him. "Pray with me," she beseeched again, her eyes awash with tears.

He bowed his head and closed his eyes, feeling her delicate hand nestle trustingly into his calloused palm.

"God, you know our weaknesses. You know without you we are consumed by our own desires. You know aside from your grace, we cannot resist temptation. Protect us from the evil one. Send your mighty angels to shelter us. Do not let evil overcome us, Lord, but let your perfect will be done in our lives. In Jesus's name we pray. Amen."

Roman opened his eyes. Her eyes shone brightly, and she smiled. He longed to explain to her the turmoil raging inside him. How he couldn't control his lust or his anger or his longing for the Americans to leave his homeland. But not her. He didn't want her to leave. Yet he dreamed of California being free. Free from Mexico. Free from the United States. Freely ruled by the *gente de razón*. How could she understand all this? How could she understand the anger that sometimes overcame him? How could she understand that he'd killed men and had his share of women? And he wanted her for his woman. Oh, how he wanted her.

She smiled up at him, her sweet innocence his undoing.

"Are you hungry?" he asked, swallowing something that felt very close to fear—an emotion he wasn't accustomed to at all.

Her stomach grumbled in response. They both laughed. Neither had eaten more than a few bites of the dried meat today on the trail. He realized he was hungry too.

"Come, you have never tasted such food as Lupe cooks." He offered his arm to her, and they left the room together.

Chapter Sixteen

When Sarita discovered Roman gone from El Rio Lobo, along with Rachel, she fasted and prayed, but Tohic was not answering her petitions these days. Perhaps because she was still angry that he'd shown her Roman's death through the bitter oak leaves in the creek last year, and so she had married the gringo. Then Roman returned to California very much alive. Sometimes Tohic toyed with people this way. His spirits of mischief and mayhem loved to tangle people's lives, but never had Tohic done this with her before. She was his chosen vessel. Perhaps Tohic was jealous of her love for Roman. Certainly, Tohic knew her allegiance was sworn to him and him alone. Roman was but a man, and though she hungered for Roman more than any other man, only Tohic could satisfy her soul.

She had belonged to him since he saved her from death years ago. The fever had taken a number of lives in California that year after the sailors brought it ashore. That was the winter both her mother and Roman's mother died, along with many others. The padre had already given Sarita, just a young girl at the time, the last rites, and everyone accepted she would die—except Chula.

In the dead of night, when everyone else was sleeping away their sorrow, her dueña had prepared the chamber for Tohic to come. Circling Sarita's bed with candles, woodpecker feathers, and tiny woven baskets made especially in Tohic's honor, Chula had cut herself, draining her own blood into the tiny baskets as an offering to Tohic. Life blood for a life. Then she chanted until the room grew very cold, very still, very mysterious.

Staring at the closed portal of the room, Chula had stiffened all of a sudden, her eyes rolling back in her head till only the whites showed in the flickering candlelight.

Burning with fever, watching Chula from her sickbed, Sarita had felt an intense rush of fear, followed by cold, like air from a grave. Something otherworldly and of great power had entered the room.

"He is here," Chula whispered, and her eyes rolled back into place. "He has come to heal you, *mi hija*." Chula had never had children of her own and treated Sarita like a beloved daughter.

"So I won't die?" Sarita asked weakly. She could barely speak and felt her life ebbing away as surely as the trees were shedding their leaves with winter's arrival.

"Pledge your allegiance to Tohic now. Offer him your soul in return for your life." Chula's voice sounded so strange, almost like a man's voice, a seductive voice.

Sweat trickled down Sarita's temples into her hair that was tangled around her on the pillow. "What will Tohic do with my soul?"

"That is Tohic's business. Do it now before he leaves us." Chula was trembling.

"I give my soul to Tohic," Sarita whispered.

Chula clapped her hands. "Make her a gatherer. She has the beauty and intelligence for that," Chula's voice pleaded with someone Sarita couldn't see. A moment later, Chula's body went rigid, and her eyes rolled in her head again.

Sarita looked away from Chula's distorted face, her fear intense, but already she could feel the fever breaking and her life returning in a rush of strangely chilling air.

After that day, Chula taught Sarita the ancient ways of Tohic. When she was well enough, they went to the oak grove on a full moon night and offered a sacrifice for the gift of Sarita's life, a newborn lamb Chula had convinced a vaquero to bring to the grove that night long ago.

After depositing the lamb into Chula's arms, the vaquero jumped on his horse and galloped away in a hurry. Everyone who'd grown up at the mission was frightened of Tohic. The padres caused this, convincing the Indians they must worship the God of the white man and forsake the gods they'd always known and trusted. Gods like Tohic, who could heal sickness.

But right now, Sarita didn't care about sickness, she cared about winning Roman back. Surely, Tohic would help her. Tohic gained as much as she did from her union with a man. She was a gatherer, and when she joined herself with a man, that man became Tohic's as well. After she'd united herself with Roman in the *mayordomo*'s quarters, she could sense he wanted to escape her. This had confused her. She knew how proud Roman was and how much he hated the Americanos. Perhaps that was why he behaved so strangely with her. She'd been in the gringo's bed. But the gringo was nothing. Tohic was everything. And Tohic would change Roman's mind. Tohic would make Roman love her again.

She gathered her herbs and her sacrifice and the bloody cloth from Roman's back, the blood she'd drawn when they were one flesh in the *mayordomo's* quarters. She also collected the gringa's hair from her hiding place beneath the loose tile in the floor of her room. Her foolish husband was still entertaining the Vasquezes downstairs. He would never know she'd left the hacienda to seek Tohic's blessing this night.

She'd noticed the way Joshua lusted for her cousin, Maria. He hungered for the girl as surely as she hungered for Roman. Let them all get drunk. Dance to the music the Indian servants played in the *sala*. Let her husband make a fool of himself with her little red-haired cousin. She no longer cared about any of them.

The puppy whined when she picked it up. That troublesome servant, Rosa, had seen her take the whelp from the litter in the barn this afternoon. Sarita wasn't concerned. The half-wild dogs at El Rio Lobo meant nothing to anyone. Surely, Rosa would not have the courage to tell Joshua. Sarita wasn't stupid. She knew why her husband kept that milky-skinned servant here.

Nobody would know she journeyed to the oak grove this night. El Rio Lobo wasn't like Rancho de los Robles in this way. The sacred groves grew very near Roman's home. Here, she must travel a considerable distance to reach a sacred grove. She would need a horse to get there.

She stuffed the puppy in one sack and the rest of the sacrificial articles in another bag. The whelp whimpered. Before she put the bloody cloth in, she pressed it to her face, her beloved's blood. Heat washed over her, pooling in her belly. Roman would belong to her again, but first she must convince Tohic to get rid of the gringa.

Why Roman had taken her pale, skinny stepdaughter when he left troubled Sarita to no end. Hopefully, he'd snatched the girl to rid himself of her, but she sensed something else. Roman could be violent toward men, but never had she seen him raise a hand against a woman. He wasn't that way, though that violent seed in him slumbered somewhere in his spirit. It had been born into him. Roman's father had been a man of pride and passion and anger so it would be easy for Tohic to awake these seeds in the son.

She'd already prayed and chanted and worshipped Tohic in the hours after rising to find the hacienda in an uproar over Roman carrying away the gringa. She felt Tohic's acceptance of her prayers even then. Even now. Before presenting a blood sacrifice.

Tonight she would get back into Tohic's good graces. Denying herself food had centered her body, mind, and soul on Tohic. The moon was right. Full and heavy in the sky like a woman about to give birth, just the way Tohic liked it. She smiled. Blood always pleased him. Roman's blood on the cloth would be a promise that one day Roman would be his. And the death of the whelp would signify the death of Rachel Tyler. With the gringa's hair, Sarita would beseech a powerful spirit of infirmity to come upon her stepdaughter, the fire of Tohic's fever to destroy her adversary.

Chapter Seventeen

Rachel woke in the middle of the night. The room felt unnaturally cold. Horribly cold. And dark. A darkness that went beyond just physical darkness. The urge to pray was so strong she got out of the bed and knelt on the planked wooden floor. Roman had given her a room down the hall from his. The chamber's painting intrigued her. It was a crucified saint, his suffering eyes raised trustingly to heaven. Before going to his own room, Roman had translated the inscription for her: *Dark Night of the Soul.*

Kneeling there beside the bed in her nightgown, she shivered, trying to ignore the chill in the room, but the cold grew overwhelming. The air was like the breath from a grave. The sinister chill wrapped around Rachel like talons as she prayed. Soon, she could no longer continue to kneel, she shivered so fiercely. Climbing back into bed, she burrowed under the covers but could not get warm. She began to feel sick and feverish, though still so terribly cold.

And on she prayed.

A longing for her grandmother overcame her. Together, her grandparents would come into her room and lay their hands upon her and pray when she was sick. Her grandfather had even anointed her with oil in the name of the Lord when she was ill as a child.

Fever raged through her now, reminding her of the days on the ship when she thought she might die. She became so sick she could no longer even pray. She fell into fitful dozing, dreaming of a terrible man on a pale horse.

Roman found her after knocking repeatedly on her door the following morning. When she did not answer, he let himself into the room. The iciness of her bedroom shocked him. Strangely, her room was much colder than the rest of the hacienda.

In the bed, she was out of her head with fever. Scooping her up, he carried her swiftly to his quarters.

An Indian maid was straightening his bed when he opened the door. In rapid Spanish, he told her to fetch Lupe.

Lupe had raised eleven children, all of them grown now, with their own families living here on Rancho de los Robles. Not only had Lupe seen her own children safely through many fevers, she'd brought healing to countless others as well, including him and his sister. When he was a boy, Lupe had nourished him and Maria, not only with her hearty food, but with her strong-handed love. After they lost their mother it was Lupe he looked to for a mother's guidance and affection. Through the years, Lupe had bound his wounds and comforted him when he needed comforting. Lupe would know what to do.

With the maid off to find Lupe, Roman tore the covers back from his bed and placed Rachel between the fine white sheets embroidered with colorful thread at the edges. She whimpered like a child when he placed her on the mattress.

Without really thinking, he kicked off his boots and lay down beside her. He pulled her into his arms, speaking to her in Spanish, hardly realizing that even in her right mind, she wouldn't understand what he said.

The heat of her body appalled him.

This was not just a fever. Her murmuring and thrashing and unawareness of him convinced him this sickness could be deadly. He stared at her flushed face, willing her to open her eyes and look at him, but she didn't. Her eyes were shut as she moaned and fought him. When Lupe hurried into the room, he jumped out of the bed.

"She was fine last night," he told Lupe in hasty Spanish.

Lupe felt her forehead. The old Indian's eyes widened. "She's on fire. We must cool her." Lupe rushed from the room and soon returned. Roman had never seen the old woman move so fast. He had no idea what age she really was; she'd come from Mission Dolores in Yerba Buena many years ago. She was the most religious person on the rancho. Lupe recited the rosary morning and night before preparing the meals for the *familia* with her host of helpers.

"*Las niñas* will bring the water." Lupe attempted to shoo him from the room.

Roman refused to budge. "You must leave, Don Roman. Her gown will be removed so we can bathe her."

"I have already seen her bathing." Roman crossed his arms, unwilling to leave.

Lupe placed her hands on her hips, her eyes afire. "Do not confess your sins to me, *mi hijo*. Go find a priest for your confession."

"I have not sinned with her. She bathed in the creek last night. All I did was keep an eye on her so a bear didn't carry her away."

"The creek is very cold. Look at how slender she is. She should not be in the water this time of year," Lupe chastised him.

Roman felt like an eight-year-old boy again. He uncrossed his arms and joined Lupe at Rachel's bedside. "Will she be all right?"

The old Indian's dark eyes softened. "I do not know, Don Roman."

A young maid rushed in with a bucket of water. The girl was Lupe's great granddaughter. Another Indian girl followed, carrying two more buckets. A third girl arrived with an armful of towels; she was related to Lupe as well.

"Do not worry, Don Roman. Your señorita is young and strong." Lupe looked at Rachel and tried to sound convincing. "If we can break the fever, she will live. I will go make a tonic out of willow bark." She attempted to push Roman from the room with her.

He wouldn't move from Rachel's bedside.

The servant girls looked at each other. Nobody smiled, especially Lupe.

"Don Roman," Lupe said sternly, "you are not her husband. Dios does not approve of you being in this bedroom with your *novia.*"

"This is my bedroom. How does anybody know what God approves of?" he said in frustration.

"My Bible," Rachel whispered from the bed.

Roman could see Rachel was still completely out of her head. "Get her Bible," he told one of the girls standing there. "It's in the crucified saint's room."

The rooms were referred to by their paintings. Not the inscriptions on the canvases, but what the *familia* had labeled each art piece years ago. Everybody knew the rooms this way. Tia Josefa called his "the devil's room," but he preferred to call it "St. Miguel's room."

Lupe's granddaughter hurried to obey him.

Roman looked at Rachel, so ill in his magnificent bed, and his anger increased. His Catholic religion always portrayed suffering saints. Dying saints. If a person was godly, they were beheaded or burned at the stake or sawed in two or nailed to a cross. All for a God who supposedly loved them. When he was young, his mother tried to explain this strange love of God to him, but he didn't understand then, and he didn't understand now. His mother had loved God, and she had suffered, and died in this very bed.

After they buried his mother, Father Santiago had done something strange. The padre placed his hands on Roman's head and prayed fiercely over him, beseeching God to save his soul. The fervent prayer, nearly as much as burying his beloved mother, had left Roman forever changed. Forever marked by God. His mother's funeral had been the typical gathering, a grand affair, like weddings and christenings always were in California.

Years later, Father Santiago had said the burial mass for his father after the Indian raid left his father lanced to the ground in the pasture. Many Californios attended the elaborate funeral. His father was a respected and revered leader of the *gente de razón,* the son of a blue-blooded solider of Spain. After Mass at the Royal Presidio Chapel, the body of Roman's father was returned to Rancho de los Robles and buried in the Vasquez cemetery alongside Roman's mother and grandparents and several infants his parents had lost. Since then, servants and friends alike had been buried in that cemetery. Death was no stranger in California.

"I will say the rosary for your *novia.*" Lupe's raspy voice stopped Roman's careening thoughts. The old woman motioned for the girls to deposit the water beside the bed, along with the towels. "She must be cooled. Her body is far too hot."

The servant girl returned with Rachel's Bible, handing it to Lupe, who handed it to Roman. Lupe patted his cheek with her gnarled hand. "Dios has the power to heal. Pray to him, *mi hijo.*"

"I will bathe her," Roman said as he knelt beside the bed.

Lupe frowned.

"I will not let her die." He placed the Bible on the bedside table and then took up a cloth and dipped it in the bucket of cold water.

"Her life is not in your hands, *mi hijo.* God alone holds the living in his hands."

"Go and say your rosary, then, for her. Take the girls with you. Leave me alone with Rachel and God." He swore under his breath. Fear more than anger drove him now.

After the servants departed, he pulled Rachel's nightgown up to her thighs and began to bathe her burning legs with towels soaked in the buckets of cool water. Then he drenched her forehead and flushed face. Eventually, he took out his knife and cut the nightgown off most of her body, removing the gown's sleeves and neck and nearly all of the skirt. He did not feel an ounce of desire as her pale skin was exposed, only a growing fear that she would die the way his mother had died.

For hours, she remained gripped by the fever. He agonized over her, soaking what was left of her thin white nightgown in the cold water and constantly bathing her body, trying to cool her. The towels quickly warmed on her burning flesh as she lay unresponsive on the sheets. Her eyelashes fanned on her cheeks as if she slept the sleep of death.

When Lupe returned to the room, Roman had covered her chastely with wet towels, which he changed frequently as they grew warm against her fevered flesh.

Lupe nodded in approval at this practice. She felt Rachel's forehead and smiled. "Her fever has lessened, but you have ruined her gown." Lupe stroked Roman's disheveled hair, her lips moving in a silent prayer, and then she departed.

Several hours later, Rachel's fever spiked again. Roman refused to leave her. Lupe finally gave up trying to persuade him to turn her care over to the female servants. The next morning, Lupe discovered he'd gone all night without sleep. "You must rest, *mi hijo*. I will sit with her," Lupe told him.

"No," he said, and that was that. He was not about to watch Rachel die as he had his mother. When she seemed aware of him, he spoke softly to her, commanding her to live. He told her stories of California. The building of the missions. The rise of the great ranchos. His own family's proud history in this pastoral land. And he read to her out of her Bible.

She calmed when he read the Bible, even slept peacefully for hours at a stretch.

At other times, she spoke in her delirium. She talked about her grandparents, the pain of her parting with them. And she spoke of someone else. Steven. The fiancé she'd left behind in

New England. She also mumbled about her father. That he had never loved her and only brought her to California to marry her off for his gain.

A storm blew in that afternoon, and Roman realized his family would not return until the weather cleared. He prayed the storm would last for many days.

That night, he bathed Rachel with one hand and read to her by candlelight, holding her Bible in his palm. He came across a story in the book of Zechariah that spoke of an angel of the Lord coming on a red horse. The story so intrigued him, he reread the chapters several times.

After the angel of the Lord appeared on the red horse, more angels on horses patrolled the land, reporting that all the earth was peaceful and quiet. There was a call to repentance, and God granted forgiveness to his people.

Around midnight, Rachel's fever finally broke for good. Grateful beyond belief, he held her as she slept peacefully in his arms. Finally, regretfully, he crawled away from the sweetness of her cool body and stretched out on top of the covers that she slept beneath. He picked up her Bible, marveling he could hold her nearly naked in his arms and not have lust overtake him. The words of the Bible bounced around his head, tangling his thoughts until he read again from Zechariah, searching for answers to his questions, bewildered as to why this story so intrigued him. Finally, worn out, he slept, holding Rachel's Bible on his chest.

Chapter Eighteen

She woke to find Roman lying beside her. She stared at his sleeping face in confusion and amazement. He looked so peaceful. And so handsome. Why on earth was he in bed with her? Moving her legs, it dawned on her she wore very little beneath the soft bedding. The realization shocked her. She peeked under the covers and saw what was left of her nightgown—next to nothing. She yanked the covers tightly up to her chin. She felt weak as a newborn babe and naked as one too. Glancing around, she recognized she wasn't in the crucified saint's room. The great battle painting hung on the wall, Michael with his foot on the devil's head. She couldn't remember a thing from the time she'd began praying beside her bed when her room had grown cold and she began to feel so sick.

Dark stubble covered Roman's face. Apparently, he hadn't shaved in days. His chest was bare except for the Bible he held there. No boots or socks covered his feet; he only had on pants. Where the sun hadn't touched his skin, it was much lighter.

His arms and chest were sculptured with taut muscle. In sleep, he still appeared incredibly strong and beautiful, but frighteningly so. Like a dangerous animal that looked magnificent right before it ate you.

The door cracked open, and Lupe strode silently into the room. The old woman carried a new nightgown and an armful of towels and fresh sheets, everything laundered and smelling of soap. When she saw Rachel awake, the old servant smiled. Without words, Rachel indicated she wanted the nightgown. The servant handed her the gown, careful not to wake Roman sleeping on the other side of the bed. Then the Indian woman left the room as quietly as she'd come, closing the door without a sound.

Rachel did her best to escape what was left of her ruined nightdress and put on the new gown under the covers. Her arms felt unbelievably heavy, and she ached all over. In the midst of her dressing ordeal, Roman awoke.

"You're alive," he said joyfully.

She stilled under the covers. "What happened to my dress?" She had finally worked what was left of the gown over her hips and now had nothing on. The process had worn her out. "Who has been taking care of me?"

His smile disappeared at her questions.

"How long have I been sick?" She clutched the covers under her chin.

"Several days." He carefully placed her Bible on the table beside the bed as he rose from the mattress.

"Days?" She glanced around the room in distress. Rain and wind pelted the window. The storm surprised her. Outside, it looked like winter again. "Where is your family?"

"I don't expect them till the storm abates." Without looking at her, he donned his shirt and stepped into his boots.

She noticed the buckets of water in the room. "What is that water for?"

Again, he didn't answer.

Several small towels floated in one of the pails. "Was my fever very bad?"

"You were out of your mind." He sounded so humble, so unlike the proud, authoritative man she'd grown accustomed to. Never had his face appeared so gentle, his manner with her so tender. "Who took care of me?"

He picked up the buckets and walked to the door. "I will send for Lupe. She will attend you now," he said before shutting the door in his wake.

She struggled into the fresh gown, tossing the destroyed one onto the floor in a huff of sudden indignation. Did her modesty mean nothing to that insufferable man? *Lupe indeed!*

Roman slept in the crucified saint's room, and Lupe attended Rachel in his chambers. Since recovering from the fever, Rachel saw very little of him. All day, he stayed away from the hacienda. Even in the storm, the vaqueros worked in the fields with the livestock. Roman rode with the Indians, tending to the cattle, horses, and sheep. The only time he appeared at the hacienda was in the evenings, usually just before bedtime.

He would knock softly upon the bedroom door while she was reading her Bible. He wouldn't come into the room, just inquire from the doorway if he could be of any service to her. The first few nights after her sickness, she tersely answered no further assistance from him was needed. In truth, she was beyond embarrassed he'd cared for her, bathed her, and nursed her through the fever. He probably knew every inch of her body now. The thought horrified her.

And now, stopping by her room, he acted like they hardly knew each other. Like he was a servant required to wait on her. After a few days, he stopped coming altogether. Her outrage soon cooled, and she began to actually long for his company, though she wouldn't admit it, even to herself. Lupe spoke not a lick of English, and neither did the other house servants, though they were much friendlier than her father's servants had been. These house servants smiled often and appeared happy and content as they carried on with their chores. By the end of the week, when Roman finally stopped by again to look in on her on his way down the hall, she asked him to stay.

"It's probably better I don't," he said from the doorway. His hair was wet from the rain and black as midnight. His damp shirt clung to his chest, reminding her of their time by the stream after she'd seen the wolf and he'd rolled her to the ground, pinning her beneath him. His passion had frightened her then, but she knew his other side now as well. This gentle, uncertain side of him standing in the doorway longing for her kindness.

"Please come in. Just for a short while. When do you think the rain will stop?" She smiled at him as he slowly walked into the room.

"Soon. Winter is playing herself out. Spring is just around the bend."

"Is the weather always like this here?"

"Unpredictable?"

"Yes. I thought it was spring."

"It is spring. Winter just wanted to say good-bye." He finally smiled, sensing her goodwill, she supposed. "Lupe tells me you are feeling much better." He ran a hand through his wet hair, almost as if he were nervous. Could he really be nervous with her after all that had passed between them?

"How would Lupe know? She speaks only Spanish." Rachel tried not to let him see how cooped up she felt by her sickness and the storm and her betrothal to him.

"Actually, Lupe speaks several languages. Her native Indian language, Spanish, and she also speaks Russian."

"Russian?" Rachel closed her Bible beside her on the bed. She sat up straighter, intrigued by this. "Where did Lupe learn Russian?"

"After she left Mission Dolores to marry her husband, she worked for a time for the Russians at Fort Ross on the north coast. Later, after her husband died, she and her children returned to Mission Dolores. That is where my father acquired them and brought the entire family down here to Rancho de los Robles."

"The Russians have a fort in California?"

"Not anymore. A few years ago, with the fur trade dwindling, the Russians gave up on their settlement and returned home."

"Tell me more." Rachel had never heard of Russians in California.

Roman walked to the window that overlooked the vineyard and the creek beyond. The windowpane was wet from the rain, no stars in the sky from the clouds overhead. "How about a Russian love story?" He didn't look at her, just kept staring out the window.

"Yes, tell me."

135

"My father's fair cousin, Concepción, lived with her parents at the presidio in Yerba Buena forty years ago. There, when she was but a girl, she fell in love with the dashing Rezanov, but Rezanov had to return to Russia. They became engaged before he departed, and the fair Concepción waited for her Russian fiancé to return for her. He never did. Nor did she hear news of what had happened to him for a long time. Finally, Concepción discovered Rezanov had died during his return to Russia before he could come back to California for her. The beautiful Concepción was only fifteen. Rezanov was a widower of forty-two when they fell in love. To this day, Concha, as she is called by her family, has never married. She remains true to her Rezanov even now."

"Such a sad tale. Waiting for a love who would never return." Rachel was fascinated by the story.

"Concha decided to become a nun. No other man could replace her Russian lover. I'm sure you understand this better than I do." He prowled the room now, appearing upset about something.

"Why would I understand this better than you?" His behavior confused her.

"You have chosen to devote yourself to God." He motioned to her Bible beside her on the bed. "Can God's love really replace that of a man's?"

"Some women and men are called to devote themselves wholly to God rather than marry. I do not think this is the path the Lord has chosen for me, but I am not married yet, so we shall see."

"Is there a man you love more than God? Perhaps a man from the east?"

"I love no man more than God."

"Then why do you marry? Why not become a nun like Concha?"

"This is not my decision to make. My father has decided that I marry. The Lord's command is to honor one's father."

Roman stepped up to the bed. His intensity took her aback. "But before you came to California, your father did not command you to marry, yet you were about to wed anyway."

"Who told you I was about to wed?"

"Why marry if you love God so much? Is your love for this man back east so great? Greater than the love you hold for God?" He scooped up her Bible, whisking it away as he walked back to the window.

Rachel bristled. "I told you, there is no man I love more than God. Who told you about Steven?"

He cradled her Bible in his hands. "You did."

"What?"

"During your fever, you talked of many things."

"What things?"

"Your grandparents. Your childhood. Your mother and father. And Steven. On and on about this Steven from the east."

Heat flooded her cheeks. She felt exposed. And angry. Not only had he seen her nearly naked, he knew her naked heart as well. "So you know all about me." She wanted to speak harshly but kept her voice soft and even as her grandparents had taught her to do.

"Yes, I know all about you." He smiled, but the gesture didn't reach his eyes. "From head to toe I know you, *pequeña*." He crossed his arms over her Bible against his chest.

"Give me back my Bible," she demanded.

"I would like to read it tonight."

Was he toying with her? "Do you not have a Bible of your own?"

"No." He looked out the window into the darkness.

"Does your family not own a Bible?"

He turned back to her. "My mother may have owned one. If she did, it's probably buried with her."

Rachel softened toward him. "I'm sorry."

Quietly, he came back to her bed. "That was a long time ago." His voice held no emotion now, but he clutched her Bible tighter.

She motioned to her book in his grasp. "God comforts us through his word," she offered, feeling a prick in her conscious for growing angry with him. He'd probably saved her life during the fever. She should thank him, but she just couldn't get over how he'd taken ownership of her body, and now her memories of Steven.

He glanced down at the Bible and then back up at her. His gaze revealed his confusion. "I do not long for comfort from a God I cannot see or feel. Nor can I hear God as you hear God." He seemed grieved as he tossed the Bible onto the bed and walked to the door.

"You do not hear God because you do not listen." She picked up the Bible, placing it gently upon her lap. "How can you live on this earth and not see the Creator's hand in all things?"

"Did God create the wolf to devour the sheep? The bear to slaughter the calves? Did God create war and famine and drought and fever and death? Did God create the ship that brought you to California? The ship that brought you to me?"

"We live in a fallen world. Man is sinful, and the devil is real. This is why Jesus came and died and rose again. The

Savior offers hope to mankind, a way for us to be rescued from the devil and our sinfulness and so we can know God."

Roman opened the door, pausing at the threshold. "If you had your choice, would you marry Steven or me?"

"I thought we were talking about God?"

"You were talking about God. I want to know if you had your choice, would you choose Steven or me?"

"You are here, and you are my father's choice. Steven is in New England."

"But if you could choose for yourself, who would you choose?"

She stared at him for a long, sad moment. "I would choose Steven."

Pain flashed across his face before he quietly closed the door behind him.

The next morning when Lupe came into the room, she found Rachel dressed and the bed made up. A bundle of her things—Roman's mother's things, really—waited beside the door.

"I'm moving to another room," she informed Lupe, though she knew the old woman did not understand English. Rachel motioned to her things. "I must have my own quarters." Picking up her pile of goods, she headed out into the tiled hallway.

Lupe trailed her down the hall, speaking Spanish with a smile on her face. Rachel went to the crucified saint's room but found Roman's belongings scattered there. At least he wasn't present in the room. She looked at Lupe. The old servant waved her on, directing her farther down to the end of the hall. Near a second set of stairs, two rooms opened across from each other.

Rachel looked in one room, and a string of Spanish spilled from Lupe's mouth.

The old servant motioned Rachel into the other room, where a painting of the Madonna graced the lovely quarters. The room was sparsely furnished, but the bed was lovely, covered with a bright brocade spread that matched the vibrant painting of the Virgin Mary on the wall. Smiling, Rachel nodded to Lupe, who grinned in return, revealing several missing teeth. Both women were pleased this would be Rachel's quarters. It was on the opposite end of the sprawling residence from Roman's master bedroom.

Downstairs, Rachel could hear the servants astir. This was clearly the functional part of the hacienda where everyone went about their daily work, which pleased her. She'd grown so lonely in such a short time. She wanted to be around people again.

An hour later, she made her way down the narrow flight of servants' stairs. The stormy weather had finally passed, leaving the land fresh and sparkling with sunshine. At the bottom of the stairs, which led to an outside courtyard, two long, covered patios stretched in opposite directions. One ran north, the other south. The northern patio was lively, filled with small brown children. Several Indian women watched the little ones at play with sticks in the yard.

The other patio stretched out in silence with no one in sight. Delighted, Rachel watched the children for a while and then walked on to the empty patio, feeling her muscles tremble from lack of exercise. She'd not been up and about since arriving at the hacienda with Roman nearly two weeks prior.

After the bout with the strange, sudden illness, she felt more grateful than usual for the air she breathed and the beauty of the Lord's handiwork this day. A large fountain in the courtyard entertained a flock of sparrows. Climbing roses covered the adobe walls, blooming red with spring back underway. At a wooden bench under the porch eves, Rachel sat for a long time watching the birds bathe in the fountain. She prayed for the Lord's guidance. What was she to do? Was she really supposed to marry Roman? Or did the Lord plan to deliver her from all this? Was it possible God would reunite her with Steven somehow?

And if so, how could she tell Steven all that had transpired here? Everything that had happened with Roman? His embraces? His intimate knowledge of her body? Her heart? The time she'd spent in his bed? In his arms?

She was most troubled by her own response to that man. Seeing him set her heart racing every time. When he touched her, she felt like swooning. The rare, tender moments they'd shared came to her mind again and again. Him sleeping beside her with her Bible on his bare chest. The times he really smiled, when those delightful dimples of his appeared in his cheeks, and his green eyes shone with pleasure. He was such an attractive man. Why did she have to find him so appealing?

These memories tangled her thoughts. Jangled her emotions. The times he seemed vulnerable and boyish, so eager for her kind words. Truth be told, she found him utterly irresistible like that, and even when he made her angry, he took her breath away, though she was just now admitting this to herself.

After sitting there on the bench for over an hour thinking about Roman, she rose and followed the patio all the way around the hacienda and up the other set of stairs on the opposite end of the house. She passed only one servant on her way, a smiling Indian girl sweeping wet leaves off the front patio.

When she reached the upper-story balcony and began making her way to her room, she noticed a large group of horses and riders in the distance. As they rode closer, she realized it was Roman's family, along with several male riders she didn't recognize. The strange men wore hats, not sombreros; clearly, they weren't Californios.

She gripped the balcony tightly when one rider in particular captured her attention. He sat tall in the saddle, exuding grace and peace even from a distance. His brown felt hat looked so familiar. Every instinct inside her came alive with dread and longing. Though she couldn't see his face, she'd ridden with him about the countryside on horseback on numerous occasions while he wore that hat.

Chapter Nineteen

Steven stepped down from his horse in front of the hacienda and came to her on the lower porch where she waited beside Roman. She was afraid to leave Roman's side, afraid of what he might do. Steven's face shone with love and excitement. "Rachel," he breathed, grasping both her hands as he reached the veranda. "I've missed you so much, my dearest."

"Steven . . . what . . . are you doing here?" She stumbled over the greeting, allowing him to draw her into his arms.

"I have found you, my darling." He wrapped her in a chaste embrace.

She tried to smile but could not. "This is such a surprise." Would Roman draw his knife from his belt and kill Steven right there on the porch? She really didn't know what would happen, and her knees trembled as she held on to Steven.

"We met these gentlemen in the midst of our ride home," Don Pedro boomed. "They were headed to Rancho El Rio Lobo. Señor Gains explained to us he was searching for his fiancée." Don Pedro's smile disappeared, and he gave Rachel a troubled stare. "Señorita Tyler, you must settle this confusion for us once and for all. Are you and Senór Gains really engaged?"

A blush seared Rachel's cheeks. She wished the ground beneath her feet would swallow her up. Heat engulfed her face and traveled down her neck, mortification making her dizzy as Steven still held her hands expectantly in his. Her legs would not stop shaking.

"The Lord helped us find you," Steven said, unaware of how his arrival affected everyone. "This is my friend, Dominic Mason." He nodded to the other American, his brown hair bouncing boyishly across his forehead. "His ship, *The White Swallow*, has brought us here from Boston. The voyage was grand. Just grand, Rachel. How was your voyage? I'd hoped for a letter to hear about it." He squeezed her hands. "But I have seen how wild California is. It must be hard to get letters back to the east."

She managed to return Dominic Mason's smile before responding to Steven's question. "My voyage was challenging. I sent you a letter. I'm sorry it didn't reach you." She wished it had, for she'd explained her father's demand that she marry Roman and how much this distressed her. Squeezing his hands as much to encourage herself as to encourage him, she continued, "Steven, I'm so sorry to tell you my father has arranged a marriage for me here in California." She paused to let her words sink in.

Steven's gaze did not waver from hers, but his face turned ashen, and he released her hands.

"Roman Vasquez is my betrothed." She nodded to him, standing stonily on the porch. "His family has brought you here." She motioned at the Vasquezes, standing there staring at them. Her eyes connected with Isabella's. Rachel sent a small smile meant to ease the child's obvious distress.

Isabella leaped forward when their gazes met, running up the porch steps to Rachel. "She is going to be my sister!" she said sharply to Steven.

Rachel stroked Isabella's black hair as the little girl grabbed her around the waist. "Steven, this is Isabella," Rachel introduced them, unsure of what else to do.

"Hello, Isabella," Steven said kindly. Though he appeared crestfallen, he smiled at the girl. She wrinkled her nose at him, her blue eyes narrowing with hostility.

Maria stepped forward. The redhead's boldness surprised Rachel. "This is Maria, Roman's other sister." Apparently, there hadn't been any introductions made on the road.

"Pleased to meet you, Señor Steven." Maria turned coquettishly to Dominic Mason. "And pleased to meet you, Señor Mason." She bowed prettily for the ship captain.

Rachel was taken aback by the redhead's flirtation. This Maria was a completely different girl than the defiant one she'd witnessed at Rancho El Rio Lobo. Maria displayed a lovely smile for the handsome, young ship captain.

Josefa came forward. "This is Doña Josefa. She is the lady of the hacienda," Rachel said.

Steven nodded to Doña Josefa, his gentleness radiating to all around him, even though Rachel could see how hurt he was. "Thank you for allowing us to visit your home." Steven's politeness never wavered, but the pain and confusion in his eyes wounded Rachel.

Don Pedro, now smiling, stepped up beside his plump, little wife. "It is our honor, Señor Gains. You and Captain Mason

are our guests for as long as you like. My home is your home."
Don Pedro made a sweeping gesture with his arms. "All we
own is at your disposal, *mis amigos.*"

"Please call me Steven." Steven shook Don Pedro's hand.

Don Pedro gestured to Roman. "Senór Steven, my nephew,
Roman."

Roman stepped forward but did not offer his hand to
Steven. "Senór Gains," he acknowledged coolly.

"Please call me Steven," Steven said graciously.

"Roman and Señorita Rachel will soon marry," Don Pedro
announced loud enough to startle the chickens scratching in
the yard.

Steven closed his eyes for a brief moment. Rachel knew
he closed them in prayer. When he opened his eyes, the smile
did not falter on his lips. He turned to Roman, laying a hand
on Roman's shoulder in a gesture of friendship. "Dominic,"
Steven said, "meet the man Rachel's father has chosen for her
to marry."

Dominic Mason stepped forward. "Señor Vasquez." The
captain politely offered his hand for a handshake. His blue-
eyed gaze was as chilly as Roman's.

With one hand on Roman's shoulder, Steven placed his
other hand on Dominic's shoulder. The two men shook hands
stiffly. Neither appeared pleased. "The Good Lord has brought
us all together. Let us be grateful for this new friendship God
has given us."

Isabella made a snorting sound. Maria shushed her.

"Don't shush me," Isabella said indignantly.

"*Pequeñas,*" Doña Josefa interrupted. "Go into the house
and tell the servants to prepare a feast for our guests. We will
have a fiesta tonight." Doña Josefa clapped her hands. Rachel

wasn't sure if it was a command to the girls to do her bidding or a gesture of delight.

"*Si,*" agreed Don Pedro, all good-natured gusto now that it had been made clear Rachel would still marry Roman. "After we eat, we shall dance."

"Dance?" Steven stared for a distracted moment at Rachel.

"*Si,*" Don Pedro insisted. "In California, we dance in celebration. Tonight's fandango will be held in your honor, Senōr Steven."

Roman moved away from Steven's affable grip, turning without a word to walk off the porch, motioning for some nearby vaqueros to help him gather the horses in the yard.

"My nephew will see that your mounts are situated in our stables. Come, let me show you to your rooms, gentlemen, so you may refresh yourselves before the evening meal." Don Pedro indicated the visitors should follow him.

Once the men departed, Maria, the smile gone from her face, stepped up to Rachel. "You look striking in my mother's dress." The redhead no longer smiled.

"Would you rather she wore your dresses?" Isabella made a face at Maria.

"Since my clothes just arrived with you, I will return your mother's garments to the chest in your brother's room right now." Rachel's legs still trembled as she walked into the house with Maria and Isabella in her wake. She couldn't believe Steven was really here.

"You've been in my brother's room?" Maria looked surprised.

"I'm sure she's been in my room and your room too, Maria," Isabella said. "Roman showed you all our paintings, didn't he?" It was more a statement than a question.

"Yes, he did. They are wonderful," Rachel answered.

"Did he show you where Señora Poppycock lives?"

"No, he did not. I would love to see where Señora Poppycock lives."

Isabella eagerly grabbed Rachel's hand to lead her to her beloved pet.

"If that stupid chicken poops on my mother's gown, I will crucify you, little goat," Maria threatened.

Isabella stuck out her tongue at her sister.

"I've been careful with your mother's clothes. I will continue to watch out for the gowns until they are safely returned to the trunk," Rachel assured Maria.

Maria's face softened before she turned and walked toward the stairs to the upper bedrooms.

"You should not treat your sister that way." Rachel told Isabella once Maria was gone.

"Did you hear what she said? She called Señora Poppycock stupid. Señora Poppycock is not stupid. She is the smartest chicken ever. You'll see."

"May I see her now?"

"She is probably out in the kitchen behind the house. Lupe takes care of Señora Poppycock when I'm away." Isabella skipped out of the house with Rachel trailing after her.

"Lupe is a wonderful cook," Rachel told Isabella as they walked around the house to the kitchen.

"Lupe likes Señora Poppycock because Señora Poppycock keeps the flies out of the kitchen."

"How wonderful," Rachel said.

Isabella gave Rachel a serious look. "Were you in love with the gringo from the east?"

"Steven?"

"Senór Gains," Isabella corrected her.

"I have always loved Steven."

"But now you love Roman."

"You are too young to concern yourself with love, Isabella."

"The maids do not think I am too young. They talk about love all the time with me around. I listen all day long and have learned much about love."

"Do the maids know you are listening when they talk?"

"No," Isabella admitted. "I like to read books under my bed. I cannot help it if the maids do not know I am there while they clean my room."

"Isabella," Rachel said gently, "you should tell the maids you are under the bed so they do not talk in front of you."

Isabella would not be distracted. "Roman loves you. He loves you more than that gringo with his funny felt hat."

"Steven is a wonderful man. You will come to love him like everyone else. Just wait and see."

"He is not nearly as handsome as my brother."

Rachel tried not to smile.

"This is true and you know it," Isabella said.

They walked through the backyard, headed for the compact building constructed well behind the hacienda so a fire in the cookhouse would not destroy the home as well.

"Roman is so handsome he steals your breath away, doesn't he?" Isabella persisted.

"He is the most handsome man I've ever met," Rachel admitted to appease the determined girl.

When Roman stepped out from behind a large magnolia tree in the backyard, crushing out his cigarillo as he did so, Isabella erupted in laughter.

"Rachel has come to meet Señora Poppycock," she informed Roman once she stopped giggling.

"Lupe has cooked your chicken." Roman ruffled Isabella's hair as she passed by.

"That isn't funny." Isabella walked faster toward the kitchen.

"Fried chicken, my favorite." Roman smacked his lips together.

"She will hear you and be frightened," Isabella said.

"Lupe will not be frightened. She knows I love fried chicken."

"Señora Poppycock will be frightened," Isabella said in exasperation. She grabbed Rachel's hand to drag her past Roman, leaning against the magnolia tree as if he had nothing better to do that afternoon.

When the girls stepped within reach, Roman captured Rachel's other hand. "I need to speak with my betrothed, Isabella. Go to the kitchen by yourself."

Isabella tugged Rachel away from him. "Rachel is spending the afternoon with me."

Roman gently tugged Rachel back. "Let her go, Izzy."

"You have been with her for two weeks while we were away," Isabella complained. "I want her to meet Señora Poppycock."

"Later, she will meet your chicken." Roman refused to release Rachel's hand.

"I promise, Isabella, I will meet Señora Poppycock as soon as your brother is finished speaking with me. I will see you in the kitchen."

"After a while," said Roman. "Go on. Señora Poppycock hasn't touched a fly since you've been gone. She's missed you so much."

"Really?"

"Really," Roman assured her.

After Isabella bounced away toward the kitchen, Roman turned to Rachel. "The storm washed away all the flies. It's too cold for them right now. That chicken won't be happy till warm weather returns the flies." Roman didn't release her hand. "Are you feeling strong enough for tonight?"

"I'm not sure what you mean by strong enough." She tugged her hand from his. He seemed regretful to let her go.

"You've been sick. My *familia* will dance all night with the Yankees here."

"They've traveled all day on horseback; certainly, they won't dance that long."

"It is the Californio way. With guests, the dancing will go on and on. I will tell Tio and Tia you've been sick. That you cannot entertain the guests tonight."

"Please, Roman, just let your family keep their customs. I will be fine."

"So you want to dance with him?"

"No. I want you and your family to enjoy your guests."

"He loves you." Roman recaptured her hand in his, holding it tightly.

Rachel held his gaze. "Yes, Steven loves me."

He pulled her close. "Do you still love him?"

"You do not understand this kind of love." She leaned away.

He pulled her back, and his lips crashed down on hers without warning. He kissed her passionately. Possessively. Yearningly. Until she yielded to his desire. Until she forgot about everything but Roman's lips on hers. Until she melted against him with a soft moan and a wildly spinning head.

It was then that he ended the kiss. "I understand," he said, his eyes bright with emotion. "It is you who does not understand love, *pequeña*." With that, he left her standing there alone under the magnolia tree.

Chapter Twenty

The music of guitars and violins filled the *sala*. The Indians played their instruments with gusto. Tio Pedro and Tia Josefa soon took to the dance floor, following the tradition of the oldest generation beginning the *baile*. They performed the stately *contradanza* while everyone sat on benches watching. All other furniture had been removed from the room. To Roman, all this was as much a part of his life as breathing. He usually enjoyed the fandangos, especially the beautiful Spanish folk dances and the dancing games that would come later in the evening, but tonight all he could think about was Rachel and Steven.

The two sat together for dinner. They interacted with such ease and affection Roman could hardly swallow his roast beef and beans. Steven had led everyone in a prayer before eating. Even now, that prayer rang in Roman's ears. Such a grateful, humble man was Steven, even though he'd lost his *novia* after sailing across an ocean to find her. He and Rachel talked quietly about her grandparents and the goings-on back home. Roman overheard them discussing the death of Steven's mother, and Rachel put her hand on his arm to comfort him.

Roman couldn't take watching them any longer and turned his attention to Maria and the ship captain. Never had he seen his sister so animated, so beguiling, so beautiful. Maria hung on Captain Mason's every word. Drinking in his tales of trading in the Orient and sailing seas all over the world. She laughed and drank wine with the Americano, encouraging him to taste the spicy peppers and refilling his wine glass again and again. It was all Roman could do not to leap across the table and knock all the gringo's perfect white teeth out so he could no longer smile at Maria. Now there would be dancing. He didn't know how long he could stomach the Yankees in his home.

After Tio and Tia had performed a series of dances to entertain their guests, Roman's sweat-drenched uncle came to him and said he and Maria should begin the waltzes. Isabella had glued herself to Rachel's side. His little sister had done a fine job of keeping Steven from Rachel since dinner. Roman noted neither Steven nor Rachel drank any wine, so he had merely sipped from his glass during the meal. He'd never liked wine much anyway. His father's drinking was enough to last him a lifetime. Roman only drank on rare occasions to drown his feelings, like the day he'd signed the betrothal papers.

Now he escorted his sister in a waltz around the floor as he'd done so many times before. He and Maria could dance in their sleep together. For years, the padres had forbidden waltzing in California due to the intimacy of the dance, but Roman could not remember those days. That was before his time. After he and Maria performed a series of waltzes, Tio, a glass of brandy in hand, came forward and told Roman and Maria to find other partners and get everyone out on the floor.

Maria didn't waste any time pulling Captain Mason to his feet.

Roman walked over to Rachel. "May I have the pleasure of your company for the next waltz?"

She wore a beautiful lavender gown that revealed her smooth, creamy neck and shoulders. Her hair was arranged in a manner that tempted him to touch the curls beside her blushing cheeks. "I have never danced with a man," she admitted.

Isabella sat beside her, tapping her small slippered foot to the music. "You must dance with him," Isabella commanded. "Everyone dances in California."

Rachel playfully tweaked Isabella's ear as she stood up to accompany Roman.

Tia Josefa had coaxed Steven out onto the floor. With Rachel leaving her, Isabella jumped up and pulled one of the young sailors out onto the dance floor too. Servant girls quickly invited the remaining sailors to dance. It wasn't long before the whole room swirled with dancers.

Rachel finally accepted the hand Roman held out to her as he put his other hand on her waist. "Just follow me." He cinched her up close. "Are you ready?" Pleasure he'd never felt before with another dancer poured through him as he swept Rachel around the room, gracefully propelling their twirling bodies past the others. Sailors stumbled along. Servant girls laughed, doing their best to teach the Americanos how to dance.

Roman only had eyes for Rachel, hardly noticing the other dancers. She followed his lead, hesitantly at first, but after several turns around the room, she began to dance with him as if they'd always been paired together. She looked as happy as he felt leading her through the intricate steps. It took a while for him to notice Captain Mason sweeping Maria around the room too. Obviously, the ship captain knew how to waltz. In the Yankee's arms, Maria glowed with beauty. Isabella appeared far too grown-up as well in the gangly arms of a youthful blond sailor.

Roman tried to hold on to the pleasure he'd first felt holding Rachel in his arms, but watching Maria and Isabella in the arms of the Americanos quickly quelled his contentment. And soon he grew angry. Americanos had no business in California. His sisters seemed to have lost their senses in the Yankees' arms. What would come next? Yankee beds for his sisters?

He led Rachel back to her seat and took command of the *baile*, ordering the musicians to begin the games. He separated the men from the women and got everyone back to the benches so his sisters were no longer in the arms of the men. He then coaxed Tio and Tia into performing the game El Borrego, where a man and a woman pretended a mock battle with a butting ram. The couple sang along with the musicians. During the chorus, Tio shook a red kerchief side to side while Tia swept her skirts back and forth in a teasing manner, resembling a bullfight.

Again and again, his aunt and uncle pretended to butt one another's kerchief and skirts in a comical way throughout the song. The Americanos laughed, especially the sailors who had consumed too much wine at dinner and now appeared to be getting drunk on Tio's brandy. Several sailors fell off the benches, they laughed so hard.

After Tio and Tia's entertainment, Maria took to the floor by herself, performing a series of graceful dance moves before approaching Captain Mason. The dashing Yankee sat on a bench beside Steven, watching Maria like a schoolboy. She executed a variety of pirouettes and other enchanting steps in front of the captain. He seemed charmed but confused as to what he should do.

Isabella raced over and placed Captain Mason's hat upon his head, whispering instructions. Maria danced a little longer for his pleasure before stealing his hat and rushing away with it.

Isabella took her turn on the floor while Roman made sure Captain Mason did not linger with Maria when the ship captain redeemed his hat with money given as a gift to Maria in return for the hat. Usually, a mere peso paid for a hat, but Roman could tell by the startled look on Maria's face that Captain Mason had placed far more than a peso in her hand. Money was hard to come by in California. This was so like the Yankees to have coins in their pocket when Californios did not.

Isabella chose the youngest sailor, the blond boy, to dance for. He too must have paid far too much money because Isabella squealed in delight when the boy redeemed his hat from her.

Roman ended the hat game and moved on to the popular pin waltz, hoping to keep his sisters away from the gringos.

Of course, Isabella and Maria chose all the Americanos as well as several of the servant girls and even Rachel to participate in this game. Those playing the game with his sisters seated themselves in a circle in the middle of the dance floor.

Roman stood back against the wall, keeping watch. He was in no mood to take part in the festivities now. Fury burned through him over his sisters' silly behavior with the gringos. Maria designated herself "it" in the game and went to another room as Isabella hid the pin on Steven's person. The musicians took note of where the pin was placed on the young minister. In his shoe. Steven was a good sport about it, even teasing Isabella, which seemed to win him Isabella's favor.

Maria then came back into the room and began waltzing around the circle as Isabella hurried to her place between Rachel and the blond sailor she appeared so taken with.

While dancing, Maria began feeling her body from head to toe—this was part of the game. The musicians were to change their tempo when she placed her hand on her body where the pin was on Steven's body. Maria went from person to person, moving on when the musicians played music that did not change.

Maria danced for a very long time in front of Captain Mason and appeared quite disappointed, giving Isabella a sharp look when the music did not rise to the occasion.

Isabella grinned, and Maria finally moved on, granting Isabella a small kick in the shin as she passed by. Isabella kicked her back, flaring Maria's skirts to reveal expensive black stockings. The sailors roared with laughter. Roman could barely harness his rising temper.

When Maria danced in front of Steven, the music played faster. His sister began her search for the pin by feeling her own body until the music rose when she neared her feet. Steven, his face red as a beet, then handed Maria the pin, apparently quite relieved to have survived the game.

Isabella snatched the pin from Maria and pushed Rachel from the room. Roman would have stopped the game right then, but Tia approached and asked him to go find Tio's stash of brandy. "Dump the remainder of it," she told him. "Your uncle is drunk, and so are the Americanos."

Tio would think he'd finished the brandy himself and finally stop drinking. Roman had done this many times for his aunt and had no trouble finding his uncle's hidden store.

The brandy was nearly gone already, but he took what little remained and poured it under a rosebush.

Upon returning to the *sala*, the pin waltz game was well underway. Rachel danced shyly around the circle, but after a while, encouraged by Isabella, she relaxed and her dancing became full of grace and charm.

The musicians did not seem to want Rachel's dancing to end, for they did not change their volume for some time, letting Rachel circle the seated ones several times before the Indians finally played louder when she passed Steven and Captain Mason, who were seated side by side.

Smiling, Rachel danced around and came back to the two men, where she danced with such ease in front of them that jealousy overwhelmed Roman. He didn't know which man held the pin on his person, and obviously neither did Rachel because she danced back and forth between the two men until it was clear by the volume of the music who held the pin.

Initially, he was relieved it wasn't Steven. Captain Mason grinned roguishly as Rachel danced in front of him. How could she look so lovely and innocent and alluring all at the same time?

The ship captain did not pull the pin out immediately and hand it to Rachel as Steven had with Maria as soon as the pin was discovered on his person. Instead, the captain let Rachel dance until there was no doubt in anyone's mind where the pin was hidden. In the breast pocket of the captain's fancy blue blouse.

Roman decided if the ship captain with all those fine white teeth laid one finger on Rachel, he would pay the devil for it.

Tio tried to stop him from pushing away from the wall, but Roman stepped around his inebriated uncle and strode right up behind Rachel as she danced in front of the captain.

The smiling Yankee removed the pin from his pocket and stood up, reaching out to hand the pin to her. Before she could take it, Roman swung her behind him and plowed his fist into the gringo's grinning face.

A bench full of men tumbled over. Several sailors landed on the floor. Roman and the captain crashed over the bench as well.

The music abruptly stopped.

The room broke out in chaos. Servant girls screamed. Benches flew out of the way, tossed aside by scrambling sailors. Steven scooped up Isabella to protect her from the fray. Tio Pedro hollered like a wild man. Tia Josefa wailed. And in some sane corner of his mind, Roman heard Rachel pleading with him to stop, but he couldn't stop. He was going to kill the Yankee.

Chapter Twenty-One

It only took a moment for Dominic Mason to realize Roman Vasquez intended him serious harm. Dominic was on his back, the Spaniard punching his face, his stomach, his kidneys. Fortunately, Vasquez exuded a small amount of dignity in not boxing below the belt, but a blow to his jaw stunned Dominic. He regretted the amount of wine he'd consumed. He couldn't seem to gain his bearings under the attack. When another blow sent searing pain to his ribs, he realized if he didn't sober up in a hurry, he might not survive.

The sudden brawl baffled him.

Feasting, dancing, pretty Spanish girls, a redhead that captivated him, and now this madman trying to kill him.

He used all his strength to flip the Spaniard off of him. The enraged Vasquez dove back at him. Dominic flipped him again, this time springing to his feet before the Spaniard could pounce on him.

A boxing match ensued with Dominic finally landing several satisfying blows to the Spaniard's face. Both men bled now. Dominic from his nose and mouth. Vasquez from a badly split eyebrow. Blood spattered the floor between them.

A woman screamed for them to stop. Dominic would have gladly accommodated her pleas if only the Spaniard would stop. But on his feet, with some distance between them, Dominic was in his element now, having boxed since he was a boy on the Boston docks.

It didn't take long to soften the Spaniard up with a series of well-aimed punches. Vasquez now bled from his nose and mouth too, along with that serious cut on his eyebrow. Satisfaction coursed through him. Apparently, the Spaniard realized he couldn't win this way and finally stopped Dominic's bruising fists by kicking his feet out from under him. Once more, they tangled on the floor like wrestlers.

The two men were nearly the same size, though Dominic outweighed the Spaniard by about ten pounds. That ten pounds of muscle helped him flip his attacker onto his back. He was about to get the upper hand when a wild woman sprang on him. Maria screamed and scratched and even clamped her teeth into Dominic, startling the two men enough to stop their fighting.

Steven attempted to pull Maria off Dominic. The girl, like her brother, was out of her mind with uncontrolled fury. When she dove into the fray, Doña Josefa screamed. Dominic waved Steven away from the fight. Steven let go of Maria and leaned down to help Roman, who was badly bleeding.

Dominic tried his best to restrain Maria without hurting her. He may as well have been attempting to tame a tiger. The girl's ferocity amazed him. Pinning her to the floor was not easy. He used his big body to hold the slim girl beneath him until she came to her senses.

"Easy," he told her. "Take it easy, Maria. I don't want to hurt you or your brother. I'm just trying to protect myself here."

Her red hair had lost every pin. It tumbled long and lush around her, tangling across her face. He considered brushing the hair off her cheeks, but he didn't dare. The girl would probably bite his hand off if he touched her.

"Do you understand that I have no intention of hurting anyone here?"

She responded in Spanish. He had no idea what she said, but she certainly was cursing him. They had conversed at dinner in perfect English, and while they waltzed, they had spoken to one another in English too. He didn't understand why she wouldn't speak English now.

"I'm sorry. I don't speak Spanish. You're going to have to use English, girl."

She cursed again in her native language.

As soon as he released her, she sprang to her feet and ran out of the room.

It hadn't taken long for his sailors to sober up under the bloody circumstances. They crowded around him like boys seeking his guidance.

Steven spoke with Vasquez in a corner of the room. The Spaniard had his head bowed and was using his shirt to stop the blood spilling from his face.

"What was she saying?" Dominic asked one of his sailors who spoke Spanish.

Jamie, his favorite deckhand, tried not to smile. "That you will surely go to hell."

"Is that all? She attacked me."

"She's probably never been beneath a man before." Jamie offered him a handkerchief for his bleeding nose.

"Just like that brother of hers. She got more than she bargained for in that brawl," said another chuckling sailor.

"You box just like my cousin from Ireland. Not a man in Boston has beaten him yet in the ring," Jamie said proudly.

Dominic placed his hand on Jamie's shoulder as a father would quiet a son. "All right, boys. That's enough. Let's get this place cleaned up."

The music kicked in, and Dominic was surprised to see Don Pedro and Doña Josefa begin a graceful waltz. Don Pedro waved to the musicians to play louder, and the Indians did so.

Roman Vasquez left the room with Steven.

Rachel held Isabella's hand and walked her from the room, both of them crying. Dominic and his sailors watched the older couple dance with dignity across the *sala*'s blood-spattered floor. Maria did not return. Neither did Roman and Steven or Rachel and Isabella.

After waltzing with nobody joining in, Don Pedro called an end to the fandango. He invited everyone to a picnic the following day, explaining feats of horsemanship would be displayed for their entertainment, and then everyone said a subdued goodnight.

Dominic couldn't wait to get away to his room. He'd been raised in a good Christian family but had wandered away from that narrow road. In his business of running a clipper ship, he spent long periods of time at sea with ungodly men. Meeting Steven on this voyage had affected him tremendously. They'd become fast friends. He deeply admired Steven's devotion to God. It was just like Steven to aid the Spaniard. He still wasn't sure what had caused the fight, though he suspected he'd gotten a little too close to the women, particularly Steven's ex-fiancée, now set to marry the Spaniard.

Wasn't this a fine mess? Steven spending months on the ocean and days on horseback searching for his fiancée, only to find her betrothed to that hotheaded Spaniard.

Discouraged and bruised, Dominic lay on the bed fully clothed, staring up at the beamed ceiling. He didn't douse the candle burning beside the bed. The last thing he wanted was to be in darkness. A spiritual darkness had settled over him. Darkness he felt like a physical presence. He thought of his mother. More than once, he'd awakened to find her praying beside his bed when he was a boy. Even after he was grown, sometimes he'd find his mother on her knees beside his bed in his room.

"A battle is going on for your heart, Dom. Please, son, pray with me," his mother said last year when he was home and found her kneeling beside his bed as he slept. He was too embarrassed to crawl out from under the covers in front of her so that he could kneel beside her. He preferred sleeping without clothes and couldn't imagine what his devout little mother would say upon discovering this. Feeling like a small, chastised boy, he reached out his hand to her.

For what seemed like a very long time, his mother prayed, holding his hand. It was cold that night, and he worried for her kneeling on the plank floor of the two-story New England cottage he'd grown up in.

He tried to offer her a blanket from the bed, but nothing seemed important to her but praying for him. Certainly, she prayed because her youngest son had not married and wasn't raising a respectable family like the rest of his siblings. His two older brothers were fine Christian men like their father.

Married to sweet, submissive women like his mother. His two older sisters were also married. They too reared busy families. Only Dominic's little sister, Chloe, remained single, as he was. She lived at home and begged him to take her on one of his voyages, which of course their parents forbid. Chloe was only fifteen years old.

Dominic knew he was a disappointment to his parents. A wry smile crossed his lips, and he winced. His lower lip was swollen and throbbed when he smiled. Out of all his siblings, he was the most successful. In a worldly sense anyway. He was by far the wealthiest. His brothers worked the Boston docks beside their father, making a living, feeding their families, going to church on Sundays, and reading their Bibles. They were soft-spoken, hardworking men. Dominic admired them, but he didn't want to be like them.

When he was thirteen, he'd decided he wanted to be wealthy. He remembered the day he'd asked his father, "Why don't we own a sailing ship like that one?" The beautiful ship had sailed into the harbor, her decks loaded with tea from the Orient, cattle hides from California, and fur from the Russians.

Dominic's father smiled, admiring the ship with her tall white sails full of wind and sunshine. "She's a fine ship, no doubt, but the Good Lord hasn't blessed me with my own ship. He's given me sons instead and daughters to raise up for the kingdom of heaven. These docks give me a steady income, and I never miss a Sunday in church with your mother. It's a life good enough for me, Dom." Patrick Mason ruffled his son's sun-bleached brown hair.

"I'm going to own my own sailing ship, Father," Dominic told him. "And when I do, I'll call her *The White Swallow*, and she will have an angel on her helm to guide me on the open sea."

"Those are fine plans, but remember, angels help us, but it is the Good Lord who guides and protects us. Don't ever lose your way, Dom. The devil is always waiting for a man to take the wrong road."

Now Dominic hurt in a hundred different places, especially his face. His nose was bruised. His mouth ached. Perhaps he'd cracked a rib. The only thing that brought him any consolation was the thought that the Spaniard may have taken a worse beating than he did. Those boxing matches on the docks when he was a youth had paid off in more ways than one. Boxing made him a lot of money back in Boston. And a lot of friends. Friends in high places who helped him become captain of a clipper ship. A ship he now owned all by himself. *The White Swallow* with her angel on the helm. His boyhood dream.

So why wasn't he a happy man?

Upon his return to Boston, he was all set to marry Sally. A sweet young woman who sat between his parents and hers each Sunday in church. Sally was kind. Smart. Appealing. So why didn't the prospect of marrying her quell his interest in other women?

Feeling a trickle of warm wetness, he rubbed his hand over a deep scratch on his neck. His fingers came away bloody. The redhead had done nearly as much damage as her brother in a much shorter time. Great seagulls, Maria Vasquez was something else. The moment he'd laid eyes on her, he could hardly catch his breath.

Now here was sin knocking on his door. The Spanish girl erased every memory of Sally from his mind. He groaned, rolling over onto his stomach, staring at the wall for a while, trying not to think about the redhead.

But it was no use.

A short while later, he rolled again onto his back to stare at the ceiling before turning his attention to the painting on the wall of Jesus being removed from the cross by several weeping men. Maria Vasquez was surely Catholic. His Protestant family would never understand if he ended up in California married to a Catholic girl.

He thought about the land he'd purchased in Yerba Buena on San Francisco Bay. What a harbor, San Francisco. The finest in the world, no doubt. He'd purchased several lots on the water, paying next to nothing for the valuable land. He imagined fine wooden docks like the ones in Boston where ships could sail right up and unload their wares. He also imagined a grand house on the piece of land he purchased on a hill overlooking Yerba Buena. A mansion like the ones back east with gables and three different shades of paint. Green, he decided. His mansion would be white and green. The same shade of green as the redhead's eyes. That's the kind of house he dreamed of settling down in one day to raise a family. Imagining a passel of little red-haired girls made him grin.

Where did Maria get those eyes? Her brother had them too, but Dominic had no desire to ever gaze into his green eyes again. But Maria. Oh, Maria. He would have drunk vinegar to sit at the table with her and look into those beautiful green eyes all night long. His stomach and head now felt like that's what he had drunk, vinegar.

His parents did not imbibe spirits. Neither did his siblings. They all believed wine was better left untouched. And spirits brought about real and frightening battles with demonic spirits, said his mother. Dominic on the other hand, had decided if Jesus drank wine, he could too. He did his best to avoid drunkenness, but sometimes it snuck up on him. Like tonight, with the redhead filling his glass again and again. By the time the dancing began, he knew he was drunk. Pleasantly inebriated, he preferred to liken it.

He stared at the painting of Jesus's body being taken down from the cross on the wall of his room. Then he rolled onto his side to stare at a different wall. The painting depressed him. He couldn't see it that well anyway in the light of just one candle. When he'd stepped into this room this afternoon, the first thing he noticed was that painting. He'd gone right over to it and tried to read the inscription, but it was in Spanish. Before going down to dinner, he'd asked Parker, his half-Mexican deckhand, to come to his room and interpret the script for him.

"It is finished," Parker read, then skedaddled out of the room in a hurry. God made his sailors uncomfortable, though in severe storms, these same sailors would pray along with Dominic for their lives and the ship to be spared.

He closed his eyes, commanding himself to sleep. He didn't want to think anymore. Didn't want to pray anymore. Certainly didn't want to look at the Savior's broken body anymore in that colorful Catholic painting. And lastly, he didn't want to think about Maria Vasquez. That was for sure.

Chapter Twenty~Two

Though the night had ended earlier than planned due to the fight, Rachel still found herself walking all alone through a sleeping hacienda the next morning. Not even the servants were up yet. Relishing the quiet sunrise and encouraged by the sparkling beauty of spring's arrival, she headed for the vineyard. Once there between the vines, she stood with her face upturned toward the sunrise, her eyes closed in prayer. Sometimes when she prayed, the Spirit illuminated her mind, and a heavenly light would swirl through her senses, so warm and soft and comforting with God's presence. For how long she stood like this savoring his goodness, she didn't know, but when she finally opened her eyes, Steven stood beside her.

"Good morning. I prayed I'd find you alone this morn."

She returned his delighted smile. "Good morning to you."

"Am I interrupting your devotions?"

In a sisterly fashion, she straightened a button on his shirt. "Of course not. You could never interrupt me, Steven." Her heart ached for him, coming all the way to California only to find her engaged to Roman.

"Has the Lord made it clear whom you are to marry?"

Straightforwardness was one of Steven's strengths. She tweaked the button on his shirtfront so it finally settled into place. Then she looked him over. He was as tall and earnest as she remembered. A fine man. A godly man. The husband she'd always dreamed of. "No, the Lord hasn't made it clear to me yet," she admitted.

"Why are you living in his home before marriage?" He did not sound condemning, just concerned for her welfare.

"He took me from my father's house."

"Against your father's wishes?"

"I don't think my father cared. He has recently married a woman not much older than me." She thought of Rosa there too at her father's beck and call. She ached over her father's sinful lifestyle. "Walk with me." She beckoned Steven to follow her.

Birds sang all around. They headed away from the house, through the vineyard, down toward the creek, where real privacy could be found. "It would not be hard for my father to come fetch me. Yet he has not. California is not what I expected. My father is not what I expected."

Steven moved closer to her, measuring his long steps to hers as they walked. "Roman shared with me last night a bit about his past. He has not had an easy life."

This surprised Rachel. "What did he tell you?"

Steven smiled. "We talked for several hours. I did not want to leave him after the fight. He was bleeding quite badly."

She stopped walking, looking toward the house. "How badly is he hurt?"

"Bruised and swollen, but he'll be fine. Lupe used a sewing needle on him. Darned his eyebrow like a sock last night. I'm grateful he's not so handsome now. It gives me a chance to have you look at me."

"Oh, Steven, the Lord made you handsome as well."

He grinned wryly. "Not like Roman Vasquez. I suspect when he heals, his face will be even more intriguing to the ladies with that new scar to admire." Steven grew serious. "Are you in love with him?"

Looking up into his kind brown eyes, she found herself fumbling for an answer.

"Don't be afraid to hurt me. Your love for him would only confirm what the Lord has already shown me."

"What has the Lord shown you?" Her heart skipped a beat.

Tears filled Steven's eyes. "I shall not marry."

She grasped his hands. "Are you sure? That can't be true!"

He pulled her into his arms. "Don't tell me you love him," he whispered huskily. "I can't bear to hear you say it."

His embrace took her aback. This wasn't like Steven at all. "In heaven, none of us will be married," she whispered back to him. "We must remember heaven is our true home." Tears filled her eyes.

He held her for a while, pressing his cheek to her hair, and then, with a deep sigh, he released her. Stepping back, he pressed his thumbs against his eyes.

She knew he fought back tears. "Ours is an eternal hope. We must keep our eyes on Jesus, the author and perfecter of our faith." She captured his hands, squeezing them in encouragement.

"I've loved you for so long. I just needed to see you again." He took a deep, shuddering breath. "You're so beautiful. I've always thought you would be my wife. The light of Christ shines through you. Pray for me, Rachel," he said hoarsely. "A battle rages in me. I don't want to let you go."

She closed her eyes, her hands tightly squeezing his. "Oh, Lord, reassure us that your plans are better than the plans we hold for ourselves. Let our lives be a sacrifice to you, dear Lord Jesus."

"Amen," Steven agreed.

Tears dripped down Rachel's cheeks. "The Lord is with us here in this place."

"Yes, he is. I did not feel God's reassurance on the ship, but I feel him now."

She felt his gaze on her before she saw him. Rising onto her tiptoes, she peered over the top of Steven's shoulder to find Roman standing amongst the vines.

Steven turned and saw him too. He waved Roman over.

"He has a terrible temper," she whispered in warning.

Steven smiled reassuringly.

Roman's bruised and swollen face was like a thundercloud when he stepped up to them there near the creek.

"We were praying. Would you like to join us?" Steven invited.

Roman glanced at Steven and then leveled his gaze on Rachel. "I understand," he said abruptly. His eyes burned over her, and then he spun on his heel to leave.

Steven captured his arm. "Don't go. Pray with us, Roman."

Roman shook off Steven's hand. "I do not pray. I'll leave you two alone with your God."

He walked stiffly away.

"See how he is?" Rachel laced her fingers together to stop from wringing her hands.

"We must show him the love of Christ." Steven stared after Roman, his face shining with compassion.

"You don't know what he has done." She bit her lip. Certainly, she couldn't tell Steven about Roman's embraces. And that he'd seen her bathing and bathed her himself when she was ill. She shuddered at the thought of how intimately he knew her. And how she responded to his touch.

"He's a man who doesn't know our Lord. We must help him see Jesus. I believe he loves you, Rachel. I think you could return his feelings in time."

"Truly, I don't know what I feel for that insufferable man."

Steven placed a gentle hand on her shoulder. "We must trust our Lord. He knows what he's doing with us here."

Steven turned and plucked some unripe grapes off one of the vines. "When the harvest comes, these grapes will be crushed to make wine." He handed Rachel the cluster of green grapes. "We must allow our Lord to ripen us like these grapes. Ultimately, we will be crushed to produce the wine God chooses to fashion from us here."

Chapter Twenty-Three

A grove of ancient oaks shaded the picnic grounds on top of a hill overlooking the hacienda. Blankets spread upon the grass provided a lovely spot to rest and eat beneath the canopy of great trees. Oxen led by vaqueros towed the wooden-wheeled carts transporting the servants holding steaming plates and baskets of food up the hill to the picnic grounds. The Vasquez family was well practiced in entertaining guests this way in the grove. As the *familia* and their visitors indulged themselves on the ridge, vaqueros assembled below on the plain, practicing feats of horsemanship for the onlookers above. Roman remained below with the cowboys, appearing every inch the vaquero on his palomino stallion.

"He is the best rider of them all," Isabella said proudly. The girl had appointed herself Rachel's dueña and refused to leave her side. Remaining close to Isabella was a smiling servant named Chatequa. Another Indian woman, not so cheerful, followed Maria around. These dueñas played a quiet role, doing little more than trailing the girls everywhere they went. Rachel smiled at Chatequa as she rested in the shade. The dark, round-faced servant with kind eyes grinned back at her.

The day was warm and vibrant, the sky sapphire blue with white puffy clouds drifting lazily along. "Will your brother come up here to eat?" Rachel asked Isabella. She hadn't seen Roman since he left her and Steven in the vineyard early that morning.

"Probably not. He prefers to be with the vaqueros. If they don't stop to eat, neither will he. This evening, the vaqueros will feast like wolves after their day is done."

Rachel was disappointed. She wanted Roman to see that Steven did not sit beside her in the shade. Steven was now keeping his distance from her, reclining with Captain Mason on the other side of the picnic grounds. Don Pedro sat with Steven and Captain Mason, eating, drinking, and watching the cowboys down below in the plain.

Hours went by. Rachel reclined back on the grass under an oak tree after eating. Nobody seemed in a hurry to do anything. And she still felt the lingering weakness of her recent sickness. A little rest would do her good. She closed her eyes just for a short while.

When she awoke, she found herself alone on top of the hill except for a handful of servants cleaning up the picnic. Startled, she sat up, looking around for the others.

"They are at a horse race down below." Eating a cold tortilla filled with meat, Roman leaned against the wide trunk of the tree she'd slept under. He was just a few feet away from her.

She scrambled to her feet. "How long have I been asleep?"

"I assured Isabella you would be safe in my care." A wry smile twisted his lips.

She smoothed down her skirts and pushed the hair off her warm cheeks in embarrassment.

"One of the Yankees has captured Isabella's attention. She's down watching him." Roman finished the tortilla and then pushed himself away from the trunk, stepping over to her side. He pointed below where everyone else had gathered. Capturing a lock of her hair, he tucked it behind her ear. "Are you feeling ill again? Is this why you sleep?"

"I'm all right." His nearness made her nervous. The servants nearby pretended not to notice them under the tree together.

"My sisters are spellbound by the blue-eyed Americanos." Roman plucked a leaf from Rachel's locks and then stared intently into her eyes.

"It is natural, I suppose, for young women to notice young men." Rachel felt breathless staring back at him.

"Maybe it is time for me to arrange suitable betrothals for my sisters. Maria especially needs a firm hand now that she is older."

"You will choose Californio husbands for them?"

"Of course." He turned away from her and walked into the open to overlook the horse race on the plain below.

Amid the dark heads of his family and Indian cowboys, the Americans stood out, along with the red-haired Maria, blond and brown-haired men with sun streaks in their hair from long days at sea. Rachel moved up beside him. Her insides knotted with apprehension as she noted his clenched jaw, that hard look overtaking his battered countenance.

"A revolution is brewing." He kept his gaze on the race. "I may ride to San Jaun Bautista tonight. General Castro has called a meeting at his home. All Americanos not married to Californios must leave California at once."

Rachel's stomach tightened with dread. "What will you do?"

He turned to her. "The *gente de razón* are in an uproar. California is on the brink of war. Things are growing dangerous for you. And for them." He pointed to the Americans at the bottom of the hill.

"Does my father know about this order for us to leave?"

"Castro is allowing those married to Californios to stay. All others must leave immediately."

"So what will you do with me?"

"I have not decided." No emotion showed on his face. "The man of God appears eager for you to return to New England with him."

"Steven?" The thought of never seeing Roman again caused a lump to form in her throat. He'd taken liberties with her she never imagined a man taking, but her feelings for him were complicated. On one hand, he infuriated her. But on the other hand, the excitement she felt with him was like nothing she'd ever experienced before. He overwhelmed her, but he protected her too. She considered the way he'd cared for her so diligently in her illness. And how he could be kind and tender and sensitive, like when they'd perused the paintings together.

"Do not look at me that way. You will have a husband. But I have not decided who that husband will be."

"You think I am merely in need of a husband?"

"All women have need of a husband unless they go to the convent." He raked a hand through his hair. She realized he always did this when he grew agitated.

"Did your grandfather choose the man of God for you in New England, or did you choose him yourself?"

"Stop calling him that. His name is Steven."

"I think he is a man who truly knows God."

"Many people know God."

"I do not think so. I have never met a man who speaks for God—except perhaps the padres. And some of them do not speak for God. They speak for Spain or Mexico. Or their own greed. Perhaps they speak for the devil."

"Knowing God is not difficult."

He laughed derisively. "You are such an innocent. The world is so much darker than you can imagine, *pequeña*."

"God is greater than any darkness. Jesus is the light of the world."

"But men prefer the darkness," he said.

"The Bible says they do."

"I am tired of all your God talk. If you stay here with me, you will learn to speak Spanish. You will teach our children about Spain where all my grandparents were born and you will not bathe in the creek without me."

She felt as if he'd slapped her. And he shamed her too by reminding her he'd seen her bathing. Here was the side of him that infuriated her. "I know nothing about Spain. I would teach our children about God." Her voice shook with indignation.

"Then you should marry the man of God." His face hardened.

"Don't you see that casting the Americans out of California will only lead to war with the United States? Men will die. Perhaps you will die."

"I would willingly die for California."

"What good would that do?"

"The Americanos want my land. They want my sisters. They want *you*." Without warning, he yanked her into his arms. "I could take you right now and make you my woman.

My servants would scatter like chickens. Your precious man of God is but a scream away, but you wouldn't scream. Right here under these oaks, I would make you moan, my little dove."

"That's not true!" Alarm swept through her. Angry heat filled her cheeks.

"It is true. I am not a boy when it comes to women. I can give you great pleasure, *pequeña*."

"You are blind!"

"Maybe it is your pride blinding you." His smile didn't reach his eyes. His face was so bruised it hurt to look at him.

"I am not prideful. You are the prideful one." She tried to pull away from him.

He wouldn't release her. "Oh, but you are prideful, little dove. You are so proud of your purity. Your holiness. You do not realize women are robbed of their purity all the time. Especially during war. You have no idea the danger you face here in California."

"You are dangerous!" Placing her hands on his chest, she pushed as hard as she could.

He pulled her tightly against his body. "I want you more than I've ever wanted any woman," he said huskily.

"Let me go," she demanded.

He barked a command in Spanish to the servants. The Indians dropped what they were doing and scurried down the hill.

"Stop! Come back! Call them back."

He used his leg to sweep her feet out from under her. They tumbled to the ground, him twisting his body to cushion her fall. His hands were everywhere at once. She opened her mouth to scream, but his mouth covered hers.

"Stop!" cried Isabella.

Roman sprang to his feet, leaving Rachel stunned on the ground.

Isabella raced over to kneel at her side. "What's wrong with you, *hermano*?" Isabella cried in outrage. "You promised not to wake her up. You promised to watch over her. You said she's been sick!"

Without a word, he spun away and strode down the hill in the wake of the departing servants.

Rachel hugged Isabella.

"My brother needs another flogging from Papa! Juan told us General Castro has ordered all the Americanos to leave California. I came to tell Roman this awful news, and I find him going crazy. Everyone is going crazy in California!" Isabella burst into tears.

Rachel put her hand on Isabella's cheek. "Roman already knows the Americans must leave."

"What is going to happen to you? You can't leave." Tears coursed down Isabella's cheeks.

"I don't know, but God knows."

"I don't want you to leave. You must marry Roman right now."

"I cannot marry your brother. He is filled with the devil."

"He loves you." Isabella defended him.

"That is not love. Lust and anger and pride are driving him." Rachel began to tremble, thinking about what might have happened had Isabella not rescued her.

"I have never seen Roman act this way. I think it is you."

"Me? What have I done?"

"You are not giving him what he wants."

"Isabella, what your brother wants is wrong. It is a sin against God to kiss me. To touch me the way he touches me. I am not his wife yet."

"That is why you must marry him now!"

Chapter Twenty-Four

Roman rode hard and fast to Castro's village. He didn't want to be away from Rancho de los Robles for very long, especially with the Americanos there. He hoped to make the meeting at General Castro's hacienda in San Juan Bautista and return home before nightfall tomorrow. San Juan Bautista wasn't far. Even if he missed the meeting, he could still speak with General Castro to find out what was really going on between the Californios and Americanos.

Revolutions in California were commonplace, but the revolutions had always been between Californios in the north and south. Or California and Mexico. Or California and Spain. Never between California and the United States. This order for all Americanos to leave California was explosive. A new decree. This revolution would certainly lead to war with America.

The hours in the saddle passed swiftly. He'd left Oro at home and brought other horses, switching them out as he traveled to ride farther and faster. The vaqueros were famous for this practice. A man could move about California very quickly this way.

He found himself thinking more about Rachel than the war in California. He'd not spoken with her since the picnic. Why he lost all control with her confounded him. Watching her dance in front of the ship captain made him insane with jealousy. Seeing her in the vineyard with the man of God sent a lance through his heart. Never had he felt like this over Sarita or any other woman. Returning from Texas to find Sarita married to Tyler made him angry, but it hadn't made him crazy.

Rachel made him crazy.

Not long ago, she lay in his arms burning with fever. His longing for her to live brought him to his knees before God. He hadn't pleaded with God since he was a boy. He thought he could live without God, but during Rachel's sickness, he discovered he would have given his very soul for God to spare her life.

Thoughts of her tormented him now. The silkiness of her skin so white under his dark hands as he washed her burning body. The firm curves of her young flesh. The softness of her long blond hair. The delicate beauty of her face. Her sweet, gentle way with people. The desire to touch her again made him tremble in the saddle. How could he let her go? But how could he marry her? She was an Americana. The daughter of his enemy, the man he held responsible for his father's death.

He spurred his mount harder. He needed to let her go. Just give her to the man of God and be done with it. Perhaps he would die in this war. And there would be war. There had to be war. No longer did the Americanos simply come to California to trap and hunt and explore as they had in the past and then return to their own land. They now brought wives and children and built farms in the north, pushing the Indians off the land in the Sacramento Valley.

Roman suspected General Vallejo might not know of General Castro's clandestine meeting. It was well known amongst the Californios that Vallejo favored an alliance with the United States. General Vallejo, it was rumored, went so far as to say California should become an American state, embracing the United States as their mother country.

The thought of this happening left Roman sick inside. Letting Rachel go sickened him even more. If General Castro himself came to Rancho de los Robles to escort Rachel and the rest of the Americanos out of California, a war would surely ensue. But Roman would not be fighting alongside the general. He would allow no man to take Rachel from his hacienda. Not General Castro. Not the Americano ship captain with his fists of stone. And not the man of God, even though he respected the man of God very much. The man of God unnerved him and intrigued him. In his life, Roman had only known a few people who truly knew God. Father Santiago, his mother, Rachel, and now the man of God. Knowing God was not a common thing. Knowing God frightened him.

Sarita knelt in the oak grove at Rancho El Rio Lobo chanting over a fire roasting a newborn lamb. Her hand clutched her womb, rubbing the blood of the lamb onto her naked abdomen. Tohic always demanded a sacrifice when she requested something from him. She wished she could offer the blood of her stepdaughter, but all she had was a few locks left of that hated blond hair.

She felt the cold of Tohic's arrival, the hair stood up on the back of her neck and her arms, the cold wrapping around her like an embrace. Moaning on her knees before the burning lamb, Sarita clutched Rachel's hair in her hand in the grip of a dark possession.

When she finally tossed the hair into the fire upon the lamb, an unearthly scream burst from her lips. Then her mouth twisted with demonic mirth as she laughed and laughed and laughed.

In her bed that night, Rachel whimpered in her sleep. That unearthly cold swirled around her room again. The hacienda creaked, though no wind pressed the tiles on the roof. The night was still but astir with something cold and sinister and dark. Oh, so very dark.

Rachel's familiar nightmare unfolded. The man on the pale horse. She twisted in the sheets, trying to escape him. The cold made her shiver in her sleep, though sweat beaded her body. Terror filled her and she called out his name above all names. Jesus! She awoke calling for Jesus.

Down the hall, Steven kneeled beside his bed, beseeching the Lord for protection for Rachel, for Roman, and for Dominic. He felt the Lord's great love for them, and that love filled him as well. The spiritual battle roared in his ears. Pounded in his heart. Rushed through his blood. *There is no greater love than to lay down one's life for his friends.* The scripture that came to his spirit, wrestling in prayer, strengthened Steven. He clung to it. Put his trust in it. Uttered it out loud into the darkness like a promise.

Chapter Twenty-Five

"Something urgent has arisen," Don Pedro told his guests and family the following evening. "Roman has been called away for government business, but that need not interrupt our festivities tonight." He raised his goblet, downing the last of his wine. By the end of dinner, he was well on his way to drunkenness. Watching the wildness fill his eyes, and the sweat bead on his forehead, Rachel began to silently pray.

Though Don Pedro did his best to encourage the Americans to drink with him, Captain Mason and his sailors consumed very little wine at dinner. Unlike the first night when they'd let their guard down, the Americans appeared prepared for whatever battle might arise tonight and hardly touched their goblets. Steven never drank.

Maria had refused to come to dinner, but she was a dutiful daughter, and when Don Pedro sent for her to dance after dinner for the guests, she finally appeared, dressed in a daring red silk gown. Captain Mason couldn't take his eyes off of her.

After Maria entertained them with her dexterity, Isabella charmed everyone with her playful dancing. Drowning himself in brandy, Don Pedro soon insisted Rachel sing for their guests. Isabella walked with Rachel to the middle of the *sala* to mollify her papa, who was growing unrulier by the hour.

After Rachel whispered in Isabella's ear, the girl rushed over to the musicians to inform them of Rachel's request. With head bowed, she waited for the music to unfurl. When it did, she began to sing for God and God alone.

One of the sailors wiped his eyes after a while. Steven wept too. In a daze, Don Pedro stumbled from the room. Rachel sang on, worshipping her God with all her heart there in the *sala*. The Spirit's presence swept in and swirled about the room, taking control of lesser spirits causing trouble there.

When she finally finished singing, Tia Josefa was wiping tears from her eyes too. Tia Josefa approached the Americans and asked them to retire to their quarters for the night. She said a time of holiness had arisen in their home.

Steven offered to pray before everyone departed. Tia Josefa, dabbing her eyes with her shawl, bowed her head as Steven prayed a beautiful prayer of peace, protection, and God's loving hand in all things.

When Don Pedro returned to the *sala,* after spending the past half hour in a frustrated search for his brandy, the long room stood empty except for the Indian musicians gathering up their instruments and Rachel and Tia Josefa straightening up the furniture.

"Who has ordered the end of the fandango?" Don Pedro demanded in outrage.

The Indians looked nervously at each other. Rachel kept setting the room in order, doing her best to stay out of Don Pedro's way.

Tia Josefa approached him. "A time of repentance has arisen among us. Our guests have gone to their beds to pray." She wrapped her shawl more firmly around her plump shoulders.

Don Pedro looked appalled. "It is not the Lenten season! No one has died. What is this you speak of, woman?"

"Something holy has descended upon our home. We cannot ignore the call of God."

"She will not sing again under my roof!" Don Pedro's voice trembled with indignation as he pointed his finger at Rachel. "She has caused this! I demand that our guests return to the *sala* at once. Go get Maria! She will dance for us."

"I will not disturb our guests," Tia Josefa replied softly but firmly. "Go to the barn. Find your vaqueros and share your brandy with them."

"What has happened to my wife? Do not speak to me this way, woman!"

"You are drunk. Drunkenness is a sin."

"Do you think you are my priest? You are not my priest, Josefa! I will not be condemned! Not in my own hacienda!"

Clutching their instruments, the wide-eyed Indians rushed from the room in the face of Don Pedro's drunken tirade.

"You're frightening the neophytes," Tia Josefa said.

"Those neophytes belong to me!" Don Pedro shouted. "I am Pedro Ramon Guadalupe Vasquez! I am the patrón of this household!"

"You are drunk. You are foaming at the mouth like a rabid dog."

"I am the grandson of a conquistador! I will not stand for this in my house!"

"I am going to bed. I will pray for you." Tia Josefa turned her back on him and motioned for Rachel to hurry from the room ahead of her.

"Do not turn your back on me, woman! Not in my hacienda! My father, a Spaniard of royal blood, built this hacienda with his own two hands!"

Tia Josefa motioned for Rachel to go quickly.

"Josefa!" Don Pedro roared after her.

In San Juan Bautista, General Castro told Roman all that had happened while he was in Texas. Roman had known some of the information, but he hadn't been told about the Yankee battleship that had sailed into Monterey Bay and boldly raised the American flag, declaring California belonged to the United States. Then, strangely, the Americanos apologized for this outrageous act and returned to the sea.

That battleship was still out there cruising up and down the California coastline. It appeared war with the United States was now inevitable.

If the United States declared war on California today could the *gente de razón* really do anything about it? Mexico, with her inept governors and *cholo* troops, certainly wouldn't be able to stop the United States. Roman doubted Mexico would even send soldiers to help them. The rabble of soldiers Mexico had already sent were known criminals and didn't help California at all. They were a blight on California's honor.

In his bed that night at Castro's house, it wasn't thoughts of the war that kept Roman awake. All he could think about was Rachel. He was weary beyond measure, but she rushed through his thoughts like water over a falls. Was her sickness completely gone? Was she safe from harm? Was she happy in his home? Was she smiling even now, out in his vineyard with the man of God at sunrise or sunset or any hour in between? He'd had a long day in the saddle, but his night missing Rachel was longer.

Sarita was delighted when a group of buckskin-clad Americanos arrived at Rancho El Rio Lobo. After several days of allowing these dirty, unshaved foreigners to rest in his hacienda, Joshua rode out with the Yankees without so as much as a word of where he was going or why. Sarita knew Joshua satisfied himself now with that stupid servant, Rosa, and that pleased her just fine. With Roman alive, all she could think about was returning to him. This war would help her.

She placed her hand on her womb, praying again to Tohic that this child growing inside her was not the gringo's. "Please let the seed be Roman's," she whispered. "Oh, Roman, soon, my love, I shall come to you, and we shall build a life together."

She hurried to her room and began to pack only her most beautiful gowns. With her body ripening with the babe, her breasts had grown fuller than ever, spilling over the necklines of her gowns in marvelous abundance.

"You won't be able to resist me, my love," she spoke to the empty room as if Roman stood there with her. "This babe is only the beginning. I will bear you many blue-blooded sons of the *gente de razón*."

Chapter

Twenty-Six

A week had passed at Rancho de los Robles. Dominic and Steven now rode the hills with Roman and his vaqueros. The two men asked to ride along as Roman set about his ranch work. After Steven informed Dominic he would be staying at Rancho de los Robles indefinitely, Dominic sent his sailors back to Yerba Buena, to *The White Swallow* at anchor in San Francisco Bay. Dominic was not about to leave Steven alone with the Spaniard. Steven, bless his soul, was determined to befriend Roman Vasquez. Dominic wanted to make sure Steven survived his unwavering love for his enemies.

He also found himself quite distracted by a certain redhead who still refused to speak to him since he'd given her brother a beating. He noticed Maria looking his way often when she thought he wasn't paying attention, but when he tried to smile at her, she immediately turned away.

Her stubborn streak both delighted and disturbed him. And her dancing at night after dinner fired his imagination.

The girl was magnificent. She deserved a stage in Paris, though he couldn't imagine sharing that infuriating little redhead with France. Men would flock to her, and she so eager for the world's attention, would be caught up in the intrigues of men.

He wondered what his parents would say if he sailed into Boston with Maria by his side. What would he do about his engagement to Sally? How could he bring a Catholic girl home to his Protestant family? His devout mother would faint dead away if she ever saw Maria dance.

If the United States took California, Dominic was certain Yerba Buena, the sleepy village on San Francisco Bay, would become one of the greatest cities in the world. His land there would be priceless. He could build his docks and charge any fee he desired for ships to unload their wares. He could also build his New England-style mansion on the heights overlooking the beautiful, wind-swept bay.

He watched Steven riding his horse alongside Vasquez. The two men talked amicably as they pressed the cattle to another pasture. Presently, the vaqueros were doing most of the work herding the cows, though Vasquez was by far the most skillful horseman Dominic had ever witnessed. Vasquez was deep in conversation with Steven. The minister could befriend anyone. Or anything. Even a snake. Dominic hated snakes. As a boy, he'd developed a fear of snakes, and to this very day, they greatly distressed him.

Vasquez hadn't really spoken to him since the fight, but he acted politely as their faces healed and bodies mended.

"It is the Lord's will for us to love Roman and share Christ with him," Steven had told Dominic that morning as they walked to the stables together to saddle their horses. As usual, they found their mounts already saddled for them. Life in

California was a pleasure in so many ways. Don Pedro treated them like the most honored guests, seeing to their every need, though Dominic suspected it was Roman who really oversaw all their needs since Don Pedro had a drinking problem and didn't get out of bed until after noon each day.

"We'll probably have to drag that Spaniard kicking and cursing to God," Dominic told Steven.

Steven smiled that patient, gentle smile of his. "Maybe you are the one kicking and cursing our Savior, my friend."

Dominic's face had heated at the rebuke. He still felt compelled to ride along to protect Steven as he went out with Vasquez, though the thought of spending another day in the saddle made him groan. His backside actually had bruises from bounding along the past several days chasing wild Mexican longhorns across the hills.

When Roman finally announced it was time to return to the hacienda after another endless day of herding cattle, Dominic felt like hugging the Spaniard.

Instead, he rode up alongside Vasquez and put his hand on his shoulder in a companionable way. "I have enjoyed these days working cattle with you," he told Vasquez. It wasn't the truth, but at that moment, knowing soon he could climb down from his horse when they reached the hacienda, Dominic really did feel a fondness for the brooding Spaniard.

Vasquez surprised him with a friendly smile.

Steven smiled too, looking up into the vast blue sky for a moment and nodding to God.

The three men rode back to the hacienda in affable conversation until they came upon a half-eaten calf near the house. Vasquez got down from his horse and stood over the remains. "A bear," the Spaniard said solemnly. "This kill is fresh and close to the hacienda. This is not good, amigos. We will have to hunt this bear."

Dominic glanced around in alarm. "How big a bear?" He tried to keep his voice steady.

Roman pointed to massive paw prints in the dirt. The claw marks on the forepaws were several inches long. "A big one. We must kill it quickly."

Dominic no longer concealed his dismay. "We are going after the bear right now?"

"It will be dark soon. It is too dangerous to hunt the bear at night. We will go at dawn. You can stay in your bed, amigo." The Spaniard grinned at him.

"We will go with you. Won't we, Dom?" Steven announced quite bravely.

Dominic nearly jumped off his horse. "Steven, this is a large bear. Have you ever seen one of these Californian bears? I have heard they are man-eaters."

"We will do as Roman does. No one will be harmed."

Dominic looked at Steven, so calm and trusting, then at Vasquez. "How will we kill it?" he asked the Spaniard.

"We will capture the bear with our riatas. Tio Pedro will be thrilled to hold a bear baiting in honor of you Yankees."

"What the devil is a bear baiting?" Dominic asked.

"A bear and bull are chained together for a fight."

"I've never heard of such a thing." Dominic shifted in his saddle, as frightened as a little boy.

"What do the animals do once they are chained together?" Steven stroked his jaw in contemplation, clearly trying to picture this practice.

"They kill each other." Vasquez walked away from the dead calf and climbed back onto his horse.

"And this honors one's guests?" Steven looked baffled.

"It is the Californio way," Vasquez replied.

"What if these animals get loose? Will we just be standing around with an enraged bull and bear trying to eat us?" Dominic couldn't believe what he was hearing.

"I will give you my riata. This rope has saved my life many times, Captain Mason." Vasquez gave him a cheeky grin.

Steven grinned too. "Maybe you should practice with this riata before we hunt the bear tomorrow, Dom."

"Steven, you can't be serious about hunting this bear." Dominic was aghast.

"Roman needs our help." The smile did not waver on Steven's face.

"They will be catching this bear with a rope! Then chaining this bear to a wild bull. A wild bull! Steven, are you hearing what he's saying?"

Steven gave Dominic a reassuring smile and then turned to the Spaniard. "Must we really chain the bear and the bull to fight?"

"Not if this disturbs you," Vasquez offered.

"Good. We will not be chaining the bear to the bull for a fight," Steven reassured Dominic.

"So what will we be doing with this bear?" Dominic squirmed in his saddle.

"We will use our riatas to capture the bear. Then either you or I or one of my vaqueros will kill it with a knife."

"A knife? Are you insane? Doesn't anyone own a blasted gun around here?"

"The knife is long. It's more like a lance," Vasquez explained.

"Hunting a bear with ropes and knives? I have just purchased the finest rifle made today. It is on my ship. How long do you think it will take for us to ride to the ship and return here with my rifle, Steven?"

"We do not need a rifle." Vasquez spoke with complete confidence. "I assure you, Captain Mason, my vaqueros and I can kill the bear this way. Only once have we lost a man on a bear hunt. And only two horses."

"You've lost a man? And two horses?" Dominic gave Steven a disbelieving look.

"That was an unfortunate year. During my father's time. I have never lost a man, myself. Nor a horse while hunting bears. Come," Vasquez said. "You must be hungry after a long day. Let's get home and eat."

Dominic urged his horse up close to Steven's mount, speaking softly but urgently to him. "I won't be able to eat or sleep tonight. We cannot go on this bear hunt in the morning. This is absurd!"

"Roman has offered you his very own riata. I have heard a man's riata is sacred in California. Isn't this true, Roman?"

"*Si.*" The Spaniard's green eyes sparkled with mirth. "My riata is like my woman, but I will give it to you tomorrow, Captain Mason."

"Please call me Dom. If we are going to die together, certainly we can be friends."

The Spaniard laughed and then grew serious. "I will not allow the bear to kill my friends. I would give my life before letting the bear harm you."

"There is no greater love than for a man to lay down his life for his friends," Steven said happily.

"Does it say anywhere in the Good Book not to hunt bears without a gun? I think the Bible should say something like that." Dominic wasn't smiling.

"When David was but a boy, he killed a bear with his sling. Samson used his own two hands to kill a lion. It is the Lord who destroys our enemies, Dom. We will trust in the Lord tomorrow to deliver the bear into our hands," said Steven.

"Well, I need time to let my hair grow like Samson's. I can't go bear hunting until my hair reaches the waistband of my britches." Dominic was still afraid, but he was laughing.

Roman and Steven laughed as well. "You don't have to go," Roman offered. "The women will be sewing tomorrow. You can fashion a dress for yourself with my sisters."

"Yes, you should do that. A blue dress to match your eyes," Steven said.

The men rode toward the house, Steven and Roman still teasing Dominic about the bear. God certainly did have a sense of humor, Dominic decided. He hated bears nearly as much as he hated snakes.

Chapter Twenty-Seven

Roman waited for everyone to seek their beds before slipping to the other side of the hacienda to find Rachel, who'd retired early to her room. He'd drunk brandy with Dominic and Tio Pedro after dinner, and the brandy gave him courage to bring her a proposal. He knocked softly upon her door until she opened it. Though she was in her nightdress, he pushed into her room, quickly closing the door behind him.

"Have you been drinking?" Her anxious gaze searched his.

"I am not drunk." He went and made himself comfortable on her bed. He didn't feel drunk—relaxed, perhaps, but not inebriated.

"This is improper." Her cheeks bloomed with color. She looked so fetching in her white nightgown with her hair flowing loose down her back, he could hardly restrain himself.

"*Si,*" he agreed, a crooked smile tugging the corners of his mouth.

"You must leave."

"I will leave after we talk." He patted the bed. "Come sit with me, *pequeña*."

"I will not come near you on that bed."

"We have shared a bed before."

"Stop this right now."

"Stop what?"

"Toying with me."

"I assure you, *pequeña*, I am not toying with you. I'm serious about my intentions. Come, sit with me, and I will tell you my proposal."

"I will not sit with you." She walked to the door, waiting there to usher him out.

He stretched out on her bed, careful to keep his spurs and boots from damaging the fine bedcover his own mother had sewn.

Her eyes widened. "What are you doing?"

"If you will not sit with me, I will make myself comfortable here." He grinned. "I have held you in my arms, all softness and warmth and nothing more. We are well past propriety, little dove."

"How dare you remind me of such a thing!"

He sat up on the bed. "I cannot forget such a thing. I close my eyes and see you in my bed. In my arms . . ."

"Stop this! We should not be alone together. This is highly improper." Her voice trembled with indignation.

He got off the bed and walked over to her beside the door.

She backed against the closed portal.

Capturing her chin, he raised her face to his. "Let me make you my woman. I will be so gentle with you, *pequeña*." His lips descended on hers. His kiss was soft and explorative and hot with brandy. His hands at her waist pulled her firmly against his body, not roughly, but with gentle, unbending strength.

After kissing her mouth for a long time, he kissed her cheeks, tasting salty tears there.

"Why are you are crying?" He rested his cheek against the top of her silky head. "I know every inch of you," he said hoarsely. "I won't hurt you, Rachel."

"You do not understand," she said tearfully.

"What is there to understand? I lie awake at night thinking about you. All day, you are in my thoughts. I have worked from dawn to dusk exhausting myself, and still I cannot escape these memories of you. Please tell me what is there to understand? I am but a man, and you are my betrothed. It is natural."

She pushed him away. Walking to her bed, she retrieved her open Bible lying there and began to read. *"My dove in the clefts of the rock, in the hiding places on the mountainside, show me your face, let me hear your voice; for your voice is sweet, and your face is lovely. Catch for us the foxes, the little foxes that ruin the vineyards, our vineyards that are in bloom."* She stopped reading.

"Go on," he said. "Read more."

"My lover is mine, and I am his; he browses among the lilies. Until the day breaks and the shadows flee, turn, my lover, and be like a gazelle or like a young stag on the rugged hills."

"These words are written in your Bible?" He was surprised.

"These are God's words of love. We cannot sin against God. Only in marriage is this kind of love allowed between a man and a woman."

"I cannot marry you," he said curtly.

"If you are not to be my husband, you have no business here with me."

Overcome by the sudden conviction that he was sinning against God trying to make her his woman without marrying her, Roman opened the door and walked from her room shaken and unsure of himself. What was happening to him?

His head hurt from the brandy he'd consumed last night. As they rode out early the next morning to search for the bear, the Gavilan Peak incident weighed heavily on Roman's mind. After the scraggy-bearded explorer Captain Fremont met with Thomas Larkin in January, Larkin brought Fremont to meet General Castro. Castro said Larkin had assured him Fremont's mission in California was peaceful. These buckskin-clad Yankees were not an American military force, but merely civilian explorers, mapmakers, and guides under the command of Captain Fremont, who happened to be a military officer, Larkin assured them. Castro allowed Fremont and his men to winter in the San Joaquin Valley out of respect for Larkin, but Fremont then brazenly ignored Castro's command to remain inland away from California's settled coastal areas.

These Americanos had committed depredations against the Californios in the valley. Fremont's soldiers had even invaded a rancho near San Juan Bautista. One of Fremont's drunken men held a gun to Don Angel Castro's head while another attempted to rape his daughter. A tough old soldier himself, Don Angel wrestled the gun away from the rascal and chased the Americanos out of his home. After this, General Castro notified Larkin of his decision to expel the Americanos from the Monterey area.

These American ruffians then built their crude fort at the top of Gavilan Peak, just thirty miles from Monterey, daring to fly an American flag on top of the peak as they defied General Castro's orders to leave the province. Castro had put together a cavalry of nearly two hundred Californios, and with three brass cannons, ran the Americanos out of the region in March. Fremont and his men then headed north to Sutter's Fort. General Castro asked Roman to join his northern forces, but the general presently seemed more bent on fighting Governor Pico in the south than the Americanos taking over the north.

Roman told Castro he would ride with him, but only against the Americanos in the north if war with the United States became imminent. He would not quarrel with Californios in the south. This had been one of California's biggest problems. The Californios in the north couldn't get along with the Californios in the south, leaving the two factions always warring for power in the province. It was the Yankees Roman wanted to fight. Until today.

He glanced at Steven riding beside him so confident in his God this morning as they hunted for the bear. Dominic rode on his other side—the ship captain with fists of stone, a man strangely terrified of bears. Roman marveled at these new friends. He truly enjoyed their company, and last night at dinner he and Dominic had discussed Yerba Buena for quite some time, agreeing San Francisco Bay was the best harbor in the world. Certainly, there would come a day when the world discovered this magnificent harbor, and the little village of Yerba Buena would explode into a booming trade center.

They searched half the day for the bear. Spring was giving way to summer. Today was one of California's perfect days—sunny skies, comfortable temperatures, a sky so blue and fair it hurt his eyes to really look at it. Roman could see for miles and felt like riding that far to get away from Rachel. She was driving him half mad with desire, and all her religion was weighing on him too. At the strangest moments he'd find himself thinking about Rachel and suddenly his thoughts would turn to God. In the early days with her, he found her devotion to religion disconcerting. Now it intrigued him. To her, Jesus was alive and very real and her whole life came under the guidance of God. Either she was crazy or she was right about Jesus Christ. Roman didn't think she was crazy.

One of his vaqueros had been following the bear's trail. The rest of them followed the vaquero, an Indian tracker very skilled in hunting bears. The bear had come back for the calf, and here and there blood littered the path the bear had taken. By the time they found the bear in a clearing in a wooded canyon, the afternoon sun shone directly down on their heads. The massive bear stood up on his hind legs when he spotted the horsemen approaching. He was a full-grown male grizzly, standing at least nine feet tall. Bears would often flee when they spotted men on horses, but this bear roared his fury.

The bear dropped down onto all fours and turned in circles as the men surrounded it on their horses in the clearing.

Roman and his vaqueros galloped their horses in a loop around the grizzly. Steven went after them, leaving Dominic no choice but to do the same. Roman whirled his riata over his head. The vaqueros whirled their riatas too as they circled the bear on their well-trained mustangs.

Before anyone could throw a rope, the bear charged Dominic's horse. Dominic's horse, not trained like Rancho de los Robles mustangs to face bears, bolted sideways. Unprepared for the horse's terror, Dominic pitched from the saddle, landing on the ground with the bear barreling toward him. His horse bolted away, empty stirrups flapping against its sweaty flanks.

Roman spurred his horse over to Dominic. He knew even if he roped the bear now, the grizzly would have Dominic in his jaws before he and his vaqueros could drag the bear away. He dropped his riata and drew his long lance.

In a feat of horsemanship, Roman swept alongside the charging grizzly, burying his long lance between the bear's rolling shoulder blades.

The grizzly roared in pain, spinning in a circle just feet away from Dominic, who was on his knees facing the bear, a look of horror on his face.

Four vaqueros threw their ropes. Every riata settled around the wounded bear's neck.

The grizzly roared and lunged at the mounted vaqueros. The palominos backed up swiftly, tightening the rawhide ropes in all directions, immobilizing the infuriated bear.

Roman rode up to Dominic and reached for his hand, commanding Dom to place his foot in the stirrup Roman vacated for him. With Dominic's boot firmly in his stirrup, Roman yanked his friend up behind him in the saddle and rode a safe distance away from the captured grizzly.

Steven went after Dominic's horse. By the time he returned, leading the fancy bay gelding Dominic had purchased in Yerba Buena, the bear was dead, and Dominic was helping Roman and the vaqueros remove the riatas from the beast's bloody neck. Roman's lance remained buried between the bear's great shoulders.

Steven dismounted his horse. "If I hadn't seen it with my own eyes, I never would have believed such a thing possible. Roman, you are a warrior!"

Roman smiled. "This was a bad bear. It is good that he is dead."

"I would like to have the hide." Dominic stared in wonder at the dead bear. "That thing almost had *my* hide."

"The hide is yours, amigo." Roman patted Dom's shoulder. "Next time, you can kill the bear."

Dominic turned and wrapped Roman in an exuberant embrace. "There will be no next time. I will never hunt another bear. Thank you for saving my life, my friend!"

"You are welcome." Roman smiled even wider.

"I spent a fortune on a horse that nearly killed me." Dominic motioned to the mount Steven held.

Roman smacked Dom on the back. "Your mount is poorly trained. Rancho de los Robles's horses are not afraid of bears. I will give you a fine stallion that will not feed you to a bear in California."

"You should have seen your face, Dom. Your eyes about bugged out of your head when that grizzly came after you." Steven began laughing and couldn't stop.

"I may have soiled myself," Dominic admitted, laughing along with Steven.

"A man of honor does not lose his bowels, even in death," Roman announced and then laughed too.

The vaqueros, skinning the bear, grinned and nodded their agreement.

"You Spaniards may not lose your bowels when a bear tries to kill you, but this Yankee may have to change his britches. I have never faced a grizzly on my knees before. I've never been that scared in my life. Even great storms at sea seem tame in comparison."

With the vaqueros laughing now, Dominic pulled out his knife to help them skin the bear. Like his fancy horse, his knife looked pretty and sharp, but the blade didn't work well on the thick bear hide.

Roman handed Dominic his knife.

"What will you do with your hide, Dom?" Steven asked.

"I think I will build a fine mansion in Yerba Buena to house my bear hide. I will lay it on the floor in front of a roaring fire and let my children play there when they are babes."

"You will have a fire in your home?" Roman was curious. "Californian adobes do not have fires." Though Roman had heard the Americanos built fireplaces in their California homes.

"Yerba Buena feels like New England," said Dominic. "The wind often rolls off the bay. It can be bitterly cold, even in summer there. I will need a fireplace in every room."

"I will come visit you in Yerba Buena. I want to see how a man burns a fire in his hacienda. I have never seen this done before." Roman smiled, feeling grateful the bear had not killed any of them. And there was no going back now. Dom and Steven had become his brothers. They were bonded to him by the blood of the bear.

Chapter Twenty-Eight

Rachel looked up from her sewing as a servant came and whispered in Tia Josefa's ear. "Señoritas, keep sewing," Tia Josefa instructed Isabella, Maria, and Rachel where they sat in the *sala*. "We have visitors."

"Who, Mama?" Isabella wanted to know.

"You may come along with me and see." Tia Josefa's smile was indulgent.

"I am tired of sewing," Maria announced.

"What have you sewn?" Tia Josefa did not look pleased.

Maria held up a cloth containing crooked stitches.

"Keep sewing," Tia Josefa commanded. "You must master this woman's art before you become the wife of some poor man."

"I do not want to be a wife. I want to travel to Spain, to New York, to the Orient."

Tia Josefa grew stern with Maria. "You will become a wife here in California, and you will know how to sew by then, Maria Domitilla Flores Vasquez."

Maria tossed down her sewing cloth in disgust. "Why is the little goat allowed to greet our guests with you, and I am not?"

"Mama, she called me a goat again."

Tia Josefa threw up her hands in front of Isabella and Maria. "You girls are as spoiled as last year's eggs. Look at Señorita Rachel, how beautifully she sews, how gentle and quiet she is with everyone. This is how a well-bred lady behaves." Tia Josefa gave Rachel an encouraging smile.

Rachel continued her sewing.

"I don't want to be a well-bred lady," Maria said.

"Me neither," Isabella agreed.

"Maria, sew! Isabella, come with me. Our guests have arrived by now."

Isabella gave Maria a triumphant look and then scampered after her mother exiting the *sala*.

"Tio and Tia spoil that child because she's adopted," Maria said. "Tell me what America is like." The redhead tossed her sewing cloth aside and focused her attention on Rachel. "Are the cities very grand?"

"I only know New England." Rachel concentrated on sewing.

"Tell me about Boston. Is it a large city?"

"The only time I've been to Boston was to sail here to California."

"You did not see how the women dress there?"

Rachel's cheeks grew warm. "I can't remember, really."

"How can you not remember a city's dresses?"

Rachel kept stitching. "I was only there a day and a night waiting for the ship to depart. I guess they dress like other women dress these days."

"Was the harbor filled with ships from around the world?" Excitement filled Maria's voice.

"There were many ships. The world is a wide and dangerous place, especially for a beautiful young woman without the chaperone of a husband or father."

Maria grinned, causing a dimple to appear in one cheek. She was an absolutely beautiful girl when she smiled that way. "I am ready for a wide and dangerous world."

"Months on the ocean is not a pleasant experience. One can become very sick. And people die all the time on these long voyages."

"I will not become sick." Maria jumped to her feet. She pulled up her skirts, revealing slender, black-stockinged ankles and calves. "I know I have sea legs. If I were a man, I would join the crew of a Yankee clipper ship so I could sail around the world."

"You do not want to marry?" Rachel laid aside her sewing, giving Maria her full attention.

"If I were to marry, a man would become my master. I do not want a master. I want to be free to do as I choose."

Rachel stretched in her seat, her muscles tight after hours of sitting there on the couch. "And what of God's choosing?"

"What of God's choosing?" Maria sat down, arranging her skirts to cover her shapely limbs. "God does not want me trapped here in this hacienda forever."

Rachel captured Maria's hands. "You live in a beautiful house with a beautiful family."

"I am tired of my family. You've sailed across an ocean. You've been in a man's arms. I want to experience this too."

Rachel's cheeks grew warm. She didn't know what to say.

Maria laughed at her blush. "Has my brother welcomed you to his bed? Has he made you his woman yet?"

"No," Rachel said sharply.

Maria clucked her tongue. "Too bad. I have heard he is a very skillful lover."

Isabella raced into the room. "Sarita is here! Mama says she will live with us now that her *Yanquio* husband has joined the rebels in the north!"

Maria's green eyes narrowed on Rachel. "You should ask Sarita about Roman's skillfulness. She knows my brother well."

"What are you talking about?" Isabella demanded. "Have you been telling Rachel lies about Roman?"

"They are not lies. I don't want her surprised when our cousin fawns all over our brother when he returns from the fields tonight."

"Sarita will be fat one day. Wait and see. She is lazy and—"

"Stop," Rachel said with her heart in her throat. "Do not speak of such things."

"See, little goat, you have upset Rachel."

"You upset her!" Isabella cried.

Maria stood up. "I am done sewing. It bores me to death. The Yankees are coming. I will sail away with one of these tall, handsome Americanos on a ship someday. Just watch and see."

"Like Captain Mason?" Isabella baited.

"Captain Mason is a beast."

"Roman no longer thinks so. Did you see him talking with the captain last night? They went on and on about Yerba Buena becoming a great city someday. They are becoming fast friends. I have never seen Roman like this. He enjoys having the Americanos here." Isabella said.

"I would not forgive Captain Mason if I were Roman. I do not forgive Captain Mason."

Isabella laughed. "You attacked the poor captain. What did you expect him to do? Waltz with you while you scratched his eyes out?"

"He threw me on the floor. His blood ruined my dress."

"I thought you liked him. He is so handsome. I know you want to kiss him." Isabella smooched her lips.

"He is not so handsome with bruises on his face."

Isabella threw up her hands. "Captain Mason is the most handsome blue-eyed man ever to come to California. Is he not the most handsome blue-eyed man ever?" she asked Rachel.

Rachel didn't respond. She couldn't stop thinking about what Maria said about Sarita and Roman together.

Maria straightened the bodice of her dress and pushed her long, red hair off her shoulders. She was slender but so shapely, and her hair was really something. Everything about her was lush. Her lips, her hair, her figure. Rachel could see how Captain Mason couldn't take his eyes off the girl.

"Captain Mason is a brute," said Maria.

"I think you liked rolling on the floor with the captain," Isabella teased.

"Watch yourself, little goat. I will throw you on the floor and ruin your dress with your blood."

"You are sisters. You should treat each other more kindly." Rachel stood up to leave the room.

"She is not really my sister," Maria announced. "Izzy is my cousin."

"I am not even really your cousin. My father was Russian. My mother a beautiful octoroon."

"An octopus," Maria said, laughing.

"Octoroon," Isabella insisted. "Do you know what that is?" she asked Rachel without giving her time to answer. "My mother was mostly Spanish with some Indian blood in her veins."

"Mostly Indian with some Spanish blood in her veins," Maria corrected.

"How do you know?" Isabella grew angry.

"Look at your skin. Is it white like Rachel's? Golden like mine? No, you are brown as a little chicken egg and you have the hair of an Indian, straight and thick and black as night."

Isabella yanked up her skirt to reveal bare brown feet and much paler legs. "My legs are not so brown," she cried. "The sun makes me brown."

Rachel went to Isabella. "You are a lovely girl made in God's image," she said, smoothing Isabella's skirts down.

"Maria is mean!" Isabella cried.

"You should tell your sister you are sorry," Rachel told Maria.

"I am sorry, little goat. You are not so brown." Maria lightly yanked one of Isabella's long black braids. "You are pretty with your blue eyes and dusky skin. The men will want you when you are older, little sister." Maria hugged Isabella and then grew serious. "Do you know why Sarita has come here?" she turned to Rachel.

Rachel shook her head. She really didn't know.

"Sarita is Tia Josefa's niece. She is our cousin by marriage. She is also Roman's former *novia*. She married your father because she thought Roman was dead. We all thought he'd been killed in Texas. I do not think Sarita's feelings have changed. She has always loved my brother."

"She used to live with us." Isabella added, wrinkling her nose. "When Mama found out Sarita and Roman were sneaking off together at night, she sent Sarita back to her brother. Sarita's father is a weak-willed man. Instead of making Roman marry Sarita then and there like any good father would have, Mama's brother allowed Roman to only become engaged to Sarita before he rode off to Texas."

"Sarita is a witch." Maria shivered. "You must be careful around her, Rachel."

"Really, she is a witch!" Isabella agreed. "She worships Tohic, but Mama won't believe it because Sarita lies about it. She says she is praying the rosary when she's really praying to Tohic." Isabella's eyes widened with fear.

With trembling hands, Rachel gathered up her sewing materials. "I am not afraid of witchcraft. God is in control."

"Sarita will cause trouble for you. Tia should not let her stay here," said Maria.

Holding her small wooden sewing chest in her arms, Rachel did her best to appear unaffected by this talk.

"Where is your rosary?" Isabella asked Maria. "Let's give our rosaries to Rachel."

Rachel did not try to talk the girls out of this practice. Like her father's servant, Rosa, Isabella and Maria were Catholic. The beaded necklaces represented God's protection to them. "I will place your rosaries beside my bed," Rachel told them.

"Under your pillow," Isabella insisted.

"Under my pillow," Rachel agreed.

Chapter Twenty-Nine

Roman sent Dominic's bear hide to the stables with the vaqueros. The hide would be cured by the Indians trained in tanning hides. Roman, Steven, and Dominic walked to the hacienda in high spirits, only to discover Sarita's arrival an hour earlier had placed everyone in an uproar.

Tio Pedro was threatening to ride north to kill Joshua Tyler. Pedro could not understand why Sarita's husband would join the rebels in the Sacramento Valley when he was a Mexican citizen married to a Californian wife. Upon her arrival, Sarita had cried and carried on about being abandoned by her traitorous gringo husband.

As soon as Roman arrived, she flew into his arms, pressing her ample curves against him even though he smelled like a dead bear. "My husband has left me! He has joined the rebels in the north," she said, then fell into a fit of sobbing.

Roman set her away from him. When she continued to weep, clutching at his shirtfront, he took her back into his arms. "Please, Sarita, stop all this weeping."

Rachel stood between Isabella and Maria, staring at him with wide, wounded eyes. He stared back at her as he held Sarita. He tried to reassure Rachel with his eyes, but she turned away, refusing to look at him. He realized in that moment that Sarita's presence at Rancho de los Robles was the worst possible thing that could happen to them aside from war.

"I will escort you to your father's rancho," he told Sarita. "We will leave at first light in the morning."

"But Tia Josefa has welcomed me here," Sarita said tearfully. "I need you to take care of me. You know how cowardly my father is. He cannot protect me from the gringos when they come to conquer us."

"Did your husband give you permission to leave Rancho El Rio Lobo in his absence?" Roman set her away from him again.

"What are you saying? You hate the Americanos! Surely, you do not expect me to remain married to my Yankee husband now that he has become an enemy to California?"

"Calm down, Sarita. We are not at war with the United States yet. I talked to General Castro just days ago. The general is more concerned about his feud with Governor Pico than war with the Americanos."

"Didn't Castro tell you he has ordered all Americanos not married to Californios to leave California at once? Why is *she* still here?" Sarita spun around to give Rachel an accusing glare.

Steven and Dominic quietly made their way to Rachel's side in a protective manner.

"What are those *Yanquios* doing here?" Sarita glared at the men.

"They are my amigos." Roman had had enough. "Sarita, you are overwrought. Come, I will see you to your room so you can gather your composure and get some rest."

She clasped Roman's elbow, rubbing her cleavage against his arm. "I knew you would take care of me, *querido*."

Isabella rushed up and squeezed herself between them. "I will see Sarita to her room!"

Sarita glared at the girl. She wouldn't let go of Roman's arm. "I prefer Roman show me to my room."

"You're coming with me!" Isabella gritted her little, white teeth and grabbed Sarita's arm, attempting to yank her away from Roman's side.

Startled by Isabella's strength, Sarita lost her balance. Both she and Isabella would have tumbled to the floor if Roman hadn't wrapped his arms around the two of them.

Maria stepped forward and inserted herself between her brother and the stunned Sarita. "We will take our cousin to her quarters." With a determined hip, Maria shoved Roman away from Sarita.

"I do not want to go with you!" Sarita tried to pull her arms from the girls' grasp, but Maria and Isabella wouldn't let go of her. "Roman, help me," she demanded.

Tia Josefa intervened. "Remember how sweetly you girls played together when you were young? Be good to each other *mi hijas*."

"I want Roman to take me to my quarters!" Sarita's voice turned shrill as she struggled to escape Maria and Isabella.

"Maria and I will see you to your room, won't we, Mama?" Isabella demanded.

"Come, *chicas*." Tia Josefa motioned for Sarita, Isabella, and Maria to follow her from the *sala*. She also waved Rachel over to join them. "Let us leave the gentlemen to clean themselves up. I would say their bear hunt was successful judging by the smell of them."

In the tussle with Isabella and Maria, Sarita's ample bosom had been liberated from its satin confinement. Roman stared at all that intriguing flesh hanging over her gown, and then his eyes collided with Rachel's. She had followed Tia Josefa's order to join the women and now stood beside Sarita, staring back at him. The hurt in her confused blue eyes pierced his heart. What did she expect of him? Wouldn't any man look at Sarita's dishevelment right now?

He glanced at Steven and Dominic for reassurance, but both men stared at the floor as Isabella and Maria dragged Sarita from the room.

I offer you an honorable wife, and you ogle a harlot instead.

The voice wasn't audible, but deep inside his soul, the rebuke pierced him. Where on earth had it come from? Was God speaking to him? Conviction that he was a sinful man tore through Roman.

He looked to Rachel, but she was following the women from the *sala*.

Utterly shaken, he walked over to Dominic and Steven. They looked up from the floor after the women departed the room.

"I feel in need of a bath," he told them, abandoning any attempt at small talk. "Would you join me in the creek, amigos?"

"Now that sounds like what each of us needs right now," Dominic agreed.

"A bath would help us all." Steven smiled reassuringly.

Roman longed to ask Steven what it sounded like when God spoke to a man. He couldn't get that thought out of his head: *I offer you an honorable wife and you ogle a harlot instead.* What he felt deep in his soul was fear. A sudden and very real fear of the Almighty had overtaken him.

Down at the creek, he got his chance alone with Steven when Dominic departed for the hacienda after they had all shaved and bathed. "See you amigos at the house," said Dom as he finished dressing and strode quickly toward the hacienda.

"How does a man hear from God?" Roman asked Steven as soon as Dominic was out of earshot.

Sitting on a rock beside the water, drying his feet with a towel, Steven looked pleased by the question. "Reading the Bible is the best way I know to hear from God."

"Are there other ways to hear God speak to a man?" What had he heard in the *sala* after he'd stared at Sarita's nakedness?

"Well," Steven said thoughtfully, "Joseph, the earthly father of Jesus, heard from God in a dream. So did Jacob and Daniel and other men from biblical times. They all had dreams where God spoke to them."

"Are the Bible and dreams the only ways God speaks?" Roman pressed.

"No." Steven grew even more thoughtful. "God can speak to a man in other ways. Through nature. Through suffering. And God gives all men a conscience. That little voice inside your head that makes you feel sorrow over your sins. It sounds like your own voice, but this is really the guidance of the Holy Spirit."

Roman leaned forward where he sat on his own rock, pulling on his boots. "That little voice is not so little sometimes."

Steven smiled that gentle smile of his. "God has sharpened your conscience to hear his voice. What has the Lord said to you, my friend?"

Roman did not want to tell Steven what he'd heard. He recalled the wounded look in Rachel's eyes and the feel of Sarita's breasts pressed against his forearm. What surprised him was that he no longer desired Sarita with all her ample charms and her flashing black eyes that promised the fulfillment of a man's dark desires. He far preferred his sweet, slender Rachel with her eyes full of light. But what surprised him most at the moment was his great longing to know God.

"The Lord always confirms his commands. If you have heard from God, our Lord will make what he has said clear to you through other ways," Steven counseled.

Roman pondered this. "So the voice of God will come again?" he asked hopefully, strapping on his rusty spurs.

"Maybe. Or God may speak to you differently. Perhaps through a person or a situation or the Bible." Obviously, the Bible was very important to Steven, like it was to Rachel.

"How will I know this is God speaking to me?"

"May I say a prayer for you to be able to hear what God is saying to you before we return to the hacienda?" Steven finished putting on his own boots and looked at him expectantly.

"I would appreciate that, thank you." Roman bowed his head, awaiting Steven's prayer.

Chapter Thirty

The days passed in turmoil with Sarita at Rancho de los Robles.
Each night after the evening meal, Don Pedro insisted on entertaining his guests with dancing. Sarita wore scandalous gowns
and danced provocatively in what appeared to be performances
solely for Roman's benefit. Don Pedro's *aguardiente*, the brandy
that inflamed him, never ran dry.

Rachel did everything she could to avoid the evenings, often
retiring right after dinner to her room. In a dark and brooding mood that would not lift, Roman spent grueling days with
the vaqueros, gathering hides for Dominic to sell in Boston as
May gave way to June. In the annual *matanza,* the slaughter
of the herds, the men rounded up hundreds of cattle, killing
and skinning the animals out in the fields. Only some of the
meat was taken, most of the carcasses were left for the vultures,
bears, coyotes, and wolves. The hides were packed to be trans-
ported to San Francisco Bay where Dominic's ship waited in
the harbor. This was California's biggest income. Cattle hides

known as California banknotes. Tallow from the slaughtered cattle was also collected and sold as well, but not to the ships bound for Boston. The tallow went to South America to make candles and soap, so it was saved at the rancho to be sold to ships in Monterey that would sail south.

When all the cattle had been slaughtered for the season, Steven and Dominic finally departed for Yerba Buena, accompanied by a dozen Rancho de los Robles vaqueros transporting the cattle hides to add to *The White Swallow's* cargo hold. Steven and Rachel had walked in the vineyard alone together before he left. Roman did not know what they'd shared, but when the two returned, Rachel's face was tear-streaked and Steven looked very sad. Steven and Roman had discussed Rachel before this. Since *The White Swallow* wouldn't be sailing away from California just yet, they decided Rachel was safest remaining at the hacienda for now.

With his friends gone, Roman grew even more unhappy. No longer could he tolerate Tio Pedro's drunken evenings and began to avoid all meals with the *familia*. Both Sarita and Rachel saw very little of him, though on two occasions, Roman had to forcefully remove Sarita from his room.

When she refused to leave the second time at his curt request, attempting to seduce him by undressing before him, Roman picked her up and dumped her, half-clothed, in the hallway, bracing a chair against the door to keep her out of his chamber.

Early one morning before dawn, after reading the Bible Steven left with him, Roman padded down the hall past his sister's rooms, past Sarita's room, around several corners of the big rectangular hacienda's upstairs until he reached the last bedroom on the left, where Rachel now resided.

Instead of knocking on the door, he quietly entered her room. It was still dark as he kneeled beside Rachel's bed. Moonlight spilled through the window, illuminating her sleeping face. The covers were tucked up to her chin, her cheek resting on her folded hands. She looked so angelic; Roman didn't want this moment alone with her to end.

He bowed his head, attempting a prayer. Castro still wanted every American out of California. Rancho de los Robles wasn't bothered by any of Castro's troops because Castro considered Roman his friend. It probably never occurred to Castro that Roman would harbor Yankees under his roof. Everyone knew how he felt about Americanos when he joined the war in Texas.

But with Rachel's father now aligned with the rebels in the north and Sarita spreading her poison here, things were only growing more dangerous for Rachel. He should have sent her with Steven and Dom a few days ago, but the thought of putting her on a ship left him undone.

When he raised his head, he was startled to find her eyes upon him.

"Why are you here?" she whispered.

"I came to pray for you."

She remained completely still, watching him with anxious eyes. "Were you praying?"

"Trying to pray."

"What were you trying to pray about?"

He cocked a half smile at her. "I was *thinking* about praying, if you really must know."

She finally returned his wry smile. "Thinking about praying is not praying."

Still kneeling, he rested his chin on his folded hands, his gaze intent on hers. "How are you feeling these days?"

"Fine."

"Are you completely well and healthy? You are always hiding in your room when I'm around."

"Do I not look completely well and healthy?"

"You look beautiful," he said huskily.

Her smile disappeared. "You should not be in my bedroom."

"Please don't ask me to leave. I wanted to speak with you about the Bible."

She raised a disbelieving brow at him.

"Who was the man riding the red horse in Zechariah?"

"The Angel of the Lord in the book of Zechariah?"

"*Sí*. He is called the Angel of the Lord in the reading."

"I believe this Angel of the Lord is Jesus. Where did you get a Bible?"

"Steven left his Bible with me. I told him upon our next meeting, I would return it to him."

"When is your next meeting?"

"Do you miss the man of God already? He has only been gone a short while." Roman's heart began to thump in his chest. His throat grew tight. What was wrong with him? All he could think about was Rachel and God, and he was torn between casting both out of his life forever or embracing them with all his heart.

"Do not be jealous of Steven. I am still here and Steven is gone." Rachel sat up in the bed, holding tightly to the covers.

He got off his knees. The moonlight pouring through the window made it easy to see her. "I miss the man of God. I do not know when we will see Steven again. This war is no good."

The longing in his own voice upset him. Every day, he was upset. What disturbed Roman the most was that his anger had given way to grief. A disturbing grief over the state of his own soul. His sins weighed heavily upon him each day now.

"I'm glad you and Steven became friends." Rachel smiled tenderly at him.

"I have never had a friend like Steven. He has become a brother to me. So has Dom. I miss them," he admitted.

"I'm sorry," she said. "I miss them too."

He didn't know how he felt about her missing Steven. He tried not to think about it. "I thought you might like to accompany me on a ride today. I must go to the Indian *rancheria* to speak with Chief Anselmo about the sheep shearing. I thought you would enjoy seeing their *jacals* and the happy little Indian children who live in these huts."

"What is a *jacal*?"

"*Jacals* are huts made from tule reeds that grow in the marshes. The Indians live in villages of these domed tule huts."

"How will we travel to see the Indians?"

"We will ride together. A mount is being readied for you; you need only dress and accompany me to the stables."

"Will you give me your word that you will not molest me in any way today?"

"You have my word," he promised.

Her small smile thrilled him. "Then wait in the hall while I dress."

• • •

A short while later, the two rode east toward the mountains. Rachel was dressed very simply with her hair braided down her back. Both she and Roman wore silk-lined sombreros to protect their heads from the summer sun that would soon overtake the horizon. Roman had tied serapes to the backs of their saddles, and leather bags held a delicious-smelling lunch. A handful of vaqueros followed them at a distance. The Rancho de los Robles cowboys stayed within eyesight but gave Roman and Rachel plenty of room to ride alone on the trail.

On the journey to the Indian *rancheria*, they spoke very little. Most of the way, they simply rode in companionable silence, enjoying the balmy June day and the abundance of wildlife, elk, antelope, deer, and coyotes, but it was the wild horse herds that delighted Rachel. The feral horses never allowed anyone too close, Roman told her. The shy animals burst into a stampede, the stallions furiously herding their mares and foals away as soon as Roman and Rachel rode near.

Upon approaching the Indian village, Rachel stared in wonder as well as mortification at the numerous naked brown bodies of the indigenous people. It was late morning, and the sun shone warm and pleasant on their backs. Some of the older men and women wore bits of cloth or fur to cover their genitals, but most of the younger Indians wore nothing but paint and beads. Rachel had never seen naked people before. She tried to keep her eyes averted from their bodies, especially the men.

The Indian chief Anselmo came forward, smiling from ear to ear. He was a tall, dark, powerfully built man who wore the most fur, beads, and feathers. Rachel was vastly relieved the chief's manhood was covered by rabbit skins sewn into a short skirt.

The language he and Roman communicated in was a mixture of Spanish and Anselmo's native Indian language, which Roman appeared to speak passably well.

Roman had told her Chief Anselmo was born and raised at a mission, but when the missions closed, he became the chief of this group of Indians, which chose to return to their pagan ways and assimilated into living in these nearby mountains.

Chief Anselmo's father had been the leader of this band of Indians before converting to Christianity and moving his people to the mission. His son's rise to leadership was easily accepted in the tribe. The band often hunted for hare and bear on Rancho de los Robles lands, and the Vasquezes allowed the Indians to take whatever they needed from the cattle and sheep herds as well.

Roman said the Indians preferred grasshoppers and angle worms to beef, so very rarely did they kill cattle and sheep for food. He also explained that during sheep-shearing season, men from Chief Anselmo's band would come and help shear the Vasquez herds. The Indians were paid for their work and happily returned every year to take part in the shearing, which was why they were here at the *rancheria* today. Roman needed to discuss the shearing with Chief Anselmo. Rachel suspected it was her confession to Isabella about wanting to see wild Indians that had driven Roman to bring her along with him.

Chief Anselmo was fascinated by Rachel. After the chief had fondly greeted Roman, the two men launched into a rapt discussion, with the chief motioning repeatedly toward her, still seated on her horse. The chief eventually brought out a parade of naked Indian women, to which Roman shook his head and firmly said the same thing again and again, much to the chief's obvious chagrin. Rachel was mortified.

Finally, a grim-faced Roman walked over to where she waited with their horses. "Chief Anselmo has never seen a woman with golden hair. He wants you as his wife. Those are his other wives." He motioned to the naked women standing shyly behind the big chief now.

The news shocked Rachel. "Certainly, you told the chief this is not possible."

"I told him you would not make a good wife. That you are a Christian and you would insist he return to the Christian ways practiced at the mission."

"What did he say?" Rachel squirmed in her saddle with the big chief's gaze intently upon her.

"He said he could not give up his other wives as the great Father in heaven would insist he do. He has many children with these wives."

Rachel looked around for the Rancho de los Robles vaqueros. To her relief, the cowboys waited in the distance upon their horses. "Are we in any danger?"

"Only your braid is in danger. I told Chief Anselmo I would retrieve some of your hair for him."

"You want to cut my hair?"

"Just a little." Roman removed a large knife from his belt. "You'll have to dismount for me to do it." His mouth was set in a grim line.

Her knees trembled as she stepped off her horse. Roman helped her down. "I'm sorry. I knew of Chief Anselmo's weakness for women, but I did not think he would dare ask for a white woman."

"It's all right." She closed her eyes, her heart pounding. Roman gathered her braid into his hand and gently sawed off the bottom four inches of it, leaving her hair hanging loose below her shoulders now, restrained only by the sombrero she wore. Wordlessly, he returned to the chief with the hair still tied at the end of the braid.

Appeased by the golden hair, the chief loaded Roman down with gifts from the village. Rachel was relieved beyond measure as they rode away from the *rancheria* a short while later. All those naked people appalled her. And the chief frightened her.

"Chief Anselmo and his people won't hurt us," he assured her. "He said he would pray for you in the presence of your hair." Roman grinned at this.

"I do not think this is funny. The chief had all those naked wives, and he looked so wild and fierce."

"Chief Anselmo is an honorable man. It is normal for a chief to have many naked wives."

Rachel ignored Roman's teasing wink. "He was raised at a mission. He must know it is a sin against God to have more than one wife."

"You should pray for him." Roman grinned at her indignation.

"I will." Rachel stiffened in the saddle.

They rode for miles in silence.

"We will stop here for lunch," he announced as they came upon a pleasant stream an hour later. The afternoon was almost hot, the sun brilliant in the cobalt-blue sky.

Roman dismounted from his horse and came to Rachel's horse to lift her down.

"I am able to dismount by myself," she informed him.

Ignoring her opposition, he reached up and captured her waist with both hands, swinging her down into his arms. "Yes, you are a wilderness woman now, having paid a wild Indian with your hair," he teased.

"I found the matter at the Indian village not funny at all." She stood stiffly in his arms.

"I did not like giving Chief Anselmo your hair, but I thought it best to make him happy. If war comes to Rancho de los Robles, Chief Anselmo has promised his band of warriors will join us in fighting the Americanos. The Indians *jaras* are deadly."

"What is a *jara*?"

"An arrow. They poison the tips of them. Come, I am famished." Roman led her over to his horse, where he unloaded the contents of his saddlebags, pressing food and a serape into her hands. He then picketed the two horses and told Rachel to follow him to the creek.

In the shade beside the creek, they spread out the serape and sat down to eat. Roman paused and bowed his head when Rachel prayed before they ate. After her offering, he quickly wolfed down the food and drank some water from the creek before lying back on the serape and closing his eyes as if greatly content.

"What are you doing?" She was still eating.

"Resting," he told her without opening his eyes. "You should rest too when you finish eating."

"Where shall I rest?"

He opened one eye to look at her. "Here beside me."

"You promised not to touch me," she reminded him.

He closed his open eye. "I'm not going to touch you. I'm going to rest."

Within minutes, he breathed evenly in sleep.

Rachel couldn't believe he could sleep so easily, though she knew he'd been working himself to the bone slaughtering the cattle and avoiding the hacienda. Cautiously, she lay down beside him, keeping a good two feet between their bodies. She'd been having nightmares regularly now, which interfered badly with her sleep.

It really was pleasant to nap beside the rushing stream in the cool shade of the big oak trees. Staring at Roman's face, so strong and striking in sleep, she was filled with a sense of well-being there beside him.

When she awoke sometime later, he was leaning over her, propped on one elbow. The jagged ends of her hair were in his fingers. "Tia Josefa can fix this," he said softly. "She cuts Tio's hair and mine. Chief Anselmo said your hair is the color of the wild wheat at harvest time."

Rachel was in no hurry to wake up. Perhaps Roman playing with her hair was only a dream. Her eyes felt so heavy. She closed them and drifted back to sleep.

Chapter Thirty-One

Ever so gently, Roman brought his lips down to hers when she closed her eyes. He kissed her cautiously, waiting for her to resist. When resistance didn't come, he deepened his kiss, edging closer to her body until he pressed his full length against hers.

She moaned with pleasure, her mouth warm and sweet from sleep.

He could not believe his good fortune. A wave of intense desire washed over him. Deepening the kiss even more, he was delighted when she responded with another throaty moan.

Trembling now, he began to run his hands over her body.

I give you a wife. Do not treat her like a harlot.

The voice so shocked him, he rolled away from Rachel, and jumped to his feet.

She sat up, rubbing her eyes, slowly coming to her senses after the nap and languorous kiss. Her face reddened. "You promised you wouldn't touch me."

"You welcomed my kiss." His own cheeks burned now with that heavenly voice ringing in his ears.

"I was asleep."

"You were awake before I kissed you."

"I was only half-awake. I thought I dreamed of you kissing me."

"Did you hear a voice?" He'd heard it so clearly. Surely, she must have heard God too.

"I heard nothing."

"You had to have heard it."

"What did you hear?"

He ran his hands through his hair. Maybe he was going *loco*.

"Tell me what you heard," she urged. She got to her feet and put her hand on his arm. "Please, Roman, I want to help you know God."

"Then pray God will reveal himself to me. I cannot believe in a God I cannot see."

"To believe without seeing is called faith. It is faith that pleases God."

"Then I cannot please God," he said in frustration. "I must see God to believe he is real."

"Jesus is real. He loves you. He died on the cross for you."

"I do not see how this is possible."

"With God, all things are possible."

Rachel began to pray out loud for him. Much to his embarrassment, his eyes burned as she prayed. He put his hands to his eyes, willing the hot tears away.

Something holy and unexplainable was happening. After praying, Rachel wrapped both arms around him and leaned her head against his chest. He pressed his face into her hair, holding on to her as if his life depended on it. He considered riding to Mission San Juan Bautista to find a priest to marry them tonight but was afraid they would run into General Castro, who lived in the village. The general might take her prisoner or ship her out of California if he took her there.

With her father now riding with the rebels in the north, marrying Rachel had become something not so easily accomplished in California.

I give you a wife. He heard the voice again, deep in his heart, reassuring this time. Like a promise. Not only did he realize he loved her, she was his only link to God with Steven gone now.

"Are you all right?"

He nodded.

She smiled tenderly at him. "We have had quite the day, haven't we?"

"Quite the day," he hoarsely agreed. "We'll have to ride hard now to return home before the sun is gone."

After they mounted their horses and had ridden for a while alone together, the vaqueros returned and trailed them once more. When the hacienda finally came into view, a group of unfamiliar horsemen were in the yard. Dogs barked unceasingly. Chickens clucked in the trees, clearly afraid of these visitors. Unease swept over Roman.

He waved his vaqueros up beside them. All the cowboys untied their lassos and laid the ropes and their long lances across their laps. Their formerly happy mood suddenly became very serious.

Upon riding into the yard, they found Tio Pedro talking with a man who had dismounted a sweat-soaked mustang. The rest of this filthy band of visitors remained seated on their horses. They appeared to be Californios, but they were poorly dressed, a rough-looking lot. Swarthy men with hard eyes and worn-down horses. All of the strangers leered at Rachel, which set Roman's teeth on edge.

"Go into the house," he told her as he swung down from his horse and helped her dismount. His eyes never left the men.

As Rachel walked past the mounted crew, they watched her like hungry wolves. One of the men even saluted her. He only had three fingers on his hand, and sweat ran down his ugly face. Roman knew this man, famous for his cruelty to horses, Indians, and women.

Rachel hurried into the house.

Sarita made her way out onto the porch as Rachel rushed inside. She was dressed in a snug red gown that made the most of her curvaceous figure.

"My fair cousin Sarita," a burly man cried, swinging down from his horse with a yellow, broken-toothed smile.

"Rachel, wait," Sarita called her back, causing the hair to rise on the back of Roman's neck. "Luis, this is my stepdaughter, Rachel Tyler. She is an Americana. Isn't she lovely?"

"Go into the house, Rachel," Roman commanded as he strode up onto the porch. "Luis Lopez," he acknowledged. "I thought you had returned to Sonora with Juan Garcia." He gave Rachel a warning look, and she turned and fled.

The three-fingered man, Juan Garcia, saluted Roman with his crippled hand the way he'd saluted Rachel. "I am still here, amigo. They won't let us back into Mexico. We are too cruel, says our government." The three-fingered man laughed. It was an ugly sound. "We are headed north to fight the Americanos. Come with us, amigo."

"Have you spoken with General Castro?" Roman asked.

"General Castro is organizing a cavalry near the southern shore of San Francisco Bay to drive the Americanos out of California," Luis said. "The Americanos stole General Castro's horses near the Cosumnes River south of Sutter's Fort. General Vallejo was sending the horses to Castro for his soldiers. Now these Americanos, calling themselves the Osos—the Bears— have captured General Vallejo. The Osos have raised a ridiculous flag made from one of their wives' petticoats in Sonoma plaza. They painted a bear that looks like a pig in pokeberry juice and a five-pointed star above the words 'California Republic' on their flag."

The news shocked Roman.

"Kill the Americanos, all of them," Sarita passionately told Luis.

"For you, I would kill them all, fair cousin." Lopez gave Sarita a brawny squeeze. The thickset man was as strong as an ox. And ugly, with small, sharp eyes in his wide, cruel face.

"So you have taken an Americana for your woman," Lopez said to Roman. "I am shocked, amigo, that you would soil yourself with a *Yanquia*, even as lovely as she is." He nodded toward the door where Rachel had disappeared.

"She is not his woman," Sarita snapped. "She is my step-daughter. Her stupid father forced a betrothal on Roman because Tio Pedro . . ." Sarita glanced over at Tio, in deep conversation with the leader of the band, and then lowered her voice. "Because Tio owes gambling debts to my husband he cannot repay."

"*Silencio*, Sarita," Roman ordered.

Lopez smiled his ugly, broken-toothed smile. "Much has changed for you, amigo, since we rode together in Texas, killing the Americanos like dogs."

With his meaty arm around Sarita's waist, Lopez turned Sarita away from Roman to speak to her privately but kept his voice loud enough for Roman to hear. "How could you marry the Americano and not my friend, Roman, fair cousin? I see you have broken his heart, but not for long, eh? He has a golden woman now. Do you think he will share this golden woman with me? I have never had a golden woman before."

"Go near her and I will kill you," Roman said.

Lopez laughed. "The Americana has made you crazy, amigo."

"I am pregnant," Sarita suddenly announced, abruptly silencing the two men.

Lopez kept his brawny arm around her waist. His other hand had dropped to the pistol tucked in the waistband of his filthy velvet pants. "Has your *Yanquio* husband planted this seed in you? Should I kill him now?"

"It is Roman's seed." She turned to Roman. "I carry your child."

"How do you know the child is mine?" Roman felt surprisingly calm despite wanting to kill Luis and never see Sarita again.

"It is yours," she insisted.

"You are sure?" He glanced around to see who else could hear them. Tio Pedro was on his way to the porch but not yet within hearing distance. His uncle's ears weren't that good to start with.

"I swear." Sarita pulled away from Luis to grab Roman's arm. "I will bear you a son. A pure-blooded *criollo*." She hung on to him in desperation now.

Lopez laughed. "She still loves you after all your whoring in Texas. You are a lucky man, amigo."

Tio Pedro arrived at the porch, accompanied by the leader of the band, Juan Padilla. "Get into the house with the other women," Tio Pedro told her sharply. "We have men's business to discuss out here. General Vallejo has been taken prisoner by a group of renegade Americanos calling themselves the Osos."

Roman yanked his arm away from Sarita and strolled into the house ahead of her, ignoring his uncle. He needed to see Rachel. He had to tell her not to leave her room until these *bandidos* departed the rancho.

Pacing into the house, his thoughts tumbling with Sarita's accusation that he'd fathered her child and General Vallejo now a prisoner in Sonoma, Roman decided he would move Rachel to his room this very hour.

Her room was near the stairs. Much too dangerous. He knew what men like Lopez and the three-fingered Juan Garcia were capable of doing to a woman. He wasn't about to leave her unguarded with such evil men roaming the hacienda tonight. He would order the maids to hide as well. And he would tell Tia Josefa to lock his sisters in their rooms until these terrible men were long gone.

Tio Pedro followed him into the house, filling his ear with talk about rescuing General Vallejo. "Ramon Carrillo is the brother of Francisca Vallejo. He is out there with those men. He is one of Castro's lieutenants along with Padilla. Padilla's band are irregulars for Castro, I tell you! We must join our brothers to free General Vallejo!"

Roman turned impatiently on his uncle. "Vallejo is probably their willing prisoner. You know the general wants the United States to annex California. Vallejo is most likely in the pot with the Americanos, stirring up war to move this acquisition forward for the United States."

"Think about what you are saying, Roman," Tio Pedro pleaded. "Padilla says the Osos are a motley, wild-eyed gang of adventurers in greasy buckskins. They admire the terrible grizzlies. This is why they call themselves the Osos. Governor Pico has accused these Americanos of the blackest treason the spirit of evil could invent in their hearts. We have all been called to arms to fight this evil. We must ride with Carrillo to free General Vallejo." Tio Pedro panted in exertion, trying to keep up with Roman striding down the hall.

Roman stopped searching for Rachel and Tia Josafa long enough to deal with his uncle. He put a hand on Tio Pedro's shoulder. "Please, Tio, you must calm down. Being upset this way is not good for your heart."

"*Si,*" Tia Josefa agreed, sweeping around a corner, holding her skirts out of the way of her rushing slippers. "Pedro, you cannot be serious about riding with these men. They are building fires in the yard even as we speak. Can't these filthy men go to the fields to set up their camp tonight?"

"No, Josefa, I will not send these men to the fields. I would invite these soldiers of California into our home if there weren't so many of them," Tio Pedro huffed.

"Not one of these ruffians will step foot in this hacienda," Tia Josefa said with a sternness that surprised Roman. "I have hidden our daughters and even the maids. These men are no good. I feel this in my bones, Pedro. I am afraid."

Relief flooded through Roman upon hearing that all of the women were safe. He'd always appreciated this about his aunt. She was wise and quick to deal with trouble.

"Do not speak unkindly about these men, Josefa." Tio Pedro straightened his shoulders and puffed out his chest. "They are Californio soldiers assembled by Castro."

"Are you sure these are Castro's men?" Roman asked grimly. "Garcia and Lopez are outlaws. I know this for certain. The rest of these men I do not know, but they do not look like *hijos del pais* to me. They appear to be highwaymen at the dawn of opportunity." Roman did not hide his disdain.

"The dawn of opportunity is to rescue General Vallejo!" Tio Pedro cried. "I will ride with these men at first light. And tonight I will share my brandy with my brothers."

"There isn't enough brandy in California to satisfy these *bandoleros* burning fires practically on our porch," said Tia Josefa. "The men are chasing the chickens. Most certainly to roast them on their fires. The dogs are scared and the servants terrified too. Please, my husband, think of your *familia*. Who will protect us from the Osos if they come here to pillage while you are off with these highwaymen?"

"These are not highwaymen, Josefa," Tio Pedro spoke passionately. "These are sons of the country, Castro's finest. I will drink with these men tonight and ride with them tomorrow. *Viva* California!" Tio Pedro shouted. Then he stomped through the hacienda yelling, "*Viva* California!"

Tia Josefa began to weep.

"Please don't cry, Tia." Roman took his aunt in his arms to comfort her.

"You must go with him, Roman. Promise me you'll ride with my foolish old husband," Tia Josefa begged him.

Roman let out a long sigh. "Tia . . . I cannot ride with these men."

"Please. You must! We have raised you as our very own son all these years. Please, *mi hijo*, you must take care of my husband," Tia Josefa pleaded tearfully.

"Enough. I will go."

Tia Josefa had always been kind to him. She did her best to keep the hacienda running smoothly, even with her husband often drunk these days. Once Tia regained her composure in his arms, Roman resumed his search for Rachel upstairs.

He found her in her room quietly reading her Bible in a chair.

"What has happened?" she asked as he silently closed the door behind him upon entering without knocking. He wanted no one else to hear their conversation. Especially not Sarita.

"A band of Americano adventurers calling themselves the Osos have captured Sonoma. They've taken General Vallejo prisoner. The ruffians claim to be Castro's soldiers. I doubt they are, but Tio is hell-bent on riding with them, so I have promised Tia Josefa I will look after my foolish uncle."

"You will be leaving with these men?" Rachel's eyes widened in alarm.

"Tia Josefa has hidden Maria and Isabella away. She has even concealed the maids for the night. I want you to come to my room, where I can protect you."

"I cannot stay in your room." Rachel sat her Bible down on the table beside the carved wooden chair and straightened her skirts quite primly.

"Then I will wait out in the hall and guard your door. Give me your chair. I know several of these men. They are desperados who hate Americanos. One of them has taken an interest in you." Roman did not want to say more. He only wanted to frighten her enough that she would agree to stay in his room tonight.

"Where will you sleep if I am in your bed?"

"I will not sleep."

"You cannot go without sleep if you must leave with these men in the morn."

"Will you accompany me to my room, then? If you come, I will try to sleep tonight," he promised.

"I hate the gringa. I want her dead," Sarita told Luis out in the darkness that night. She pulled out a golden cross, holding it upside down in the firelight as she handed it to him. "If you kill Rachel, I will give you this cross. It was given to me by Chula who taught me the dark magic of Tohic. She stole it from the mission the day the Indians rose up and murdered the padre. It is the death cross."

Lopez took the cross, weighing the gold in his hand. "I cannot kill the gringa right now. I must ride north with Padilla. But I will come back, and we will decide how to get rid of her then." Holding the cross upside down, just as she had, Lopez returned it to Sarita.

"You must kill her now," Sarita insisted.

Lopez laughed. "I am not so wasteful. I will not kill her until I have had my fill of her. Perhaps then I will kill her."

Part Three

Your enemy the devil prowls around like a roaring lion looking for someone to devour.

1 Peter 5:8

Chapter Thirty-Two

Neither Rachel nor Roman undressed that night. They slept in their clothes. Outside, the men's raucous laughter around the campfires kept the dogs barking till well after midnight. Roman went to the elaborately carved chair in the corner of the room and tried to make himself comfortable. After kneeling in prayer beside the four-poster, velvet curtain-draped bed for some time, Rachel finally lay down on the feather-filled mattress. Roman blew out the candles and returned to the chair. They remained silent for a while before he quietly spoke, "I won't let anyone hurt you, *pequeña*." With moonlight pouring through the window, Roman could see her lying on her side, wide awake, watching him.

"You look uncomfortable in that chair," she said. "There is room here for the both of us." She scooted as far as she could to one side as he came and stretched out beside her.

The whoops and hollers and boisterous laughter outside around the fires carried through the open window. Roman felt sick inside. He knew how Lopez had treated women in Texas, saw how Lopez and the rest of the men leered at Rachel this afternoon. She was an enemy woman, desired and hated at the same time. To those men, this made her irresistible. If the desperados stormed the hacienda, he could not stop all of them. He closed his eyes. *Do not let them come,* he prayed. *Please keep Rachel safe tonight. Keep all the women safe, God.*

After the simple but heartfelt prayer, he opened his eyes, turning his head to look at Rachel lying beside him so quietly. Why should God answer his prayer? As a boy, he had prayed for God to save his mother from the dreaded fever. She died anyway.

Did God merely toy with men when they prayed? Sometimes granting them mercy, sometimes taking away what they loved most in this world?

He felt toyed with tonight while staring into Rachel's soft blue eyes, knowing that if she died, he would die too.

"What are you thinking?" she asked.

"That God entertains himself with mankind."

"Satan entertains himself with mankind. God intervenes on man's behalf."

She looked toward the window. "Satan is entertaining himself tonight with those men out there. The devil will tempt them to do evil. If God does not intervene, wickedness will have its way tonight."

Roman reached out to feather his fingers down her cheek. "You are so full of goodness and light."

She turned her cheek into his hand and pressed it there, closing her eyes, appearing to savor his touch.

He cupped her face. She smiled against his fingers. His throat tightened. He realized he no longer cared that she was

American. Looking at her face, all he cared about was keeping her safe. Circumstances unfolding now had turned destiny against them. War had come to California, just as he'd known it would. And then there was Sarita's claim that she carried his child. Perhaps Sarita did have his son or daughter in her womb. He removed his hand from Rachel's face. "*Buenas nochas, Yanquia pequeña,*" he said, rolling onto his back, aching inside like he'd never ached before in his life.

"Do not doubt God's goodness," she whispered.

Not knowing what to say, he lay there until he knew for certain she'd fallen asleep. Once her breathing evened out, he rolled over onto his side and tried his best to memorize her sleeping features. Light from the full summer moon poured into the window, turning her blond hair silver. Turning his heart inside out by her beauty. Tomorrow he would leave her. The wheels of war and his sin with Sarita turned sharply now. Tearing them apart. How he wanted to hold her. Love her. Never leave her. All these things that could not happen now.

He thought of Steven. The man of God who loved her too. He should send for Steven. Ask him to take Rachel back to New England, where she'd be safe from war and Sarita's wrath. Ask Steven to marry her and protect her forever. That would be the right thing to do, but he couldn't bring himself to do it.

During the night, Rachel had a nightmare. He pulled her close and cradled her in his arms. "Shush, *chica,*" he whispered in her ear. "It's just a bad dream. I won't let anyone hurt you. I would die to keep you safe, *mi amor.*"

He kissed her temple, wondering why someone so full of light would have such dark dreams. To his surprise, she fell back to sleep like a trusting child in his embrace. He lay there holding her, with sleep eluding him.

Just before dawn, he kissed her lips lightly. He did not want to wake her. Then he rose and, without making a sound, gathered his things and departed the hacienda.

The band rode hard, bent on destroying the Osos in Sonoma. Tio Pedro, on one of Rancho de los Robles's finest palominos, galloped in the rear of the party. Roman rode at his uncle's side, cursing the dust, his uncle, and these ill-bred Californios they accompanied north.

He tried to pray for Rachel's safety, but this ride with Padilla's band troubled him so much his thoughts careened in all directions. Every twenty miles or so, the band stopped and traded out horses. Roman was grateful he'd left Oro at home. The horses on this journey were being ridden into the ground. The ones that broke down were left on the side of the road.

Tio Pedro had insisted on taking a dozen Rancho de los Robles horses along, all magnificent palominos. The farther they rode, the angrier Roman grew over the treatment of the horses. Riding hard this way was common in California. Horses were branded and, if found abandoned along the road, returned to their owners by helpful neighbors. But these men rode the horses so hard some would certainly die on this trail.

Hours into the journey, as horses began to break down, rather than leaving them along the road as they had earlier, both the three-fingered Garcia and Lopez began shooting the horses that could no longer run with pistols they kept in their waistbands.

When Garcia and Lopez chose Rancho de los Robles palominos to ride into the Sonoma Valley, Roman used every ounce of self-control he could muster not to interfere with the outlaws saddling his stallions.

"I will not tolerate the killing of our palominos," he warned Tio Pedro.

"Horses are but horses, Roman. Do not fight with these soldiers. Save your fire to liberate General Vallejo."

"These men are not soldiers. They are desperados. You should not have brought our palominos along." Roman untied his riata from his saddle and laid it around his saddle horn as the band moved out once more.

"Do not draw attention to us," Tio Pedro ordered. "Why do you prepare your rope?"

"You have already drawn attention to us by bringing our horses." Roman spurred his mount to the front of Juan Padilla's band, where Lopez and Garcia raced his palominos. If one of these men attempted to shoot his horse, Roman would use his rope. Dragging a man a mile or so behind a horse usually took the devil right out of him.

Chapter Thirty-Three

In Sonoma, the Bears had swiftly formed the Republic of California, flying their homemade flag with its pig-like grizzly over Sonoma square. Joshua Tyler found the whole thing wearisome but necessary. Sweating in their greasy buckskin hunting shirts under the warm June sun, the Bears gathered to discuss how to defend themselves against the Californios now that they'd declared war on the Mexican province. Unlike Joshua, who had come by ship years earlier and assimilated by patiently adopting the Catholic religion and Californio ways, many of these settlers and adventurers had made the long trek overland across the rugged mountains and unforgiving deserts and weren't about to let Castro tell them what to do in California.

Especially not with Captain John Fremont with his impressive troops of mountain men and Delaware Indian bodyguards representing the United States of America, now camped in the north end of the Sacramento Valley, giving advice and egging the Bears on in their rebellion against Mexican authorities. Captain Fremont and his troops had just finished punishing the Maidu Indians along the Sacramento River, going from one village to the next, slaughtering men, women, and children as a precautionary warning that any Indians helping General Castro and the Californios resist the Americans would be dealt with in the same brutal manner.

Though emboldened by Captain Fremont's war with the California Indians, their hero, Fremont, had not shown up in Sonoma as of yet to help the Bears, and the rebels were running short on ammunition and arms. Joshua warned the leaders they did not have enough men to defend themselves in a full-scale attack by Castro, but nobody wanted to hear about Castro's forces running Fremont off Gavilan Peak. And after overtaking Vallejo's garrison, the Bears quickly discovered Mexico had not sent arms to the Californios. The meager supply of ammunition in Sonoma consisted of nothing more than a nine brass cannon, two hundred muskets, and a hundred pounds of gunpowder. To Joshua's quiet satisfaction, this dismayed the Bears. Certainly, the Sonoma stash wasn't enough powder to hold off an attack from General Castro's troops. He'd already told them that.

During the Bears' meeting that warm June day, Lieutenant Henry Ford decided William Todd, the Bears' young flag maker, would be sent to Bodega in search of gunpower. Two other Bears, Thomas Cowie and George Fowler, were sent toward the Russian River to contact Kit Carson's half-brother Moses, *majordomo* of Henry Fitch's rancho. Kit Carson was Fremont's right-hand man. The Bears knew Moses Carson could help them.

• • •

Roman saw the two Yankees on the road ahead and felt relief and dread tangle inside him. Lopez and Garcia would not shoot Rancho de los Robles's palominos now that they'd found more agreeable victims on which to vent their wrath. The band surrounded the two just outside of Santa Rosa, taking them prisoner there on the road. Padilla announced they would camp for the night in a nearby glen. The prisoners, Thomas Cowie and George Fowler, were tied to trees while the band settled into the camp.

Roman held on to his riata as Lopez and Garcia swung off the sweat-soaked palominos. The stallions had held up well under the hard riding. Roman breathed a sigh of relief when both men left the palominos without a backward glace, heading straight for the Americanos tied to the trees.

Gathering the palominos, Roman went about the camp collecting Rancho de los Robles horses. Some of the men silently watched him, but nobody confronted him as he rounded up his herd.

He came upon Tio Pedro lying on the ground, soaked in sweat like the horses.

"Tio, are you all right?"

Tio Pedro only grunted.

"After I feed the horses, I will return." Roman was still too angry with his uncle to feel much sympathy for him. Tio deserved all the pain he got for making this decision to join with the *bandidos*.

Roman led the horses out into the fields to graze. He would not water the animals until they cooled off. All but one of the palominos were too tired to graze.

In the distance, Roman watched the band make camp as Lopez and Garcia tormented the prisoners. He turned away when Lopez kicked one of the prisoners in the belly as the Americano stood helplessly tied to the tree. The young blond-haired Yankee yelped in pain upon receiving the vicious kick.

Why did that boy have to be blond like Rachel?

A dozen Californios soon gathered around the trees where the Americanos were tied. The Californios began to throw stones at the prisoners. The tormentors laughed as the bloodied *Yanquios* begged for mercy.

Roman gathered the palominos and led them to the creek. The horses drank thirstily, as did Roman. He ignored the screams of the prisoners as best he could, washing his face in the cool water, trying to ignore the torture in the trees. Padilla's band was probably seeking information about the Osos, torturing the prisoners to get it.

Roman reached into his pocket and pulled out the small golden rosary he'd carried all these years. He'd believed his mother's rosary would keep him safe. And it had. Many times, he should have died, but he had not. He stared at the crucifix on the bottom of the string of beads. Jesus hanging on the cross. The sight grieved him.

One of the horses stopped drinking and looked at him. "The Americanos are the bears," Roman said to the horse. "They kill, steal, and destroy like the grizzlies. The Americanos deserve what they are getting."

But the torture of the prisoners weighed heavy on his mind. Especially the blond boy with hair like Rachel's.

When they had their fill of water, Roman led the horses out of the creek and over to an open meadow. After picketing the palominos there, he returned to Tio Pedro. His uncle was lying on the ground where he'd left him.

Tio Pedro drank brandy from a *bota* he'd stashed in his pantaloons.

"I cannot move," he told Roman. "Never have I traveled so far so fast. What is wrong with these men? Mexican soldiers do not ride this way. Killing their horses as they go. These men have gone mad."

"You said they were Castro's soldiers," Roman reminded him.

In response, Tio Pedro drank more brandy.

Campfires now burned amid the trees. The men roasted and ate beef taken from a nearby rancho. The Americanos tied to the trees were still being tortured by Garcia and Lopez and others in the band. The rest of the Californios stood around the campfires with their leaders, Padilla and Carrillo.

Roman realized the Americanos would probably be killed because the leaders did not seem to care about them.

A sharp pang of remorse hit him when he realized those two men being tortured in the moonlight could, in a twist of fate, be Steven and Dominic. And that blond boy could be Rachel's brother, had she a brother.

The Californios bragged at the campfires about how Garcia and Lopez no longer used stones to abuse the Yankees. Their methods had improved in brutality. Padilla's men now sharpened their knives by the fire for the game of slicing without killing that they would play next with their Americano prisoners.

Roman did not attempt to eat the roasted beef he was offered by Padilla. With a sickness in his stomach that somehow reached all the way to his soul, he waved off the Californio leader's attempt at friendship and returned to Tio Pedro, still lying in the grass where he'd dismounted when they first arrived at camp.

Tio Pedro's serape was pulled over his head, the empty skin of brandy tossed aside near where he slept.

Roman longed to kick his uncle awake so Tio could see for himself the terrible things being done to the Americanos. Instead, he rounded up the palominos and saddled two of the strongest looking animals. He then went to Padilla and told the lieutenant his uncle was in no condition to continue with this quest to free General Vallejo. Roman reassured Padilla that after returning his uncle to Rancho de los Robles, he would ride in search of General Castro to inform him of the capture of the two Americanos.

Padilla said the prisoners were Osos. The two had confessed to taking part in the Sonoma siege. One of the prisoners had even helped make that audacious bear flag. Roman knew they'd be dead by morning.

Returning to where Tio Pedro slept, Roman shook his uncle awake. "Mount up. We are leaving."

Tio Pedro protested, his words slurred from the brandy, but Roman informed him Padilla expected the two of them to find General Castro and tell the general Americano rebels had been captured near Santa Rosa and to relay the information taken from these prisoners.

Stumbling to his feet, Tio Pedro struggled into his serape. "How far must we ride to reach General Castro?"

"Not far." Roman held the palomino so Tio Pedro could mount the horse. The lie came easy. Roman would say anything to get his uncle on the back of that horse so they could get away from these evil men.

"*Viva* California!" Tio Pedro shouted upon sinking into the saddle, causing the horse to shy sideways.

Pedro pitched out of the saddle, hitting the ground with a terrible thud. The horse would have bolted away had Roman not restrained it with the lead rope.

"*Viva* California!" Shouts came from the campfires.

Swearing in Spanish, Roman said, "Get up, Tio, before they see you on the ground."

Tio Pedro stumbled to his feet, untangling himself from his serape. "*Viva* California," he repeated, this time in an absolute daze.

Roman grabbed Tio Pedro's elbow and propelled his uncle toward the stirrup. "Mount like a man," he commanded. "Padilla and Carrillo are on their way over to speak to us."

With Roman's help, Tio Pedro managed to get back on the horse.

Roman then mounted his own horse while still holding Tio Pedro's horse's rope. He also held another rope with the other palominos tied pack train-fashion for travel.

Padilla and his lieutenant, Ramon Carrillo, walked faster to reach them as they departed.

"What are you doing with those horses?" Padilla demanded.

"Taking them to General Castro," Roman answered.

Carrillo and Padilla looked at each other. Both men had their hands on pistols tucked into their pantaloons.

"I heard your men talking about Lieutenants Francisco Arce and Jose Maria Alviso bringing horses to General Castro from General Vallejo. The men said buckskin-clad Americanos took the horses from Arce and Alviso before the Osos overtook Sonoma. Vallejo's horses never reached Castro," Roman explained.

"This is true," Padilla agreed.

Unwilling to conceal his anger now over the horses destroyed on the ride, Roman continued, "Your men shoot good horses after riding them into the ground. Castro is in need of horses. Your men obviously are not."

Tio Pedro hastily joined in. "If you want the horses . . . they are . . . yours," he slurred drunkenly.

"I told you, my uncle is ill. He has suffered some kind of head injury. You can see he is sick." Roman motioned for them to look at Tio Pedro, a sad sight in the saddle.

"Tell the general we have gotten all the information we need from the prisoners. They are dead, and we have moved on to Sonoma," Padilla said.

"The prisoners are dead?" Remorse swept over Roman.

"Not yet. But soon they will be. We will rest in camp another day or so, killing these Osos slowly."

Roman nodded stiffly to Padilla and then spurred his horse forward, leading Tio Pedro and the rest of the palominos to the road, where they turned for home.

Chapter Thirty-Four

At Rancho de los Robles, Sarita paced her room, chanting in a fierce, unintelligible language for Tohic to avenge her. Roman had rejected her even after she'd told him she carried his child. He seemed blind to her now; all he did was watch the skinny gringa with hungry eyes.

How could Roman lust for that pale slip of a girl? Sarita saw no beauty in her stepdaughter. Her hate for Rachel intensified as each day passed. Tohic was doing nothing to help. Sarita danced her heart out, and Roman hardly noticed. She undressed for him, and he picked her up and carried her from his room, dumping her in the hall like a sack of grain. Then he locked her out of his bedchamber.

What was the matter with him? He was so different these days. Where was all that passion and rage she used to see in him? The violence that delighted her? The lust she'd used to control him?

Tohic was doing nothing to make Roman return to her. The sacrifice of the newborn lamb must not have pleased him.

This battle for Roman was bigger than Sarita ever imagined. She knew she was losing him as surely as the sun rose in the east. She realized another sacrifice must be presented to Tohic. Something special that would please him enough that he would unleash all his power on her behalf so that she would gain Roman back.

She began to search for blood. Blood that was special. Greatly loved blood, for this is what she wanted Tohic to give her. Roman's love in return for this sacrifice.

That night, she searched the barns and the servants' quarters for a sacrifice worthy of this love. She even considered snatching an Indian baby to burn in the fire under the sacred oaks, but she could find no infants amongst the Rancho de los Robles servants. A small boy of about two years old captured her eye, but after watching him with his mother for a while, she felt the boy wasn't valued enough to merit Tohic's favor.

In the stables, she hoped to find a treasured pet, a dog favored by one of the vaqueros or a young goat or lamb a shepherd showered with affection, but she saw no man attached to an animal.

Discouraged, she returned to the hacienda to gather the charms and idols she always carried with her. She had to worship Tohic, perhaps cutting herself to release her own blood for him if no other sacrificial blood could be found.

On her way to her room, Sarita passed Isabella's quarters. Behind the closed door, she heard the girl singing sweetly to someone and wondered who was in the room with the child.

A pet, perhaps.

Sarita burst into the room without knocking. A smile lit her face when she saw Isabella in her nightgown, sitting on the bed holding a chicken in her lap. A little red hen. Sarita momentarily felt disappointment. Only a chicken.

"Is this chicken your pet?" She walked over for a better look at the little hen.

"You do not know how to knock?" Isabella petted the chicken to settle her down. Sarita's harsh entrance had startled the bird.

"Your singing was so pretty I just had to see who you sang the lullaby to." Sarita eyed the hen with growing interest. Isabella held it so tenderly.

"Señora Poppycock does not like strangers." Isabella tucked the hen's head under her wing so she wouldn't see Sarita. The chicken obediently remained this way in the girl's lap. Sarita was charmed.

"Such a lovely little hen. Have you had her very long?"

"For two years. She is a wonderful chicken. The smartest ever."

"You must love her a great deal."

"Señora Poppycock is my best friend."

"Do you sing to your little chicken every night?" Sarita gazed intently at the girl and her chicken.

"Every night," Isabella answered. "Señora Poppycock is afraid of the dark. My singing helps her go to sleep."

"That is lovely. Does Señora Poppycock sleep in your room with you?"

"Yes. We take care of each other at night."

"So where does your little hen go during the day?"

"She goes to the kitchen, where Lupe takes care of her while I do my chores and sew with Mama. Then I go fetch her, and we take walks together looking for flies."

"Well, I better let you continue with your singing. We don't want your dear little hen to be frightened tonight."

"After I sing, I pray for Señora Poppycock, and then she is not frightened any longer."

"I will pray for you and your little hen too. Tohic cares about you. He can make your nights oh so sweet, little cousin. Tohic is the king of the darkness. With him as your lord, you will never be afraid."

"Is Tohic real?" Isabella's blue eyes grew wide with fear and wonder.

"Of course he is real. Tohic can do great things. He rules the earth. All you must do is worship Tohic, and he will give you whatever your heart desires."

Isabella wrinkled her nose. "Do you have to be a witch to worship Tohic?"

Sarita laughed. "You think I am a witch?"

Isabella shrugged her shoulders, continuing to stroke Señora Poppycock.

"I use the power Tohic gives me to gather the souls of men. These souls I bring to Tohic. I am not a witch. I am a gatherer."

Isabella's eyes widened even more. "What does Tohic do with these souls of men?"

Sarita smiled. "That is Tohic's business."

"Tohic sounds like the devil to me."

Sarita laughed. "The devil is not who the padres teach he is. He is not bad. He is prince of this earth. He can make you powerful. The greatest weakness of men is women. A beautiful woman can rule over men. If she is beautiful and a gatherer, she can have any man she wants."

"How do you gather a man?" Isabella asked.

Sarita smiled. "I must spend some time teaching you Tohic's ways. You have everything it takes to become a gatherer. Your face is pretty, and your eyes, they are like running water. Pray to Tohic that your breasts grow. Men love the soft flesh of a woman."

Isabella sat up straighter, squaring her petite shoulders, thrusting out her budding bosom. "Can Tohic bring me true love?" she asked in excitement.

"Yes." Sarita's smile disappeared. "But Tohic always requires a sacrifice worthy of the gift."

"What kind of sacrifice?" Isabella's face fell. She held Señora Poppycock more closely against her.

"That is between you and Tohic. He will speak to you through your thoughts. It takes time to understand how to hear Tohic, but once you learn his voice, you will know what he requires of you."

Sarita walked to the door, giving the little red hen a final triumphant glance. Tohic spoke to her at that very moment. He not only requested the chicken, he wanted Isabella too. The chicken for the fire. Isabella for his use.

She is a gatherer, said Tohic. *I will make the girl irresistible, and men will break themselves apart over her. She will have their hearts, and I will have their souls.*

A fierce jealousy sprang up in Sarita as Tohic spoke this prophecy over her cousin. After leaving Isabella's room, Sarita stood in the hall listening to Isabella sing once more. The girl had a siren's voice. Jealousy was fierce in Sarita. The little half-breed didn't deserve such favor from Tohic. She was a dirty little Indian harlot's daughter. Why was she special to Tohic?

She has the crystal eyes of her father. He belonged to me. He was from a long line of those who have served me. The padres took her mother from me. They put the shadow of the cross on the mother so I could no longer touch her, but this girl is mine. Claim her for me, Sarita.

"You promised me Roman," Sarita whispered to Tohic as she stood in the hall while Isabella sang to her stupid little chicken inside the room.

After you bring me the red hen, set aside some of its blood to be mixed with the blood of the girl with the crystal eyes, and I will give you Roman.

"How do I get her blood?" Sarita asked.

I will present the opportunity to you. Ask a servant to steal the chicken from the kitchen in the morning. Do not let the girl know it is you who has killed her precious hen. I want you to befriend Isabella. Teach her my ways.

"Promise Roman will love me again," Sarita pleaded.

You must kill the gringa first. When Rachel Tyler is dead, Roman will be yours again.

"You hate my stepdaughter as much as I do," Sarita whispered in delight, struck with this knowledge that Tohic despised Rachel even more than she did.

She hurried down the hall to gather what she would need to sacrifice the little red hen tomorrow. All night, she planned and worshiped and the next morning found an Indian who took the chicken from the kitchen when the old cook was distracted by another servant Sarita paid for the service.

After killing the little hen and draining blood from its neck into a small leather *bota* out in the oak grove on the hill, Sarita burned every last feather, chanting a wicked song that sounded nothing like Isabella's pretty lullaby the night before.

When Sarita returned to the hacienda hours later, she came upon Isabella crying and bleeding at the bottom of the stairs on the backside of the hacienda.

Rachel was with the girl, trying to comfort her while pressing her skirt to the girl's forehead in an attempt to stop the bleeding.

"What has happened?" Sarita rushed to her cousin's side, thrilled at the sight of Isabella's blood.

"Señora Poppycock is gone. I cannot find her," Isabella sobbed.

"She fell down the stairs while running in search of her hen," Rachel explained. "She needs Lupe's help."

"You fetch Lupe. I'll stay here with Isabella." Sarita hid her smile. Tohic made this so easy.

"You must hold tightly to the wound to stop the flow," Rachel instructed, her hands and skirt covered with Isabella's blood.

"I will." Sarita lifted her skirt to cover Isabella's wound when Rachel pulled her own skirt away from the girl's forehead.

As soon as Rachel rushed away, Sarita took the small leather bag from her dress pocket. "Blood is precious to Tohic. Give me some of your blood so we can make you a gatherer."

"Will becoming a gatherer help me find Señora Poppycock?" Isabella asked tearfully.

"I don't know. But being a gatherer is certain to bring you true love. No man will be able to resist you once you belong to Tohic."

Isabella allowed Sarita to collect the blood flowing from a small gash near her temple. "I have to find Señora Poppycock.

I think maybe one of those terrible men who were here the other night came back and took her. Do you think one of the *bandoleros* could have returned and taken her?"

"I did see them after the chickens," Sarita said sympathetically. She corked the *bota* with Isabella's blood and hastily returned it to her dress pocket. Then she used her skirt once more to stanch the flow spurting from the gash.

Isabella sobbed harder. "I've even prayed to God . . . asking him . . . begging him to bring . . . Señora Poppycock . . . back to me." Isabella cried so brokenly she could hardly speak.

"This is why years ago I pledged my life to Tohic," Sarita told the distraught girl. "This God of the black-robed padres did not get off his cross to help me. But Tohic has helped me. He will help you too, little cousin. I will give him your blood, and you will belong to him forever."

"Why is my daughter bleeding!" Tia Josefa rushed over to where Isabella and Sarita sat on the bloodstained stairs.

Rachel and Lupe came too, Lupe carrying her bag of herbs and fresh cloths to bind the wound.

"Señora Poppycock is missing. Isabella fell down the stairs while searching for her."

"I told Pedro those men came here with evil intent. Most of our chickens are missing from the yard," Tia Josefa said.

Isabella collapsed against Sarita in a burst of heart-wrenching sobs.

Rachel rushed to her side. "Let me pray for you." She got on her knees beside Sarita and Isabella, her skirt stained with Isabella's bright red blood.

"I have already prayed for her." Sarita tightened her hold on Isabella.

Rachel rose to her feet, stepping out of the way so Lupe could care for Isabella.

"I will keep looking for Señora Poppycock," Rachel promised Isabella.

"Yes, do keep looking, my dear." A smile curved Sarita's lips.

Chapter Thirty-Five

Roman found Rachel with a tear-streaked face walking up the road that led to Rancho de los Robles with a tear-streaked face. "Go on without us," he told Tio Pedro, dismounting there beside her on the road.

"What has happened?" Tio Pedro asked. "Have the Americanos attacked the hacienda?"

"No. Isabella has lost Señora Poppycock."

"You cry over a chicken?" Tio Pedro asked incredulously.

Roman turned his horse loose, along with the string of palominos he led. When the horses trotted toward the rancho's buildings, Tio Pedro's horse reared up on hind legs, straining to go with them.

Tio Pedro nearly lost his seat in the saddle. "You are a foolish woman to act this way over a chicken," he said, surprising both Rachel and Roman with his harshness. "We are at war with the Americanos. War is worthy of tears. Not chickens!"

He spurred his horse after the palominos, kicking up dust on the road as he rode off.

"You know a Californio never walks where he can ride a horse," Roman told Rachel.

"Then why are you walking?" She wiped tears from her cheeks.

"Because you are walking." He pulled out a handkerchief and used the cloth to dry her face. "I don't think you will find Señora Poppycock out here, *pequeña*."

"I know, but I cannot bear to be at the hacienda any longer. Sarita hates me, and she will not leave Isabella's side. She is turning Isabella against me."

"Isabella wants Sarita over you? I cannot believe this."

"I'm not sure what is happening. Isabella won't let me pray with her. She says God isn't good. That God allowed a bad thing to happen to Señora Poppycock and she will never pray to God again."

Roman tried to take her in his arms.

"Please don't touch me."

"*Chica*, let me hold you." He tried again to enfold her in his embrace.

"If you touch me . . . I won't be able to . . ." She broke into sobs.

Roman scooped her up into his arms and carried her down the road to the shade of a massive oak tree. He sat down holding her in his lap. "Please, little dove, do not cry. Your God will make everything right."

"I do not know if he will," Rachel breathed between sobs.

"He will," Roman assured her.

A rider approached on the road. A smile burst across Roman's face when he recognized Steven in his felt hat. "You have returned, amigo!" he called, taking Rachel's hand to lead her over to welcome Steven.

Steven climbed down from his horse, hugged both Rachel and Roman, and then walked beside them as they proceeded toward the hacienda. "In Yerba Buena, everyone is talking about war. U.S. ships are in the harbor ready for battle. Dominic is preaching restraint to anyone who will listen." Steven smiled, but his brown eyes were troubled.

"So what brings you back to Rancho de los Robles so soon, amigo?"

Steven looked at Rachel, and then returned his attention to Roman. "I have decided to return to New England. I was going to send a message of farewell, but the Lord made it clear to me that I should come in person to say goodbye to both of you."

Roman captured Rachel's hand and pulled her closer to his side. "California is not safe for Americanos any longer. It is better for you in New England right now."

The thought of Steven in the hands of the likes of Lopez and Garcia chilled Roman. He could not escape the memory of those screams of the Yankee prisoners as they were tortured. The Americanos were surely dead now. "You should not be traveling alone," he told Steven. "Not all Californios are honorable men. There are some in the province who are outlaws. They use the excuse of war to spread their evil."

"I did not see anyone as I traveled here." Steven wiped sweat from his neck with his handkerchief. "The land I rode through was quiet and uncommonly beautiful."

"Castro's soldiers are roaming the countryside. You are lucky not to have run into these troops."

"I don't believe in luck. The Lord orders my steps. I have arrived here safely because it is the Lord's will that I do so."

Roman envied Steven's faith. Was it true God cared about a man's steps enough to order them? He was grateful Steven had returned. Together, they could talk more about God. Roman had many questions.

At the hacienda, Roman told Rachel, "Please tell Tia Josefa to have a feast prepared. We will celebrate Steven's safe return."

"Steven, come with me. We will see to your horse together."

At dinner that evening, the men ate with gusto while the women picked at their food. Isabella's head remained bandaged. She ate only what Tia Josefa commanded her to consume. Isabella grieved terribly over her lost hen.

Rachel pushed the food around her plate, taking small bites here and there, but eating hardly anything. Roman knew she grieved over Isabella and wondered if she felt saddened over Steven's decision to return to Boston soon.

He tried not to think about her feelings for Steven. The two appeared so chaste together Roman had almost convinced himself their relationship posed no threat to him at all. Maria did not appear hungry either. Roman knew Steven's arrival without Dom greatly disappointed her.

After they finished eating, with the women quietly listening, Roman asked Steven about the happenings in Yerba Buena.

"The sloop of war, Portsmouth, rides at anchor in San Francisco Bay. Her commander, John Montgomery, is sending supplies up the Sacramento and Feather Rivers on the Portsmouth's launches." Roman could see Steven did not like giving such news. Both men knew what this meant. The American rebels in the north were now being supplied by the United States military.

Roman asked Steven to walk with him out to the vineyard to continue their discussion of war without the ladies present. He did not want to frighten Rachel, his sisters, and Tia Josefa. War belonged to men, but women often suffered for it.

Chapter Thirty-Six

"I do not trust the Protestant," Sarita said as soon as the men walked out of earshot. "How do we know he is not a spy for the Americanos? Maybe he has come here to set a trap for Roman?"

"He is not a spy," Rachel said. "Steven has returned only to say good-bye. He's going back to Boston."

Sarita laughed. "Are you so stupid you cannot see why Roman entertains the *Yanquio*? He is but using him to gather information for General Castro. I would not be surprised if Roman kills the Protestant before this war is over."

Tia Josefa stood up, waving her finger warningly at Sarita. "Do not talk this way," she commanded. "Senõr Steven is our dear friend. God does not want us to fight with each other. He wants us to live together in harmony with the Americanos."

"I think God wants the Yankees to rule California," Maria spoke up.

"What is this my women speak of?" Tio Pedro demanded as he returned to the *sala* with a bottle of brandy.

"I'm going to bed." Maria jumped to her feet to leave the room.

"Me too." Isabella rushed after Maria, swooshing past Tio Pedro in a flurry of skirts.

"You girls will say the rosary before bed," Tia Josefa ordered.

Avoiding Tio Pedro, Rachel followed the girls out of the *sala*.

"Yes, Tia," Maria called. "We will say our rosaries."

Sarita left the *sala* too. "Do not trust the Protestant," she told Tio Pedro as she passed by.

"Just a moment," Rachel called, laying aside her Bible and rising from the chair to walk over and open her bedroom door. When she saw who stood there her heart sank.

"May I come in?"

Rachel stepped aside without a word.

Sarita rushed into the room. "Close the door. I do not want anyone else to hear what I must tell you."

Rachel hesitated, holding open the door in protest.

"Close the door. It's in your best interest," Sarita assured her.

Against her better instincts, Rachel complied. "What is it you have to say?"

Sarita prowled the room, a wild look in her eyes. "I am pregnant. The baby I carry is not your father's."

A sick feeling rose up in Rachel. Before Sarita spoke the words, she knew what her stepmother would say.

"I carry Roman's child. I am here because when Castro's soldiers kill your father, Roman will take me for his wife. I do not know what Roman plans to do with you, but he knows I carry his child, and it is only his pride keeping us apart. Once your father is dead, Roman will marry me. I want to help you. Your Protestant friend is returning to Boston. I have brought money so you can sail home with him."

Sarita stopped pacing the room. She came to Rachel with a bag of coins. Smiling in sympathy, she pushed the sack into Rachel's trembling hands. "Your fare for the ship."

Sarita circled the room once more. "I want you to know everything. The night you became betrothed, Roman returned to me. The only reason I married your father was because I thought Roman was dead. I allowed Tio Pedro and your father to force me into the marriage. They said a union would protect both our families. I should not have listened to these foolish old men. General Castro will destroy the *Yanquios,* and your father will die with the rest of the traitors in the north."

Rachel opened her door. "I have heard enough. Please leave." She handed Sarita back the coins.

Sarita laughed. "I will bear Roman a son, many sons who will kill every Americano who comes to California." She snatched the coins from Rachel's trembling hands.

Her knuckles white on the door latch, Rachel waited for Sarita to depart. Her stepmother's confession shocked and hurt her beyond measure. And she realized in that moment of heartbreak she truly loved Roman.

"Please," she requested again, this time more firmly. "Leave."

Sarita walked out the door. "Tohic will kill you," she whispered with such venom Rachel was taken aback. Sarita turned down the hall and ran headlong into Roman.

"Are you threatening Rachel?" Roman's gaze seared Sarita.

"I have told her the truth is all."

He looked over Sarita's head to Rachel, still standing there holding the door open.

"Is she telling the truth?" Everything in Rachel longed for him to say it wasn't so.

He took a deep breath. "I may have fathered the child," he admitted.

"Of course it is true!" Sarita put a hand on her expanding waistline.

"Go to your room," Roman commanded Sarita.

"I carry your son. She doesn't belong here. Make her leave."

"Go to your room," he repeated more harshly.

Sarita moved a short ways down the hall. When Roman stepped toward Rachel, she slammed the door in his face.

"Open the door," he insisted, knocking fiercely on the wood.

She latched it.

"Open the door, Rachel!"

He beat on the door. "If you do not unlatch the door, I will break it down," he threatened. "This door cannot stop me."

Fear and anger tangled inside of Rachel. She walked away from the door, and went and knelt beside her bed. Tears burned her eyes as she bowed her head.

"If I come through this door by force, you will regret not opening it for me."

Even with the door closed, she could hear him raging in the hall. Let him rage. How could he have impregnated Sarita?

"You are my betrothed!" he roared, kicking the door with all of his might. The wood exploded, splintering open, the broken door banging against the adobe wall.

Rachel did not lift her head as Roman burst into the room.

He strode over and lifted her to her feet. The tears on her face didn't distract him. "Don't ever lock me out of my own hacienda." He kissed her roughly, possessively, before pushing her onto the bed.

"You are full of the devil!" she cried. Fear coursed through her, but anger filled her as well. How dare he barge into her room and attack her. He was the one guilty of sin, not she. He had committed adultery with Sarita. A vile iniquity against God. An act that rent Rachel's heart in two.

He leaned over her, his arms braced on either side of the bed to keep her beneath him. "I have decided we will marry. Before I join Castro's forces, you will become my wife. It is the only way to keep you safe."

"I will not marry you. You are an adulterer. Sarita carries your child. Get away from me. The two of you deserve each other."

Roman grabbed her wrists, pinning her to the bed. "You must listen to me! I do not want Sarita. I don't even know if the child she carries is mine. You will marry me! It is the only way to protect you."

"The protection I need is protection from you. Let me go!" Rachel began to fight him with every fiber of her being. "Help me! Someone, please help me!" she screamed, struggling to escape him.

"Be quiet," he ordered. "You are my betrothed. You will listen to me!" He shook her on the bed in a fit of frustration.

"Roman, stop," Steven ordered from the doorway. Tio Pedro and Tia Josefa stood behind Steven, eyes wide in distress.

"What is going on?" Tio Pedro bellowed. "Have you lost your mind, *mi hijo*?"

Tia Josefa carried her rosary beads, furiously fingering the necklace.

"You are a minister, Steven. You will marry us right now," Roman announced, climbing off of Rachel.

"Sarita carries his child. I will not marry him." Rachel sat up on the bed, her hair tangled and torn from its pins, her face ashen.

"Is this true, *mi hijo*?" Tio Pedro demanded.

"Yes," Sarita said, standing at the door behind Steven. "I will bear Roman a son come winter."

"Is this true? Does she carry your child?" Steven asked Roman. Steven was an anchor of calm in the midst of the chaos.

Roman now appeared grief-stricken. Rachel felt the same way he looked. Shattered.

Sarita smiled.

"Is it true, Roman?" Tio Pedro asked.

Ignoring his uncle, Roman stared at Steven, "It may be true."

"You cannot marry Rachel if Sarita carries your child," Steven said gently.

Roman nodded. A tear slipped out of the corner of his eye and trailed down his cheek. Rachel had never seen him look so defeated.

Turning to Pedro, Steven said, "Senór Pedro, please take Sarita back to her room."

Steven urged Tio Pedro out into the hall, pushing Sarita out of the room as well. Maria and Isabella scurried away from the broken door where they'd been listening in the hall.

Steven returned to the room and shut the others out by closing the broken door as best he could.

Rachel told Steven, "Tomorrow you will take me to Yerba Buena. I cannot stay here any longer, and I don't know where my father is. I must return to New England with you."

"You are not leaving." Roman clenched his fists. His face hardened once more. "It is too dangerous away from the hacienda. California is at war, and you are an Americana. There are men out there who would hurt you. They would kill Steven."

Rachel got off the bed, shaking out her skirts in determination. "I am leaving, Roman. You no longer have any say in what I do."

He spun around and punched the broken door. It banged against the wall again, splintering further.

"Easy, Roman," Steven said. "Do not give in to anger. Let Jesus lead you through this storm, my friend."

Roman turned to Steven. "Maybe she wants to marry you. Perhaps she has always wanted you, amigo."

"Rachel has just learned you have been unfaithful in your betrothal agreement. She is upset. As you would be if she had done this to you. Come, we will walk and talk in the vineyard." Steven motioned for Roman to follow him out the door.

Once they were gone, Rachel fell apart. Somewhere along the way, she'd come to count on Roman. To trust in his strength. To surrender to his passion. She saw him struggling to know Christ. He read Steven's Bible every day now. She had begun to think perhaps they could build a life together. With a sob, she collapsed on the bed.

Never had someone made her feel the way Roman did. She cared deeply for Steven, but Steven did not fill her with longing. She didn't want Steven to hold her, to kiss her. When Roman touched her, it was all she could do not lose herself in him. Being in his arms thrilled her. She hungered for his company. The realization that Sarita might carry his child sickened her beyond belief.

Tia Josefa soon returned to comfort her. "I know Roman," she said. "He no longer cares for Sarita. He loves you, *chica*. You have softened his heart. Do not break it now."

"I cannot marry an adulterer," Rachel told Tia Josefa. "He has been with my stepmother. This is an abomination in the eyes of God."

"God's eyes are merciful." Tia Josefa held up her rosary, showing Rachel the crucifix. "It is the cross that brings us mercy. Lean on the cross, *mi hija*."

Part Four

Even though I walk through the valley
of the shadow of death,
I will fear no evil, for you are with me;
your rod and your staff,
they comfort me.

Psalm 23:4

Chapter Thirty-Seven

"If you are meant to marry Rachel," Steven assured Roman, "the Lord will bring it to pass. Right now, you must work through this ordeal with Sarita. If she carries your child, you must stand by her. You must accept this child and the mother as well."

"I know you are right," Roman agreed as they walked through the vineyard under a blanket of the stars. "I have been so blind. How could I not see Sarita for what she was? Even after she married another man, I could not keep her at bay. She came to me when I was drunk and wanting revenge against her husband. I see how wicked we both were to do such a thing. I am sorry for my sins with Sarita. My sins with other women. My sins with Rachel. Though she was untouched, I wanted Rachel for my woman. I have never taken no for an answer in all my life. I take what I want, thinking only of myself. I have been my own god. I deserve God's punishment."

"God doesn't always have to punish us. We are often punished by our own sins. The consequences of our actions bring us suffering. You have confessed your sins to me. You must also confess these sins to God. I will pray for forgiveness for you and that your suffering is borne in the light of the Lord's great love for you."

Roman stopped walking. He took Steven by the shoulders. "I want you to marry Rachel. You are the kind of man she deserves."

Steven's smile was full of sadness. "I would like that very much," he admitted. "But perhaps, like Paul, it is better I do not marry."

"Who is Paul?" Roman released his hold on Steven and took a deep breath. He was so tired of fighting everyone and everything. Most of all, he was tired of fighting God.

"Saint Paul wrote many letters in the Bible. He was converted after watching another saint put to death. I am named for this saint." Steven smiled.

Roman looked at his dear face, feeling unease sweep over him. He worried for Steven's safety. Steven was such a peaceful man, but California was not peaceful.

"When we give our troubles to Jesus, he will make all things right," said Steven. "If Sarita is lying about the child, this too will be brought into the light. Wait and pray, Roman." Steven put his hand on Roman's shoulder, looking with great affection into his eyes. "You will know Jesus, my friend. The Lord has promised me you will know him well."

• • •

"This child you carry better be mine," Roman warned Sarita the next morning out in the stables. "If you are deceiving me, God will deal with you."

"I swear it's yours. I know you want sons. I will give you sons. I will. . ."

Roman silenced her. "It is important I tell you this." He took a deep breath, reminding himself Steven said this must be done. "I am sorry. I never should have lain with you. It was a sin against God and against you."

Sarita threw herself into his arms. "What are you saying? I am not sorry! I love you. I am your woman. I have always been your woman." She tried to kiss him. "Please let's return to the way we were before Texas. Before the gringos came to California."

He set her away from him. "I am no longer that man who left for Texas. I never want to be that man again." He despised her now, though he knew these feelings of hatred toward her were wrong. And he hated himself for ever having slept with her. Steven had promised him God would help him if he trusted God to deliver him. He pulled the cinch tight on Oro, and then saddled Steven's horse, and then Rachel's mount as Sarita continued to ramble on about how the Americanos had ruined their lives.

"We have done this to ourselves," Roman told her. "Adultery is a sin. We are sinners, Sarita."

"What has happened to you? God let your mother die! He let my mother die! The only reason I lived was that Tohic healed me. You know this! We must worship Tohic, not the God of the padres. The padres brought only disease and death to California. Tohic has always brought life and healing and . . ."

"Be quiet! Do not speak to me about your devils." Roman bridled the horses and led them out of the stables. Sarita trailed after him, but when she saw he headed towards the hacienda where the family had gathered on the porch to see him off, she walked the other way. "I will be here waiting for you when you return," she called as she left him.

Roman did not answer her. He continued to the hacienda where he found Steven waiting in the yard for Rachel to appear with her belongings. The three were to ride together till the fork in the road. Roman would head south to join Castro's forces while Steven and Rachel continued north to Yerba Buena.

Rachel was set on leaving him. And his feelings for her were so volatile right now, he agreed with Steven that she was safest returning to Boston in the midst of war in California. Roman did not trust her father. Nor Sarita. Even his drunken Tio Pedro. And he felt it his duty to ride down to meet Castro and join in the effort to set California free to govern herself. He could not escape this war, just as he could not escape Sarita's pregnancy.

He had not spoken with Rachel since kicking down her door last night. Steven had worked out the details with her for departure. It was all Roman could do this morning to maintain his composure as he waited for her to come out of the hacienda. Perhaps he would never see her again. Though he believed Steven meant what he said about not marrying, Steven's intentions surely would change when they returned to New England together. Roman couldn't begrudge him that. Steven loved her first.

When she appeared on the porch, Roman thought she'd never looked so lovely. Her hair was in a single braid down her back, like the day they'd visited the Indian village together, but shorter now thanks to his knife. She wore simple clothes—a black skirt and white blouse draped by a sturdy shawl. Peasant clothes. He smiled in spite of himself. For all her beauty, she was such a humble human being, more concerned with others than herself. By the look on her face, he could see this parting caused her great pain. She held tightly to Isabella's hand. Both of them had been weeping.

Maria, Tia Josefa, and Tio Pedro stood on the porch with sad faces. Rachel looked at him with tear-filled eyes as he waited with the horses. After hugging Isabella, she embraced Maria, and then Tia Josefa, and said a kindly goodbye to Tio Pedro, and then she walked down the steps and handed her satchel to Steven.

She would not acknowledge Roman as he came quietly to her side to assist her onto her palomino mare. On her own, she climbed into the saddle without meeting his gaze.

Roman walked over and mounted his own horse as Steven settled himself in his saddle too.

The three rode out of the yard as the morning sun rose over the mountains. During the hour it took to reach the fork in the road, Steven and Roman talked about the ship journey. The long months at sea. Steven's plans once he returned to New England. Rachel said nothing. She wouldn't even look at Roman.

When they reached the fork, Roman dismounted and walked purposefully to her horse. He wasn't about to let her leave this way. Reaching up, he swept her off the palomino into his arms. He captured her chin, forcing her to look at him. "I only want to say good-bye," he said tenderly.

"Good-bye," she said, trying to escape him.

He held her more surely, staring into her eyes. He longed to tell her he loved her, but the words would not come. *"Vaya con Dios,"* he said instead with a knot in his throat choking him. The same words he'd spoken to his mother all those years ago before she died.

Suddenly, he felt like a lost little boy. Hot tears scalded his eyes and spilled down his cheeks. Overwhelmed by emotion, he drew Rachel against him and held on to her with his heart breaking.

"God will go with us," she whispered in his ear. "And God will go with you, Roman."

He finally pushed away from her, his jaw clenched tight. Tears blurred his vision. "God took my mother. Now he's taking you as well."

"God is not who you think he is, Roman. God loves you. He loved your mother. I will pray in time you know God."

At that moment, he wanted to rage against God. And shake Rachel senseless. Tears coursed down his cheeks. He wasn't used to grief and wanted to destroy something. Anything to make the pain go away.

Steven came and put his hand on Roman's shoulder. "Trust God," he said. "The Lord will not abandon you, Roman."

"If you are stopped by anyone on the road, tell them you are my friend." Roman pulled a paper from his shirt pocket. It was written in Spanish. Roman's signature was there along with General Castro's. "These are orders General Castro wrote for me. This should be enough for the soldiers to let you continue on to Yerba Buena in safety."

Steven nodded. "Thank you, Roman."

Roman reached out to shake Steven's hand.

Steven enfolded Roman in his embrace, holding him tightly. "I will miss you, amigo."

"I will miss you as well, my friend." Roman hugged him back with all his strength and then pushed Steven away. He walked briskly to his horse and swung into the saddle. With a last nod to Steven, he galloped away without looking again at Rachel.

Chapter Thirty-Eight

Rachel watched Roman go through a blur of tears. Steven held the stirrup for her to mount her horse. He did not seem pleased with her, which confused Rachel. She stepped into the stirrup and climbed into the saddle. Steven handed her the reins. "You ignored him all morning. Then, when he laid his heart bare for you, you told him you would pray for him. That was really something."

Rachel was taken aback by Steven's chastisement. "What was I supposed to do? He bedded my stepmother."

"You are supposed to forgive him."

"I will forgive him."

"You did not offer forgiveness. You offered him a stiff back all morning."

"That is not fair, Steven."

"Christ does not say life is fair. At the cross, Jesus proved life isn't fair. He took our place under God's wrath. If life were fair, you and I would hang on that cross instead of Christ."

"For heaven's sake, do you not understand how I feel? Sarita will bear Roman a child."

Steven smiled, a bittersweet twisting of his mouth. "I understand more than you know. You love him. If you did not love him you would not act so foolishly. You would offer Roman mercy instead of this righteous anger I have never seen in you."

"I am angry. I have never known people like these Californios. They eat sin and wipe their mouths in satisfaction."

"Are you their judge?"

"We are called to lead holy lives before God. Are we not?"

"True. But we are also called to gently lead the lost to Christ. The lost do not understand holiness. We must awaken them with Christ's great love. That love comes through us, Rachel."

They rode for the better part of the day without speaking. Rachel prayed for Roman and for herself and for Steven. She could now see the mistakes she'd made. From the beginning, she'd thought herself better than Roman because she was a Christian and he was not. She realized her sin of pride and also the sin of unbelief.

Unbelief because she never truly considered Roman could come to Christ. He was a man driven by the flesh. Full of fury and lust and a longing for war. The worst of sinners, she'd told herself.

And yet Steven was right. She'd fallen in love with him. Absolutely, completely fallen in love with Roman. And now she had let him go. Rejected him, really.

"Steven, when two or more of God's people request something on earth it will be done in heaven."

Steven finally smiled at her as they rode along the narrow dirt road. "What shall we request?"

"That Roman be saved."

"Let's stop and rest the horses under that oak grove. We can pray there."

Once they were settled beneath the shade of a mighty tree, and the horses left to graze nearby, Steven reached out and took Rachel's hand in his. He bowed his head. "Lord, we come to you because salvation belongs to you and you alone. We know we can do nothing to save a man's soul. Only you can bring salvation. Humbly, we ask you to save Roman. Not because we love him, but because you love him. In the name of your one and only son, Jesus, we pray. Amen."

Steven and Rachel opened their eyes at the same time, their faces shining with light.

"He has heard us," Rachel said.

"Indeed he has," Steven agreed.

As Roman rode south a great battle raged inside him. The farther away from Rachel and Steven he traveled, the more convinced he became the two would soon forget all about him. Once they returned to New England, they would certainly resume their lives, with California only a distant memory. Perhaps they would marry on the ship and become lovers under the "approval" of their Almighty God.

Roman rode hard for miles, thoughts of Steven and Rachel battering his mind and bruising his heart. The idea of the two intertwined in a lover's embrace tortured him. He couldn't get the image out of his head.

Rachel and Steven are probably lying together even now in the cool of the shade of some great tree, their bodies soaked with sweat and passion. Remember how easy it was for you to kindle desire in her . . .

"No," Roman said hoarsely, startling himself that he spoke out loud against the barrage of wicked thoughts. Steven and Rachel were not like this. They were not unrepentant sinners like he and Sarita. Their faith and dedication to God was real. Steven was his friend. Rachel was pure and lovely and untouched by any man except him. They would not do these dark things he envisioned them doing.

Turn around. Return to Steven and Rachel. I will be with you.

Roman recognized that voice deep inside him.

The voice of God.

Relief and elation bloomed in his chest. After a day of riding south, he skidded to a halt. Turning his horse around, he headed north. The meeting with Castro would have to wait. He would escort Steven and Rachel to Yerba Buena. Perhaps in Yerba Buena, Rachel would agree to wait for him. He could find a safe place for her to stay until the war was over. She could live in Yerba Buena with his great uncle and aunt. If he remembered correctly, they were devout Catholics. Once Sarita gave birth to the child, if God was merciful, the baby may very well favor Rachel's blond Yankee father.

Hope soared in Roman. He rode to a nearby rancho in search of fresh horses. He wanted to travel at the greatest possible speed. He could leave Oro at the rancho with the assurance he would return with the rancho's horses in the near future to trade them back for his stallion.

At the rancho, Roman discovered only Indian vaqueros and servants there. The *gente de razón* family had headed to Monterey to seek protection from the war. Usually, Californios generously provided horses to one and all, but the vaqueros said they could part with no horses. General Castro's troops had taken most of the rancho's horses already.

In California before the Americanos came, no one needed money to travel. A man could ride the vastness of the country from one rancho to the next with everything for his journey provided for him. Food, fresh horses, supplies—whatever he required, the *gente de razón* would gladly give to their guests.

Roman had never traveled in California with money, but before leaving this morning, he'd been prompted by the thought that he needed gold in his saddlebags. Enough to buy his way to Mexico and back. Fortunately, he had this gold hidden away from Tio Pedro.

"I will pay you for horses," he told the vaqueros. "This war has changed California. A man needs gold now to survive here."

"*Si,*" one of the vaqueros agreed. "The Americanos cannot see past their coins. Everything is money to them."

Roman bought two horses at the rancho and switched his saddle onto one of the fresh stallions, tying Oro to the back. He wouldn't leave Oro in this new, inhospitable California.

By the time he reached the fork in the road that led to Rancho de los Robles, it was well past midnight. There, he turned Oro loose. The stallion would go home on his own. He changed out his saddle and led the other horse he'd brought north with him.

After releasing Oro, he rode like the devil was on his heels. It felt that way to Roman as terrible thoughts attacked his mind.

You will find her in Steven's arms. He has already bedded her. You are a fool to put your faith in a God who took your mother.

Roman raced on, doing his best to outrun the torment of his imagination. He rode at breakneck speed, unsure of why he felt such a great urgency, but he knew once he found Rachel and Steven, he would know the truth and the truth would set him free.

Chapter Thirty-Nine

Not long after Roman, Rachel, and Steven left the rancho, Luis Lopez arrived at the hacienda. Sarita couldn't believe her good fortune. Certainly Tohic was helping them. "You will have no problem tracking Rachel and Steven down," she told Luis. "Roman has headed south to join Castro. It will be easy for you to overtake the Americanos and do away with them in the wilderness before they reach Yerba Buena."

"Why do you still want the gringa dead now that she has left Rancho de los Robles?" Lopez wanted to know.

"Roman might decide after the war to go after her. I don't want any possibility of him returning to her. I want her dead. I want the birds of the air to pick her bones clean. And the Protestant too."

Lopez laughed. "Such sinister plans you have for your stepdaughter."

"If my husband does not die in this war, I want you to kill him too, cousin."

"What will I get for all this killing for you?" Lopez used his fierce-looking knife to clean the dirt out from under his long, ugly fingernails, and then he motioned for Sarita to follow him. "I must water my horse if I will be riding the rest of the day to do your killing. You owe me something."

"What do you want?" Sarita asked as she left the yard with him.

"I have not had a woman in many days." He gave her a leering grin, his teeth a rotten mess.

"Take the gringa before you kill her. Take her as many times as you wish before she's dead. She is a virgin. Surely, that will satisfy you."

Lopez laughed. "I am not so easily satisfied."

"I am your cousin," Sarita argued.

"You are Roman's cousin too. That has not stopped you from lying with him."

They'd reached the creek, alone in the trees now where no one could see them from the hacienda. "I am pregnant with Roman's son," Sarita reminded him.

"How do you know the child is not a girl, and not your gringo husband's?" Lopez tied his big albino stallion to a willow limb after watering the animal in the stream.

"I don't know whose child I carry," Sarita admitted. "It doesn't matter. If the child comes forth fair like the Americano, I will drown it before Roman sees the whelp."

After tying his horse, Lopez walked toward Sarita standing there on the bank. "I will kill the gringos for you, but not for free." He smiled wolfishly as he unbuckled his belt, dropping two pistols and his savage-looking knife onto the ground as he grabbed Sarita's arm. "I'll be quick taking my pleasure," he assured her. "And quick to make sure you do not bear an Americano's whelp, fair cousin."

Steven and Rachel stopped for the night in a picturesque canyon with oaks and pines and some magnificent redwood trees guarding the glade. They prayed together before eating and then read their Bibles beside the light of their crackling campfire.

Roman had tied bedrolls to the backs of their saddles. The food he'd packed for them proved generous and tasty. It would be several days until they reached Yerba Buena. But it was summertime and the night balmy when they lay down to sleep.

Yet within a few hours, an eerie fog from the ocean engulfed their camp, and wolves began to howl. Rachel tossed and turned and prayed, and when she did manage to sleep a little, she had that awful nightmare of the man on the pale horse pursuing her.

When dawn finally arrived, she was incredibly grateful for the break of day.

Steven got up and rebuilt the fire and then crawled back into his bedroll, waiting for the morning sun to warm the glade, but the fog wouldn't relent.

Rachel pulled her Bible out from under the covers of her bedroll and began reading Zechariah. *"During the night I had a vision—and there before me was a man riding a red horse. He was standing among the myrtle trees in a ravine."*

"Steven, read Zechariah and tell me if the Lord reveals anything to you from this passage." She waited for Steven to read the scripture as she looked out over the fog-shrouded ravine.

After reading, he asked her, "Did you have a vision during the night?"

"I keep having the same dream. A terrible dream about a man on a pale horse."

Steven was thoughtful for a moment. "Are you sure the horse is pale?"

"I am certain it is pale."

Steven flipped through his Bible till he came to Revelation. He began to read, "I looked, and there before me was a pale horse. Its rider was named Death, and Hades was following close behind him."

They lay there silently for a long time, each praying fervently because of the unease they both felt. The morning sun finally began to push the fog back toward the ocean. Birds sang in the trees, and the fire crackled when Steven got up and tossed more wood upon it.

"Are you hungry?" he asked.

"No. Not at all." She sat up in her bedroll, fully dressed, having chosen to sleep in her clothes for warmth as well as modesty. "I'm so troubled, Steven."

"Our Lord never said our lives on this earth would be easy. Jesus said he would be with us. That he would never forsake nor abandon us no matter what comes our way."

"What if death comes our way?"

"Then we will see our Lord face-to-face," Steven replied confidently. "Death is but a doorway into the presence of God. We are not to fear death, Rachel. The apostle Paul said, 'To live is Christ, and to die is gain.'"

She stood and shook out her skirts. "You are right. I should not fear death."

"I will pray this dream troubles you no more. We should be on our way to Yerba Buena soon." Steven began packing up the camp.

"Is the ocean beautiful there?" Rachel walked toward the trees for some private time.

"Magnificent," Steven called. "Blue as your eyes, Rachel."

Smiling, Rachel disappeared into the woods.

Steven rolled up their bedrolls and tied them to the back of their saddles. He wasn't hungry either, so he saddled the horses and packed all their goods upon them. Then he kicked dirt on the fire until it smoldered down to nothing but smoke.

It was this smoke drifting up into the sky that led Lopez right to them.

Steven was helping Rachel into the saddle when he galloped into the clearing. Lopez swung his riata around his head. As he raced into their midst on his big albino stallion, he threw the rope. It snaked around Steven's upper body, settling around his chest, pinning his arms to his sides.

Lopez jerked the rope tight, yanking Steven off his feet.

He hit the ground with a sickening thud and was then dragged through the camp by the triumphant Lopez.

Rachel screamed as Lopez laughed like a madman. Steven never made a sound as he was dragged behind the pale horse.

Lopez leaped to the ground and swiftly tied Steven to a tree. Steven bled badly from a cut on his forehead. Bruises soon formed on his face and neck and arms.

Rachel jumped from her horse and tried to help Steven. When she reached the tree with Steven there on his knees, Lopez backhanded her across the cheek.

She sprawled in the dirt and then crawled on hands and knees back to Steven. He was tied to the tree now, a disorientated look upon his battered face.

Lopez kicked Rachel away from him. She cried out in pain.

"Don't hurt her," Steven begged.

Lopez kicked Rachel again, not hard, but hard enough to knock her onto her back in the dirt. He then walked over and yanked her to her feet.

Rachel had braided her hair in a single plait down her back. Lopez grabbed hold of the braid and yanked the leather binding off the end, then shook her hair free. "I have found gold," he exclaimed, a wild look in his wicked eyes.

"Don't hurt her," Steven pleaded once more.

Lopez dragged Rachel by her hair over to Steven. "The golden woman is mine now," he sneered, and then kicked Steven in the stomach.

Steven grunted in pain.

Several more times, Lopez kicked Steven in the midsection until Steven's head hung low and he no longer responded to the beating.

"Please," Rachel cried. "Please don't hurt him anymore."

"Don't hurt him," Lopez mocked her. Still holding her by the hair, he shook her roughly and then yanked her head back to breathe his hot, foul breath on her face.

Swinging an arm with all her might, Rachel managed to punch him in the mouth.

He growled in fury and threw her to the ground. "You will pay for drawing that blood, little gringa!" He wiped his split lip across his sleeve, viciously kicking her in the hip.

She rolled and whimpered, desperately trying to crawl away from him.

Smiling, his crooked yellow teeth covered in blood, Lopez stalked her. Grabbing her hair, he jerked her back on to her feet.

He carried her over to the horses. Pulling a rope from Steven's horse, he used it to bind Rachel to the saddle after he'd tossed her up onto the palomino mare she'd ridden since leaving the rancho.

Rachel wept as Lopez walked back to Steven. The monstrous man stopped to retrieve another riata from his horse before going to the tree where Steven was tied.

Approaching hoof beats caused Lopez to dive into the trees. When Roman rode into the clearing, Lopez roped him just as he had Steven. Rachel screamed his name as he was yanked off his horse. Seeing him filled her with shock and then soaring hope. She couldn't believe Roman was really here. Her love for him overwhelmed her.

Lopez stepped from the trees. The horses Roman had been leading raced away. The horse Roman rode galloped off as well, causing Rachel's mare to bolt after them.

Lopez let out a string of curses as Rachel, screaming for Roman, was carried away with the runaway horses.

Steven's horse, tied to a tree limb by its reins, went wild when the other horses bolted away. Rearing back, it broke free from the tree, and then raced after the other horses. Lopez's big pale horse remained where Lopez had left it, though the stallion pawed the dirt and whinnied repeatedly after the departing animals.

Lopez ran to his stallion, holding the end of the long rope that had captured Roman. Leaping into the saddle, he wrapped the end of his riata around the saddle horn.

Roman was up on his feet now. Still wrapped in the riata, he ran after Lopez, but the pale horse sprang forward under Lopez's spurs, yanking Roman off his feet again.

Lopez galloped his horse around the clearing, dragging Roman behind him. Roman kicked wildly to free himself from the rope, but to no avail.

Lopez dragged Roman until he stopped fighting.

Roman was bruised and bleeding when Lopez stopped at the tree where Steven was tied.

Leaping off his pale horse and laughing in glee, Lopez hauled Roman over to the tree next to Steven's and swiftly bound Roman there.

Steven was bleeding badly from his mouth and forehead. He looked at Roman with grieving eyes while Lopez bound Roman beside him.

"Which one of you shall die?" Lopez asked, pulling his dagger from his belt with a wide smile. "I am in a generous mood. I will let one of you live to play with the wolves tonight."

Steven coughed, spitting blood from his lips. "Kill me," he told Lopez. Steven turned to Roman, his gaze piercing Roman's soul for a moment that lasted a lifetime. "Trust your life to Jesus, amigo."

"No! Don't kill him," Roman begged.

Grinning, Lopez sliced Steven's cheek open.

With great calmness and courage, Steven looked steadily into Lopez's hate-filled eyes. "I forgive you," he told Lopez. "You don't know what you're doing, but I forgive you."

With a growl, Lopez plunged his knife deep into Steven's stomach.

"Lord Jesus!" Steven cried out.

"NO!" Roman screamed in agony.

Growling like an enraged animal, Lopez sawed the knife down, cutting Steven's insides out.

Steven died very quickly.

Bloody knife in hand, Lopez stepped over to Roman. "Your friend died a strange death." Lopez appeared shaken. He took several deep breaths as if trying to regain his composure.

Roman bit back his grief as rage rose up in him. "You have killed a man of God."

Lopez ignored this. "Do you love the little golden gringa?" He leered into Roman's face.

Roman gritted his teeth to keep from saying anything Lopez might enjoy.

Lopez laughed wickedly. "Sarita tells me the Americana is a virgin. Is this true, amigo? You have kept this golden woman in your hacienda all these days without touching her? I find this hard to believe. Perhaps you are no longer the man you once were in Texas."

Roman strained against the rope binding him to the tree. "I will kill you," he told Lopez. "If you touch her, I will skin the ugly hide off your body the way I skin cattle."

Lopez laughed again and raised his knife. "Speaking of skinning, I wonder how many ways I can slice you without killing you?"

"Start slicing. The longer you remain here with me, the better."

The delight left Lopez's face. "This is true. My golden woman is galloping away."

"Cut me!" Roman cried.

Lopez sliced Roman's arm open. "That should bring in the wolves but keep you alive long enough to entertain my pets when they come."

"I am hardly bleeding," Roman taunted. "Perhaps you are not the man *you* once were in Texas. Surely, you can cut me better than this, Luis."

"So we are amigos again?" Lopez wiped the bloody knife on his pant leg before holstering it in his belt. "You use my name in such a friendly manner. How can I cut you now that you call me Luis? Like we are old friends again."

"Cut me!" Roman did his best to hold Lopez's attention so Rachel could escape.

Lopez shook his head. "My golden woman awaits me. I will cut her instead." A wicked smile lit his face. "She will bleed her virgin blood so sweetly."

Roman went crazy, wrestling the rope that pinned him to the tree. "I will kill you," he yelled as Lopez walked toward his albino horse. "Luis! I will kill you! I promise you will die!"

After mounting up, Lopez saluted Roman. "Good-bye, amigo," he called, spurring his pale horse out of the ravine.

Roman fought the rope until exhaustion set in. Looking over at Steven, a supernatural calm finally settled over him. "Did you really see Jesus before you died?"

Steven's body remained hanging limply against the tree.

Roman felt light-headed from his own blood loss.

"Trust your life to Jesus, amigo." Steven's words came back now more powerfully than when Steven spoke them when he was alive.

"Jesus!" Roman cried, causing a flock of birds to burst out of the trees across the clearing. "Jesus!" he screamed again and again. Then, his throat raw from all his yelling, he finally bowed his head and began to weep.

As he hung there, Roman recalled the scripture from the Bible out of Zechariah, the verse he'd read over and over while Rachel was sick with fever.

During the night, I had a vision, and there before me was a man riding a red horse.

He heard Rachel's sweet, gentle voice telling him, "The man on the red horse is Jesus."

When Roman looked up, he saw Jesus riding up the ravine on a red horse. He must be dying with Jesus coming for him now.

Chapter Forty

Dominic couldn't sleep aboard *The White Swallow* anchored in San Francisco Bay. His unrest was so great he left his bed and paced his cabin, then went up on deck and paced some more. No stars shone that night. The ship was engulfed in a cold, damp fog that enveloped everything. Why was he so disturbed this night?

After several hours prowling his ship, he realized he kept thinking of Steven. Maybe God was trying to tell him Steven needed his help. He prayed for some time and felt even more strongly that Steven needed him.

By dawn, Dominic knew he had to ride after his friend. Jamie rowed him to shore, and he went to the village stables and saddled his horse. He planned to take only the one horse, but that little voice inside persisted that he needed two horses.

Maybe the Holy Spirit was trying to tell him Steven had lost his horse. Giving up on his human reasoning, Dominic trusted that persistent inner voice and bargained with the horse trader to buy another horse for his journey to Rancho de los Robles.

He packed his bedroll and the food he would need to ride to the rancho in a hurry and left Yerba Buena on the same route he and Steven took on their previous trip there.

Dominic arrived at the ravine two days later. He would not have ridden into the little canyon off the main road had he not heard a man yelling Jesus' name.

Such a strange thing to hear, someone hollering for the Savior that way. He urged his horse up the canyon until he saw two men tied to trees there. From a distance, both men appeared dead.

His heart pounding, Dominic rode closer until recognition knocked the breath from him. "Roman, Steven!" He spurred his horse over to his friends and jumped off his mount.

"You came." Roman smiled at Dominic, tears coursing down his stubble-covered cheeks.

Dominic fell to his knees in front of him. "What has happened?" He could see Steven was already dead.

Roman came to his senses. "Luis Lopez killed him."

Roman was bleeding badly from his arm. Dominic took off his flannel shirt and ripped the sleeve from it, using it to bind Roman's wound.

"Jesus brought you here." Roman's voice was filled with awe and wonder.

Dominic couldn't speak, so great was his grief over Steven's death.

"Just before he died, Steven saw Jesus. I know he saw Jesus. I thought you were Jesus riding up on that red horse."

"You're not going to die." Dominic found his stern captain's voice. He took out his knife and began cutting the rawhide rope that bound Roman to the tree. "Jesus isn't coming for you yet, amigo. My horse isn't red. It's a sorrel."

"Dom." Roman waited until Dominic looked him square in the eye. "Jesus was here. He came for Steven. I know Steven saw him." Tears streamed down Roman's bruised face.

Dominic sat back on his heels.

Roman took a shuddering breath, looking up into the sky. "Jesus died for me just like Steven died for me."

Tears rushed to Dominic's eyes. He went back to sawing on the rope.

"I believe," Roman rasped. He returned his gaze to Dominic. "I believe in Jesus."

"Tears rolled freely down Dominic's cheeks now too. "Steven died so you could believe." Dominic's voice was hoarse with emotion.

Roman closed his eyes. His shoulders shook with sobs, though the rope restrained him. When he finally got control, he said, "Lopez is after Rachel. We need to find her before he does."

Dominic sawed harder on the rope.

When the rope finally burst loose, Roman pushed himself off the tree and nearly fell face down on the ground.

Dominic caught him in his arms. "You've lost a lot of blood. Are you sure you can ride?"

"I can ride." Roman got his bearings. "We will come back for Steven after we find Rachel."

Dominic swiftly unpacked the other horse and helped Roman into the saddle.

He then mounted his own horse and pointed to the long gun tied to the side of his saddle. "I brought my rifle this time. I'm a crack shot, you know."

The two galloped out of the ravine, following the torn-up dirt trail the fleeing horses had made. Dominic kept an eye on Roman, but after watching him for a while, he decided the Spaniard rode better than he did even with a wounded arm and blood loss.

They traveled south as sundown neared. It was obvious Rachel's horse was headed home to Rancho de los Robles.

It was Rachel's worst nightmare. In the distance, she could see the evil man on his pale horse. Roman must be dead if the man now pursued her.

The wind whipped the tears off her face as the little mare she was tied to ran for all her worth on the same road she and Steven had taken the day before. The mare was racing back to Rancho de los Robles, running like Rachel had never seen a horse run. If she hadn't been bound to the saddle, she surely would have lost her seat miles ago.

Glancing over her shoulder, she saw the evil man gaining on her. The big albino stallion was finally overtaking her swift little mare.

"Why have you forsaken me?" she cried into the wind. "I've lived my whole life for you, Lord! Why have you forsaken me!"

Crying brokenly, Rachel could see the rider on the pale horse, so close now his leering grin was evident. Such an evil face, like looking into the eyes of the devil himself.

She leaned over the mare's sweat-soaked neck, the sound of the pale horse's hooves pounding in her ears as her mare galloped into a meadow surrounded by trees.

"Give it up, little gringa!" the evil man called out. "You are no match for me!"

I am no match for him, Jesus. Rachel wept into the mare's mane. *Only you can save me. Only my God can save me now.*

A rifle shot rang out in the meadow.

The evil man pitched from his saddle just as he reached out for Rachel's horse. The mare was yanked to a halt by the sprawling outlaw. The barrel-chested man lay face down in the grass, his body restraining the rope attached to Rachel's trembling mare.

Rachel stared at the dead man in horror and wonder with the words of the Lord ringing inside her head. *Deliverance belongs to the Lord.*

Two men emerged from the trees. One of the men ran toward Rachel. His white shirt was bloodstained. A piece of blue flannel bound one arm.

"Roman!" Rachel cried when she recognized him.

The second man wore a torn blue shirt and carried a long rifle, the setting sun gleaming off the gun barrel.

Roman ran across the meadow to her, using his good arm to cut her loose with a knife before sweeping her off the lathered mare into his arms.

He lowered his face to hers for a tender kiss. They did not part until Dominic cleared his throat.

"What should we do with him?" Dominic pointed to the dead man.

"Leave him," said Roman. "We need to get back to Steven before the wolves find him."

"Steven?" Rachel asked hopefully.

"Is gone," Roman said gently. "He gave his life for mine. It was Steven's sacrifice that opened my eyes to see our Lord."

"You know Jesus." It wasn't a question. Rachel put her hand on his cheek, crying and smiling at the same time.

Roman smiled too, tears rolling out of his soft green eyes. "Yes, I've come to know our Lord Jesus, Rachel."

She launched herself back into his arms, and together they wept.

Chapter Forty-One

Bleeding from her womb, Sarita managed to make her way to her room after her brutal encounter with Lopez. When Isabella found her several hours later, Sarita was weak from blood loss, the bed soaked red.

"He has forsaken me," Sarita said when Isabella leaned over her.

"Who has forsaken you?" Isabella was horrified.

"Tohic wants you instead . . . of . . . me," Sarita whispered.

"I'll get Lupe and Mama to help you." Terror filled Isabella's face as she backed out of the bloody room.

"Tohic wants . . . you," Sarita insisted.

Isabella ran for help. She returned to Sarita's room with her mother and Lupe.

"What has happened?" Tia Josefa leaned over Sarita, smoothing the raven hair back from Sarita's deathly pale face.

"He . . . has . . . forsaken . . . me," Sarita whispered.

"Who has forsaken you?" Tia Josefa asked.

"Tohic."

Lupe made the sign of the cross upon hearing that name. "Who is Tohic?"

"Tohic is the evil one," Lupe said. The old Indian woman surveyed the bloody room, her solemn eyes resting on the carved images, speckled woodpecker feathers, and tiny woven baskets set up as a shrine in one corner. Then Lupe left the room without another word.

Tia Josefa pulled the rosary from her skirt pocket.

"Get . . . that . . . away . . . from . . . me," Sarita said weakly.

"You must pray for God to have mercy on your soul."

"Tohic is my god. Tohic will heal me." Sarita tried to bat Tia Josefa's rosary away from her, but she was too weak.

"Ask God to forgive you so you do not go to hell," Tia Josefa insisted, her shaking hands holding the rosary.

Sarita looked around the room until she spotted Isabella, appearing scared to death, standing near the door. "Come to me, Izzy," Sarita whispered.

When Isabella stepped forward, Tia Josefa shooed her away by waving the rosary at her. "Go! Get to your room and say your rosary until I come for you."

"Tohic . . . has . . . chosen . . . her." Sarita used the last of her strength to point to Isabella. Then she closed her eyes, her life ebbing away.

"Get out of here," Tia Josefa ordered Isabella when she remained rooted to the floor beside the door.

Wide-eyed, Isabella finally ran from the room.

With fierce determination, Tia Josefa recited the rosary until Sarita died that afternoon.

• • •

The following morning, they buried Sarita in Rancho de los Robles cemetery on the hill behind the creek. As the funeral procession returned to the hacienda in their black mourning attire, a handful of Californio soldiers rode into the yard.

"We are recruiting men for Castro's army," the leader of the troop spoke to everyone. "Word has come that Mexico is now at war with the United States."

"Our son has joined with Castro," Don Pedro assured them. "I am an old man. Too old to ride with soldiers now."

"You do not look too old," one of the mounted Californios challenged.

"I have just returned from riding with Castro's lieutenants, Padilla and Carrillo, in the north. I was injured on the journey with those men. I am no longer fit to ride."

"Give us your horses, then," said the man in charge.

Don Pedro waved two of his vaqueros over to where he spoke with the soldiers in the yard. "Help these men gather the horses they need."

"Your Indians," said the Californio leading the group. "They look fit and strong. They will take your place fighting for California. Tell them they must come with us."

Several Indian women in the mourning party, wives of the vaqueros, began to weep. Tia Josefa wept too. Maria grabbed Isabella's hand and pulled her close to her side.

Tears filled Don Pedro's eyes as well as they all watched the herd of palominos driven away by Rancho de los Robles's loyal vaqueros in the wake of the Californio soldiers.

When the dogs began to bark again that evening, Don Pedro was too drunk to venture out of the hacienda to greet the arrivals.

Isabella's squeal of joy from the porch alerted the family that these riders were welcome.

Tia Josefa and Maria rushed out onto the porch with Isabella as Roman, Rachel, and Dominic rode into the yard with the sun setting behind the mountains, the sky awash in golden splendor.

"Roman is home," Isabella cried. "With Rachel!"

When Roman swung down from the saddle, Isabella threw herself into his arms. He held her with his good arm, walking over to Rachel's horse with Isabella clinging to him. Isabella stepped back and waited until Roman helped Rachel to the ground so Isabella could eagerly embrace her as well.

"What is that?" Isabella pointed to the roll of blankets tied over the saddle of one of the horses. Having buried Sarita that very morning, her body wrapped in a colorful serape, this form draped across the saddle looked all too familiar.

"We will bury Steven tomorrow." Roman's voice was hoarse with emotion.

Isabella was horrified. "Everyone is dying!" she wailed.

Tia Josefa rushed off the porch and wrapped her arms around Isabella. "We laid Sarita to rest today," Tia Josefa whispered to Roman. "She bled to death miscarrying the babe."

Roman was shocked. He couldn't speak. Rachel came over and put her hand on his arm. "Is everything all right?"

"Sarita has died," Tia Josefa said, wiping the tears that came to her eyes.

Rachel put her hand over her mouth. Tia Josefa embraced her.

Dominic had begun to remove Steven's body from the horse. Roman walked over and helped Dominic without saying a word. Together, they carried Steven into the hacienda.

The two of them took Steven to a downstairs bedroom and placed his wrapped body on the bed. The painting in the room was a depiction of heaven with angels surrounding a flaming throne.

The following morning, Steven was buried in the cemetery on the hill overlooking the creek near the other fresh grave there. Rachel sang several hymns. Dominic joined in, the only one who knew the words to the Protestant songs. After it was over, Roman stayed behind at the graves. He asked everyone to leave him alone for a while.

It was a beautiful summer day, the sky very blue, the creek sparkling with sun diamonds in the distance at the bottom of the hill. Roman walked over to Sarita's grave and stood there for a while filled with regret. When they were young, he thought he might have loved her. She was beautiful and vivacious with her flashing black eyes and aside from Maria, she'd been his main dance partner at the fandangos. Had she carried his child? He would never know. "I'm sorry, Sarita," he said, before returning to Steven's grave. He stood there a while longer at Steven's mound with tears streaking his cheeks.

Upon returning to the hacienda, he joined the feast arranged in honor of the dead that afternoon. All of Rancho de los Robles's Indian servants attended the gathering along with the *familia* as was the tradition of a Californian wake. Tio Pedro ordered the musicians to play all afternoon, and by nightfall, the patio was filled with the mournful songs of the servants. None of the Indians knew Steven, nor did they grieve

Sarita's parting, but the vaqueros taken into the army left every family grieving.

Finally, at nightfall, the Indians gathered their children to return to the small adobe outbuildings they called home.

Roman escorted Rachel to her room.

"Dominic tells me Yerba Buena is growing by the day. That the harbor is full of ships, and the Californios and Americanos are mixing amiably there. After talking with Dom, I believe this would be the best place for us to marry. San Juan Bautista is Castro's town. Monterey is a cradle for rebellion. Dom says we can spend as much time as we like on his ship in the harbor." He squeezed her hands. "God will go before us, Rachel. This war will pass. I have given this much thought, and I think it best for us to quietly marry in Yerba Buena. I have an aunt and uncle there at the mission of San Francisco Dolores three miles from Yerba Buena. My relatives are humble, god-fearing people. They will help us."

"When will we leave for Yerba Buena?"

"As soon as you are ready." Roman smiled down at her, but sadness still filled his eyes.

She returned his tender smile. "Tomorrow?"

"Will you marry me so soon, *pequeña?*"

"Yes," she answered, pressing against him. "I know Steven would want that."

Instead of kissing her, he leaned his forehead against hers for a long moment before pushing her gently away from him. "Go," he said. "Pick out your favorite dress. Pack enough to see you through several weeks in Yerba Buena."

"So we will leave in the morning?"

"*Si.* I hope to find a padre willing to marry us there."

"You have never said that you love me." Her words were soft, uncertain. "Are you marrying me because Steven is gone? Did you make a promise to him to care for me before he died?"

He pulled her back into his arms. "I am marrying you because I love you. I have loved you since the moment I laid eyes on you at your father's hacienda wading in the fountain."

"You should not remind me of that." But a smile lit her face, her eyes sparkling.

"It is my favorite memory of you." His smile slipped away, and he grew serious. "You have not professed your love for me, *pequeña.*"

She raised her hand to touch his cheek. "I love you, Roman." Slipping both hands around his neck, she tugged his head down to press her lips to his.

Chapter Forty-Two

That night, Maria could not sleep. Thoughts of Captain Mason kept her awake. Lighting a candle, she wrapped a *rebozo* around her nightgown and, slipping past her softly snoring dueña, left her room. She padded down the hall and used the servants' stairs to escape out into the night.

A full moon lit the vineyard. Maria decided to go for a walk there. It was close enough to the house to keep the wild animals at bay but far enough from the hacienda to spend time alone on a soft, summer night.

In the vineyard, she strolled between the vines, where emerald clusters of grapes now dangled from the branches. After walking a short while, she sensed she wasn't alone. Turning around, she saw a tall figure one row over beyond the vines.

"Who is following me?" she called out, her heart pounding faster.

"You are out here alone? It is well past midnight. A girl like you should be safe in her bed."

"I am not a girl."

He lowered himself under the row of vines to step over into her path. Captain Mason smiled, his teeth flashing white in the moonlight. "You are not so old," he countered. "And not so big that a wolf or a bear could not drag you off in the blink of an eye."

She did not return his smile. "Rarely do bears or wolves come into the vineyard. The scent of man is here. The wild beasts do not like man's scent."

"It appears you do not like man's scent either."

"*Si.* The scent of one particular man displeases me."

"Roman holds no ill will toward me. We are like brothers now. Why do you persist in hating me?"

"I do not hate you." She wrapped her *rebozo* more snugly around her nightdress. "I would have to care to hate you."

Captain Mason gave her a wry smile. "You are like Cape Horn. Sailing around you is dangerous, my lady."

"You think because you are a tall, blue-eyed Yankee with your own ship the señoritas will fawn all over you. Well, think again, Senór Mason."

"I will take that as a compliment." He lifted a cluster of grapes, inspecting the ripening fruit in the moonlight. "When will these rubies be ripe?"

"Long after you are gone from here."

"Your tongue is as sharp as your claws." He dropped the grapes back to the vine and began walking toward the hacienda.

"You insulted me that night you fought with my brother." Maria hurried after him.

He halted. "Why are you pursuing me if I insulted you?"

"I am not pursuing you," she said in outrage.

"Yes, you are." He grinned, distracting her for a moment. "Here you are at my heels."

"I am not at your heels!"

"Do you want to wake the hacienda so we are found out here alone together in the middle of the night? Speak softly, my dear."

She laughed, her mirth twinkling like a bell. "Senõr Mason, your ship? Are the sails very large on her?"

"Like snow-covered mountains."

"Have you sailed all over the world?" She hurried to match his stride as he walked once more amongst the vines.

"Yes. The world beyond California's shore is as wide as the heavens."

"Really?" Her eyes sparkled with excitement.

"Not really," he answered. "The heavens stretch far beyond what we see with our earthly eyes. This earth man can explore. The heavens belong to God."

"You are a Protestant. I can tell."

"And you are Catholic. Let's not talk about religion. God is a much finer subject."

Maria tossed her head, sending a wave of red hair cascading over her shoulder. "Aren't they the same thing? God and religion?"

Captain Mason stopped walking. "I hope not. Religion is full of man's plans. God's plans are much better." He looked up at the stars. "I could not sleep. I have never known a man like Steven. He was so full of God. People would say Steven was religious, being a minister and all, but he was not religious. Steven loved God. He died for your brother. Did you know that?"

"No. I didn't know. But something has changed Roman. He's so different now." Truthfully, it unnerved her. Just as Steven had unnerved her with his Protestant prayers.

"Your brother accepted Christ as his Savior after Steven died." Captain Mason searched her eyes, discomforting her a great deal.

Her face growing warm, she looked away, remaining silent for a long moment while staring at the shadowy vineyard. When she finally turned back to him, she said, "Tell me of your travels. I want to hear all about the great cities you have seen."

"The cities I have seen?"

"Yes. I am made for more than this wilderness. I want to travel the world. See all the great cities of the earth. Meet all kinds of people. Dance in all kinds of places." She swept her arm out in front of her, pointing across the land, and her *robozo* fell from her shoulders. She didn't bother to pick up the shawl, just stood there in her sheer white nightdress before Captain Mason like a queen. Perhaps the captain would find her so lovely he would take her on his ship with him and sail her to all the fair cities.

"California is the future." Captain Mason turned away from her, looking out across the vineyard. "By far the richest shore I have ever visited. I would not call this place a wilderness. This land is a paradise."

She laughed, mostly because she knew he found her attractive. "California is but one place. I want to visit many places."

He scooped up her shawl and presented it to her. She took her time returning the wrap to her shoulders. He kept his eyes carefully on her face. "Months on the ocean are needed to visit other shores. I doubt a girl like you would enjoy living at sea for so long."

"A girl like me?" She quirked one of her brows at him. "What is a girl like me?"

"A girl like you longs for the city." He walked some more with her at his side. "She wears fashionable clothes and meets fashionable people. Sailors are not fashionable. They are wet, salty dogs, and so is their captain."

Maria laughed, her amusement rippling through the night like quicksilver. "Captain Mason, you are not a salty dog." She captured his hand, pulling him deeper into the vineyard. "You are the most interesting man I have ever met." She spoke in a low, throaty voice. "Take me with you when you leave California. I will cause you no trouble. I am a capable woman. I have ridden with the vaqueros capturing bears, branding cattle, helping bring in the hides. I am good with a knife and a riata. I could help on your ship. You must use ropes out at sea. I am good with ropes."

Dominic pulled his hand free from hers. "I'm sorry. I cannot take you with me."

She moved closer until she stood toe to toe with him. She tilted her head back to look up into his face, her hair rippling down her back. "Why not?"

"You have no idea what it is like to live at sea. A grand hacienda is the place for you my lady. The wild ocean belongs to men who may live or die in every storm."

"Men such as yourself, Captain Mason?" She raised up on tiptoes to get even closer to him. "Why should I stay here? You won't be here." She draped her arms around his neck.

He took her by the waist, held her for a moment, and then gently but firmly set her away from him. "Because you are safe here with your family."

"I don't want to be safe." She moved right back against him, dropping the shawl as she reached up and wrapped her arms tightly around his neck, molding her body to his in a marvelous way. Though she had never kissed a man before, Maria boldly pulled his face down to hers. When she pressed her lips to his, he kissed her back, holding her snugly against his body, groaning in pleasure when she opened her mouth under his.

Maria had seen the servants kiss. She'd been planning her first kiss most of her life. This was nothing like she'd planned. It was far more thrilling than anything she'd ever dared imagine a kiss could be. She was drowning in delight.

Dominic finally tore his mouth from hers. "I'm sorry," he said, breathing deeply. "I should not be out here with you. I have a fiancée in Boston."

"What? You just kissed me and you are to be married?" Maria's voice rose.

"I did not kiss you. You kissed me."

She slapped him as hard as she could across the cheek.

"I did not deserve that." He looked shocked by her wrath.

"Yes, you did. You can save your spittle for your meek-mouthed *Yanquia*."

"You leave Sally out of this. She is a proper lady who minds her manners, unlike you, Little Miss Hothead." Dominic fingered his cheek.

"You are probably marrying Sally just to please your mama. I'm sure this Sally grovels at your feet when you return from your travels, mighty ship captain."

Dominic took a step toward her. Maria stood her ground, not the least bit intimidated that he outweighed her by nearly a hundred pounds of muscle and stood a head taller than she.

"Sally does not grovel at my feet. She sits prettily upon my lap, listening to my stories of the high seas. Stories I will never share with you," Dominic said with a temper of his own.

"I do not care about your tales! And I don't need your pathetic stories of the high seas. I will see for myself what life on a ship is like, and it will not be with the likes of you."

"I pity the poor captain that takes you aboard his vessel." He stepped away from her, rubbing his cheek.

She spun on her heel and headed for the hacienda in a flash of white nightgown. She didn't bother to retrieve her shawl on the ground. Let him pick it up and carry it to the house.

Stupid man. A fiancée? Tears sprang to Maria's eyes. Not a day had gone by that she had not thought about him since he'd arrived at Rancho de los Robles, and all this time he'd had a fiancée!

Chapter Forty-Three

"We will all travel together to Mission San Francisco Dolores. It will be like the old days," Tio Pedro said. "We will bring our servants and have a great caravan of celebration."

"No." Roman raked a hand thought his hair. "It is too dangerous for all of us to travel with war going on. It is best for the rest of you to remain here. Tio and Tia Renaldo will witness for us. We will lodge with them in Yerba Buena."

"They live in a hovel!" Tio Pedro cried. "A hovel is no place for a Vasquez bride and groom."

"I have prayed about this," Roman said firmly. "I believe Yerba Buena is the safest place for us to wed right now."

"You have prayed?" Tio Pedro replied scornfully. "Since when do you pray, *mi hijo*?"

"Since I came to know my Lord." Roman held his temper in the face of his uncle's anger, which was quite unlike him. "You should pray for this to happen to you, Tio."

Tio Pedro lowered his voice so nobody would overhear them speaking in the *sala*. "Perhaps you should not marry her. We can make other plans to align ourselves with the Americanos. It concerns me that the *Yanquia* has changed you."

"The Lord has changed me." Roman walked away from his uncle. "Do not fret, all will be well. Dios is in control," he called over his shoulder as he left the room.

"God does not want you to marry a Protestant!" Tio Pedro cried out, no longer caring who heard him.

Joshua Tyler traveled south toward Rancho El Rio Lobo. No war had materialized in Sonoma. General Vallejo languished in a prison cell at Sutter's Fort in the Sacramento Valley. The crude bear flag had been replaced by the stars and stripes of the United States just this afternoon in the Sonoma plaza. Lieutenant Revere, grandson of the famed Paul Revere, came to Sonoma accompanied by a large party of sailors and marines from the sloop of war Portsmouth, anchored in San Francisco Bay. The military raised the American flag not only in Sonoma, but also in Yerba Buena. Monterey was now in the hands of the Americans as well. So was Bodega Bay.

When Joshua heard General Castro had fled and was headed south, he decided returning home was the wisest thing to do. Upon arriving at his rancho, he discovered Sarita gone. The servants said she'd packed up the day he departed for Sonoma and headed for Rancho de los Robles. She'd been there ever since.

With Rachel there as well, Joshua gathered his vaqueros to ride to the Vasquez hacienda. He would take both his wife and daughter back and perhaps end the betrothal agreement between the two families, considering this war would make the Californios a conquered people. Certainly, he could find a better match for his daughter if she hadn't been ruined by that hot-blooded Spaniard.

Pedro Vasquez owed him more than the family could ever hope to repay. Once the United States was firmly in power and California became a state, he would simply take over Rancho de los Robles with the support of his government and send the Spaniards packing.

When Joshua reached Rancho de los Robles two days later in the heat of the day, he found three chickens scratching in the sleepy yard and a few dogs barking. He saw none of the valuable palomino herds grazing in the fields near the hacienda as they once had. Only one old vaquero lazed in the shade near the stables when he arrived during the afternoon siesta.

Joshua waited in the yard with his army of mounted vaqueros a long time before Don Pedro, rumpled from sleep, came out onto the veranda to greet him.

"Hello, amigo," Don Pedro called as if the two were the best of friends.

Without returning the welcome, Joshua stepped down from his horse, and walked up onto the porch. Sweating under his hat and shirt, he did not shake Don Pedro's hand. "I've come for my wife and daughter."

"Come inside," Don Pedro said with great sadness. "I must tell you what has happened to Sarita."

Joshua followed Don Pedro out of the heat into the cool of the *sala*. Doña Josefa quietly sewed in the parlor, along with the girls, Maria and Isabella.

Joshua's gaze lingered on Maria. The redhead refused to look up at him, which rankled him, as it always did. The striking young woman ignored him. He didn't like it one bit.

"What has happened to my wife?" he demanded to know.

Doña Josefa rose to her feet. "I will bring some wine," she told Don Pedro, hurrying from the room.

The girls quickly followed the older woman from the *sala*. Joshua was sad to see Maria go. "What is going on? Where is Sarita?"

"She is gone," Don Pedro said, his face filled with grief.

"Gone where?" Joshua refused the chair Don Pedro offered him.

"When she lost the child, she lost her life. I am sorry, amigo."

Joshua returned to the chair and sat down with a thud. "What child?"

Don Pedro lowered himself into the chair beside Joshua. "Sarita was with child when she came to us."

"Where is my daughter?" Joshua's mind was spinning.

"Roman has taken her to Yerba Buena."

"Yerba Buena?" Joshua tried his best to recover from the shock of Sarita's death. This wasn't the first wife he'd lost. And it was nothing like losing Rachel's mother—a woman he'd actually loved—but still, it unsettled him. Things had gone sour with Sarita mere days into their marriage. Perhaps it was a relief to come home to find her dead and buried. Now he could start over. This time, he wouldn't take no for an answer concerning Maria.

Don Pedro tried to explain the journey to Yerba Buena. "Roman believes your daughter will be safer living there with the war going on."

Joshua scoffed. "California has already lost the war."

"What do you know of the war?" Don Pedro asked eagerly.

"The United States is winning. Fremont can find no one to fight. A few Californio lancers here and there hiding in the bushes like bobcats. Other than that, the American flag has been run up peacefully all over the province. The Californios are just standing around with their hands under their serapes."

Don Pedro buried his head in his hands.

"I want the betrothal ended between my daughter and your nephew. Things have changed in California. I do not think my daughter is safe in your nephew's care. I heard he's been riding with Castro's forces. Of course you understand, Don Pedro."

Don Pedro looked up from his hands. "This is not possible. Perhaps they have already married in Yerba Buena. You know a betrothal agreement in California is as binding as the wedding union."

"Did your nephew defile my daughter?"

"Of course not," Don Pedro said in outrage. "We are an honorable family. You insult me, Senõr Tyler."

"Are you certain?"

"Nothing dishonorable has happened in my hacienda." Don Pedro puffed up like a peacock.

"My wife died in your hacienda. She was young and strong and healthy the last time I saw her. She couldn't have been far along with child. I don't understand how a miscarriage killed her."

"She bled to death. Sometimes these things happen." Don Pedro arose from his chair to huff around the room.

"You owe me a great deal of money." Joshua rose from his chair as well. "The way I see it, you also owe me a wife. I am willing to cancel both these debts if you give me Maria."

Joshua knew it wasn't the time to ask for the girl with Sarita so recently deceased, but he wasn't about to wait in the midst of a war. Who knew what would happen to the girl when American soldiers arrived here?

Excitement surged through him. The redhead was several years older now. Certainly old enough to marry, even in her uncle's drunken estimation. He could smell the brandy wafting off the disheveled old Spaniard. He'd become a worthless drunk.

Don Pedro stood up to accept the wine his wife carried into the room on a wooden platter. "Gracias," the don mumbled, whipping the wine from his wife's hands and drinking a full glass without taking a breath.

His plump little wife looked at him sternly, but said nothing. After glancing at Joshua with eyes full of trepidation, the Californiana in black mourning clothes hustled from the room.

Don Pedro handed Joshua a glass of wine and then poured himself another from the decanter. Don Pedro drank that too before returning his attention to Joshua.

"I have been considering a betrothal for Maria," the Spaniard admitted as if the demise of California lay squarely on his shoulders.

Joshua smiled. "I will personally see that Colonel Fremont and his soldiers do not bother Rancho de los Robles. With Maria at my side, I will guard your land as if it were my very own. You will have no problem with the Americans. I give you my word."

Don Pedro poured himself more wine before saying, "Then we will draw up the betrothal agreement—"

"There will be no betrothal agreement," Joshua interrupted him. "Maria will leave with me today. I will marry her the same way my daughter and your nephew are seeking their vows. We will ride to the mission and meet with the padre as soon as possible."

Don Pedro dropped his wine glass on the pine-planked floor. It shattered, and wine seeped into the wood. "No betrothal?"

"No betrothal," Joshua said firmly. "We are at war, Don Pedro. I see no need for a Californian betrothal agreement when the California government is fleeing south for Mexico even as we speak."

"Maria may not accept this marriage," Don Pedro warned, staring at his broken wine glass, appearing on the verge of weeping.

Joshua placed a condescending arm around the Spaniard's shoulder. "Come, my old amigo, I want to show you something." He handed Don Pedro his own full glass of wine as he led the old don out of the *sala* and onto the veranda.

The Spaniard gazed at the army of hard-faced vaqueros mounted on their horses, waiting patiently for their boss in the hot summer sun. Joshua did not employ ordinary vaqueros. These were not tame Indians turned cowboys. They were *mestizos* with long rifles tied to their saddles, along with their ever-present riatas and knifes. Some of the half-breeds even sported pistols strapped to their waists, as did Joshua. These were paid desperados with blood on their hands.

"My own little army," Joshua spoke softly, almost tenderly to Don Pedro.

The don hung his head in defeat.

"Do not fret, my friend. I will take good care of Maria. Much better care of her than you did Sarita." Joshua pounded Don Pedro on the back and stepped off the porch with a wide smile. "I have learned a man my age should not leave a bride to go off and fight a war. Let the younger men fight these wars. A man of my years should stay in bed with his wife and produce sons to help in his old age. Tell Maria to pack her belongings. We will depart within the hour."

Chapter Forty-Four

Roman, Rachel, Dominic, and two old Indian vaqueros who hadn't been enlisted into Castro's army, reached Mission San Francisco Dolores just before sunset on the third day. The mission sprawled at the foot of the eastern side of the mountains skirting San Francisco Bay. A creek flowed through the mission lands providing fresh water, before the stream emptied into the bay three miles from the village of Yerba Buena. Though the church and main buildings remained somewhat maintained, the mission was no longer in service, and the outlying buildings were falling apart.

Roman's relatives lived in a one room house in one of the rundown squares of the mission. With great delight, they welcomed Roman and his guests into their humble adobe. Several crosses hung on their walls. Their furniture was sparse but well cared for. The place was very peaceful.

"Is there a padre here?" Roman asked after embracing the elderly couple.

Tio Pablo Renaldo, Roman's great uncle on his mother's side, shook his white-haired old head. "Only Mormons. These families arrived on the ship *Brooklyn* from New York and had no place to stay. We have given them the mission housing. A priest has not lived here in many years."

"Is there a padre in Yerba Buena?" Roman asked, feeling a keen disappointment.

"I do not think so." Tio Pablo looked pensive. "There are many ships in the harbor now. Several days ago, the American flag was raised over the town. Most of our padres have returned to Spain. Why do you need a priest, *mi hijo*?"

Roman ushered Rachel forward. "This is my betrothed, Señorita Rachel Tyler. We long to marry, Tio."

Tio Pablo clapped his gnarled hands in excitement. His shrunken little wife, Teresa, displayed pleasure as well. "We will pray for a priest," Tio Pablo said with great confidence. "The Lord will provide. Come, you must rest after your long journey."

"Let me settle the horses and my vaqueros for the night," Roman said. "Tio, this is my amigo, Dominic Mason. He is like a brother to me. Show Dom and Señorita Rachel into your casa. I will return shortly."

"Behind the church you will find lodging for your men," Tio Pablo told Roman before he ushered Rachel and Dominic into the small but hospitable house with the smell of onions and garlic wafting in the air.

That night, Roman and Dominic spread their bedrolls on the house's earthen floor. Across the room, Rachel slept on Pablo's pallet beside Teresa. Pablo slept on a serape near the men.

Before settling down for the night, Pablo said a series of long, earnest prayers in Spanish that Rachel and Dominic could not understand. But a spirit of goodwill permeated the dwelling. Everyone did a lot of smiling.

Early the next morning, Roman had everyone mounted on their horses to continue on to Yerba Buena, journeying over rolling sand hills covered in gooseberry and wild currant bushes. Native rosebushes thrived as well, as did scrubby evergreen oak and hawthorn brambles. On the steep ridges of the coast range magnificent redwood trees rustled in the breeze from the bay.

The sun steadily climbed in the sky, the morning clear and beautiful when they reached Yerba Buena. The bay shimmered like sapphires surrounded by wooded hills. Dozens of ships, whalemen, merchantmen, and the U.S. sloop of war Portsmouth, stood at anchor in the harbor, along with a host of smaller crafts. Dominic pointed out his clipper, *The White Swallow*.

"So many ships." Roman was taken aback. The last time he'd visited Yerba Buena only two trading vessels were in the harbor. Several rocky islands made white by the droppings of waterfowl rose out of the middle of the bay, and beyond the bay, steep hills forested with redwoods rose on the other side of the harbor.

"I've never seen a bay like this one," Dominic said. "I believe this may be the finest harbor in all the world."

"Apparently, the world has discovered it." Roman looked out over a sea of vessels from around the globe. "No longer is San Francisco Bay California's best kept secret."

Leaning from her horse, Rachel touched his arm. "The Lord has promised us a hope and a future here," she said reassuringly. "This war will pass. California will be at peace again."

"A hope and a future," Roman agreed with a smile, though his eyes remained somber.

"I'll find a place for your vaqueros to rest in the village," Dominic offered. "You two can search for a padre."

"Thank you." Roman gave Rachel's hand a reassuring squeeze.

Roman and Rachel rode from house to house in the village. Less than three hundred people resided in Yerba Buena, most of the inhabitants foreigners, predominantly Americans. Only a few Spanish families remained in the town. No priest was there.

Dominic waited at the village horse trader's house. It was nothing more than an old man's adobe, where several horses stood tied to posts in front of the tiny hacienda. Behind the little adobe, horses wandered about with ropes hanging from their necks. Roman and Rachel arrived in a short while, discouraged.

"This is not the Yerba Buena I remember," Roman told Dominic. "Nearly all the Californios are gone. There is not one padre amongst the people."

"Where is the nearest church?" Dominic asked.

"Monterey," said Roman.

Dominic smiled. "Just a sail away."

Roman raised his eyebrows.

"We will cruise down the coast in my ship this afternoon, and you can wed by tomorrow eve."

Rachel smiled in relief.

Roman thought long and hard for a moment. "I do not like the looks of things here," he admitted. "I did not expect the American military to be here. Perhaps Monterey is a better place for us," he told Rachel.

"You have an uncle and aunt in Monterey," Dominic guessed with a grin.

"And plenty of cousins." Roman returned Dominic's smile.

After arranging for Rancho de los Robles's vaqueros to ride down the coast to meet them with the horses after a day of rest for the cowboys, Roman and Rachel and Dominic rowed out to *The White Swallow* in a little boat.

As the morning gave way in San Francisco Bay, the breeze picked up. By the afternoon, a brisk wind blew off the ocean, carrying *The White Swallow* with all of her billowing sails swiftly down the coast toward Monterey.

Roman and Rachel stood with Dominic on deck under the summer sun as he good-naturedly captained his men while entertaining his guests by pointing out whales and sea lions and dolphins and all sorts of sightings as *The White Swallow* followed the coastline.

Dominic had a special meal prepared for Roman and Rachel, and that night after supper, they stargazed from the deck. Rachel then retired alone to the wood-paneled captain's quarters as Roman and Dominic remained on deck the rest of the night sailing the ship.

The morning found *The White Swallow* in the blue-green waters of Monterey Bay. Rachel went up on deck with Roman and Dominic as the picturesque town with its red-roofed, whitewashed adobes came into view.

Roman was taken aback to see the American flag waving over the presidio. He hadn't known Monterey had fallen to the Americanos as well.

Concealing his dismay, he said a silent prayer that God would protect them this day and that by nightfall, he and Rachel would be husband and wife.

Dominic's deckhand, Jamie, the curly haired, blond boy who had captured Isabella's fancy, rowed Roman to shore after *The White Swallow* anchored in the harbor.

Rachel and Dominic remained on the ship. Dominic to watch the crew, and Rachel to await Roman's return.

Dominic sent his first mate, a red-haired bear of a man, Jack Andrews, along in the rowboat in case Roman met with any resistance from the American soldiers now in charge of Monterey harbor.

On shore, the burly first mate wasted no time ordering the young deckhand to run ahead to the church to warn the padre they were coming and wanted a wedding performed that afternoon.

Roman kept quiet, though the first mate's high-handedness disturbed him. Californios did not appreciate such brusqueness. A Spanish padre would not take kindly to being told he must perform a wedding on a moment's notice.

Praying the Lord would smooth the way, Roman walked from the docks to the church to speak to the padre himself. It had been years since he'd been in Monterey. The sun felt warm on his face. Seagulls swooped overhead, their squawks filling his ears. He thought of his mother, a sought-after belle in Monterey, until his father married her and whisked her away to Rancho de los Robles.

By the time he reached the Royal Presidio Chapel, entering the sandstone sanctuary with a prayer on his lips, the deckhand, Jamie, was all but pleading with the grim-faced padre near the altar. Roman was grateful the blustering first mate had stopped at the customhouse to announce *The White Swallow's* arrival and had not appeared here yet.

"*Por favor, Padre,*" Roman interrupted in Spanish. "I am Roman Miguel Vicente Vasquez . . ."

"My boy," cried the old priest, a smile splitting his ancient face. "Come closer so I can look at you, *mi hijo.* You have become a fine man."

Roman recognized the bent old padre. "Father Santiago!" He strode forward and embraced the priest.

The padre laughed with joy. "You still have your mother's green eyes. And her sweet smile as well." The padre held Roman by the cheeks, gazing up at him with great pleasure.

Tears flowed out of Roman's eyes, dampening the padre's wrinkled hands. "I was just thinking of my mother as I walked here from the harbor."

"God has reconciled you to her death, then?"

"He has," Roman said with wonder in his voice. His mother's death had always been so painful for him. To have peace about it now after all these years surprised him.

"You have met our Lord Jesus, I see. The light of his Spirit shines on your face, my son."

"*Si.*" Roman no longer cared that he couldn't stop the tears.

Father Santiago patted Roman's wet cheek. "My prayers all these years for you have not been in vain. God has purchased you with the blood of his precious Son, our Lord Jesus Christ."

"You have prayed for me?" Roman found it hard to believe.

"Since your mother's passing. Your courage at her graveside broke my heart. I told our Lord I would pray all my life for

Domitilla's green-eyed boy." The old priest smiled. "Now I can die in peace knowing your soul is safe with him."

Jamie cleared his throat. Both Roman and Father Santiago had forgotten about the boy. "Should I tell the captain the wedding will take place this afternoon, then?"

"These Americanos," Father Santiago said in Spanish. "They are so impatient. They marry like they do everything else, swift as sand dries in the sun."

"I am sorry," Roman apologized. "The wedding he speaks of is my wedding."

"Yours!" Father Santiago cried, a wide smile taking over his wrinkled face. The padre turned to the deckhand. "By all means, tell your captain I will perform the wedding at dusk. Roman will remain here with me until then. We need time to prepare for this holy union."

"Please have Captain Mason bring my sack of belongings so I can change into my wedding attire when he escorts Rachel here." Roman spoke with Jamie.

The deckhand nodded and hurried from the church, appearing much relieved to escape the place.

Father Santiago laughed. "Our Lord has brought you to me for your marriage. I am so pleased, *mi hijo*." The padre began to cry, tears dripping down his weathered old face.

"May I confess my sins to you, Father Santiago, so that you can pray with me to walk uprightly before God the rest of my days?"

"By all means." The little priest waved Roman toward the confessional.

"Can we kneel here at the foot of the cross instead?" Roman looked toward the altar with its crucifix hanging there.

"Of course, *mi hijo.*" Father Santiago knelt down on the hard tile in front of the altar. He waved Roman down beside him.

On his knees, Roman bowed his head. He had lived in sin for so many years. He had much to confess. The Americanos he killed in Texas. The adultery he'd committed with Sarita. His coupling with other women. At every turn, he had rebelled against God, leading a godless life among godless people.

He told Father Santiago of his loathing for Sarita. His relief and grief at the news of her death along with, perhaps, his child. The fierce hatred he still carried for Luis Lopez. And his heartbreak over Steven giving his life for him. Once he finished, Father Santiago began to pray. On and on the priest prayed until Roman lost track of time and space and all his sins.

Finally, Father Santiago blessed Roman, and the two men rose to their feet. He helped Father Santiago to stand as the old priest struggled to rise after kneeling for so long.

"These arthritic bones don't move like they used to." Father Santiago smiled.

"I am sorry my sin kept you so long on your knees," Roman apologized, smiling too.

"You did not keep us there. Our Lord kept us there. He is purifying your heart, *mi hijo.* Time on one's knees is required for cleansing."

"I do feel cleaner. Like a newborn lamb."

"You are clean. The blood of Christ has washed all your sins away. As far as the east is to the west, your sins have been removed, *mi hijo.* You are white as washed wool now."

Father Santiago led Roman over to sit on one of the wooden benches. "Tell me about your betrothed. Will her confession take as long as yours?" the old padre teased.

Roman smiled. "She will probably not confess to you at all. She is a devout Protestant, though she's been baptized into the Catholic faith."

"Does your señorita know our Lord?"

"She knows Jesus quite well," Roman assured Father Santiago.

"Then she will confess her sins before I marry you. Confession is an essential part of every believer's life. I must find my best robe. We will light every candle in the church. When your señorita arrives you will wait in my room until I have heard her confession. Then you may come out to meet her at our Lord's altar where the two of you will become one flesh." Father Santiago clapped his hands in anticipation.

Chapter Forty-Five

Aboard *The White Swallow*, Rachel dressed for the wedding in the captain's quarters, brushing her hair until it shone, putting on her best gown—the lovely rose-colored silk and lace gown she'd worn for the signing of the betrothal papers. It was the only fancy dress she had carried with her. Her other ball gowns remained at Rancho de los Robles. Someday she hoped to live there with Roman. It was his home, a home he loved. She'd grown to love Rancho de los Robles too. She couldn't wait to become Roman's wife. His strong arms around her always. His ardent kisses never having to stop.

She wanted to look her loveliest today. Dominic had an impressive mirror in his cabin, something rare indeed in California. Rachel pinned her hair up as best she could, leaving tendrils hanging around her face and down her back, mostly because she only had a handful of hairpins with her.

The results of a lack of pins pleased her. She picked up her Bible, taking time to pray and read Song of Songs there in the quiet of the captain's quarters. *My lover is mine and I am his; he browses among the lilies. Until the day breaks and the shadows flee . . .*

Finally, the day was really breaking. She praised the Lord for his faithfulness and asked him to bless their marriage. And to take care of Steven. Surely, Steven was at the Lord's side in heaven now, smiling down on them.

As afternoon gave way to early evening, Dominic knocked on the door to tell her it was time to row ashore. When she opened the portal, he stepped back with a beaming smile.

"You look beautiful," he said with such sincerity Rachel blushed all the way to her toes.

"Thank you," she answered softly, wishing Steven was here with them too.

"You're thinking of Steven, aren't you?" The smile left Dominic's face.

"I do wish Steven was with us. Roman adored him, you know."

"Steven was easy to adore. It doesn't seem like he's gone. I keep thinking he's going to join us at any moment." Dominic stepped out of Rachel's way, waving her to walk before him, up the stairs to the top deck.

"I feel like that too. He isn't gone, just waiting for us to greet him again one day soon. I believe he will be there to walk us through the gates of heaven."

Dominic sighed with regret when they reached the upper deck and looked out over the ocean. "I took it for granted that Steven would sail back to Boston with me. Having a minister on *The White Swallow* changed my crew. They minded their manners and talked about their mothers for a change. Many a night, Steven and I charted the stars and spoke of God. I will miss our talks, and my crew will miss Steven's Sabbath services on the deck." Dominic smiled wistfully.

Rachel smiled too and dabbed at her tears.

Every man on deck stopped what he was doing to stare at her as she made her way to the rowboat, her gown and hair shimmering in the sinking sun as she swished past the speechless sailors. Men smiled, but not a word was said until the rowboat was well out in the water.

"My men will be useless for the rest of the day," Dominic said as he rowed the dinghy through the gentle swells of Monterey Bay.

Pelicans flew overhead. The blond boy, Jamie, sat with his back to Dominic and Rachel. "I doubt any of them have seen a bride on her way to her wedding. Jamie, have you ever seen a bride off to her wedding in a rowboat?"

"No, and there's nothing prettier," he shyly replied.

"Thank you." Rachel's cheeks reddened. "Do you ever allow your men to venture ashore, Captain Mason?" She hoped small talk would quiet the fluttering in her stomach.

"Usually I do, but with this war going on, I'm hesitant to release the crew into town. I think it safer for the men to stay aboard the ship for now."

"Is there any trouble in Monterey?" Rachel craned her neck to view the waterfront. The beautiful village surrounded by a forest of pines was still a ways in the distance.

"My first mate tells me all is calm in the village. A curfew has been placed on the people. I guess nobody put up a fight when the navy arrived. The American flag has been flying for several days now without interference."

"Do you think California will become part of the United States?" Rachel asked.

"I hope so. San Francisco Bay alone is worth the war. I believe a great city will spring up by the bay. I plan to make that city my home someday, God willing."

"That would be wonderful. You could visit us at the rancho from time to time. Maria would be happy to see you." Rachel couldn't resist teasing him for a moment.

"She's as obstinate as her brother used to be. That girl could light a man's world on fire."

"You must pray for the Lord to save her as he saved Roman. I have gotten to know Maria, and underneath her fieriness, she is rather sweet and vulnerable and very smart."

A rueful smile twisted Dominic's mouth. "I see nothing sweet and vulnerable in that young woman. Smart, yes, give her a stage and she could rule the world."

"Would you have ever guessed Roman could become the man he is today? A follower of Christ, and your friend?"

"Not in a million years," Dominic conceded with a laugh.

Rachel turned serious. "Do you think Roman is in danger with the town ruled by American forces?"

Dominic appeared to measure his words carefully. "During a war everyone is in danger. Violence breeds violence, but God is in control. If the Lord wants Roman safe, he will be kept safe."

Dominic's faith calmed her. She gazed at the lovely little town, in close range now. The village was situated in a large cove surrounded by all those tall pines trees, everything lush and green, with the village's houses plastered white and topped by red tile roofs. Such a pretty pastoral scene. An old man wearing a serape walked slowly past the customhouse. A few dogs trotted down a dirt road. Several American soldiers strolled along in front of the presidio, but the men smiled, appearing relaxed in their uniforms.

"The church isn't far, Captain," Jamie said. "Should I find a horse for the lady, or would she prefer to walk through the village?"

"I'll walk." Rachel smiled at the curly haired boy.

Jamie's face reddened under her attention.

"May I lift you out of the boat and carry you through the surf so you don't soak your comely dress?" Dominic waited expectantly.

Rachel looked at the foamy water washing against the sides of the boat. "That would be fine." Her face turned as red as Jamie's, considering Dominic would have to hoist her into his arms.

"Here goes." He scooped her up, carrying her to shore with ease. "Let me get you through the sand," he said, continuing to bear her all the way up the beach until they hit the hard, dry dirt of the street.

She'd gotten somewhat accustomed to Roman putting his hands on her, but in Dominic's arms she felt painfully self-conscious. "Thank you," she said when he placed her on the ground.

"My pleasure." He surveyed the sleepy village.

"The church is at this end of town." Jamie led the way up the street.

"After my lady." Dominic waved her to walk between him and Jamie.

As they strolled through the village, the voice of a child cried out. "Rachel!" The little red-haired girl ran to catch up with them. "Rachel! I knew t'was you!" Molly threw herself against Rachel's legs.

Tears filled Rachel's eyes. "Molly!" She bent down to embrace the little girl.

"Ma sent me to fetch fish from the docks. When I saw you, I couldn't believe my bloomin' eyes." Molly's eyes shone with joy. "You're all dressed up. Where you goin'?"

"I'm getting married." Rachel surveyed the child, noting with great pleasure Molly's rounded cheeks and glowing health. Nearly six months ago, departing the ship and saying good-bye had been so difficult. Walking off the dock after hugging Molly and her mother, she wondered if she'd ever see them again.

"Can I come to your wedding?" Molly clung to Rachel, her freckled arms wrapped around Rachel's satin waist.

"Go fetch your ma right now and meet us at the Royal Presidio Chapel," Rachel told her.

"Can I bring my pa and brothers too?"

"You found your father?" Pleasure poured through Rachel. God had answered her prayers for Molly!

The smile wavered on Molly's face for only a moment. "My old pa is buried in the cemetery. That's where we found him when we got here. My new pa is the town blacksmith. He's a widower, and I got me two brothers now!"

"Oh my," Rachel said. "God has blessed you with a brand new family."

"He sure has." The smile shone once more on Molly's precious face. "My new pa's a God-fearin' man. And Ma is happy now."

"What wonderful news, Molly. Why don't you go see if your family can join us for the wedding." Rachel looked up at Dominic and Jamie. "Where's the church?"

"Over yonder." Jamie pointed to the sandstone building up the street as the sinking sun cast a golden glow over the entire town.

"I still got them pretty dresses you made me on the ship." Molly walked backward. "I don't live far from here. I'll go fetch everyone and be back in a lick." The little girl waved happily and then turned and raced down the street, her skirts flying.

Rachel swept tears off her cheeks. Only God could have arranged this meeting with Molly. She said a grateful prayer as they continued on to the church, where Dominic opened the heavy wooden door for her to slip inside the sanctuary. That's when she noticed Dominic, in his finest captain's garb, was all wet from the knees down due to carrying her through the surf. "Thank you for all you've done for us," she told him, tearing up once more. Her heart felt so full, happiness expanding inside her.

"You're welcome. Personally, I can't wait to see the look on Roman's face when he sets his eyes on you. And meets your Irish family when they arrive."

Rachel returned Dominic's wide smile. "It's a miracle, really, meeting Molly on the road."

"God is good at miracles," Dominic said as they stepped into the church.

It was darker inside the building, but candles glowed throughout the sanctuary. A little old padre came down the center aisle to greet them.

"I am Father Santiago," the diminutive priest said with a heavy Spanish accent. He nodded to Dominic and Jamie behind her and then focused on Rachel. "You are Roman's betrothed." It wasn't a question.

She liked the padre's kind brown eyes that shone with intelligence. To her relief, she sensed the Holy Spirit in him.

"It is time for your confession," Father Santiago announced. "Come, we will kneel before the altar as your *novio* and I did earlier."

Dominic and Jamie turned and would have fled the church had Father Santiago not halted them. "Please, senõrs," he said with gentle firmness. "Have a seat. I will come for you shortly so you too may confess your sins before the ceremony."

Jamie looked at his captain with fear-filled eyes. "I ain't confessin' my sins to no man. The wrong I done is between me and God."

"You heard the padre, Jamie. Take a seat over there. I'll join you shortly." Dominic pointed to a bench at the back of the church.

Clearing his throat, he continued, "Padre, I'm a Protestant. We believe in confessing our sins directly to God." Though Dominic stood two heads taller than the little priest, it was apparent he was a bit unnerved by the padre in his flowing robes.

"The Bible says we are to confess our sins to one another so that we may be healed," Father Santiago said. "We read the same Bible, do we not, Captain?"

Dominic nodded in agreement.

"There will be confession today by all who are here to celebrate one of God's greatest sacraments, marriage."

"So be it, Father." Dominic gave Rachel an aren't-you-lucky-to-go-first look.

She raised her eyebrows at him before following Father Santiago up the aisle.

• • •

Rachel remained waiting at the altar as Father Santiago held confessions with Dominic and Jamie. As she stood there, Molly and her family slipped into the church, Anne wearing one of the dresses Rachel had given her on the ship. Anne's head was covered by a shawl of lace. Molly looked so winsome in the little gown Rachel made for dining with the captain on the *Rainbow*. She'd cut the gown out of one of her own best gowns on the ship, and seeing it now, a smaller version on the child, filled Rachel's heart with a longing to make tiny dresses for her own daughters. She prayed God would bless them with many children. She imagined dark-haired little ones with their father's green eyes.

A tall, friendly looking man and two small boys with freshly scrubbed faces trailed Molly down the aisle, slipping onto a bench in the middle of the sanctuary. Rachel smiled and waved to Molly.

Full of exuberance, Molly waved back.

A short while later, Dominic and Father Santiago joined Rachel at the altar. Jamie was nowhere in sight.

"It is time. I will return with your groom," Father Santiago said happily. "Captain Mason, you may kneel here." The padre pointed out a place on the floor to Dominic. "The couple will kneel here." He indicated where Rachel was to kneel with Roman in front of the altar before he walked away.

Rachel wore a white lace shawl over her head that Father Santiago had given her. Women kept their hair covered in the Catholic church no matter the occasion. Rachel hadn't known this until Father Santiago explained it to her and loaned her the shawl. She wondered if Anne was of Catholic descent since the Irish woman had entered the church with her head already covered. Perhaps the padre wouldn't even notice Molly's little family sitting quietly in the shadows of the church.

Rachel hid her face under the lace shawl when Roman finally approached with Father Santiago, but she peeked up enough to see Dominic, kneeling nearby, giving Roman a huge smile. Roman smiled back like the happiest man in the world. He wore the ensemble of a Californio don—a velvet jacket over a white silk shirt with a bright red sash tied around his waist and black velvet britches, along with embroidered deerskin boots that reached nearly to his knees.

Reverently, he knelt down beside her. The ceremony proceeded in Spanish, but when speaking directly to Rachel, Father Santiago used his broken English.

At the end of the lengthy event, Father Santiago looped a sash over Roman's and Rachel's shoulders, signifying the two had become one flesh.

They all rose to their feet rather stiffly, having kneeled the whole time on the tile, and then the pleased padre insisted on a feast in the mission dining room in honor of the occasion. Molly's family joined them there.

By the time they returned to the beach hours later, having said good-bye to Molly's family and the gregarious Father Santiago, the moon was rising over the water. They found Jamie asleep in the bottom of the rowboat.

Roman carried Rachel through the surf to place her on one of the benches in the dinghy. After that, he helped Dominic push the rowboat into deeper water until they both hopped in. Roman sat beside Rachel, careful not to dampen her dress with his wet boots.

Back on board the ship, Roman surprised Dominic with a hug. "Thank you, Dom. I'm grateful it was you who stood by me for my wedding." Roman could not stop smiling.

It made Rachel so happy to see him happy.

"Who was standing? My knees will never be the same." Dominic grinned with pain and pleasure.

Roman and Rachel laughed, admitting their knees were sore as well.

Dominic made a bow. "Allow me to escort you newlyweds to your quarters." With the full moon lighting the deck and shining off the tranquil waters of the bay, Dominic led Roman and Rachel down to his cabin.

When he opened the door for them, Rachel was taken aback by the smell of flowers. "I had my men hunt down a bit of flora. It appears they stripped every garden in the town."

Awestruck, Rachel walked into the flower-filled room. Brass whale lanterns lit the quarters, warming the polished wood walls even more. "It's so beautiful," she said, tears filling her eyes.

"A cabin fit for a bride. Have a wonderful evening, my friends." Dominic winked before shutting the door behind him.

They were finally alone. Both of them took a shaky breath.

"Shall we say a prayer of thanks?" Roman gazed at her.

"Yes. I would like that." He took her hand and walked her over to the large bed draped in fine fabric. Waves lapped the side of the ship, creating a soothing sound. After looking into her eyes for a long, heartfelt moment, he bowed his head. "Lord Jesus, we thank you for your tender care for us. Let this time tonight glorify you. Amen."

"That was short." Rachel couldn't hide how nervous she felt.

A smile settled on Roman's face. "Our Lord understands." He reached out and plucked a pin from her hair. And then, one by one, he removed them all until her hair tumbled down her back in glorious splendor.

He was different now that he was a believer. Still, there was so much Rachel didn't know about pleasing a man. So much she had to learn as a wife. Her heart hammered in her chest, and her breathing quickened. Fear and excitement left her light-headed.

He moved in closer, and she stepped back until her legs bumped the bed. "Maybe we should read the Bible for a while together," she suggested.

"Really?" His gaze swept her face, settling on her mouth. Placing his hands on her waist, he gently turned her around and deftly loosened the stays on her dress and then pushed her hair aside, kissing the back of her neck.

"Please, I want to share this with you," she said, shivering.

She spun around to face him and flattened her palms against his chest, looking shyly up at him. "It won't take long." She ducked under his arm and crawled across the soft mattress to the table on the other side. Her Bible lay open there where she'd left it before the ceremony. "My lover is mine, and I am his; he browses among the lilies until the day breaks and the shadows flee, turn, my lover, and be like a gazelle or like a young stag on the rugged hills." Her voice caught with emotion as she read the scripture.

Roman removed his wet deerskin boots and stripped down to just his pants before joining her on the bed, where she sat amid the pillows in her wedding gown that matched the color of the blush heating her cheeks.

She continued to read, "All night long on my bed, I looked for the one my heart loves." She glanced up to find him intently watching her. His chest was bare and all muscle. One forearm remained bandaged. Lupe had stitched him up, and he was healing. Her husband was so strong and handsome it stole her breath away.

Roman took the Bible from her trembling hands. "God is no longer between us, *pequeña*. He has made us one flesh now." He raised the Good Book to his lips and kissed the leather and then placed the Bible back on the bedside table before sweeping her into his embrace.

THE END

Excerpt from *Far Side of the Sea*
California Rising Book II

Chapter One

Monterey, California, 1846

Maria rode into town alongside Joshua Tyler. An army of vaqueros followed in their wake, the sound of hooves like thunder on the street. The moon shone so brightly she could see every ship silhouetted in the harbor. Joshua led them directly to the church. By now, American soldiers had noted their arrival. With guns drawn, the soldiers surrounded them in the churchyard.

"Why are you here?" demanded the leader of the U.S. Army detachment, a large man with long, bushy sideburns.

Joshua stepped down from his horse with an easy smile. "I've come to marry my fiancée." He motioned to Maria, perched in a sidesaddle on her mare. "We've ridden a long way today."

"The padre's asleep. You'll have to wait till morning."

Joshua reached into his saddlebags and pulled out a sack of coins.

The soldiers looked at one another speculatively. "The padre isn't going to like this. He's a pious old guy," said the soldier in charge.

Joshua retrieved a handful of silver coins from the pouch, showing them to the soldiers. "My bride is a gently bred Californiana. Certainly, the good padre will understand the need for vows before we take a room for the night."

The soldiers stared unabashedly at Maria. She glared back. Her fiery auburn hair tumbled down her back, tangled with dirt and leaves from a fall from her horse while trying to escape after leaving the hacienda.

"Does she understand English?" asked the soldier, thoughtfully stroking his sideburns. "Do you speak English, señorita?" He walked toward Maria, tucking the silver Joshua handed him into the pocket of his uniform.

"She speaks only Spanish." Joshua gave Maria a warning glare. She reined her horse away from the approaching soldier about the same time one of Joshua's vaqueros cut him off. The other vaqueros circled Maria with their horses.

"Gavilan, go rouse the good padre," Joshua told one of his men.

The vaquero with a tall, muscular build stepped down from his mount. He looked more Spanish than Indian, with European features. He'd picked Maria off the ground after her tumble. His big hands had been gentle but unbending as steel. Maria had seen a flash of compassion in his dark eyes as he helped her back onto her horse. She had hoped he would feel sorry enough for her to help her escape. He walked past the soldiers without any fear.

All of Joshua's men exhibited an absolute disregard for any authority beyond Tyler's. Several of the soldiers moved to intercept the vaquero, but the soldier in charge waved them off. "Let him go. This is a civilian matter. Return to your posts."

The soldiers lowered their guns and slowly left the square. Soon it was only Maria, Joshua, and his cowboys waiting for the padre. He never came out of the church. Gavilan returned, shaking his head.

"He refuses to do the ceremony?" Irritation edged Joshua's words.

"I could not find him." Gavilan spoke in English without much of an accent, which surprised Maria. "Nobody is in the church or the living quarters in the back."

Joshua looked at her. She met his eyes, and a triumphant little smile tilted her lips. She would not marry him. Ever. He stepped down from his horse and walked to hers. Gripping her arm, he yanked her down from the saddle. "Find a place to see to your horses and get some sleep," he told his men. "Gavilan, come with us."

Leading Maria by the arm, he marched her into the sandstone chapel. Candles burned before an altar of a saint; aside from that, the sanctuary was dark. "Wait for us here," he told Gavilan, motioning for the vaquero to sit on one of the long benches that seated the congregation. "I'll find the priest myself." He handed the vaquero the bag of coins he'd saved for the priest.

Maria attempted to pull away, but Joshua drew her closer to his side. "I realize you are young and unaware of what this war means for your family, but believe me, you will thank me for this marriage one day."

"I will never thank you." Maria spit in his face.

Joshua's mouth tightened into a grim line as he wiped the spittle from his cheek. He pulled her over to the candles in front of the saint and picked one up, then propelled her past the altar and through a door that led to the padre's private quarters in the back.

The modest chamber was empty. Joshua pushed Maria inside the room and shut the door behind them. He forced her onto the padre's narrow bunk, and then sat the flickering candle on the little table in the center of the room. "I have wanted you for a long time," he said while removing his hat and gun belt, then his vest and shirt. He kept his pants on, with his long knife tucked into his waistband.

Maria couldn't believe this was happening. The last time she'd been in this church, her cousin, Donatella, had been getting married. It had been a lavish affair with laughter and happiness and over a hundred family and friends. Her mother's and father's funerals had also been held here. She was too young to really remember her mother's passing, but her father's burial she recalled quite well. It was his death that had stolen her freedom. He'd allowed her to accompany him all over the rancho as he worked the cattle and oversaw their vast sheep herds after her mother had died from a fever. Maria's childhood had been spent in a saddle, a sombrero pulled low on her brow to protect her fair, golden skin from the California sun, a riata in her hand just like the cowboys. Under her skirts, she'd worn pantaloons and boots like her father's, with spurs strapped on, along with every other man in California. She could rope as well as anyone, and during the *Matanzas*, skinned cattle better than most of her father's men. That had ended when her padre died during an Indian raid, lanced to the ground when a handful of their golden horses were taken from the field.

"I will not marry you. I have no desire for this union." She looked around for a way to escape, but only the door he stood in front of offered any kind of exit. What was he thinking? Why was he undressing? Did he have marriage attire he wanted to put on? She didn't see how this was possible considering they'd carried nothing into the church with them but the bag of coins he'd left with his vaquero.

"Your uncle owes me a lot of money, more than he can ever hope to repay. If you do not marry me, I will take Rancho de los Robles, and your family will be destitute. The United States has run up her flag in every town along the coast. Soon more soldiers will arrive here. Men who have no regard for your welfare. Marrying me is the best thing to do, Maria."

She did not like the way he said her name. Like an endearment as he removed his spurs and boots. "What are you doing? Will you wear the padre's robes for our wedding? There are no other clothes here."

"So you will marry me?" His smile returned.

She had no plans to marry him; she was only trying to discover why he undressed in her presence. Fear had begun to claw in her stomach, rising like a wild thing trying to dig its way out of a very deep hole. She knew little about men, but instinct warned she would need a weapon. She rose from where Joshua had made her sit on the hard, narrow bunk the padre slept on. Perhaps with all these rough American soldiers in town, the padre had headed south. She saw nothing to defend herself with in the sparse, little room and turned her gaze back to him, measuring his size and strength against her own.

In his forties, Joshua was still a handsome man with a lean, hard frame and a thick head of blond hair that waved off his high, tanned forehead. Maria had never liked him, even though he was Rachel's father.

Joshua had asked for her hand in marriage several years ago, but Tio Pedro had proposed her older cousin Sarita instead. Now Sarita was dead after miscarrying her babe. Even though she was older now, Maria had no desire to marry anyone yet, least of all this high-handed Yankee who'd always made her skin crawl when he looked at her.

"We should find the padre. He will want a confession from both of us before performing the marriage rites."

Joshua's lips spread into a smile. "I am planning my confession even now," he said, stepping toward her.

She realized his intent, and it sickened her. Her suspicion had been growing as he undressed, but she wouldn't accept it. He was a landowner. She was a daughter of the *gente de razón*. Things like this did not happen in her world. She could see there would be no vows spoken tonight, but he intended to have her anyway. "I will not marry you, no matter what you do to me."

"You will change your mind after tonight, my dear."

A Note From Paula

When I first began writing *Until the Day Breaks*, I was twenty-four years old with a baby on my hip and a baby on the way. This was my second attempt at a novel. My first book was also a historical romance that Harlequin considered acquiring when I was twenty-two years old. In the end, the editor decided my hero was too mean. I had no idea that when an editor was interested in a book, you were supposed to fix the problems they mentioned and then resubmit the story. Instead, I began researching California history and wrote book number two, the first draft of this novel. My husband, Scott, was in the military, and we lived in Germany at the time, and reading about California helped my homesickness.

I wasn't a born-again believer back then, but I was raised in the Catholic Church and loved my religion. My best friend, Christy, was a Protestant, and we had long talks about the differences and similarities of our faiths. The clash between Catholics and Protestants has always fascinated me, especially since we all worship Jesus. I knew historical romances needed conflict, and putting a Catholic guy with a Protestant girl in an arranged engagement in the middle of a revolution sounded interesting to me. Looking back, what really interested me was God.

I'm a fifth-generation Californian, and I fell in love with California's beautiful missions when I was a little girl. In high school, I began reading historical romances. I just couldn't get enough of these exciting books. A high school English teacher, Mrs. Bonnie Newton, my earliest critique partner, took me under her wing and drove me to my first writers' conference. As Mrs. Newton aged, I drove her to several more conferences. She asked me to call her Bonnie after I graduated high school, but I never could get there. I tried to teach Mrs. Newton how to put gas in her car, but she said she'd never touched a gas pump in her life and never planned on doing so. Her husband always filled her gas tank. I happily pumped the gas on our way to and from the conferences and marveled that a woman in the 1990's had never put gas in her car. We remained great writing buddies until her death when I was in my thirties.

Along with Mrs. Newton, many special people encouraged me along the way, and I'm so grateful to those who took the time to help me grow as a writer. High school teachers, college professors, and of course, my amazing family. My mom has always been my biggest fan. Her unwavering support has carried me through many long years of writing discouragement. Thanks, Mom!

My dad read my first book and edited it for me too. I was twenty-one years old, the wife of an equally young army lieutenant, and we were flat broke when Scott was in flight school in Alabama. My dad paid me four hundred dollars to write that first historical romance I set in the South. Daddy called it an investment in his future. When the book didn't sell to Harlequin, I called it a waste of Daddy's money, but looking back, I see growing up with parents who loved reading books, and who wanted me to become a novelist, set me on this long road to publication. I'm so grateful they never gave up on me. And, of course, my big brother, Patrick. Thank you for believing in me and financing this novel. You've always taken care of me, even when we were little and your love for our Savior inspires me. Hoping together we can help World Vision meet the needs of many more precious children in the coming years.

Back to my writing journey, my third book, not a historical romance, a love story set in 1972, landed me a New York literary agent. I am thankful Peter Miller gave me a shot at the big time when I was a young, stupid, starry-eyed writer, but it was really Jennifer Robinson, who worked for Peter, who put the writing wind in my sails when she said, "You have that something special I can't teach you, so let's get to work, and I'll teach you the rest!"

I learned so much from Jennifer with my third novel, and I hope to thank her someday for helping a baby writer learn to walk.

A few years later, I was born again. All of a sudden, I couldn't write anymore. Actually, I strongly sensed God didn't want me to write anymore. Laying down writing felt like giving up my legs. Where would I go? How would I walk? Heartsick, I left Peter's agency and quit writing feature stories for newspapers. I stopped working on my novels, put my laptop away, and planted my first garden.

I also picked up a Bible.

I haven't put the Bible down since. Each year for the past fifteen years, I've read the Bible straight through in a year. One year, I read through the Bible several times. I was pregnant and stuck on bedrest and decided I'd only read the Bible and no other books that year. Talk about eye-opening. The Bible is not a shy book. The Bible rocked my world.

God is very passionate, and he often compares our unfaithfulness to sexual infidelity. True love began with God in the garden where two humans were naked and felt no shame. Don't be confused, sexuality is very meaningful to God. We are the ones who mess up sex.

So back to planting my first garden. While growing that garden and taking care of our three young children, I began to grow another baby. On bedrest with my fourth baby, God whispered, "You can write again."

I was thrilled! By the time I gave birth, I'd finished my first attempt at a Christian novel, but I tucked that book—a murder mystery set on a peach farm—away and kept reading the Bible. After having a fifth baby, I contacted a Christian literary agent, Les Stobbe. I found him in the library in a book listing all the Christian agents. I said a prayer and chose Les because I liked what he said in his bio.

Les and I immediately hit it off, probably because when he called out of the blue one morning, I was shocked to hear a man's voice introduce himself as Leslie Stobbe. I'd assumed Leslie was a woman—I wanted a female literary agent—and here Les was telling me how much he liked my writing and that I needed to get email. "Writers today correspond by Internet, not snail mail," he informed me. This was 2005. I told Scott that night I needed to learn how to use email pronto. So I took over our joint account, the account only Scott used until that day, and P.S. Bicknell was born. Scott opened another email account using just his initials.

Les and I later laughed about him being a man with a woman's name, and then he did his best to sell my first Christian novel after warning me it was probably too secular for the Christian market.

Les was right, that book didn't sell, so I got to work rewriting my California historical romance novel with the plan of turning it into a series of three novels. Les loved the storyline and suggested the California Rising series name. Thank you, Les, California Rising was perfect! You are a great encourager to writers and a wonderful man of God. I love you and am so thankful for you!

When the rejections began pouring in on *Until the Day Breaks*, Les wasn't discouraged. One editor gave Les an earful because Roman had damned God in the story. I grew up with people who'd damned God on a regular basis, men who kicked down doors when they were angry, and I watched one of these men give his life to Christ on his deathbed. Jesus graciously forgave this man—my grandpa—and took him home to heaven, and I didn't get why I couldn't write about real men like this in my novels.

I wanted to write raw and honest, and I figured if it was in the Bible, I could put it in my stories. Maybe I wasn't writing this stuff the right way, but if you've read this far, hopefully you're okay with how I write. I love history, and I love Jesus, and I love writing about sinners who really meet the Savior and it stops them in their tracks.

This happened to me. At thirty-three-years-old, I had a personal encounter with Jesus. If you haven't met Jesus, I'm hoping with all my heart that you do. Jesus loves you so much that he died for you. It's not a joke. It's not a tale. It's the truth. And it's for you.

I want to thank my daughters, Cami and Lacy, for pushing me to publish this novel. For the past several years when I've asked Cami what she wanted for her birthday, she has said, "I want you to make *Until the Day Breaks* into a book for me."

I never intended do anything more with this novel after it was rejected by Christian publishers nearly a decade ago because I didn't want to change it for the Christian market, and honestly, I was afraid it might offend Christians, so I thought it better to keep it tucked away in my computer. But I wrote a memoir last year that Scott has decided he's putting on Amazon. I was hoping to sell this memoir to traditional publishers, but like my other books, my story doesn't quite fit the Christian market.

"You need to give me one of your novels to practice with on Amazon before we publish your memoir," Scott said a few months ago. The thought horrified me. Practicing with my novels on Amazon sounded about like going to church without my pants on. I cried, I prayed, I did everything I could to convince my husband this was the dumbest idea ever, but I've never been able to say "no" to Scott for long. He's the love of my life, my great romance. This is why I chose Paula Scott for my pen name.

"Pick a novel," Scott ordered. "We are going to Amazon with your books this year."

The Bible says to obey your husband, so I chose *Until the Day Breaks* for Cami and Lacy. I figured if nobody else enjoyed the book at least my girls would appreciate it, and this could be Cami's birthday present. So happy twenty-fifth birthday, Cami! Thank you for being so sweet, so strong, and so persistent. Rachel reminds me so much of you, honey. And thank you, Lacy. That vein in Rachel's forehead is your vein, and when I picture Rachel's eyes, I see your big, beautiful blue-green eyes my precious girl.

I need to thank my critique partners, Michelle Shocklee and Katherine Scott Jones, for all your help working the kinks out of the story. I met you ladies at my first Christian writers' conference but came home from that conference so discouraged about my writing, not realizing meeting you ladies was an incredible gift. At that conference, I also met Lisa Buffaloe, my beloved writing prayer partner, and Jeff Gerke, who helped me typeset this book. Jeff was an editor representing a publishing house at the time, and I was so nervous I introduced myself to him as Les Stobbe's agent. Jeff laughed and told me to relax. Thanks, Jeff!

How blessed I was at that conference and didn't even know it!

Also, a mountain of thanks to Kay Andrus, my daily prayer partner. Can't live without you, Miss Kay! To Laura Frantz, my dear soul sister, our phone talks and prayers are my favorite! To Karen Ball, my mentor and my friend. I love you, Karen. And a shout-out to my brilliant editor, Jenny Q of Historical Editorial. Thanks for all your help, Jenny! Looking forward to working with you on book number two. You're amazing!

If you enjoyed this novel, please consider leaving a review on Amazon. Leaving reviews is a great way to connect with writers and other readers. I actually met Laura Frantz by leaving an Amazon review for one of her books. She contacted me to thank me for my review, and we became friends. Leaving a review is also a great way to be friendly to writers. Thanks so much!

Made in the USA
San Bernardino, CA
09 August 2016